SONG OF BATOCHE

SONG *of* BATOCHE

Maia Caron

RONSDALE PRESS

SONG OF BATOCHE
Copyright © 2017 Maia Caron

RONSDALE PRESS
3350 West 21st Avenue
Vancouver, B.C. Canada V6S 1G7
www.ronsdalepress.com

Typesetting: Julie Cochrane, in Granjon 11.5 pt on 15
Cover Design: Marijke Friesen
Paper: 55 lb. Enviro Book Antique Natural (FSC), 100% post-consumer waste, totally chlorine-free and acid-free.

Ronsdale Press wishes to thank the following for their support of its publishing program: the Canada Council for the Arts, the Government of Canada, the British Columbia Arts Council, and the Province of British Columbia through the British Columbia Book Publishing Tax Credit program.

Library and Archives Canada Cataloguing in Publication

Caron, Maia, 1960–, author
  Song of Batoche / Maia Caron.

Issued in print and electronic formats.
ISBN 978-1-55380-499-4 (softcover)
ISBN 978-1-55380-500-7 (ebook) / ISBN 978-1-55380-501-4 (pdf)

  1. Riel Rebellion, 1885 — Fiction. 2. Métis — Fiction. 3. Saskatchewan — Fiction. 4. Historical fiction. I. Title.

PS8605.A763S66 2017   C813'.6   C2017-903928-8   C2017-903929-6

At Ronsdale Press we are committed to protecting the environment. To this end we are working with Canopy and printers to phase out our use of paper produced from ancient forests. This book is one step towards that goal.

Printed in Canada by Marquis Printing, Quebec

For my father Allan Caron
and for C.M.

"Medea, you struggle in vain:
some god, I do not know which, opposes you.
I wonder if this, or something, like this,
is what people indeed call love?"

— Ovid, *Metamorphoses*

I

a small one

IT WAS A BAD SIGN to almost lose her son the night before Riel arrived. He was miles away yet, but Josette could feel him, a spider at the outer edge of its web and her a fly in the centre, waiting. She laid a hand to her son's forehead and stared at him a long while in the light of a candle that flashed shadows up the walls. Only hours ago she had boiled water to bathe his lifeless body, yet here he breathed, black lashes upon his cheek mocking existence. The priest would say it pleased God to raise him up again.

Air in the backroom was stale, humid. When she blew out the candle, the bundled shapes of her four sleeping children faded into darkness. Even the whippoorwills were silent in the trees behind the house, just a yard of luminous moon glancing off the sod roof and sweated heat rising in the eaves.

Out on the porch, she lifted her dress around her thighs and let the front door swing wide to clear the smell of vomit and fever. She closed her eyes, whispering prayers to the Cree spirits for rain. A full moon rose in a sky pricked with stars—Thunder Moon her people called it—the colour of ripe wheat, lurid and immense. Mosquitoes buzzed at her neck; she could feel the strange touch upon her skin, flickering wings and then some low dull sound near the barn that made her turn and drop her skirts. But it was no more than night wind stirring the trees. Norbert's four sled dogs had disappeared, only a skunk scent that rose from the parched fields, the sunburnt pigweed, and her grandfather's voice in her head.

Drought smell's not far off from death.

Wahsis cried out, but he had settled by the time she reached the backroom door. She wanted to wring a fresh cloth with river water for his brow but when she went to the pail, found that her eldest daughter had forgotten to fill it before dark. The scar ached between her legs, a tear the midwife had sewn closed with a beading needle less than three years ago. Josette touched herself there, not in desire—she had put that away from her—but in memory of how Wahsis had been yanked from her womb. The blood had rushed out like a river at spring melt. To save her life, the midwife pushed her hand in and worked it to the place the baby had come only moments before.

When the bleeding finally slowed, the midwife met her eyes, fist still in her body and said, "The next one will kill you."

Josette picked up the pail and went down the porch steps, the earth nearly as bright with moon as it was that day with sun. The handle abraded her palm. Her long black skirts trailed in the dust of the yard, now in dead grass, almost soundless. Once her husband had admitted that he craved the sweet mystery of her, that he lived there. He said it was something like hunger. She was captured, like one of the animals in his traps, the wild escaped from it, leaving only what it showed to the world.

Near the bluff, she passed a hallowed place, pickets stark against the sky, and small wooden crosses darkening over bones, now powdered and mute. She imagined taking out her knife, drawing it down the blue veins of her wrists. The blood would drip from her arms and sink into the dirt as Eve's had in the first days of creation. Blood in shame for her sin, blood for the mortal stain left on woman.

Heat issued from the earth, a smell of wolf willow and sweet grass on the sloping trail to the river. A high-pitched snarl came from below; most likely a pack of dogs, some Norbert's, were hunting down the bank. Stars flared in an arc above her head, the path of light on the river sure as his hands had been, pressing her in a more urgent manner than before, and her rising from the body with helpless judgement. At the river's edge, she stood in the reeds, the hem of her skirt and her moccasins wet and cool in the lapping damp. The current seemed languid. Last week, a Hudson's Bay steamer on its way to Prince Albert had its hull ripped out by rocks and lay stranded not far upstream from here.

When she waded in, the river pulled at her knees. One version of her kept walking until it caught her skirts and carried her under, but she thought of her children lying up in the house. She lowered the pail, let it fill, and brought it up the trail. Yards from the barn, four spectres gleamed and hovered, staring sightless to the night sky, blunt vertiginous snouts that had once snuffed prairie grass. Their empty eyes sought stars. As she grew closer they revealed themselves: buffalo skulls on each fence post of her garden, the bones bleached white as a stone from years in the sun. The fence was purposeless. No rabbit would bother with carrots and potatoes reduced to the earth by weather.

She put her hand to the paddock gate and looked south. Smoke still coiled from the Dumonts' summer kitchen chimney, the front meadow awash in moonlight. Louis Riel would stand there tomorrow before the feast tables. How could she face him? She wouldn't. It was men he had come to see, and he'd take no mind of her or any other woman. The Old Crows would stand there too, urging him to taste their *boulettes* and bannock, close to peeing themselves that the great Métis hero was finally among them. The Old Crows, who did not fear for their lives when their husbands came to bed.

She set the pail by the door and dipped a cloth to lay on Wahsis' brow, her wet skirt cool against her legs. She let herself down next to him, hot, tired, ready to sleep, but no sleep would come. *Ôyêhâ*, she whispered in Cree, to the one no longer there. A light had gone out in her when she'd found her daughter, still and cold, taken in the night. She had carried that wasting body out of the house, arms heavy with more than the weight of her. So many died they were expected not to mourn.

Through the thin straw mattress, a loose set of planks that served as a floor, and the hard-packed dirt below, the sound of a horse came long before it galloped into the yard. On the other side of the room, Cleophile's eyes flicked open.

"Go back to sleep," Josette whispered. Her daughter turned to face the wall. Josette lay stiff on her side, listening. She counted the moments, Norbert leading his mount to the barn. Now removing its saddle and bridle. Rubbing it down. Of late, her husband had sat on the porch staring out at the dry fields, ignoring her when she dared speak, then taking off on his stallion, coming back with the horse foaming and close to death. He would not feed the dogs for days until they were half-starved and looked at the children as prey. He might be on the edge of one of his headaches that would keep him in bed for days.

He might be on the edge of something else.

When he looked at her in a certain way, she knew what was coming, sometimes even sparked his anger to control one small thing.

His great shadow appeared at the door. "Cleophile," he said, his voice slurred. "Unsaddle the horse."

The girl roused herself quickly. She slipped her bare feet into moccasins and walked past Josette, her eyes down.

When Cleophile had closed the front door, Norbert said, "Come out."

"Wahsis is still sick," Josette said, her back rigid.

"He's asleep. Come out."

When she did, Norbert had struck a match to a candle and was sitting at the table, his face bloated with drink. Her eyes lighted a moment on a blooded cut at his lip. Two dead rabbits lay in front of him, their necks twisted from the snares.

Norbert saw her looking at them and said, "I do not neglect my duty."

She had watered the backfields by hand while he drank himself stupid in Batoche, and he expected her to praise him. This man she'd once loved, tall and thickly built. A jutting chin and dark hair that twisted at the scalp and fell across his eyes prompted the women to call him fine-looking, when they didn't think she was near enough to hear. Then their voices would hush. "*Tant pis*—that one's not right in the head."

"Make a fire," he said.

"The house is hot," she said in a quiet voice. "Wahsis burns with fever."

"A small one."

She turned, fingernails digging at her palm. He needed to see her move through the room and then blame her for stirring his desire. She lighted a few sticks of kindling in the stove to keep the flames low. Cleophile came in and went to the backroom without looking at either of them. She closed the door behind her.

Josette gathered the collar of her dress close around her throat and turned to face Norbert. Then she was kneeling, struggling with the ceinture fléchée that held up his pants, praying he was too drunk to care how he arrived at his relief, but he pushed her hand away. She got up and faced the table, offering her backside. He wrestled with her skirts, his frustration mixed with mounting excitement. If she closed her eyes, she could will a kind of want that would make it tolerable, a desire she once had for him. Finally, he exposed her and spit into his hand.

She did not make a sound as he stabbed at her, tearing the small scabbed gashes. He pulled away and put a knee to her ribs, turning her as he would a calf for branding. She was winded, her chest bruised, and could feel the limp bodies of the rabbits beneath her. His face went slack with desire as he looked down between her legs, as a man would after months on the trail, spurring his horse upon seeing home.

"Michel Dumas says his wife lets him have it when he wants."

Norbert entered the place she'd kept from him, and she bit down on her tongue, felt the midwife's stitched scar splitting open like wood to the axe. He held her shoulder with one hand, was drunk, had killed to prove his worth and would not be turned. If she fought him, the children would hear. She turned her face to the candle, a lone flame guttering in a sudden draft, its small heat making the air shudder.

"Spill outside of me," she whispered, but he buried himself deeper, his back rounded and hard. She thought she would not stand another moment when he finished with a whimpering cry.

Josette got off the table and lowered her dress around her ankles, resisting the urge to clean the mess between her legs. At her back throbbed a dull, hammering ache made worse by the sight of the rabbits, their legs shamefully distorted by death, glassed eyes staring.

He pulled up his pants, spoke of riding out at dawn to meet Riel on the trail, and wanted something to eat from what she had cooked for the feast. She looked at the floor, wooden slats that he had found discarded in someone's midden heap and laid so poorly they shifted, revealing crude gaps of beaten earth. Norbert was tying his ceinture fléchée, and its long fringe flicked the back of her wrist. The feel of it, like a lash, or something that would finally bury her.

"I have made nothing."

Norbert snatched at the rabbits once, twice, finally getting his hands on them and swept them off the table. She closed her eyes as the broken bodies fell at her feet.

"You will cook for him," he said. "And be there when we bring him in."

scorn, or
something worse

MADELEINE DUMONT CAME out on her porch, squinting and wiping her hands on a cloth. The armpits of her black dress were ringed with sweat, but despite the heat, she'd pinned a new lace collar at her neck. *By God*, she thought, *when would it rain?*

The Saskatchewan wound like a great snake below the bluff, green-blue water dim in the shallows where it eddied in a gentle motion. To the south, slanting banks levelled to a grassy terrace at the crossing where the Humboldt Trail exited a thick stand of cottonwoods. Riel's wagon train approached, and she marked its progress by a cloud of dust sifting over the trees. She took hold of the rosary at her neck and turned her eyes to Josette Lavoie, who was on her knees in the garden, apron tented in one hand. Josette, who God had blessed with a fertile womb while striking hers barren.

Over the past six weeks, Madeleine had watered her garden from the river, awaiting her husband Gabriel, who had gone south across the boundary line. Even in the days of the buffalo hunts, he would not have ridden three hundred miles into the Montana Territory but for Louis Riel. Since word had come that Riel had agreed to help them, her neighbour Josette had been difficult, apt to strange silences. There might be good reason, but what kind of mother did not look up when a shout came from her four children playing at the bluff? Josette's two daughters minded the young boys, calling out when they braved the edge. By the look of Wahsis, it did not seem he'd been near death these last few days. In the way of children, he'd thrown off his sickness and run, chasing his older brother as if he'd never been ill.

Josette got up from her crouch in the garden and looked north with an ireful gaze. The Old Crows were on their way down from Batoche in Red River carts as they had in the buffalo hunts. Their wagon train and Riel's would converge in the front pasture before the sun moved another pace across the sky.

"Pull the small ones, too," Madeleine called to her before going back in the house.

"They're all small ones," Josette said and shaded her eyes to look south, as if a storm were coming.

Madeleine went to the stove and flipped a round of bannock in a fry pan with practised fingers that were immune to scalding heat. She would not normally have a fire going in the house on a hot day, but the stove in her summer kitchen out back was covered with pots of stew and *boulettes* she had made for the feast.

Josette came into the kitchen and tipped an apron-full of sad carrots and potatoes onto the table. She said, "You would think God was coming."

Madeleine frowned. "Best look glad to see your saviour." It had been eight summers since she'd first seen Josette and Norbert standing up near the old house abandoned by the Pilons. A girl herself still, heavy with child, a *bibi* in arms and another one at her skirts—the husband good looking and a skilled marksman. But after Norbert's fall from a horse on one of the last buffalo hunts, there had been changes.

Josette was rubbing dirt off the carrots, lost in her thoughts. Madeleine would like to wipe the look from her face. What was it? Scorn, or something worse. She could not put that to nights up with a sick boy. She said, "I'd pay to look on the face of that dog Macdonald when he hears Riel is back with his people."

"Macdonald?" Josette said in a quiet and even voice. "He is the one who drove Riel out of the country."

Madeleine hesitated. She knew nothing of politics, only that Riel's five-year exile to the States had somehow become fifteen. "Macdonald will listen," she said, to appease herself.

"He will punish us for Riel's sins in Red River."

Madeleine turned to pat another round of bannock for the pan. Sometime after they had become friends, Josette had told her that Riel was to blame for her father's death and made her promise: *do not say this to Gabriel or the women.* Why would she? If they knew Josette spoke the great man's name in vain, she would be driven from the country, shunned, banished. Or stoned like Shelomith's son for blaspheming the name of the Lord.

Years ago, Josette made enemies of the godly women of Batoche who gathered at the river to smoke their pipes and wash clothes. Once, a young girl had been in the water, lifting her skirts, and her mother told her stop, that she was too much like Eve. Josette—bent to soap one of Norbert's shirts—had laughed, said that Eve seemed the smart one. The women were silent as she scrubbed, telling how she'd behave if she were in the Garden of Eden at the beginning of creation, eating all the fruit she could stomach. And then the thing that damned her: "What strange God made man and woman in His image yet punished them for wanting to become more like Him?"

From then on, she was called La Vieille, a mocking nickname used behind the back of a quarrelsome mother-in-law, or for a young woman with too high an opinion of herself.

"If you watered your garden instead of your fields," Madeleine said, "you would not look so hard for carrots in mine." Josette remained quiet, which galled her. What had she provided for Riel's feast? A small pot of rabbit stewed in a watery broth. Something her Cree relations would serve up. And she defiantly wore a faded blue house dress, when only her Sunday best would do.

Madeleine went to the doorway, but the wagon train had yet to appear on the plain by the river. This withered land and the sky bright and hard against it. Even on the trap lines all these years, she'd gone out with her husband. Tonight, in the hushed dark of their bed, he'd hold her and make her cry out the way only he could do. Would he notice in his time gone that her breasts were smaller and had lost their shape? She flapped her skirts to bring some air to her legs. Her good Sunday dress had served for years, and it was not lack of food that made it too big. In her youth, she'd kept a healthful frame, too much so the women might say, and would have welcomed a slighter one. Now, in her fortieth year, she'd lost some of the fullness and would soon be the size of Josette, who, despite bearing five children, had a form slim as a woman unmarried. Madeleine's wasting was for another reason, but she would not think on it, this of all days.

Josette chopped at the carrots, which were stunted, uneven, and she struggled with the knife.

"Remember not to speak of Riel's time in exile," Madeleine warned.

"I will not speak to him at all."

Madeleine crossed herself. She would not abide such talk of the great Riel. "You'll be here. What will Norbert think?"

Josette stared out the window, where the first carts of women were leaving the trail and coming through the back fields. "I don't care what he thinks."

She wanted to laugh. Of course, Josette cared what he thought. She cared too much. Madeleine reached for the knife and the girl let her have it, her fingers thin and resigned. Who could blame Norbert for losing his patience? Josette was too sensitive. A woman with wits about her would choose a man with a head hard enough to survive a fall from a horse, or one not weak enough to go down in the first place.

When Josette lifted a pot to the stove she winced, and Madeleine gave her an appraising look. While in childbed with Wahsis three years ago, she had almost bled to death. The midwife declared that another pregnancy would kill her. Josette had suffered two miscarriages since then, but the Old Crows continued to watch her womb with a morbid fascination.

Fearing the answer, Madeleine asked, "You're not pregnant?"

"Norbert's horse knocked me against the barn stall."

"He should feed his own horse. That one is too strong for you."

A volley of rifle shots issued from the south, and they went to the porch in time to see the first few riders and wagons emerge from the trees at the crossing. Riel's wagon train was half a mile away yet, but she could not mistake Gabriel at its head, astride his chestnut roan. A plug felt hat was set low over his brow, the deep-set eyes missing nothing. And there was Riel, she was sure of it, on the high seat of the first wagon, spine straight despite the three-hundred-mile journey he had made from the Montana Territory. Beside him on the buckboard, a woman with a small child in her lap, and one between them on the seat.

"I wager Riel's put on a stomach," said Josette. "Or his hair has turned white." She followed Madeleine back into the kitchen and fidgeted with a cloth used for drying dishes. In a small voice, she said, "Norbert was at me last night."

Madeleine coughed into a handkerchief and tucked it into the pocket of her dress before Josette could see that it was specked with blood. "At you? How will you live with the sin of refusing him?"

Josette went to the stove. Madeleine could not bear the sight of her standing there, staring at the pots, arms at her sides like a child. Deep in the melancholy she was prone to suffer. The Old Crows judged her for continuing to grieve over a daughter who had died from the lung disease. Madeleine had also been overly fond of *P'tite Marie*, a sweet child, but most women had lost *les bibis*. It was sinful to question God's will in taking them.

Madeleine returned to the porch where the first women's carts were arriving, children spilling out—running for the bluff and a first view of Riel's wagon train. She should not be so hard on Josette when she herself suffered and could not control the black moods that seemed to come upon her more often now, losing her temper at the slightest irritation. She had blamed it on Gabriel's absence, missing him too much, but she could not discount that consumption was eating away at more than her lungs.

Amid jokes and laughter from the women, ancient Grandmother

Pétchèse, in her long black dress, was handed down from a cart. Henriette Parenteau, a big-bosomed matriarch, climbed the porch steps with a crockery bowl in her gnarled hands.

"I saw La Vieille just now. Where is she to help?"

Madeleine turned to find the kitchen empty and made for the back door. Josette had untied her horse near the barn and swung up on its back, skirts lifted to the moccasins lashed beneath her knees. She turned her head and laughed, but her jaw was set at an angle that Madeleine knew was far from a matter of joy.

"Eh, what do you expect," said Henriette, who had come to the back door as Josette took up the reins and forced her mare into a gallop, shawl flying out behind her. "Like her grandfather two times over."

Cleophile had run to the pasture gate, the young ones coming up behind her. She stood, short of breath and glaring after her mother. Josette often said Cleophile resembled her grandmother, Little Feather, who lived in Big Bear's camp—dark complexioned and slight, with weighted eyes.

Madeleine looked sharp at Alexandre, who had followed. She thought he'd ridden south to meet Riel. Although Alex had come to them only last year from the Fagnant family, learning to trap and help Gabriel with the saloon, he was dear as a son to her.

"You two bring the milk. *Vite, vite.*"

The Old Crows had taken over Madeleine's kitchen. They ruled their husbands and had broods of children, still pregnant into their late forties. She was in constant awe of them. If a woman could survive the birth of more than ten *bibis*, nothing could kill her.

Louise Boucher was at the window. "Where goes La Vieille in a hurry?"

"She does not like us," said Henriette, and the women laughed.

"Or she is off to dig up her roots," said Pélagie Gervais.

Domatilde Ledoux made the sign of the cross. Métis women learned the value of herbs and roots from their mothers—which tree bark was good for coughs and toothache, and what spit-chewed flower would break a fever. But Josette's Cree mother and grandmother had taught her a medicine woman's herb lore. The girl knew the use of every weed that grew on the prairie and in the bush along the river. Although the Old Crows considered it a sin to meddle too much with God's will, they were at Josette's door when a child was gravely ill with the strangling cough, or a husband returned from his winter trap lines with snow blindness.

Madeleine's chest tightened with a familiar, niggling pain and she slipped a hand into her pocket by habit. Henriette looked her way, and with effort, Madeleine choked back the cough. One day it would be impossible to hide, but until then she would not give them the satisfaction.

"God saved Josette from death in childbed," said Domatilde, shaking her head. "Only to take her daughter with the lung disease."

Madeleine went out on the porch. Riel's welcoming party had finally appeared over the bluff from the river. The wagons rolled up to the house, men whooping and shooting their guns in the air. Gabriel was already off his horse and helping Madame Riel from the buckboard, a little girl clinging to her neck. Louis Riel had climbed down with his son and stood, taller than Madeleine had expected, the sun like a star behind him. When Gabriel introduced them, she looked up at him with a dazzled grin.

Josette, he has not put on a stomach, he has not gone grey.

A photograph of him hung in her kitchen, one from his days in Red River, a serious young man with a frank and confident air. But now in his eyes there was a flash of distrust or wariness, a certain apprehension. Despite ten days on the trail, Riel was dressed in a suit, a tie knotted at his throat, hair brushed back from his wide forehead. He introduced his wife Marguerite and his two children and turned to the men who now surrounded him, eager to shake his hand.

Gabriel stepped back to make way for Riel, treating him with deference. *Oui*, it was there in the way he looked at him. Like a dog that showed its belly to another dog it took for the stronger. But her husband was a Métis chief; men made way for *him*. He would not bring the great man if there would be trouble, yet Josette's words came at her like a threat.

Macdonald will punish us for Riel's sins in Red River.

She took his youngest from Marguerite's hip, but as she showed her to the house, a gang of Métis men arrived on horseback. It was plain to see they'd followed Riel's train, drinking.

One of them brought his horse almost to the porch, and shouted, "Where is my wife?"

Madeleine turned to find Norbert staring her down. "She's in the summer kitchen," she said to relieve her guilt at speaking harshly to Josette earlier. "In the root cellar . . ."

But Patrice, Josette's six-year-old son, was already pointing in the direction she'd disappeared.

Cleophile and Alexandre were coming from the root cellar with pails of milk. Norbert pulled the reins of his horse. It reared, hooves pawing the air. The stallion sprang into a dead gallop, and Cleophile drew back, as if he'd raised a hand to strike her.

Norbert was at me last night. What had the girl heard of this business?

Gabriel was distracted, but he glanced in the direction of Norbert's receding figure. "Where has Josette gone?"

It was hot, too hot. Louis Riel stood in Madeleine's front pasture, and she held his youngest child in her arms. She had promised Josette not to tell even Gabriel, and yet her husband would know if she lied.

She leaned to him and whispered, "Away from Riel."

he has come

AT THE RIVER'S EDGE, a few miles north, Josette left her horse in a cluster of willow. She went up the cut-bank, her body tilted forward by gravity, an ache in the bones of her chest. At the top of the bluff, she skirted a mound of snowberry bush and ran her fingers along a crevice in the rock. There was the old tea tin that contained the *Spinoza*. Josette lifted it out and removed a stub of pencil that marked her place. She opened the book and flipped quickly past the dedication, written in a man's hand.

My dear Josette—I like to think I have put you back in God's grace.

She shut her eyes. What if Norbert had done his man business well? He tried to heed the midwife's warning that another *bibi* would kill her. But whenever he took her in frustration, she feared the worst and had been forced to end two pregnancies with the aid of yarrow and devil's club roots. The midwife's death sentence and the state of Josette Lavoie's womb preoccupied Norbert's female relations and the Old Crows, who had come around each time she was bed-ridden, curious as to why she had not been seen in the village. They would suspect something if she lost another *bibi*. Josette only attended church to please them. The Old Crows expected a Métis mother to lead her children by example and love the true faith. She did not care about being excommunicated from their church, but if she was caught aborting a child, she risked losing her four others.

She walked through the trees, searching for one of her favoured passages in the book. *Anything can be the cause of sorrow or joy.* Her lips formed each word, blotting the memory of last night, Madeleine's betrayal, and Cleophile's face, the look on it when she rode away. The *Spinoza* was more than a book pressed into service as diary, more than a place she wrote her thoughts in tight script in the margins. It transformed her, lifted her from brood mare to a woman of letters.

Her body might betray her, but Madeleine . . . *How will you live with the sin of refusing him?* She had taken the side of Church and God. Madeleine had drawn her in over the years, making her love her like a little mother. They'd relished goading the Old Crows, but now she was one of them.

The killing heat even here over the river, in the trees, and clouds bunched on the horizon in the shape of yarrow flowers in full bloom. She had never seen mountains, but imagined them like earth rising before her to the sky. Sun broke through and sent a ray of sudden light to the river's surface. In a margin of the *Spinoza*, Josette made a note of the date and wrote,

He has come. Not He as in Jesus, but close.

She'd let Norbert, despite not wanting to, and kept some small piece for herself. How was that refusing?

There was a sharp report of guns in the distance, one after the other, and in a moment, puffs of smoke appeared in the south. By now, Norbert would have discovered her missing, but she had been careful to ride in the river shallows, and he had never tracked her to this place. From a pouch at her hip, she took out a pinch of chopped red willow bark and offered it to the four directions, then earth and sky. Josette would not find herself in childbed again, death song on her lips and blood draining from a body determined yet to live. She prayed to make her womb cold.

Grandmothers, these words I send to you—if a spirit seeks me, find another more deserving.

The birch grove high above the river had always been a kind of church to her, but now the trees loomed too close, their pale trunks scarred with black, fading into the canopy of leaves above. She could feel Riel's presence, even here. The last fifteen years he had remained a distant enemy. It was said that he and his family would stay in St. Laurent and she would not be tempted to make him listen to how the *Anglais* soldiers, desperate for revenge, had taken it out on her father.

Shadows flew across the ground. She looked up as a flock of white pelicans soared in a V pattern toward the river. They swooped down, beating their massive wings against the water to drive fish to the shallows, and, in a wide semi-circle, dipped their large scooped bills, gobbling fish until the circle was so tight the ends of their bright orange bills almost touched.

There was a sudden crash and snapping of branches on the trail below, and she brushed the willow bark out of her hand. Dropping the *Spinoza* behind a rock, she forced breath into her lungs. In a moment, Norbert, mounted on his stallion, charged over the rise. He yanked the horse's reins, the only sound its frantic blowing.

"Now I must track my own wife." He dismounted and tipped his chin toward the river. "La Noire drags her reins in the water—if you leave on her again, I will sell her."

"She's my horse."

He removed his hat, and she saw that he struggled with himself, desperate to have her trust him again. When he took a step toward her, she edged away, held out her hand to ward him off. His pupils were wide, the first sign. "I won't take another drink." He came closer, circling. She put her back against a tree and closed her eyes. But he went to his knees before her, fingers reaching for the hem of her dress.

She looked down from outside herself, a hand drifting over his bowed head, and flinched as he got hold of her around the legs. His face pressed to her thighs, the heat of his breath through her dress. In a moment, he would lift her skirts, expect to take her here against this tree, and she caught at his hands, agreed to go back.

He kissed her palms in gratitude, turning them upward.

a tender creature

MARGUERITE RIEL STOOD near the window in Gabriel and Madame Dumont's bedroom. The sun was directly over the house and the air in the small room so close, she swayed on her feet, yet Madame Dumont insisted on pressing her, asking this and that about the journey.

Oui, Marguerite wanted to shout, it was hot and dusty, *oui* of course it was difficult. In camp this morning and despite the heat, Louis had insisted she put on a white lace collar over her dress to meet the Métis of the South Branch. But a prickly rash had broken out across her chest, small agonizing blisters also at her groin and in the elbow creases, thankfully hidden by her dress, but aggravated by it, too.

Madame Dumont fussed with Marguerite's daughter, Angélique, ten months old and not yet walking. Young Jean had climbed up on the bed, his cheek pressed against a pillow, fighting sleep. Marguerite put her hand to the curtain. Hundreds of miles from home, in a house with two floors, a room with a real bed and feather mattress. And yet she craved solitude.

In the front pasture, more horses were arriving: Métis from all over, eager to see the great Louis Riel. Women were in and out of the house, setting up feast tables. Her husband stood outside of Gabriel's saloon, a crowd of men around him. Louis wore the only suit he owned—a dark blue worsted he had traded three buffalo robes for in the Montana Territory. How he held himself while she wilted, sad and wretched. She slipped a hand into her skirt pocket and found her rosary.

Hail Mary full of grace, forgive me the sin of begrudging my husband's proud frame.

A smartly dressed Métis embraced Louis and held his hand a moment longer than necessary. The man said something low in Louis' ear that disturbed him—she could see it by the way he held himself—but they were interrupted by Gabriel Dumont, who had brought another Métis and a white man to meet him. The four of them spoke briefly, and Louis followed the small group into the saloon.

Marguerite had not cried since she was a child, but she felt like crying now. They were poor in Sun River, but at least she had him to herself. Since Gabriel Dumont had arrived, inviting him to the Saskatchewan, Louis spent hours talking to him and when she asked him something, he regarded her with a peculiar, bewildered expression.

There was a noise at the door, and Marguerite turned to find another woman in the room, a beauty with long black hair unbound around her face. Madame Dumont introduced them, and Marguerite extended her hand as she had many times downstairs, greeting the women whose names she would not remember. But Josette Lavoie looked away, and Marguerite let her hand drop. By Josette's wild-eyed look, she thought something must be wrong with her head.

Marguerite lifted a hand to her hair. It was a tangled matt, much as it had been when Louis had first seen her seated on a pony, the sun's rays directly upon her. He often said he knew then that he'd found his Virgin Mary, but she had lost her innocence on a buffalo hunt many years before and was prone to melancholy. She kept her secret well, modulating her voice to sweetness, pretending that she was above anger and opinions of her own.

The thought of coming to the North-West had terrified her, leaving family and the familiar, yet Louis did not ask her thoughts when making his decision. She had tried to convince him to stay, using his own words.

"You once told me," she said, as Gabriel Dumont waited outside their house, "that it was best for your health not to be in the North-West, mixed up with the Métis politics."

"Their sacred cause reclaims me," he replied. "I cannot refuse them my life and my blood."

Madame Dumont was suddenly there, unbuttoning Marguerite's coat. Her face loomed, black hair parted low over her forehead, expression grim, and a double-beaded rosary at her neck. Marguerite wanted to push her away, but let herself be undressed, like a child. She was in awe of those hands, the fingers swollen from years of hard work and large as a man's.

"So much dust," Madame Dumont said as she got her out of the coat. "I will wash it for you."

She started in on the dress and Marguerite burned with shame that she would soon stand in her underthings before these strange women. Madame Dumont spoke with pride of her hand-crank washing machine, the only one in the South Branch. Josette stood in the corner, fidgeting. She and Madame Dumont exchanged a private glance, almost imperceptible. Marguerite had seen this look among the women in Sun River and imagined their whispers.

That dark one, too plain, she is not good enough for the great Riel.

"Where are the men?" Madame Dumont asked.

"In Gabriel's saloon," said Josette. "Drinking and talking politics."

"Louis does not drink," Marguerite said with a smile.

Josette gave a short laugh. "He does now."

Marguerite's smile faded. Josette came to the window and looked down from behind the curtain, as if searching for someone. Marguerite did not care for her blunt manner, but she sized up Josette as if seeing her through Louis' eyes. The other Métis women she'd met downstairs wore their good black church dresses. Josette's was faded blue, the hem frayed and thick with dust, her apron stained. A pair of moccasins on her feet looked as though they'd been recently in water. Her long dark hair almost hid eyes that were shrouded in an expression somewhere between sadness and hate. And yet her face was thin and beautiful.

Louis will notice this one, she thought, glancing toward the saloon. Louis, who had surprised her shortly after their marriage with talk of the prophets Abraham and Moses, men whom God had granted many wives. Marguerite had listened, appalled, obsessed first with jealousy and fear, and then a thought that she could live with: her husband was too poor to support more than one wife.

Madame Dumont cleared her throat and nodded toward a bucket near the door. Josette moved reluctantly, pouring water into a crockery bowl on the dresser. She took up a comb and loosened the knot at the nape of Marguerite's neck but it snagged and her head was yanked back.

"*Pardon,*" Josette said.

"It's nothing." Before she had married Louis, Marguerite's sister had combed her hair. This kind of treatment was reserved for brides or women who had died in childbirth, readying them for burial.

Madame Dumont had thrown Marguerite's coat on the bed and picked up Angélique. Josette stepped around, and Marguerite cast her eyes to the floor, uncomfortable at having her so close. There was something absurd about having her hair fixed by a woman whose own was in worse shape.

"You have lost your *pêpîm* to Madeleine now." Josette said this in Cree, switching easily from French.

Madame Dumont cooed at Angélique. "We will let your *maman* rest before the feast." She stifled a cough. "It is the dust," she said before rushing out with the little girl. Besides the muffled sound of a coughing fit from the hallway, it was silent in the room. Marguerite wanted to go after them, take her daughter back into her arms, for she recognized the signs. She had watched the old ones suffer with lung disease before they passed with blood fits, yet now she too had the beginnings of the same affliction. It had become another secret she kept from Louis, blaming it on drafts or dust.

Josette began to fashion three curls over her forehead. "I wish my hair was straight," Marguerite said, in a fit of frustration, "like yours."

"You can have it if you like."

Marguerite's mouth twisted into a smile. She had not made friends in Sun River, and felt that maybe here she would find someone to share her fears, and the burdens only the wife of a great man was forced to bear.

But just as suddenly, Josette, as she gathered her hair back to fasten in a bun, crushed these hopes by asking a simple question. "Did you bring books?"

Marguerite looked down, confused. "Louis has brought some."

Josette's eyes came alive for the first time. "Which ones have you read?"

Marguerite took the comb out of her hand. "Women do not read." It was for men to do the thoughts and read the words. Then an awful thing occurred to her. *Women in the Saskatchewan could read. And write.* She felt she could not breathe, that she was too much under the eyes of those who saw her as a country simpleton.

Louis had written a poem about her. When he first read it aloud, she was moved to tears, but now the line, "Ah . . . she is a tender creature, always attentive to her duty," made her feel profoundly inadequate in the eyes of Josette.

the enemy

JOSETTE WENT QUIETLY down the stairs. If it were possible, Riel had sunk lower in her estimation. *Women do not read*. She thought of her diary, her Spinoza, lying behind a rock in the birch grove. With her luck, rain would fall for the first time in months and ruin it.

In the kitchen, women crowded around Madeleine's stove, warming the dishes they had brought. Others were taking food out to the feast tables. Louise Boucher held Riel's youngest in her arms. Madeleine was likely in the summer kitchen in a fluster of last minute preparations.

Josette meant to slip unnoticed out the back door, but the sound of horses arriving drew the women out on the porch. She followed, hesitating in the doorway. Lean Crow's band had come in on their ragged ponies, Lakota Sioux who had been in the South Branch for the past four years, freighting and trapping with the Métis.

Lean Crow and two of his men dismounted, their long, leather-bound braids swinging. Josette did not think it strange that the Sioux were here to greet Riel, but one of the braves had his face painted red and black, as if going to war. His name was Little Ghost, a boy of nineteen, who wore a buckskin war shirt fringed with horsehair and red handprints beaded up the sides. Despite his youth, he owned an elaborately beaded pair of leggings, with two decorated scalp locks sewn to the panels.

The crowd parted and there was Riel. Josette drew back behind the door, heart pounding at her ribs. He seemed taller than she remembered, but she'd been fourteen the last time she'd set eyes on him in Red River. He was older too, of course, creases around the eyes, which were intense, almost black and brooding, older than the man who had attended meetings at their house late at night, speaking of politics with her father and other supporters. She could not recall his light skin and *Anglais* manner of dress, or the pomade that had been applied to tame his waved hair. If it weren't for the moccasins on his feet, she'd think he was a Frenchman. The suit he wore must have caused him grief in this heat, but he would not remove the jacket, although a wicked sun beat down upon his head. He had grown a beard on the trail and it was untrimmed, something he seemed to regret, for his hand went to it as he strode forward to speak with Lean Crow.

But it was Little Ghost who greeted him. The warrior unleashed a string of declarations in Sioux, gesturing widely to his people. Gabriel acted as a go-between, translating the language he'd known from his trading days.

"He says that if the white soldiers come, they cannot kill him, for he is a ghost," Gabriel said in French. He seemed almost reluctant to add the rest of it. "He has come to show you his men. They will fight with you against the great white chief."

Josette thought that Riel hesitated to clasp Little Ghost's hand. "You have many fine men," he said, his face suddenly flushed. "But there will be no fight. We need your marks on our petition so the white chief will hear us."

Father Moulin had come down from Batoche and pushed his way through the crowd. He watched the proceedings as if he'd come across sinning and meant to force a confession.

Little Ghost cut his eyes at the priest then back to Riel. He said, "You have business with that one?"

"The White Queen loves his God." Riel exchanged a brief look with Gabriel. "We need his support as much as we need yours."

Gabriel translated this to Little Ghost, who nodded and accepted an invitation to join them. The Sioux were off their horses and eyeing food that had come out on the tables. Father Moulin stood with his cross in hand ready to bless the feast, but Riel was hurried off to Gabriel's saloon by some English half-breeds from Prince Albert.

Josette stared after him. Despite the heat, she felt a shiver go up her spine. Riel was already taking oaths of allegiance and speaking of petitions, as he had in Red River. She went out the back door and past the summer kitchen to the paddock where Norbert had tied their horses. After unlashing La Noire's reins, she paused for a long moment. If Norbert found that she had escaped again, there would be consequences, but she would rather face his wrath than suffer another moment in Riel's presence. Her fingers twisted into her horse's thick mane and for the second time that day, she leaped on its back.

they are all
going to hell

FATHER MOULIN STOOD near the feast tables where the Sioux dog
was skulking and giving him the evil eye. Moulin stared back at the
Indian youth, his blood boiling. Riel had accepted help from painted
heathens. Not just any Indians, but ones who wore the scalps of white
men they'd massacred at the Battle of the Little Bighorn.

Father André, head priest in the South Branch, had called him up to
Prince Albert last week after learning that Gabriel would return from
the Montana Territory with the legendary half-breed leader. André had
said, "Keep an eye on Riel. He can't be trusted. If you catch a whiff of
trouble, let me know immediately."

This was a whiff of trouble if he'd ever seen it. Riel had studied to be
a priest himself, but a man of God would not be, at this very moment, in
a saloon. Already Moulin had caught hints of immorality. In the front
pasture, men were passing bottles of homebrew from pocket to pocket.
For over fifty years, many good priests had accompanied the half-breeds

on their buffalo hunts. Blood and suffering they had endured, weeding out pagan ceremonies and belief in *Kisê-Manitow*. It was a blessing that the buffalo had died out and the half-breeds had settled to farm, but the old ways were still plain to see in the hide bags some of the men carried. These contained the games of their Indian ancestors, which Moulin strictly forbade—throwing buffalo bones etched in pagan symbols, drinking and wagering their horses—but they would do it later, after he went home. His rectory was eight miles north in Batoche, far enough that he would not be forced to lie abed and listen to the scrape of their fiddles, the stomping of many feet and think, *they are all going to hell.*

He had unhooked the large wooden cross that was tucked into his belt, anxious to bless the feast, but everyone was made to wait. Half-breeds had arrived from all over the South Branch. They were devoted to God, but when they came for the sacraments, they still whispered of superstitions and talked of omens and dreams. Moulin expected Riel to turn up in the confessional as well as Mass on Sunday. John A. Macdonald had forced him into a five-year exile. By choice, Riel had stayed away another ten. Macdonald might think fifteen years was punishment enough for Riel's part in the execution of Thomas Scott, but God had a longer memory.

Many tents had been pitched on the bluff overlooking the river, and children ran across the yard, eager to fill their bellies with dishes made only for celebrations. It was sweltering hot where he stood, sweat building under his wool cap, but Moulin would not remove the only protection he had from the blistering sun. His long black soutane had seen many years of service and was a point of contention for the Batoche matriarchs, who competed with each other to get it off his back and into a wash tub. The same good women who now arranged their dishes on the feast tables. Flies were getting to the food, and they whisked them away with their shawls. This waiting. And the Sioux war chief, paint not dry on his face. The squaws and children had tagged along behind on foot, anticipating a feast, and would lay waste to it if the half-breeds let them.

Lean Crow, their headman, stood in the long shadow cast by the house, his dour expression revealing nothing. That he had let an insolent young buck greet Riel was both symbolic and disturbing. Little Ghost possessed an air of authority, and Riel had taken notice. It was clear that Gabriel Dumont had arranged this welcoming party of savage Indians originally from south of the line—rag-tag fugitives without a reserve, who had made a permanent camp across the river at Batoche. Once, when he had thought Lean Crow was out hunting, Moulin had gone over there with a Bible to convert a few of the squaws, but Lean Crow returned and chased him out with a horse whip, saying he did not want the white man's religion. It didn't bode well that he was here pledging to fight with the Métis "against the great white chief."

Riel finally emerged from the saloon, followed by a group of men. He shook hands as he approached, and the people crowded close, impatient for a glimpse of him. Moulin was pleased to see that Riel had on simple moccasins, free of the elaborate beading he would have expected.

Moulin narrowed his eyes at Gabriel Dumont, who followed him in a deferential manner. He had a healthy respect for Dumont, who he had seen dedicate meat from his kills on the buffalo hunts to poor half-breed families. He was often called "Uncle Gabriel" by men older than him by many years. Men had entrusted their lives to him as captain of the hunts and on the trail. He was considered a judge in the district; if men had a dispute, they would visit him to solve it. He could not read or write but had organized petitions to Ottawa for the past ten years with the help of the priests. That he had given over that task to Riel impressed itself upon Moulin as significant. If Gabriel wanted Riel here, everyone wanted Riel here.

Riel stepped up to the feast tables and praised the bounty. Father Moulin watched as he made an effort to commend each woman, a politician through and through. He had a fine way with the French tongue. Moulin waited for him to finish so that he could administer the blessing. Stomachs were growling. What was he waiting for?

Riel presented himself to Moulin with reverence, and to the old priest's surprise, got down on one knee before him. The priest cleared his throat. *Eh bien*, this was a promising start. Riel crossed himself and kissed a rosary he'd taken from his pocket.

The good, pious half-breeds like Letendre and Goulet, merchants in

Batoche, expected him to sanctify the work Riel would do here. Moulin was about to place his hand on the man's head, but Riel suddenly rose and turned to the tables, lifting his hand to recite a blessing only a priest could make.

"Glory be to the Father, and to the Son, and to the Holy Spirit." Riel made the sign of the cross over the food. The half-breeds bowed their heads. "As it was in the beginning, is now, and ever shall be, world without end . . . Amen."

Moulin stood with his mouth open. *Le culot.* This was not the proper order of things.

Riel had started on the traditional mealtime blessing, "Bless us, O Lord, and these Thy gifts which we are about to receive from Thy bounty."

Moulin walked forward and raised his hand higher in benediction. A few heads lifted and Riel mumbled, losing his place. Moulin over-powered the man's voice with his own, almost shouting, "In the name of the Father, and of the Son, and of the Holy Spirit."

With some hesitation, the people murmured, "Amen." Already doubt crept into their eyes, questioning Church authority. Father André had been right. *He can't be trusted.*

After an awkward pause, Moulin turned to face him. "Monsieur Riel," he said, "I bless your service to the half-breeds." Riel returned his gaze with eyes dark beneath a furrowed brow. Steeling his jaw, Moulin added, "And may you be free of evil influence."

Riel's rosary was wound so tightly around his left fingers the knuckles had turned white.

Only when Letendre announced, "Come *mes amis, allons manger,*" did the moment pass, and Riel turned with a laugh.

"*Oui,* let us eat."

david

It had not rained in months, but every grass and rock was holy. To-

LATER THAT NIGHT, Louis Riel stood with Gabriel Dumont beside a smudge fire on the bluff overlooking the river. A tangle of willow and small aspen sloped to the banks of the Saskatchewan. He imagined it not unlike the great river Jordan, running silent in the dark, and he lifted his face to the sky. *I have returned, Lord.*

It had not rained in months, but every grass and rock was holy. To-day they had ridden out of a forest of poplar onto a wide plain when a kind of whirlwind kicked up, and the Saviour was there in the mounting sky, dust in the hair, in the eyes, wind raking the earth with fury then descending until He was little more than a breath in the trees.

For the past fifteen years, Riel had dreamed of coming back to his people, and they had welcomed him as a hero, but his stomach was cramping from the rich food, and he felt distinctly overcome by what had happened before the feast. A Sioux warrior had openly declared his allegiance, if *the white soldiers come*. At first, Riel had panicked, fearing an omen, but in the next moment, he had heard the voice of God.

Here are the Indians, come to your side.

With so many eyes on him, he had recovered and said there was no need of a fight, but the local priest had soon checked his elation and had the nerve to suggest that he was under the influence of the devil.

Gabriel stood on the other side of the fire, smoking and watching him with an odd expression. Riel guessed that many a man had been the target of the buffalo hunter's intense gaze, and many a man had looked away. Even in this heat, Gabriel wore a faded wool ceinture fléchée around his waist. On the buffalo hunts, his sash had kept out the cold and held a skinning knife, or was used to haul meat back to the carts. But Riel suspected that Gabriel and some of his old *capitaines* wore them in nostalgia for the days when the herds had been the centre of their existence. If it were not for Gabriel's unkempt beard and long hair, he would resemble an Indian chief. *His nose is French*, Louis thought, but facial features aside, he was left with the feeling that here was a beautiful animal.

Riel tried to calm himself yet his mind rebounded with possibilities. When Gabriel had arrived in Sun River, he brought a letter of welcome from the Métis, and Riel had read the words with anticipation and pride.

Where is the half-breed who does not feel the blow of your banishment and is not ready to defend you to the last drop of his blood? The whole race is calling for you!

It would be simple to get Métis signatures on his petition. But that would not be enough. God had told him the government would listen only if they feared the Indians were involved.

"I did not expect to see the Sioux," Gabriel said, taking the pipe from between his teeth. "Pray Ottawa will not hear the men that killed Custer have thrown their support behind you."

Riel felt nauseous, sweating as the fire blazed higher. The night was hotter than the day in this country. And *Custer?* He had not expected to hear that name. These were fierce warriors then, men he would want on his side. Of course, there would be no rebellion, but he had learned the hard way in Red River: Macdonald responded only to impending threats. Despite the gratifying sound of a fiddler tuning his instrument around a large fire that burned in Gabriel's front pasture, the pressure was building in Riel's chest, the old, dangerous pressure. He removed his tie as a harmonium joined the fiddle, and watched more Métis drawn by the music, already forming into couples as a reel started up.

There was a time when only the fear of the straitjacket, or being chained to the bed with men screaming down the halls, had kept Riel from expressing his suffocating frustration. On those lonely dark nights, he had learned to control a disappointment so profound it was like blood in his mouth.

He noticed that the Sioux had begun to dance in the outer circle where sparks rained down among them. "Their chief is young," he said, straining his eyes to pick out Little Ghost.

"Lean Crow is the headman," Gabriel said. "Little Ghost is his war chief."

Riel glanced quickly up at him. "The scalps on his leggings . . ."

"His father was Inkpaduta, one of the war chiefs at Little Bighorn." Gabriel eyed him, his gaze direct. "Little Ghost was only a boy, but he shot his arrows into the dying soldiers and took their hair."

The wind changed direction, and Riel moved to escape the trailing smoke. Gabriel's eyes moved with him. The buffalo hunter was like a dog that studied a man to see not where he looked, but what he might be thinking while he looked. Riel was fascinated with those eyes. Integrity there, but also the suggestion of danger. When they were on the trail, he'd seen the scar that ran across the left side of Gabriel's forehead. If a Blackfoot had once tried to take his scalp, Riel was certain the man had died trying.

"Inkpaduta's sons are protected north of the line," Gabriel said. "Lean Crow's band brought Little Ghost here. Some of our men have married their women."

Riel said a silent prayer to God for this blessing. "When Macdonald hears that Sitting Bull's braves from the Battle of the Little Bighorn have pledged their allegiance to me on my first day in the South Branch, he will take notice."

There it was. *Macdonald*. It had been years since he had spoken aloud the name of that foul vampire who had left him for dead. The man who had offered him money to disappear and not show his face again. Fifteen years without a country, but Macdonald's name had been in his head that long, turning his blood cold. Now Riel had come up to Jerusalem, crossed magnificent plains without end, rolling hills, sloughs filled with wild fowl. Bounty. That was why Macdonald wanted it, too.

Gabriel's deep-set eyes were on him again. "We will watch the Sioux while you write a petition that the English half-breeds and men like Charles Nolin will sign."

Nolin. Another name that made Riel flinch. Before the feast, Charles Nolin had embraced him and said in his ear, "I had been told you were ill, but you look good, my cousin. Have you come back to finish the job?" Riel had brought Manitoba into Confederation and won land claims for the Métis, only to have Macdonald chase him out like a criminal. Yet he was still haunted by his failures. Somehow Nolin had heard of the illness—one he had kept even from Marguerite. *Mososkwan*, he said to himself in Cree, the private nickname he had always used to describe Nolin. *Moose nose*. He knew the man would harbour his secret until it suited him to tell.

Nolin had written the welcome letter Gabriel had brought, but he'd always resented his leadership in Red River. "It is *Nolin* who needs to be watched," Riel said.

Gabriel took the pipe stem out of his mouth. "What did he say to you earlier? Something you did not like."

Riel hesitated before answering. "He heard I'd been ill." His doctors had warned him to avoid excitement, avoid talk of his health and competence and lead a quiet life. And yet words from his old mentor, Bishop Bourget, echoed in his head.

God has given you a mission, which you must fulfill in all respects.

Ten years ago the Spirit of God had come upon him in a cloud of flames and revealed his true purpose. But when he had shared the revelations with friends and family, they'd sent him to a madhouse. If Gabriel heard of this through Nolin, Riel would lose his loyalty. *Non*, if he wanted the man's trust, it must be done now. He breathed, his skin prickling, tried to find the right words to begin. As if sensing the change in his mood, Gabriel squinted through the smoke at him, waiting.

"In the years after I was exiled, I prayed to God," Riel said carefully. "It was thought that perhaps . . . I prayed too much, that I was possessed with an unnatural affliction of faith." Firelight played across Gabriel's face and those resolute eyes that bore down on him. It was a candid look of admiration from one of the most admired men in the North-West. It was right to tell him. Riel ignored the rising panic in his throat. "What I want to tell you is—my friends felt I went mad with all this praying. They committed me to an asylum . . . a madhouse."

Gabriel's gaze slipped back to the fire. He blinked a few times, appeared to be thinking. In a moment, he said, "I take a man as I find him. And it doesn't matter—"

"*Oui*, it does."

Gabriel took a deep draw on his pipe, inhaling and exhaling with enviable rhythm. "How long were you in this place?"

With the toe of his moccasin, Riel poked at a log that had fallen off the fire. "Long enough." Memories rushed at him and he pushed them down. *The Métis are like the Children of Israel*—he wanted to tell Gabriel—*persecuted, deprived of their heritage, and I will be like a second David to them, wrest justice from the tyrant*. Instead, he forced himself to think of those two tortured years in the Beauport Asylum. "That time," he said, "made me love the Métis more and strengthened my mission. We must obtain our rights, what is promised us. Do you understand?"

He hated himself for rambling, but he was still unnerved, perhaps cowed. Yes, he might as well admit it. This was the kind of man who could sniff out lies and conceit. And he was moved by Gabriel's devotion. Perhaps the great Métis warrior should know all of what God had said to him. He would understand when others hadn't. But the hand of God held him back. *It is not yet time*.

"I tell you because you are my Métis brother," he said. "I bare my soul to you. And we must go with conviction." He fought the need to explain himself. "I will tell you of the Night Watchers at Beauport. Every hour, they would walk the floors—" He broke off, for he had noticed lights advancing toward them, the eyes of otherworldly creatures. Coyotes and wolves had bothered their camps travelling north, and Riel had lain awake listening to them, arms around his wife and children.

Muscles tightened in his chest, and he forced himself to take a full breath. Many times he'd camped on the high Missouri and not heard such packs hunting at night. The red eyes grew closer, and Riel could now see these were not coyotes or wolves, but the light from four men's pipes, men who had left the main fire and were making their way to the bluff. Suddenly the weight of his mission seemed impossibly heavy. He slipped a hand into his breast coat pocket, where he carried the letter from his mentor, a letter that he kept with him at all times. He let the words wash over him.

I have the deep conviction that you will receive in this world, and sooner than you think, the reward for all your mental sacrifices, a thousand times more crushing than the sacrifices of material and visible life.

Three weeks ago, before their delegation left the Montana Territory, Riel had gone to the local priest, said that his people had sent for him and asked for his blessing. When he knelt before Father Eberschweiler, the priest had hesitated, saying, "I see your trip to the North-West ending in bloodshed and defeat." This had almost shaken his resolve, but the priest would have said the same thing to Christ himself as He came out of the desert. Now that Riel was in the North-West, he must establish himself as a prophet to the Métis. What did Christ do when he prepared to share his message with the world? Chose disciples. Gabriel was already here as Peter, firmly loyal, resolute. But he needed more.

He looked upon the four figures as they made their way to the mount. Here were Maxime Lépine, Michel Dumas, and Damase Carrière, old friends and Gabriel's inner circle of scouts. Men he'd trusted on the buffalo hunts. More would show themselves worthy in time. The last man came into sight. Charles Nolin. Riel closed his eyes.

And immediately, while he yet spake, cometh Judas.

le maudit anglais

GABRIEL DUMONT'S MIND raced as the men joined them at the fire. Each had influence in the Saskatchewan. Lépine had been a supporter of Riel in Red River, and Nolin too, although he was up in Prince Albert doing business with white men more than he was in Batoche. Dumas served as One Arrow Reserve's Indian agent, and Carrière had just rode in from Fort Pitt where he'd been cutting and squaring timber. Gabriel wanted to speak to him and hear news of the North Saskatchewan.

But first he needed to think. He was a man of the plains, of the hunt, and knew nothing of insanity among men. His experience with madness was limited to horses or dogs. If their eyes rolled and mouths foamed, Gabriel shot them in the head without a second thought. Among the Indians, if someone started a rant and tore their hair—that was a haunting, a *Wîhtikow* had taken them. Move to the next camp and leave them behind. But here was Riel admitting he'd been in a lunatic asylum, looking and sounding saner than any of them.

The men had brought out plugs of tobacco by the time Gabriel's adopted son, Alexandre, arrived carrying a billycan of water. The boy set it on a hooked branch over the fire and shook loose-leaf tea and some sugar into the water. Michel Dumas produced a flask of whiskey and offered it around, his eyes swimming. *Le Rat*, drinking all day. Any excuse to get in the bottle. Other men wore their longish hair loose about the ears, but Dumas had his smoothed back in town fashion— even a damn handkerchief tied around his throat.

Riel refused the flask, and said he'd wait for his favourite drink— black tea, sweet and hot. He hadn't wet his lips in the saloon earlier, but it didn't stop the others from nipping at Dumas' flask while they waited for the tea to boil. Maxime Lépine stood beside Riel as he had in Red River, a godly man, modest and restrained. Not a fighter, but one you'd want to have with you in a fight, regardless. Alexandre hung back just out of the fire's halo, gazing at the Métis hero he'd grown up hearing stories about. There was the first touch of beard on his son's raw-boned face, but he was too young to be invited to sit with them.

Could you be insane and the next moment not? Gabriel looked at Riel speaking with the men and thought of his neighbour, Norbert Lavoie, fallen from a horse and hurt his head. Now he was lazy, didn't care for work, and like a dog that lived under the porch, snarled at those that passed by, too dangerous to let in the house, too useful yet to take out and shoot.

The tea had boiled and Riel dipped a tin cup into the billycan. By reflex or habit, Gabriel put his hand to the chiseled grip of his hunting knife in the leather sheath at his waist. He had made the sheath as a boy, from the hide of his first kill. Riel didn't look crazy, but you wouldn't guess a buffalo bull could react before you turned in the saddle—he'd get your horse on the jump and outrun it too.

Whites in the east called the Métis "buffalo hunters" or "miserable French half-breeds." When Ottawa tried to push them out of Red River fifteen years ago, it was Riel pushed back. He'd brought Métis, English half-breeds, and white settlers together to draft a bill of rights. Gabriel admired Riel, how he'd forced Macdonald to make Red River a province and offer title to their lands. Riel had come to them rested, both champion and hero. He would challenge the old man in Ottawa again, the way a young bull defied the ailing leader for his cows—growl low and deep, scent the ground, make himself known.

He and Riel had been ten days on the trail from Montana Territory. Plenty of time for him to share that he'd been in an asylum. Why now? Gabriel glanced up at Charles Nolin, who was at his third swig of Dumas' whiskey. Nolin had a nose that gave him the look of barnyard or pasture and too much drink. His left hand, two fingers blown off from a misfired gun, rested on his barrel chest. Slippery *bâtard* profited from any situation, good or bad. Riel had seemed troubled, maybe angry, when Nolin greeted him today. Gabriel suspected that just the three of them knew about the asylum, and he wanted to keep it that way.

"Macdonald ignores your petitions," Riel was saying to the men. "Just as he did in Red River."

Nolin lowered the flask and wiped his mouth. "In time, he will give us what we want."

Gabriel wanted to leap the fire and grab Nolin by the throat. But it was four years since the buffalo had disappeared across the boundary line, with him captain of the chase. The days long over when he held the power to enforce hunt rules with his fist.

Riel had his head down but raised his eyes in a glare. "In *time*? Macdonald promised Métis rights would be secured in the North-West. Has this been done? Ottawa does not intend to govern this territory so much as to plunder it."

Gabriel was relieved to see that Riel had settled. He had not liked the look on his face earlier—roused at the idea of Lean Crow and Little Ghost's pledge of allegiance. The Métis needed a man who knew the words to make a petition, not accept support from Indians with scalps on their leggings.

"A claim in Duck Lake was jumped last month by a white settler," Michel Dumas said.

"Macdonald wants we should move west," Damase Carrière offered, and then fell silent, a man of few words.

"Or roll over like dogs," added Lépine. He swatted at a mosquito with his hat, then put it back on and crossed his arms, staring into the flames.

"Louis will make *le maudit Anglais* listen," Gabriel said.

"When my brother Ambroise arrives," Maxime said, "the other Métis leaders in the Saskatchewan will come to us."

Gabriel nodded. Before they had left Sun River on the return trip to Batoche, Riel had said he wished for his old supporters around him, and could not do without his loyal Métis, André Nault and his war lieutenant, Ambroise Lépine, who had been by his side during the Red River troubles. Gabriel had sent a messenger on a fast horse to Manitoba to bring Nault and Ambroise to Batoche.

"We need the *Anglais* half-breeds in Prince Albert," Riel said, sipping at his tea. "But we need the Indians more."

Gabriel studied the broad vault above, bright with moonlight. There might be weather starting up in the east. But the sky was clear, not a wisp of cloud across the stars. A prairie chicken gave one last, low call on the bluff and another answered in the backfields. Madeleine said the garden was dry to the finger, and women were obliged to wander the plains and coulees rooting up prairie turnip and bugleweed. He spat into the flames and watched it sizzle on a burning log. "Sioux marks on your petition are useless. We need a powerful Plains Cree chief to bring the Saskatchewan chiefs and their warriors to our side."

Riel fished in his pocket, bringing out a pipe. "Chief Piapot was always a rebel. Send runners to him and all the chiefs within a hundred miles," he said, unrolling some plug tobacco. "The more of us grumbling and growling, the better."

"Piapot's been brought to his knees by Ottawa," Gabriel said. "He was forced to take a reserve last year."

"Big Bear's the only holdout," said Carrière, his eyes on the fire.

"I thought he took treaty." Riel tamped the tobacco into his pipe bowl and struck a match against a rock to light it.

"He did," offered Dumas. "A reserve's been parcelled off for him at Frog Lake, but he refuses to move on it until Ottawa delivers their treaty promises."

"Ottawa's punishing him the way they did Piapot, to force him on," said Carrière. "The Indian agent there's a son of a bitch."

Gabriel admired Big Bear for holding out. But it bothered him that one of the old eagles of the Cree was begging for treaty rations. "Big Bear's like a fox circling the trap," he said to Riel. "He knows the food in it will save his people, but to take it . . . he'll lose the only power he has to change the treaties."

"He's legend to young braves in the territory," said Lépine. "Many have snuck off their reserves to join his band."

"*How* many?"

"We can't go to him," Lépine said. "Ottawa watches him too close."

"Get into his camp," said Riel. "Tell him we'll add his grievances to our petition if he signs his mark."

Nolin put up his hands. "No more talk of Indians. Macdonald has gone to great expense to pick lands for the last rebel chiefs. Their reserves are far apart for good reason. If word gets to Ottawa you're meeting Big Bear, Sir John will take it as an act of war."

"*Ah-hai!*" Dumas said in Cree. "Macdonald needs to hear."

Riel scowled and looked to Nolin, as if he wanted to say something, then thought better of it. He turned to Gabriel. "Ride out in the morning and find Big Bear. Ask him to come south."

Gabriel took one last draw on his pipe and knocked the remaining charred bits of tobacco against a log. "We'd have to feed his band. This drought . . ." He shook his head. "We'll be snaring muskrats and gophers soon enough. He doesn't trust whites—and half-breeds have too much white in them." A thought occurred to him and he raised his eyes to Riel. "He might listen to Josette Lavoie—his granddaughter. She and her husband have the land north of me. The Indians call her She Is So."

Riel looked at the dancers around the main fire, as if he expected that she would somehow appear.

Gabriel turned to Alexandre. "Go find Norbert's wife. Tell her Louis Riel wants to meet her."

Riel laughed as he watched the boy go. "This morning I prayed for a way to approach the Indians, and here is Big Bear's granddaughter under my nose."

"*Oui,*" said Gabriel. "It won't hurt to remind the old chief he has some blood in Batoche." He remembered that there was something to do with Josette earlier, after the cart brigade came in—Norbert looking for his wife and riding like a demon after her. When Gabriel asked Madeleine where Josette had gone, she gave him a strange answer. What was it? Now he remembered.

"Away from Riel."

he saves that
for you

⁓

AT FIRST LIGHT, Josette stood among an aspen grove north of her house. Already she sweated in her long dress. She leaned against La Noire's muscled withers and waved her hand to ward off the swarm of mosquitoes that had found her, rising out of the grass. The sky was bright and cloudless, sun filtering through the trees. Soon it would heat the dew-covered banks and pastures and drive the bugs away. One of Norbert's dogs had caught her scent. When it trotted up to investigate, she took a quick step toward it, for Cleophile had just come out of the house. Her daughter hesitated on the porch and Josette moved behind a tree, hand on her horse's reins. She would not show herself until she knew that Norbert had left.

What had her children thought when they awoke this morning to find her gone? Cleophile headed to the summer kitchen with matches in her hand to make a fire. Josette had almost convinced herself that Norbert was not around, when he emerged from the house and disappeared into the bush on the other side of the barn to check the snares. She would wait for him to saddle his horse and ride out before showing herself and avoid punishment for disobeying him twice.

Last night she had ridden north a mile or so and tied La Noire to a tree. She had pushed herself into the centre of a thick stand of wolf willow and watched the moon rise like some fell sign, listening to the strains of fiddle music from Riel's welcome celebration. At one point, she heard Norbert's horse plunge through the brush near the riverbank, her husband swearing and calling her name. Wrapped in her shawl, she had stayed there all night, sleeping in fits and starts.

Norbert reappeared from behind the barn. The body of a prairie chicken dangled from his hand, its head almost twisted off. His four dogs barked to get at it, and he yelled for them to quiet. His anger would be less from killing something, but he seemed to brood. She stood still, praying that she and La Noire blended into the trees.

As if satisfied that he was not being observed, Norbert went into the summer kitchen, closing the door behind him. Josette thought of Cleophile in there, starting the fire. But Norbert would not bother her, for he would be intent on the trap door in the centre of the room, which hid steps to the root cellar where he kept a bottle of rum. Last year, she had made the mistake of following him down and caught him drinking. He'd almost knocked her out, but she had never seen him raise a hand against the children.

A wave of nausea swept through her. Was it more than hunger that made her feel faint? Only two days had passed since Norbert had forced her. *Two days.* But she'd prayed to the ancestors to make her womb cold. It was fearful thinking that convinced her she was pregnant. She had stores of gumweed and devil's club in the root cellar. There was no harm in taking them as a preventative.

She had begun to worry over her three youngest in the house—Eulalie was nine, not old enough to be left so long with her younger brothers—when the door of the summer kitchen flew open and her daughter hurried out. Josette bolted from the trees, heading across the pasture toward Cleophile, who raised her head, wiping away tears, and ran past her to the house. Josette stopped short near the garden. She turned toward the summer kitchen and lifted a hand against a glare of sun in her eyes. If she hadn't been away all night, Norbert would not have punished the children.

He came out of the summer kitchen, his face red, as though shocked to see her, and she braced herself, ready to face his wrath. The dead prairie chicken still in his hand, he turned and went into the barn. She wanted to see the children, but Norbert had already come out, leading his horse and the saddle slung over his arm.

She took a step toward him. "If you hit her," she said, "I'll kill you."

Norbert heaved the saddle onto his horse's back. He did not look at her as he threw the reins across its neck, and she ducked to avoid being hit. He reached for the dead chicken and draped it over the saddle, making his horse baulk. Wahsis had come out of the house and stood on the porch, crying when he spotted her.

"Your son is hungry," she said, glancing at the prairie chicken. "You will not leave us without meat."

He kneed his horse in the stomach, and cinched the saddle tight over its heart. There were oats enough for the cow that it still gave milk, but Norbert knew the flour sack was almost empty and most of the yard chickens had escaped the heat of the henhouse and roosted in the bush, making it difficult to find eggs. He swung himself onto the horse and she tried to get out of the way, but a stirrup hit her across the cheek. She reeled back, yet resisted putting a hand to her face.

He looked down at her. "You make a fool of me at the feast," he said, "after I ask you not to. After I ask you *not* to. There is talk that you rule the house. What do you think was said when Louis Riel himself asks for Josette Lavoie and you are not there?" He wheeled his horse. "I am a laughingstock—Norbert Lavoie cannot keep his own wife."

She felt herself spinning. "Did he ask to meet the other women?"

"I was Gabriel's first captain on the hunts," he said, lifting his head. "Riel will ask me to be part of his council when it is established." His horse danced, mouthing the bit. Only after Norbert rode off in the direction of Batoche, his four dogs running after him, did Josette realize that she had been holding her breath.

She stared blankly at the ground, her mind working feverishly. Riel asked to meet her last night. Had he wanted to apologize, even beg forgiveness for causing her father's death? *Non*. Something else. The impulse to run again was overwhelming. She went back to the house and climbed the steps, picked up Wahsis. When she entered the kitchen, Cleophile stood at the table pouring boiling water from the kettle into a tin tub to do the dishes, her arm shaking from the strain. Wahsis ran to his brother and sister playing in the corner.

Josette lifted a tentative hand to Cleophile. "Where did he hit you?"

Her eyes went to her mother's cheek, where a welt had begun to rise, and said, "He saves that for you."

"Was he drinking in the root cellar?"

Cleophile shook her head and turned away.

"You must have seen him. Did he have a bottle?"

A wedge of bannock had been left on the table, and Josette took a bite of it, enough to keep herself from fainting. She touched her throbbing cheek. Louis Riel had asked to meet her. *Riel*. He had heard that she was the daughter of Guillaume Desjarlais and wanted to honour his sacrifice. Nothing more. She put a hand to her belly. There had been enough bad omens in two days to last a lifetime. By taking her, Norbert had shown that he no longer cared whether she lived or died. Her mother had been raised in Big Bear's camp, on stories of *Wîhtikow*, a monster that craved the flesh of those who looked to their own selfish needs rather than those of the band. Her *Nôhkom*, grandmother, would say this drought had brought the creature, or perhaps Josette herself was possessed. Hadn't she prayed to keep her womb cold? It was told that within the *Wîhtikow* beat a heart of ice.

The Old Crows knew that Louis Riel had asked for Josette Lavoie. Their contempt for her had most likely turned to a kind of obsession. She could disguise the vomiting from devil's club and yarrow as food poisoning, but it would be near impossible to conceal a third miscarriage. The old gossips were like dogs on the hunt when it came to sniffing out a pregnancy and might suspect that she had committed a mortal sin. How to throw them off the scent? She took up a cloth for the dishes, a plan forming in her mind. She did not believe in their God, but of all the possibilities available to her, there now seemed to be only one.

an indulgence

AROUND MIDDAY, FATHER MOULIN lowered himself into a chair at his kitchen table in the rectory. It was a relief to be indoors, but he could feel the temperature build in the house, the walls almost expanding and pulsing with heat. He crossed himself with a sigh, praying for rain. And for something to fill his stomach. He had eaten well at the feast, but that was almost a week past, and the ruthless prairie sun had destroyed his garden. "Dirty weather," the white settlers called it. Even the udders of his milch cow had dried up and festered with bloat.

The episode with Riel still stung him. A priest's blessing from a rebel! For years, the half-breeds had relied on the Church to help them understand new laws that had come into the territory from Ottawa, complex rules on land surveys and local governance. It had taken time and great effort to build their trust and dependence on the clergy for more than spiritual guidance.

Absently, he bit at the fingernails on his right hand until the cuticles were bloody. When he realized what he was doing, he sat on his hand to deny himself, muttering a prayer for moderation. *Consider the lilies how they grow: they toil not, they spin not.*

He would chew his nails down to bleeding stumps if not for the grace of God. Father André had sent word that Riel had held meetings in Prince Albert for the English half-breeds and white settlers, and had barred him from attending. Father André had enlisted both Charles Nolin and Lawrence Clarke, the Hudson's Bay Company Factor, to watch Riel, but André had directed Moulin, "Find someone else in Batoche to watch him, someone who can be trusted."

This morning, Moulin was woken early by a few traders forced by their wives to beg confession before they left on a freighting expedition to Qu'Appelle. He had tested their allegiance, hinting that Riel was dangerous, but they listened only long enough to receive penance before hurrying off.

Most of the breeds had kinship ties going back generations to Quebec, Red River, and a multitude of Indian tribes. When the buffalo died out, they had found ways to survive. Some had established stores in the village and become prosperous from freighting. Men like Xavier Letendre, who had been here longest, counted their wealth in cattle and horses. Moulin could depend on the farmers and carpenters and blacksmiths to show up at Mass. But the buffalo hunters like Gabriel Dumont followed the old ways of the plains, and were undisciplined, operating the ferries or saloons.

There was a knock at the door and he opened it to one of the half-breed wives, only her eyes showing over a shawl wrapped around her head against dust on the trail. When she removed it, he gave a start to see that it was Josette Lavoie, and with a purple bruise across her cheek.

"*Oui*," he said to cover his surprise. "This is why I did not see you at Riel's feast." She coloured, made some excuse of getting in the way of a horse rearing in its stall and handed him a small hide medicine bag.

He quickly tucked the bag behind a book on the table. A year ago, Josette had observed him scratching through his soutane during a sermon and guessed that he suffered from carbuncles. Shortly after, she had brought him the powder of *salsepareille* root with instructions on how to make a poultice. She had insisted that he surrender his soutane to be washed. He had refused her the soutane and the powder—the painful boils on his back and sides were God's punishment for sins that he had committed as a young man—but she'd pressed it into his hand, and the root had given him blessed relief. He should be glad of Josette's concern, yet there was something about her that was anything but charitable.

"*Bon*," he said, when Josette brought out a chunk of bannock wrapped in cloth. He accepted a straggle of carrots she offered, too. His parishioners would not let him go hungry, although Josette was not one of the women who came to the rectory to feed him. She was the product of *à la façon du pays*, a marriage in the fashion of the country, her parents flaunting their disregard for the Church. The devout women in the South Branch had half-breed mothers and grandmothers. Josette's mother was a Cree who had married an untamed French breed somewhere out on the plains. The man had most likely paid a bride price of horse or cow to her mother's people and a pipe was smoked to mark the deal, the couple left free to separate at any time. Yet they had not been so heathen in their ways to deny Josette schooling from the Grey Nuns in Red River.

There had been a Church project of sorts, at the time, to educate Métis girls. The priests had hand-picked those with aptitude to become nuns, planning to send them out and minister to the Cree tribes on the prairies. Josette had found it impossible to give up her heathen spirits and remained half in and half out of the true Church, no more than an odious heretic who thought she could freely interpret scripture and avoid the Sacrament of Penance. She attended Mass only to appease the pious matriarchs—who called her La Vieille—and her eldest daughter, Cleophile, whose admirable devotion made up for her mother's lack of faith. Moulin had tried to reach out to Josette, for he had never seen a more wretched soul. She was like one of the old witches: either kept to herself during the Métis gatherings or danced with her skirts around her knees, and could often be seen riding out into the woods, hair flying, to root up herbs. She was as the Magdalene, imprisoned in her own sorrows. Or like Eve, consigned to a lifetime of suffering for her sins.

He expected her to leave, but she made the sign of the cross and said, "Bless me father, for I have sinned."

Father Moulin tried not to look shocked. "How have you sinned, child?"

"I refused my husband."

"Refusing the marriage debt is a mortal sin!" He had been livid to hear that the midwife Caroline Arcand had told Josette her life was at risk if she became pregnant again. It was time to visit Madame Arcand with a reminder that God would punish her for warning women of danger in childbed, when any choice to avoid pregnancy was sinful.

Josette had managed to lower her eyes. "It is a cruel God who would wish me dead."

"*Non!* A wife hath no power of her own body, but the husband—"

"He should take another woman," she said bitterly.

Moulin shook his head, searching for the right words to help her find the strength to live as a good Catholic wife. "David said in the Psalm: Behold, children are a heritage from the Lord."

"If I become pregnant again, I'll die."

She looked so miserable, he was tempted to pat her hand but thought better of it. "If it be so you should die in childbed, that is God's will."

"You sound like one of the Old Crows."

Moulin bristled. The pious women judged her harshly, but she brought this on herself. A devout wife was the centre of the family. If her fear of God was not plain, she was regarded with suspicion, considered a threat. Rightly so. The half-breeds demanded strong hearts from their women. And the priests required a controlling influence over men who would rather be on the trail hunting than on their knees in church. It was rare for one of them to openly question divine authority; even Gabriel Dumont and some of his faithful scouts, who did not attend Mass regularly, were brought to heel by their wives.

He started up the stairs to the chapel on the second floor of the rectory, with Josette following close behind. The church was a stone's throw from the rectory, but the half-breeds did not like to wait until Sunday for him to hear their confessions. She sat in one of the chairs arranged in front of the table that served as a makeshift altar. Moulin dispensed five Paters and five Aves. Josette took out a rosary he recognized as Cleophile's and knelt on the prayer bench. She began to whisper her penance, thumbing a bead each time she finished a verse. Her head was not bowed as deeply as he might like and she did not demonstrate true sorrow, but she was here at least. He hoped that one of the good women of Batoche had seen her come in and stay. They would soon have their heads together, trying to guess what sin was so grave that she begged God for forgiveness.

Josette, her eyes closed, swayed on her knees and murmured in Cree, "*Êha, êkâkîsimoyân.*" Yes, I am praying.

His blood boiled to hear her say this. She was one of the few women breeds in Batoche who still wore a painted hide bag at her waist, and he was certain it contained more than tobacco. Most likely an old buffalo bone or wolf claw, and a lock of her dead daughter's hair. Pagan talismans to appease the spirits. She would not dare pray to them here! Moulin decided that if the women hadn't seen her, he would let slip (perhaps when one of them came to confession of her own), that La Vieille had finally let God into her heart. The ensuing gossip would keep them from thinking too much on Riel.

Josette had rushed through her rosary and sat with one eye open, observing him. He shot her a warning look, but she opened the other eye and gave him her full, uncomfortable stare. He had overheard a chance comment the other day—that Riel had called for Josette at the feast. Why? Obviously for her relation to Chief Big Bear.

"Have you met the great man?" he asked. There was a distracted, secretive look on her face and her breathing seemed to slow. Sweat had broken out on her forehead. "Are you ill?"

Her rosary dropped to the floor and he bent to pick it up. When he gave it to her, she took it with trembling fingers and said, "I am thinking of something I read in the *Spinoza.*"

He shut his eyes. She knew he would not tolerate mention of that evil book, one she had told him about years ago, hoping that he, like the Red River priest who had given it to her, would enjoy discussion on the heretical subject matter. What had possessed a man of God to give his student a book written by a Jew bent on fouling scripture? He had been required to read the book himself in seminary, but all this talk of reason! The priests were meant to dismiss these books, not gift them to Indian children under their care.

"That book," he said. "A vile attack on divine revelation."

"*We* are revelation."

Father Moulin slapped his leg. "Heresy."

She inclined her head. "Spinoza said the essence of that thing which can be conceived as *not existed* does not involve existence. If God exists as an essence, where is he?"

He was not an ignorant man, but this kind of thinking was impossible to follow. "God exists," he heard himself say. "He watches over us every moment."

"He must have many things to do. What use is someone like me, a small woman, to Him?"

Somehow, she had steered the conversation away from her wifely sin *and* Riel. He could almost see her with an apple in her hand, one that she had plucked from the tree of knowledge. He caught a small louse that had broken free of a seam in his soutane and crushed it deftly between his nubbed fingers. "What do you think of Riel?" he asked, observing her carefully.

She got up, her shawl trailing from her hand. "I think nothing of him." Her lips were pale, bloodless, the expression on her face one of contempt.

"Riel wanted you at the feast," he persevered. "Why?" Still she did not answer. It occurred to him that she might think Riel was a bad one. At least one of the breeds had seen his true nature. Moulin was now sitting on the edge of his chair. "We wouldn't wish for him to do more harm than good."

"He has already done enough harm."

Moulin started. She was a puzzle. Why did she hate Riel? He did not trust Josette, but here was his chance. "The Bishop himself would put you in his prayers if you let us know what Riel plots behind our backs."

Josette looked down at him as if she were a queen and he a mere subject who dared insult her. "I might let you know—if you offer me an indulgence."

He was stunned, first that she had agreed and second, the presumption to plead for such a thing. She had never before confessed to him and yet here she was, a woman Riel wanted to see, who had agreed to spy on him for the Church. It felt as if he were about to make a deal with the devil, but he stood reluctantly and placed a hand upon her head, whispering a lesser indulgence.

She smiled distractedly while receiving it, as if the blessing was for his benefit not hers. After he finished, she turned to the window. When he made a comment about looking forward to Riel's presence at Mass on Sunday, she said she was tired of hearing about the man, and hurried off without so much as an *à bientôt*.

He watched her slight form as she went across the meadow in front of the church and did not notice that one of his hands was at his mouth again, fingers creeping past his lips. Nolin and Clarke could be trusted to keep their counsel, not like this Jezebel.

I might let you know.

He bit at what was left of his nails. Josette could not possibly think her future sins were pardoned or that she had avoided hell by appealing to God's eternal mercy. She was already in hell. Her fate was set.

she is so

THAT SUNDAY, RIEL STEPPED into the church vestibule and shook Father Moulin's hand. "I enjoyed your sermon, Père Moulin." When the priest tried to pull his hand away, Riel used it to draw him closer. "'Just as through the disobedience of the one man, the many were made sinners,'" he said with a smile. "Such a message for the day I am in your congregation."

Riel stared into Moulin's pale blue eyes and thought he looked too much like one of his old teachers from the seminary in Montreal. Father Moulin raised his chin to meet his gaze, but blinked and looked away. "So also," the priest managed, "through the obedience of the one man the many will be made righteous."

Riel masked his uneasiness with a laugh before moving outside. Christ had been hounded by priests during the three years He travelled preaching the Lord's gospel. And He had also been betrayed by His disciples.

Riel was still recovering from an unexpected blow to his pride. The Métis runner, whom Gabriel had dispatched before they had left Sun

River, rode in yesterday from Manitoba, saying that André Nault and Ambroise Lépine would not come, but had pledged to send a delegation of Red River Métis to form a religious society of support for the cause. Riel did not want to hear of delegations and societies. He needed his old patriots *now*. He suspected they had been talked out of coming by Archbishop Taché and Father Ritchot, men of the cloth who had once been his trusted allies.

New purpose shone in Riel like a flame. God was showing him that he was being tested by the clergy here and in Red River for a reason. He must finally prove his own abilities. These good Métis, *his* people, were being manipulated by the tyrant, Macdonald. They were at risk of losing their language and culture, driven from the promised land.

He closed his eyes, entreating the Spirit who guided him. *They will not agree to leave their church.*

Without hesitation, the answer came. *Arouse their wonder.*

Clouds had gathered and there was an air of excitement among the parishioners. Months with no rain and their farms were scorched dry as a desert. It could just as quickly turn and pour for weeks, filling the brackish sloughs with alkaline water that would stink of rotting flesh and give their horses and cattle the scours. Yet in January, great sheets of snow would shift across the plains. Enough water for them all to drown in when it melted come spring.

The country was uncommonly beautiful. A majestic bluff over the river, poplar and birch and willow ringing the small prairie meadows that pitched in rises and draws. The lots were staked in the old French seigneurial system, allowing each farmer access to the river. Beyond the whitewashed houses and neatly plowed fields, beyond the trees that shaped the borderland, flat prairie stretched to the horizon. Across the river, a few stores and more farms dotting the bank. Progress.

A group of older Métis women surrounded his wife and children, and Riel used the moment to scan the parishioners who had come out of the church. Key to the Indians was Big Bear, the only chief who still clung to his freedom in the North-West. The only way to him was a woman who had so far proved elusive, but whose determined figure was heading out on the grassy meadow in front of the church and rectory with her children. Maxime Lépine had pointed out Josette Lavoie to him earlier, and when Father Moulin had droned on in his sermon, Riel observed her and her children in the row across from him. He had not been able to take his eyes from her profile as she stared down at a Bible, strands of dark hair escaping the knot at the back of her head. Maxime had told him that she was viewed as an outsider in the community because of her beauty and education. The men desired her and the women thought her too full of herself.

When he had first heard that she was rebellious, often flouting the priest's authority and dancing madly at the Métis celebrations, Riel had been dismayed. He hoped the woman he needed above all others here would be an exemplary Christian, a devoted wife and mother. But as he looked at Josette now, wind whipping her long skirts, he thought of Christ's greatest disciple, the Magdalene, who had also been an outcast before Jesus brought her into His fold. God had showed him that he would find no better woman to fulfill this role. He thought of how the Magdalene might have appeared when Christ first saw her: wild hair and eyes tortured by sin, not unlike Josette Lavoie's.

Mary loved the Lord, who called her to a new life.

Mary Magdalene, the lost rebel, had been with Jesus from the moment He cast out her demons, had accompanied Him throughout His ministry, and been at Golgotha when He was nailed to the cross. She was there when the other disciples ran away in fear. There to the end.

A group of Métis from Duck Lake headed his way, but he held up his hand with a smile and called Josette's name as he walked toward her through the prairie grass. She turned, and her expression gave way to a frown, which disturbed him. Surely, she would find him intimidating. He imagined that even white men, with their British ideals of beauty, must have given her a second look. He met her gaze and was stunned. *Marie-Julie.* The resemblance was there in Josette's eyes, the colour of a cat's, and in the look of them—both willful and tragic. He could not recall the happiness in his heart when he and his first love had signed a contract of marriage in Montreal, only the devastation that followed when her parents forbade the union. *You will never marry a half-breed.*

Josette's eyes also said that she would not tolerate a fool, and the old fear gripped him. "Gabriel tells me you are the granddaughter of Big Bear." He waited, but Josette said nothing, and his glance lingered on the shadow of a bruise on her cheek. "I admire him for being the last Cree chief to take treaty." Josette stared at her hands, which still held her Bible. Was she stubborn or simply shy? "Do you have influence with your grandfather?" he persevered. "Does he listen to you?"

She waved her young sons away from her skirts and shot her daughters a look. The girls took their brothers off to the trees near the rectory, where other children were playing. "Influence?" she replied carefully. "He welcomes me to camp when I come in."

He smiled, relieved to hear her finally speak. "If you could talk to him—"

Josette seemed taken aback. "Why?"

"To support our petition."

"My father followed you in Red River and came to regret it," she said with sullen reproach.

"Who was your father?"

She said his name and Riel's stomach cramped violently. For a moment, he was back in one of his nightmares, the prairie around him disappearing, this woman, the parishioners, like ghosts haunting a deserted house and him alone there. After he had escaped Red River, some Métis had suffered at the hands of the soldiers sent by Macdonald to punish him. Of all the people that God could have chosen, why the daughter of one of these men?

He looked up to find Josette looking at him strangely. "Papa suffered because of you—for what you did to Thomas Scott."

Thomas Scott. Riel resisted the urge to shout, what *I* did? *Me?* Images flew at him—Scott dragging Norbert Parisien to death behind a horse . . . Scott lunging from his prison cell as Riel passed. He could still feel the man's fingers tight around his throat. His Métis guards saying, "Get rid of him, or we'll murder him in the night." Riel had agreed to form a tribunal, as they had in the days of the hunts, and the council had voted in favour of execution. It had been carried out the next morning. Riel had not voted, nor pulled the trigger, yet he would be blamed for Scott's death for the rest of his days.

Churchgoers had congregated in the meadow, visiting, but some were now close enough to hear this talk about Thomas Scott. Who else would condemn him? Riel took Josette by the elbow and steered her out of earshot. He feared losing his temper and turned to search for the figure of his wife, who still stood in front of the church. Marguerite was already looking at him, and although he was too far away to see her eyes, he imagined her kindness, was soothed by the thought of her soft hand on his brow.

"I was forced to leave Red River," he said, trying to keep the sting out of his voice. "And rode for my life—exiled and hunted by assassins."

She pulled her arm away and rubbed the place where his hand had been. "Papa was beaten to death on the riverbank by soldiers."

He stared down at his moccasins, prairie grass waving against his knees, and could feel his anger fade, only to be replaced by a kind of loneliness. It struck him that he and Josette were alike, some part of them regretful and tortured, dark with anguish. The way she stood there, wind blowing the strands of her hair. It would not be easy to convince her, but when she finally came to him, she would prove his closest ally.

"Do you remember the names of the soldiers who killed your father?" he asked. "Were *they* arrested for their crime?" He did not like to think on his years at the insane asylum, locked in a barren room. His doctor had refused him a Bible, and he had sought comfort in the few books of poetry allowed to him. "Grief knits two hearts in closer bonds," he muttered to himself, "than happiness ever can."

She gave him a curious look. "Lamartine."

Marvellous are thy works. A woman in this wilderness who knew of the French poet. He would not deny the miracle. Mention of poetry caused a profound change in her. She drifted closer, light in her eyes, and wanted to know if he'd brought any books from the Montana Territory. He heard himself confess to bringing too many and writing verse of his own. When he saw the look of wistful interest on her face, he asked if she wrote poetry.

She smiled and said a shade cautiously that such a thing wasn't possible without the use of paper. But her smile disappeared as quickly as it had come, and she broke away from him without ceremony or propriety, wading with bitter disdain through the grass.

Riel could feel the people's eyes on him, their judgement.

And his undeniable need for her.

mistahi-maskwa

⌒

MARGUERITE RIEL WAS besieged by well-wishers after Mass, but it did not prevent her from keeping an eye on her husband, who watched Josette Lavoie stalk away from him out on the meadow. Louis, like all men, was not above noticing a pretty woman, but when his gaze had turned to Josette again and again during Mass, Marguerite's heart had churned with resentment at Josette's beauty, anger at Louis' disrespect, and a kind of shame, too, for not being good enough to keep him from wanting better.

After the service, she watched with a rising sense of dread as he went after Josette and spoke to her with surprising deference. It had been obvious by her insolent stance that she refused to give him the respect he was due. But there was a moment when Josette stepped closer to Louis, her hair blowing across her face.

Her husband had stared back at Josette, obviously agitated, and Marguerite thought of the day, not two moons past, when the delegation from the North-West had arrived in Sun River. Louis had sat at the kitchen table long after supper, brooding over a letter they had brought. That night, he had woken out of a nightmare, speaking of his sacred cause and whispering scripture. *His life and his blood.* Would it come to that? The thought frightened her and she shifted Angélique on her hip, still feeling the ache in her back from the long wagon ride north.

Louis now walked across the meadow toward her and the children, his hat in hand. He was a difficult man to understand in certain ways— ways of the mind—yet she yearned to protect him now as she did when he was taken by one of his fits, tested by God, and she would put out her hand or look at him and feel his struggle, his great effort pass through her.

He stopped to exchange greetings with a group of people who waited to speak to him. Marguerite stood with the children, impatient to have him back to herself. Josette lived near Gabriel Dumont, eight miles south of Batoche. Moise Ouellette, one of Louis' closest supporters, and husband to Gabriel's sister, had recently built a fine home for his large family in St. Laurent, and had invited them to use his old log house on the property. Marguerite had thought it too far for Louis to go back and forth from Batoche ten miles south, but now it did not seem far enough.

As her husband approached, she decided she would not let him know that she had already met Josette. But she could not resist asking, "Why were you speaking to that woman?"

"Who?" he said, still distracted. "*Oui*, Big Bear's granddaughter."

When Marguerite was a child on one of her father's buffalo hunts, they'd come across a band of Indians gathered at a crossing on the high Missouri, and her father had pointed out a man seated on a spotted pony, the saddle ornately beaded. "That is *Mistahi-maskwa*, Big Bear," he had said to her, "a man that will not listen to anyone but himself."

She had studied the old chief then and thought he was the most dig- nified man she'd ever laid eyes on. To think that Josette was his grand- daughter somehow added insult to injury.

"Strange she doesn't look like him." Although fine in bearing, Big Bear was not a handsome man. Compared to some of the Sioux she'd known in the Montana Territory, he was homely, his pock-marked face creased with wrinkles from many summers on the plains.

"*Non*," Louis said, "but she's going to bring me Big Bear."

The prick of sudden panic, sweat under her arms and at the back of her neck. When Louis had told her that God permitted a man more than one wife, he had seen her horrified reaction, and never spoke of it again, but there had not been women like Josette Lavoie in Sun River. "Why were you smiling after her?"

"I mean to gift her paper," he replied, "to write her poems." He turned to greet a Métis from St. Laurent who had come toward him, hand outstretched, anxious to meet the famous Riel.

Poems. The word was like a brand on her heart. Although she was proud of Louis, she could not read his poems, much less write her own. Now here was a woman, admittedly married, but with the same passions as her husband.

She's going to bring me Big Bear. This statement bothered her with its vague threat of future contact. She watched as Josette and her children drove south in their wagon. If her husband was to "need" someone, Marguerite would rather she not be a beautiful woman who could read, write poetry, and might very well test his faith.

take genesis

MIMOUX PLANTED HER hooves over the milking bucket and brayed. In the dimly lit barn, Josette examined her swollen udder with dismay. *Mastitis*. Most likely carelessness on behalf of Cleophile, whose chore it was to keep the hay for the cow's bed clean and dry. Mimoux had slept in a puddle of her own urine, contaminating her teats. For once, Josette did not curse the extra work. This morning, Norbert had made a production of dragging out his saddle bags and packing a pair of work gloves and some bannock from breakfast. She had watched with trepidation and followed him outside.

"I go to Fort Battleford," he said as he drew the bridle over his horse's head. "They're building a new outpost and need wood cutters."

It was like him to make work a sacrifice, when he most likely had cabin fever and wanted to be with his *amis* on the trail. Or perhaps he *had* taken up with an Indian woman on one of the nearby reserves. In any case, he hadn't touched her the last few weeks.

When Norbert had ridden away, the dust from his horse's hooves made Josette gag, and she had run to the latrines in time to lean over the hole and heave up her breakfast. Positive now that she was pregnant, she had begun to desperately mix her herbal abortives. She could tolerate feeling dizzy and weak, but tremors and nightmares were signs that she might be harming herself. The only solution was to visit her grandfather's band. Her *Nôhkom* was a medicine woman with the right herbs to stop Norbert's seed from taking greater hold in her womb. Tears stung Josette's eyes. She yearned for another *bibi*, but the thought of leaving her children with a man like Norbert firmed her resolve to end the pregnancy.

Mimoux kicked over the empty pail. Josette leaned to stroke her belly, applying a salve of garlic to her teats. Even a cow suffered to give milk. With this drought, there would be less hay in the back fields for winter feed, and diminished milk production as a result. If Norbert stuck to his work in Battleford, it might keep them going over the winter.

When Josette had visited Father Moulin, she had not planned to ask for an indulgence, but when he was so arrogant as to use her to spy on Louis Riel for the Church, she could not resist. She had underestimated the old priest. Two days after her confession, Madeleine had visited her with a freshly baked flan, in guilt, Josette thought, for speaking to her harshly on the day of Riel's arrival.

"The Old Crows think you have seen the error of your ways," she had said, and waited to hear an explanation as to why her neighbour had, without warning, found God. But Josette now considered Madeleine an Old Crow. It would not occur to her that a woman who had humbled herself before God and received an indulgence might commit the mortal sin of abortion.

The Old Crows had eyed her when Riel had come across the field after Mass on Sunday, inching closer to hear why he had singled her out. When she'd said her father's name and Thomas Scott's too, Riel had looked to his wife with the eyes of a drowning man. It had thrown him when she knew the name of the poet who had written the words he quoted. Lamartine had been a favourite of Father Dubois in Red River. But Riel had acted as if she were a genius. And yet there was something he had said that stuck with her:

Do you remember the names of the soldiers who killed your father?

Fixing blame on the men who had beaten him to death had not occurred to her. She leaned back on the milking stool and called for Cleophile. A few minutes later, the girl appeared in silhouette at the barn door, Norbert's dogs bounding after her. Josette was about to tell her that they would go to Big Bear's camp and to get their things together, when she saw a figure on horseback riding away from Gabriel and Madeleine's house. She squinted to see who it might be and stood up quickly, overturning the stool. On Sunday, she had walked away from Louis Riel, showing him she could not be easily won over, but here he was again. Would he not leave her alone? Wiping her hands on her skirt, she came out of the barn.

Riel got off his horse and ignored the barking dogs, removing a tied bundle of foolscap paper from his saddle bag.

When he gave it to her, she said, "*Bien,*" and put her hand to the paper. She would not let him see how delighted she was to touch its smooth surface.

He brought out a blunt pencil. "Not the finest, but it will do for now." He bent his head to look into her eyes, and she turned her face, still conscious of her bruised cheek. "I once had my papers and books taken from me," he said. "I know how precious these things are to one of a sensitive nature."

He followed her back into the barn, and Josette could not decide if he considered a *sensitive nature* a blessing or a kind of weakness. Cleophile had disappeared, too shy to meet the great Riel. Josette felt his eyes on her as she straddled the milking stool. She set the paper and pencil beside the grubby feed pails to show him that the gift would not change her feelings toward him.

"I have just been to Gabriel's." He paused, but she said nothing. "We leave tomorrow. Big Bear is on the trail to Battleford. They say he wants to meet Poundmaker and hold a sun dance . . ." He trailed off, his face reddening as she let the silence grow. After a long moment, he drew himself up and said, "There is talk that Ottawa will send police from Fort Carlton—to find your grandfather before I do." She granted him a brief look and he continued with greater confidence. "They will bribe him with rations to stay away from me."

Riel had shaved off his beard since she had last seen him and his moustache was carefully trimmed. There was a deep cleft in his chin that made him seem less imposing. Yet she could not look long into those dark, secretive eyes. "Why do you want my *Mosom*'s allegiance?" she finally said in English. "He does not give it easily."

"Big Bear should hear how Macdonald has been plotting."

"How do you know?"

"I have political contacts in Ottawa."

A tremor shook her hand, an effect of the herbs, and she pulled at one of the cow's teats to hide it. Although she had just decided to ride north to her people, she wanted to see how far Riel would go to convince her.

"Not many Métisse learned English or poetry," he said. "What else did you study in Red River?"

She did not like to remember her time in school. The Grey Nuns had thought they could make her love Jesus, transform her into a nun. She had tried, and found some solace in the Bible. But it had been a priest who opened her mind by giving her Spinoza's *Ethics*. "I spent a lot of time on my knees," she said, surprised to hear bitterness in her voice. "Father Dubois taught me science and arithmetic."

"Good, good," Riel said. "When I went to school, only boys studied those things."

"Yes—a girl must learn to be a wife."

He laughed. "What did you read, besides Lamartine?"

"I asked too many questions of the nuns. Father Dubois lent me his books."

"He must have thought you remarkable."

Had the old priest found her remarkable? She recalled Father Dubois' face when she had come to him after reading Spinoza, so pleased to have discovered a thing called "reason."

"You do not yearn for reason," he had said. "You yearn for God."

She thought of this often and it still confused her, for she did not yearn for *any* god, much less the heartless, punishing one that seemed resolved on making her suffer.

Riel asked what her Cree mother had thought of a religious education. Josette would not tell him that her mother had been forced, out of propriety, to attend church in Red River, but remained at odds with the Catholic God. A sudden bout of morning sickness rose in her throat and she panicked at the thought of retching in front of Louis Riel. "*Maman* has thoughts of how the world was made," she said, as the moment passed, "that do not resemble Genesis."

"The children I taught in Sun River said their 'Our Fathers' but would not forsake their mothers' superstitions." He smiled indulgently. "They whispered prayers to spirits of the Cree."

Josette hid her face behind the cow's rump. She had not taken him for another religious fanatic. "I learned my scripture to please the nuns and Father Dubois," she said. "As a piece of poetry, yes, but there were inconsistencies."

"Where?"

She stole a look at him. When Father Moulin had called the *Spinoza* a "vile attack on divine revelation," she had enjoyed baiting him with heretical talk and could not resist doing the same with Louis Riel. "Genesis—that is like the Cree stories. How the world was made."

A spark of disapproval in his eyes, then it was gone. "Genesis came directly from the hand of God."

Last year, four Grey Nuns had come from the east to teach school at St. Laurent. Josette had anticipated having them in the district, hoping that at least one of them would have an open mind. But they had regarded her as Riel did now, asking polite questions to trip up her mistaken logic.

She patted her cow. "Why can't there be a cause for Mimoux that's contained in her own nature?" Riel's colour was rising. It amused her that he would not stomach such blasphemy if he did not need her.

He took off his hat and kneaded it in his hands. "I'm curious how Genesis resembles the Cree creation myth."

Josette felt the muscles tighten in her jaw to hear him speak of her people's stories as *myths*. "Well, it doesn't," she said. "I was mistaken."

He put his hat back on and adjusted the brim. He looked at the far wall—as if he had found something of interest there—and then directly at her. "What kind of poetry do you write?"

She wanted to hate him, but it was impossible. Not since Father Dubois had someone, man or woman, spoken to her of poetry. "I write nothing that would interest you."

Riel raised his eyebrows. "Blessed is she who does not profane her talents."

The corner of her mouth lifted in a reluctant smile. He was close-minded, yet engaging, different from any man she had ever met. There was something about the set of his nose and the way he stood, hands idle yet dynamic, like a Roman statue she had seen in one of Father Dubois' books.

Riel fumbled in his pocket, asked if she would read a poem that he had written. She took the paper he held out to her. His expression as he watched her fold the poem and put it in her skirt pocket was that of a hopeful child. As a learned man, he must long, as she did, to converse with an educated member of his people. Maxime Lépine and a few other men could read and write, but Gabriel and the rest could not.

What harm would it do to go north with him? The idea fascinated her, that he would be forced to listen to Spinoza's theories of existence or risk ruining his chance at wooing Big Bear. She got up from the stool. "I will go with you tomorrow," she said, leading the cow by its halter.

When she passed Riel, his eyes betrayed a fleeting look of relief or triumph, as if he'd won her over, and her heart hardened toward him. She would let him think that he'd succeeded due to his charm. And perhaps she would take up Father Moulin's suggestion, that she get inside the great man's head.

Josette let go of Mimoux's halter, and they watched as she ambled toward the back pasture. Riel told her that a wagon would slow them down on the journey north tomorrow, and Madeleine had already volunteered to take her children. She was indignant that others had been so sure of her answer, they had made plans without her knowledge, but she said nothing. Riel studied her a moment. "What happened there?" he asked, his eyes going to her cheek.

She put her hand to it without thinking, and offered the same excuse she'd given Father Moulin. "Norbert's horse," she muttered. "Reared in its stall."

Riel nodded and she watched him leave from between a gap in the barn door. He mounted his horse, jerking the reins. Then he stopped and looked around; his expression seemed a mix of doubt as to the truth of her story and gratitude for accepting his offer. If he discovered that she travelled north with him to end an unwanted pregnancy, he would think her soul forever banned to purgatory. Riel could not possibly see her, but she drew back, an unspeakable grief descending on her like the beat of a raven's wing.

bestow on me
the grace

JOSETTE THRASHED HER way through a thicket of wolf willow, taking no notice that her shawl had been torn off on a thorny bush. When she was far enough from the trail, she leaned against a tree and heaved up what was in her stomach, retching until tears ran down her face. How could a ruined man like Norbert have such a strong seed?

Louis Riel waited for her, but they were hours away from making camp for the night. It was early afternoon, the sun hidden behind a thick haze of cloud. Diffused light slanted through a stand of birch trees, lined up in rows here as if someone had planted them in a garden. Josette undid the top buttons of her dress and fanned herself. Her anxiety had been building since yesterday, thinking more of her father, who had died because he supported Riel. That she now went to persuade her grandfather to his side seemed a betrayal of his memory. Not that she thought *Mosom* would listen. Many Cree chiefs had distinguished themselves as warriors against the Blackfoot, which Big Bear had done in his youth, but her grandfather was known to guide his people with spiritual visions and prophetic dreams. He already knew what was in Riel's heart.

Her hand slipped into her pocket to feel for the poem Riel had given her yesterday. After his visit to her farm, she had gone about her chores. Only after the children were in bed and she was alone, did she unfold the paper and hold it close to a candle in the kitchen. Since then, she'd committed it to memory.

"O My God, help Thou my fate.
Rescue me, no longer wait;
Bestow on me the grace
Not to frighten men away;
And teach me how to trace
The path which is Your holy way.

Support me, so men take
Me seriously. And see
That my words in them awake
Respect for my authority.

Oh, let me have such charm
That in speaking to men,
Both they and their chiefs will open
Their hearts and salute my designs
Without alarm."

Riel obviously hoped his poetic words would impress her that God had His imperious hand in the affair. Yet she had been struck by the mention of two words: "designs" and "charm," which resonated more with contrivance than integrity of vision.

She broke off a birch twig and chewed it, spitting out the pulp. There were better times to harvest, but she could not pass by these fine trees without gathering bark to make tea for her daughter, who had been born ailing and often fell sick with deadly coughs in winter. Josette feared losing her and experimented with combinations of remedies to strengthen her heart. After carefully cutting several branches, she left a pinch of red willow tobacco at the base of a trunk, singing to the spirit of the tree. At the sound of movement behind her, she turned to find Gabriel standing quietly, her shawl draped over the tip of his rifle.

"Riel did not want you lost," he said, handing her the shawl. The Métis of Batoche spoke French among themselves, but Gabriel addressed her in Cree, the language of his grandmothers. His eyes followed a game trail, one finger almost caressing the smooth wooden stock of his gun, as though he would rather be on the hunt.

"I am not lost," she said, moved that the leader of the South Branch Métis, the best with a horse and a gun, had come out to find her in the woods. In Red River, Gabriel had been spoken of with reverence as the greatest buffalo hunter and warrior in the North-West Territories. Even his rifle was legendary. Men were known to visit his saloon just to see *le Petit*. When she and Norbert had moved to the South Branch, Josette had been in awe to discover that the great Dumont was their neighbour. But he had not seemed to notice her beyond a cursory nod when she was in the company of Madeleine.

"You are afraid of speaking to your grandfather of Riel," he said. She raised her head with defiance to prove him wrong, but Gabriel fixed her with a look she found bold and assuming, as if he were taking her measure. "Riel said after he left Red River, your father was killed by the English."

Startled by this turn in conversation, she took up the edges of her apron in one hand and began to gather the cut birch branches. "I doubt *Mosom* will agree to put his mark on a half-breed petition."

"The police are looking for his band. It's said they will bribe him with rations to stay away from us."

"My grandfather cannot be bribed, either by the English or Riel."

"The warriors in your grandfather's camp are on edge. They're tired of being hungry."

She paused, bent to reach for a branch. Was he suggesting that they were ready to set up a soldier's lodge? *Never*. But she could not discount the fear that her uncles and the warriors had grown weary of Big Bear's strategy of dealing with the government. "They trust in his leadership without question," she said, then looked up to meet his eye. "As you do Riel's."

A flicker of a smile showed on Gabriel's face. "Riel is *Mistahi-maskwa*'s only chance to change the treaties. With his name on the petition, Poundmaker and other chiefs in the Saskatchewan will come to our side."

"Riel was our only chance in Red River, too."

Gabriel's smile had disappeared. "Riel united the Métis, English half-breeds, and white settlers—forced Macdonald to make a province under their terms. They made him promise title to their lands."

She placed a hand in her pocket to feel for Riel's poem. How could she be so bold as to contradict the great Gabriel Dumont? "Riel had a man executed," she reminded him. "Macdonald ran him out like a criminal, and we suffered for it."

Gabriel's eyes had grown dark, not so much in anger but blunt inquiry, a force that felt like a bullet had passed right through her. "*Âhâw*," he said, "I will not let him fail."

She held his gaze for a long moment, and felt a flush creeping up her neck. He looked at her with a kind of veiled defiance, as if he would like to dismiss her, then his expression changed, a softening, and it seemed that he saw her loneliness, all the secrets she had kept even from herself, the many moments of doubt and depression. The one no longer there.

Finally, she looked away, and he turned to lead her back to the trail. She faltered, recovering the breath that had gone out of her lungs, the smell of the freshly cut birch sap rising, and air that had become overwhelmingly close. Her hand, still in her pocket, finally released Riel's poem.

Rescue me, no longer wait. These words hinted at deficiency, written by a man pleading for recognition from his heedless God. If she were to respect anyone's authority, it would be Gabriel Dumont's, who had run the buffalo hunts. A man of reason who succeeded at every cause he had ever committed to in his heart.

━ ━

The sun was setting behind the trees when they stopped near a stream to make camp, a place that had been used by freighters, marked by a pit in the middle of a clearing where many fires had burned. Josette had gone out in a grove of cottonwoods, and made her way back with an armload of deadfall kindling. As she approached the clearing, she heard Riel before she saw him.

"Who are the head men in Big Bear's camp?"

She passed quietly through the trees until she could see Gabriel as he bent to start a fire with grass and small sticks.

"Lone Man is still good with him." He looked over his shoulder at Riel, who stood with one foot up on a rock. "Thunder Child and Lucky Man are gone. Twin Wolverine left last month, but he had a change of heart and is back. I hear that Big Bear's other son, Imasees, is making it hard for him. His war chief's a new one that joined camp from the Chipewyan—name of Wandering Spirit."

Riel laughed again. "That's the one I should speak to."

She stepped into the clearing and threw the kindling to the ground, daring him to look at her. "You said you wanted to speak to *Mosom*."

"Of course," Riel answered, evasively. "And the other head men, whoever they might be."

"The head man *is* Big Bear," she said, breath loud in her ears.

Gabriel piled some branches on his small fire then edged away. He picked up his rifle, looking at Riel as if to say, *I leave her to you*, and melted into the trees.

Riel eyed her with caution. "It's no secret that your *Mosom*'s band has attracted rebellious young warriors. They're not happy with the broken treaty promises and want to do something about it."

"*Mosom* has reasons not to go to his reserve," she said stubbornly. "His men will respect that."

The fire caught at the dry branches, illuminating Riel's face. "If Big Bear thinks he will find an honourable soul in a government man, he's mistaken."

"He has dreams of meeting the Queen herself." A gust of wind blew the flames toward her and she took a step back.

"He does not understand the white man's ways in politics—or their laws," Riel said, thrusting his hands deep into his pockets. "They'll starve his band to get him on that reserve."

She had been sure that her grandfather would not agree to speak to Riel, but both he and Gabriel insisted that his band was on the brink of starvation. If this were true, she did not like to think of her mother and relations suffering when the petition might help them. "What would you have me say to him?"

"Remind him that the Métis and Indians are still the true owners of the North-West."

"He knows that above all others."

Riel lifted his eyes to study her. "The Indians and Métis must stand together."

She looked away. "*Mosom* will not give his allegiance to a half-breed. You have Indian blood, but you are also of the whites, and he does not trust them."

Riel began to pace on the opposite side of the fire, his colour high. "God said to King David, 'I will appoint a place for my people Israel and plant them, so that they may dwell in their own place and not be moved again. I will subdue all your enemies.'" He paused and added in a low voice, "Josette, *He* has asked me to create a sovereign state of Métis and Indians, independent of the Dominion and with my new church at its head."

The picture that sprang to her mind was of the prophet Elijah raising the dead and bringing down fire from heaven. Did Riel think he had these powers? Although her *Mosom* also had visions of a large reserve where each band could roam free and govern itself, he would die before agreeing to it ruled by the white man's God.

Riel stopped pacing and put a hand to his forehead, as if reluctant to say what was in his mind. "God told me a woman would assist in my mission here, a woman in the South Branch. I know that woman is you." He looked at her and she stared back at him in fascination. "God said that you would share the burden of this mission," he went on. "And keep it secret until the time was right."

The sky had turned that rare, surprising blue, which only occurred at dusk. She looked up as a flock of birds flew from the trees and abruptly shifted direction. It was like the wind blowing over a field of grass.

Her first thought was what the Old Crows would say if they heard that Riel had chosen La Vieille to help him. But her good sense came into play. What kind of God wanted a heathen to assist the great Louis Riel? Not the one who had left her helpless in a war with Norbert over her own body.

Riel was watching her with obvious regret that she hadn't been moved by his talk of missions and secrets. "Tell Big Bear it saddens you to see his land stolen," he added. "Tell him that the government means to steal the half-breed lands too, and *you*—his own blood—are half-breed. The government will listen to our grievances if we stand with one voice."

Josette was surprised to find herself close to tears. Riel was a conundrum. One moment she had dismissed him as a religious fanatic and in the next he had moved her with his compassion and demand for justice. She wanted her lands as much as anyone. And none other than Gabriel Dumont was on his side. But how could she follow a man who believed the Métis were the children of Israel? It was an impossible dream, creating a sovereign nation ruled by Métis and Indians with his church at its head. Macdonald would no sooner agree to a separate state than the Métis would leave their beloved Catholic Church.

a sovereign state

⁀⁀

THAT NIGHT AT THE campfire, Gabriel Dumont watched Riel finish a piece of bannock and lick his fingers. The Métis leader dipped his tin cup into the billycan of tea and leaned back against his saddle. He closed his eyes and seemed to pray. When he opened them, Gabriel could see him look directly at Josette, who sat on the other side of the fire, speaking with Maxime Lépine. She held one of the birch branches she had harvested on the trail and traced its length with her knife edge until the limb was stripped to bare wood and curled shavings of bark lay on a blanket before her.

There was something compelling about Josette that he hadn't noticed when he had run across her in his kitchen with his wife or saw her moving between her house and barn with the children, doing chores. He was still unsettled by their earlier encounter. He had sensed her reluctance to involve Big Bear and followed her into the woods, thinking to encourage her, but she had quickly turned the conversation to Riel's misfortunes in Red River. It had been necessary to persuade her of his great successes, yet she had mentioned the messy execution business and suggested that he was mistaken to follow Riel without question. Gabriel did not make promises he could not keep and had been confident in the one he made to her: *I will not let him fail.*

But he had not bargained for the look she had given him. A look that had put him in mind of a magnificent grey mare he'd seen years ago at the head of a wild herd on the plains. Mane and tail black as midnight. He had gone out for days after to find the herd, meaning to take the grey mare for his own, but he had not found them. That horse still haunted him like some kind of phantom.

After they made camp, it had been unfortunate when Josette overheard Riel say that Big Bear was no longer the head man of his own band. Gabriel had not gone far after leaving them. He'd lingered in the bush, curious to hear how the great man would handle himself. Riel had tried to shift Josette's mood, appeal to her love of country. But one of his proclamations still rang in Gabriel's ears.

He has asked me to create a sovereign state of Métis and Indians, independent of the Dominion and with my new church at its head.

He'd brought Riel here to petition Macdonald for title to Métis lands, not to push for some idea that had come from his time in the crazy house or out of his disappointments in Red River. Gabriel had listened as Riel had made a beautiful speech. When Josette argued with him, he claimed that God had chosen her to assist him in his mission. Yet she had said nothing, as if confounded by it all. The way Riel looked at her now, Gabriel knew that he was not done trying to win her over.

Josette had gone to work on another branch, wedging it between her skirted lap and the blanket. Her hands, the nails broken, were finely shaped. They'd been too much in water, too much in the hardship of running a farm. Riel was telling of his schooling in Montreal and she listened, head to the side, her eyes molten in the firelight. Gabriel had heard how people were made. Adam. And Eve from his rib. It seemed unlikely that Josette had such a beginning. Her face was carved by a natural force. The bones of her cheek close under the skin, put him in mind of shale cut in the riverbank above Clark's Crossing, and women who had lived on those lands many years ago, working at the fires.

Maxime Lépine had wandered away from them, smoking his pipe. "Look," he said. The night sky was lit with bands of green and red, bright stars shining through the shimmering haze.

"*Kanimihtocik*," Gabriel said in Cree. The spirits dance.

"God Himself blesses our journey," Maxime replied.

"Each time something beautiful occurs in nature," Josette said amiably, "we must give credit to God."

Gabriel smiled before he could stop himself. He was far from pious and considered Métis women too influenced by the Church, his wife included.

Riel stared into the fire, as if he hadn't heard her comment. When Maxime went off into the shadows to relieve himself, Riel's expression lightened, as if an idea was beginning to form in his mind. "A leader must prove his abilities. Louis 'David' Riel will show the Métis that he is their prophet. You are my Peter," he said, speaking directly to Gabriel. "And Christ himself had two Marys, did he not?"

"Two Marys?" Gabriel said in the voice he used to quiet a horse. "We have the priests, but not our lands."

Riel stood up quickly. "*Oui*, you are right."

Gabriel frowned. Riel was unpredictable as a trapped wolverine. "You must write the petition as soon as you can."

Riel's eyes ranged around the fire until they found Josette. "Marguerite is my Mother Mary," he said, "and Josette will be my Magdalene."

Riel would not permit blasphemy, so Gabriel threw some wood onto the fire to hide his oath. "*Crisse*." Over the past month, Riel had spoken only of Métis politics. Why suddenly this talk of prophets and Marys?

Riel gazed at Josette with almost tender regard. "You have suffered—fallen angels surround you."

She set aside the branch she'd been working on and returned his look. Gabriel thought of a buffalo cow he'd once chased in the hunts, galloping alongside it on the prairie, getting closer, and her turning that massive head, a dark, liquid eye. How had she suffered? He did not listen to women gossiping about childbirth stories, but now recalled Madeleine coming down from the Lavoie's three years ago muttering of a collapsed womb and bleeding, that Josette had come close to death.

"Your husband . . ." Riel paused, with a strange, sudden look ". . . has hurt you."

Her eyes had slipped back to the fire, and she drew her shawl close around her. Norbert wasn't right in the head, but it had not occurred to Gabriel that he would hit his wife. He was up in Battleford. When he got back, Gabriel vowed to pay him a visit.

Riel was not finished. "Josette, God has told me that He means to save you."

Josette set about placing each piece of bark she had shaved from the branches into a hide bag that she kept for the purpose. She did not seem to like this talk of God either, and her expression was closed, secretive.

"God has chosen you," Riel said, nodding at them both. "To help me fight the tyrant for our lands. God will make the Métis Nation strong again."

Her hand that held the shawl to her breast plucked absently at a bit of thickly knitted wool that had come loose from the weave. Gabriel had been unable to look away as she glanced up at Riel. Strange that Big Bear's granddaughter, long slighted by the women of Batoche, and himself, a buffalo hunter that just wanted his land, had found themselves here, some kind of disciples to a prophet.

Riel went to his knees by the fire. He clasped his hands tightly together. "Jesus, Mary, Joseph, and Saint John the Baptist," he prayed. "Forgive the mistakes I made among the Crees—send them to help me."

Josette looked at Gabriel. Her face had turned pale, her breathing irregular. He could see the pulse at her throat. Firelight reflected in her eyes, and the warning: do not forget your promise. Again, he thought of the buffalo hunts. How the men had run the herds and the women waited for dust to settle before kneeling to skin the still-warm bodies. The sounds they made at the first cut, an old song, tongue at the roof of the mouth again and again. She took up the hide bag and rose to her feet. When she went to her tent, Gabriel stood, unnerved and afraid of what Riel might say next. Mumbling something about checking the horses, he walked quickly away from the fire.

The northern lights pulsed a vivid green on the horizon. As he approached the horses, they shifted to look around at him. His chestnut roan turned her head and he laid his hand on her neck, stroked the length of her muscled shoulder, letting it rest on her withers. He wanted to be out hunting, not listening to Riel speak of fallen angels and God.

An image from Gabriel's past continued to haunt him: a scene on the Grand Coteau in the Montana Territory, almost twenty years ago. He'd been scouting out with a small band of Métis when they came upon a group of white hide hunters setting fire around a herd, waiting for the buffalo to panic and stampede. The hide hunters ran down the trapped animals, air full of smoke from their rifles. He and his men had made camp a short distance away and the next morning, all that was left on the plains were mound after mound of bloody, glistening flesh. The white hunters had stripped the buffalo hides, cut out tongues and humps, and left the rest to rot. The Métis had harvested what meat they could, and Gabriel looked back as they rode away, some part of him dead, too. Later they heard this was the government's doing; keep the herds from moving north, break the Indian spirit. They'd done it well enough. Not one buffalo could be found between here and the Americas. Métis were forced to beg Ottawa for their lands to farm and Big Bear and his band starved free in the bush rather than be held captive on a reserve.

The northern lights had faded and only the moon remained, a sliver in the night sky. He felt the end of things—this boundless land now parcelled off like something that could be sold. Beneath his moccasins, the ground still threw heat from the day's sun. The air smelled of goldenrod and sage.

He thought of the look Josette had just given him as Riel prayed for help from the Cree. Gabriel felt off balance, that Riel was planning something beyond his control. And maybe by Josette herself. He, a man who loved his wife, a man with a job to do, had let down his guard and been mesmerized by her beauty. He shook his head, determined to clear his mind of Josette's sorrowful face and Riel's troubling talk of prophets and disciples.

Some part of him wanted to believe that Macdonald would answer a petition signed by Indians, Métis, English half-breeds, and white settlers in Prince Albert. A petition from Louis 'David' Riel, who said that God would not allow the Métis to be moved from their lands again. If Macdonald refused to agree to their demands and they were forced to rebel, Gabriel did not have faith that God would protect them. He believed in his gun and the need, one day, to fight the tyrant.

the spirit is not good
with him

JOSETTE LIFTED THE coyote skin flap. Inside *Nôhkom*'s tipi, a pot of water hung over the small fire, now eased to glowing embers. The air filled with the cloying pungency of sage smoke that drifted up to the opening in the tipi poles, where roots and herbs had been hung to dry.

Nôhkom sat cross-legged on the other side of the fire, eyes closed as if in a trance. She was Big Bear's first wife, the band's healer and medicine woman. Two years ago, Josette had come to her when her daughter was dying. But the lung disease could not be stopped by any medicine.

Grandmother opened her eyes. Her face was etched with lines fine as those on a map, wrinkled from years of walking miles in sun or driving snow. The dress she wore was made of gingham and old-fashioned in style, her neck encircled with ropes of beads she'd likely not removed since Big Bear had traded for them many years past.

He was out on a hunt, and Josette was thankful to visit *Nôhkom* without him in camp. And she was relieved to have another day to think, plan an approach. That morning, the men had left her outside the camp and ridden on for Prince Albert. Her eyes had followed Gabriel, who turned briefly in his saddle, as if to remind her that he had not forgotten his promise.

Josette knelt before her grandmother on an ancient, tanned buffalo hide that was heavily beaded along the edges. Power coursed through her body, and she felt dizzy with the force of this sacred place. After lighting a braid of sweet grass, *Nôhkom* palmed the smoke over her face and body then passed the braid to Josette, who did the same. The old woman lifted her chin, as if waiting for a sign, then crumbled a sharp-smelling herb into her palm. Holding her hand over the smudge, she scattered the herb into the simmering pot of water.

Josette thought of how Gabriel had struggled within himself at the fire last night, reminding Riel to concentrate on the petition, even swearing in frustration, something he had not seemed to notice. Riel, who had asked her to keep his vision a secret, the idea of a separate state run by his own church, because he obviously knew it was inconceivable. The talk of her becoming his Mary Magdalene had put her off. Then she had walked into *Mosom*'s camp, expecting to be met by children, excited to see her. But the cooking fires had not been lit and the women sat outside their tipis, glancing sidelong at her, their faces gaunt, morose. Children, too weak to play, squatted in the dust, eyes red-rimmed and defeated. She admitted the only hope for them was to join forces with Riel. She would not tell him of Riel's dream, but she could at least convince him to sign his petition.

Her grandmother sang in Cree as the tea steeped. Josette shut her eyes, the familiar incantation pulling her under, and the memory of Riel's claim in her mind: *God has told me He means to save you.* If God had wanted to save her, He would already have done it. Yet she could not dismiss Riel's accusation.

Fallen angels surround you.

It was an insult, but perhaps he knew the blackness in her heart—look where she was: on her knees, waiting for what Father Moulin would call an evil potion, ending a life to save her own. Riel had seen the bruise and presumed that Norbert was abusing her. Did he know that he had also taken her against her will and she was pregnant? There was one truth he hadn't guessed. She was not a blood relation of Big Bear. *Mosom* called her *Nôsisim*, my granddaughter, but Josette's mother had been adopted as a child. It had not seemed to matter until Riel said, "tell him that *you*—his own blood—is half-breed." What would he do if he discovered she was not related to the man whose mark on his petition was considered more precious than gold?

Nôhkom had dipped a cup into the decoction. Josette hesitated before bringing it to her lips, the midwife's words in her head: *The next one will kill you.* She drank it down, coughing at its bitterness.

Grandmother beckoned, and Josette knelt beside her, let her place her hands on her stomach, rocking as she prayed, eyes closed. "Great Mother who gives and takes without warning," she sang, "bring this one back to your breast. Do it now before the earth womb of my *Nôsisim* makes it fast."

Without warning she opened her eyes and her gaze was direct. "Your womb is weak," she said. "I cannot give these again."

—— ——

The next morning Josette woke with painful cramps and went out into the bush to gather moss for the bleeding to come. She discovered some plants that could not be found in Batoche and rooted them up, her thoughts in turmoil. *Bring back a young woman of Mosom's tribe, one with a strong womb who will take your place in Norbert's bed.* Such a thing occurred only among the Indians. It would not be tolerated by the Old Crows. She knelt quietly in the trees, her hands black with dirt, when she heard Big Bear and his warriors pass on a nearby game trail, returning from their hunt. Her first impulse was to make herself known, greet him, but she did not yet have the courage.

Later, when she had gone out on the prairie with the women to dig for dandelions, her mother came to find her. Big Bear was in his lodge and wanted to see his granddaughter. She went back with her, trying not to notice that her mother had lost weight she could not spare, and that her step was heavy, moccasins stirring the dust. Heat hung like a pall in the air. A sudden cramp made Josette wince, and for a moment she panicked, could not force herself to walk through the depressed camp, quiet on the banks of the North Saskatchewan. She had been here with them before, the river water running low over tumbled rocks and stones, the sound of drought.

The village dog pack loped ahead of them. A black cur bolted across her path, and she wavered, suddenly weak-kneed and dizzy. Most likely the herbs *Nôhkom* had given her and not an omen or a sign. What had Riel said of Big Bear's new war chief Wandering Spirit? "That's the one I should talk to." Yet he had spoken of his plans, heartfelt, honest. "The government will listen to our grievances if we stand with one voice." She could not forget him praying in his next breath to the saints for making mistakes among the Crees.

Big Bear's lodge was in the centre of camp, and they passed other tipis, once grand but now in tatters. In the days of the buffalo, the skins had been replaced every few years, but now they were ragged and threadbare—stinking like creek mud from the many times they had been rolled for transport, still wet from rain or snow.

Josette's mother had been telling her of the Indian agent at Frog Lake, who took pleasure in withholding their rations and pawed at the young women. When Little Feather said the man's name, Josette committed it to memory. She would ask Riel to look into this agent with the last name of Quinn. Her mother's expression had turned bitter. "Your grandfather asks why you ride with Riel. After your father's death . . ."

"White soldiers killed papa," she said. "Not Riel."

Her mother's eyes darkened. "How can you remember? You were a girl the day Riel had Thomas Scott taken out and shot—"

"It was the council's vote that he should die."

Little Feather glanced at her. "A great chief throws the stone into the lake and knows it will splash. He knows before he lifts his hand what it will mean to his people."

Josette did not answer. She had reminded Gabriel that the Métis had suffered for Riel's choice in refusing to stay Scott's execution. Had she been too quick to accept his promise that he wouldn't let it happen again?

They stood in front of Big Bear's lodge. His standard snapped in the wind at the top of the tipi poles. Once brightly painted, it had long since faded to grey. Josette ducked her head to enter the tipi, and was greeted by the potent smell of woodsmoke and sweat and hide. There he sat, cross-legged at the other side of the fire. Directly behind him, the medicine man held the band's pipe bag on his knees. Big Bear wore a dark flannel shirt, a pair of worn moccasins, and threadbare pants bound with an old rope. He too had lost weight, and despite heat from the fire, had a Hudson's Bay four-point blanket over his shoulders. His hands— veined and large knuckled—lay across his knees.

In the circle around the fire were a few of his counsellors—Four Sky Thunder and Josette's uncles, Big Bear's two elder sons. Imasees sat at his left and Twin Wolverine to his right. Close by were *Mosom*'s other two wives. Little Feather went to sit beside Big Bear's youngest wife and their son, Horse Child, who was almost the same age as her own son Patrice. *Nôhkom* was there, blinking slowly and studying Josette with eyes that did not betray their secret.

Among the younger men was one she did not recognize. He was handsome—eyes black as his hair, which fell down his back in long waves. A grey cap of lynx fur was draped over his head, the dead creature's eyes glittering, its teeth bared as if in final battle. The long tail dangled across his muscled shoulders. Over a dozen eagle feathers were sewn to the headdress, yellowed with age. A cartridge belt was strung across his chest, and he fingered it while eyeing her narrowly. So, this was Wandering Spirit, Big Bear's new war chief.

She knelt on one of the moth-eaten buffalo hides strewn on the floor and suspected many had been brought from other tipis, for her grandfather was too proud to show his relations how poor they really were.

Big Bear looked up at her. "Welcome *Nôsisim*. Is it well for you?"

Josette nodded and after he accepted her gifts of tobacco, sugar, and tea, she asked, "Did you make a good hunt, *Mosom*?"

"Our medicine was good. We got some rats in the bush."

Josette knew well enough what kind of hunt he had made. She had helped the women gut the muskrats earlier. The disagreeable task of skinning a carcass, holding the long, rigid tail and removing musk glands and fat from the dark meat. It pained her to hear that Big Bear, one of the great buffalo hunters of the plains, now considered these unpalatable creatures, "good medicine."

They spoke briefly of news from Batoche and of her children. He looked across the fire at her, his familiar wizened face, scarred years ago by the pox, shadowed in its light. "You have come to speak for Riel. Does he hold his spirit well?"

Josette forced herself to meet his eyes. "Riel has come to right wrongs done to his people by the government," she said carefully.

"*Âhâw.*" Big Bear nodded.

"He seeks your influence with the other bands in the Eagle Hills and Battleford." He stared long into the fire, and she took his silence as an invitation to continue. "Your people are starving, *Mosom*. You and Poundmaker can join with the half-breeds. Riel will put your grievances on his petition, and the one who is higher will listen to his words."

"I have tried to find a way to the one who is higher, and to the White Mother," he said, "but it is difficult to find her. If I do not have power to bring a new treaty, Riel has no power to bring a new treaty." He raised his eyes and squinted through smoke rising from the fire. "I am thinking of our last meeting. It was years ago. We were camped at Milk River, following the buffalo to the south feeding grounds. Hungry. Riel sent a messenger asking us to come eat with him—more like to hear him talk." He chuckled. "We went to hear what we could hear—and get some grub. He sat across the fire as you are now and asked me to bring men to him. I nodded and ate his grub. It was good. I will eat his food again, but not his words."

Did Riel consider this the "mistake" he had made among the Crees? She faltered, reluctant to reveal his prophetic dream to her grandfather, but not wishing to hide it, either. "He has visions of our people and the half-breeds living in one large territory under our own control."

Big Bear rubbed his chin for a moment. "Riel, his words filled my ears, but not my heart. I have seen him wander through the mists of my dream journeys. The spirit is not good with him." He gestured at the fire. "His vision for our people is smoke. He says he is like us, but he is not. Too much white blood in his veins."

She forced herself to breathe and not look at the men who waited for her response. To not look at the face of Big Bear, a man she had long respected and loved, who had just confirmed the same concerns she'd had about Riel. The image came to her, of a painting of Mary Magdalene in one of Father Dubois' books—naked and swooning before the Lord, her modesty covered by long, golden red hair. Impossibly beautiful.

"I am half-breed," she said. "I have white blood too."

He bent his head, appeared to weigh her words. "Because you have come," he said finally, "I will open my ears to him. We will see then if what you say is true."

Josette said that Riel waited for him in Prince Albert, and Wandering Spirit leaned forward. "*Cêskwa!* Our own territory? We must join with Riel."

Imasees turned to his father. "He cannot fill our bellies. Take a reserve and we will eat."

Big Bear seemed mesmerized by the flames. "I have not taken a reserve, it is true. I fear I will lose the power I have now as a wanderer to change the treaty. The whites think we will move to small bits of land and learn to farm, even as the rain does not fall or the winter winds blow snow down our backs."

There was a long silence and Four Sky Thunder rose, as if he had heard this speech too many times. Big Bear finally stood and exited the tipi with his counsellors around him. When she went out with her mother, the men had mounted their horses. She looked after her grandfather's figure as he rode away. The striped blanket around him seemed too heavy on his shoulders, or perhaps he was disheartened at what lay ahead—the testing of Riel and her own judgement.

That night, Wandering Spirit and the other young braves took advantage of Big Bear's absence and made a grass dance, painting themselves up. They drummed and strutted around a fire in the centre of camp telling stories of their past exploits and what they would like to do to the whites. They had not the nerve to set up a soldier's lodge, taking over from Big Bear, but Wandering Spirit danced like a war chief, swinging a sharp-bladed club around his head and uttering high, thin cries of his Chipewyan people, the fire throwing his shadow.

Josette dipped her tin cup into a large pot of stew over the cooking fire, the smell of wet fur and ripe flesh rising to greet her. As she drew the cup to the surface, a muskrat's head—its lips drawn back over yellow teeth—rolled in the broth. It was considered a good omen to draw a head on the first dip—a great delicacy and an insult to refuse it. Boiling in a stew for hours had not improved the look of the creature. The head turned in her cup, a lustrous eye staring. When the broth was consumed, she would be expected to take it up and gnaw the greasy meat off the skull. If she had not been ravenous, it would have turned her stomach.

The broth was thin, with no potatoes to thicken it, so she downed it quickly and was obliged to start on the head. As the men danced and stabbed at the air with their knives and rifles, she felt the first stirring of blood between her legs. Her womb cramped violently. She doubled over and made for her mother's tipi, crawling with relief to a buffalo robe.

Her mother opened the flap and looked in, the silhouette of her face against the hide. "She is So. It does not go well with you. The child must have a strong spirit." She clapped her hands around Josette, chasing away evil influence, "*Awas, awas!*"

"*Nôhkom* said I would suffer." The drum's steady beat pulsed from the ground beneath her. Blood seeped between her legs as if from an old wound and her pelvis ached. The familiar rough smell and feel of a buffalo hide at her cheek, worn past usefulness yet kept by her people out of nostalgia, grief. Soon, these things would be gone to dust.

She had been moved at her grandfather's quiet resistance and done her best to persuade him, if only to save the band from starvation. Perhaps Riel would use his eloquence and win the last rebel Cree chief's mark on his petition. But it was Gabriel's face that persisted in her memory. She had looked at him over the fire last night, daring him to deliver on his promise. *I will not let him fail.* Could she support Riel with that kind of passionate confidence? If she did, it would be because the best man in the South Branch had pledged his allegiance. But Gabriel did not know of Riel's secret vision. If he did, would he still be willing to follow him to the end?

god has told me

IT WAS LATE MORNING, the sky free of clouds, threatening another day of heat. Josette stood in a thicket of Saskatoon bushes. A willow basket was hung around her neck, leaving both of her hands free to pick. The berries were purplish red, not yet ripe, blighted by the never-ending drought. Josette's children ranged along the thicket, even young Wahsis contributing his share. The plain behind them was dotted with white tents. When these berries were gathered, the women and children would move, and move again, until the entire region was picked clean.

Madeleine Dumont tipped some of her berries into Patrice's basket when he wasn't looking, a smile on her redoubtable face. Her dark, thick hair fell in a braid down her back and was smeared with creek mud to keep away the flies. She had on the same long-sleeved, unforgiving dress all Métis women wore, even in the worst of heat, and set about stripping branches clean of berries, her jaw set and decisive eyes fixed on the bush—as they did on those who came across her path—incapable of suffering a fool.

The sun climbed higher in the sky, the women sweating and joking amongst themselves that the only benefit of heat was the absence of mosquitoes that had bothered them earlier. Josette was hit with a cramp so violent she almost cried out. She bent over with the dry heaves, and turned to avoid Madeleine's eyes on her, but could see the forbidding figure of Father Moulin standing in his black soutane, down by the creek. He accompanied the women on berry-picking expeditions, as he had to the buffalo hunts, and eyed her suspiciously.

She looked toward Eulalie and Cleophile, who were searching for Seneca snakeroot in the nearby bush. Eulalie went to her knees, digging at a root. When she worked it free, she lifted it to her nose and inhaled, rubbed off the dirt and nibbled at it, as *Nôhkom* had taught her, to test its potency. Cleophile had already taken a pinch of tobacco from her medicine bag for the spirit of the plant before her sister filled the hole.

Josette plucked at a branch laden with berries, so absorbed in her thoughts, she did not notice that Moulin had come up behind her.

"What is your sickness?" he said, his breath on her neck.

"I ate bad meat in my grandfather's camp," she said carefully, a cluster of berries in her hand. "Muskrat does not agree with me."

"What did you learn on the trail with Riel?"

She turned to find him staring at her angrily. "Nothing."

"I'm told he met with your grandfather and has brought a white man back from Prince Albert. That the two of them are holed up there in St. Laurent, writing a petition." Moulin moved closer. "You forget our agreement."

Josette dropped her eyes to avoid his accusing look. She imagined his outrage if she told him that Riel wished to create a separate state here in the North-West, with his own church at its head.

Henriette Parenteau was nearby and had overheard Moulin's remark. "Leave her be," she scolded and nodded to Josette before moving away to pick another bush.

He bit at his nails and Josette hid a smile, pleased that the leader of the Old Crows had defended her. But the priest took her arm, "Do not affront God," he muttered and she waited, suffering the feel of those cracked and bloody fingers on her. Did he suspect her of mortal sin? "You would do well to confess again," he went on, "for it is plain you are rejecting good and choosing evil by following Riel."

Moulin stalked away on his bandy legs, and Josette let her breath out in relief. She opened her hand to find the crushed berries, juice staining her fingers. She knelt to wipe her hand in the grass, looking up to call her daughters, but was met by the sight of a familiar form on the other side of the meadow. Louis Riel was getting out of a wagon, accompanied by the white man from Prince Albert. She watched as they walked directly toward her.

"Eh," she called out to them, "men are not allowed."

Riel laughed gamely, and took off his hat to the women, who stared, curious as to why he had invaded their berry-picking camp. He stood before Josette, his smile dissolving. "God sent me here today—he has told me that you are troubled."

She stood rooted to the earth. The white man had dropped back, suit jacket draped over his shoulder. His face, partly shaded by a felt hat, was kind, almost despondent, the heavy-lidded eyes dark and apologetic.

Riel put his arm around her and turned her to face Madeleine and the few women nearby. "I see into Josette's heart," he said in a formal voice. "I hear her cries for freedom." More women hurried across the open field, eager to hear what was happening. Riel paused when he saw Father Moulin, but in a moment, went on. "Josette has suffered much. Perhaps she is being punished by God."

The feel of his arm on her shoulder, and the Old Crows murmuring to each other in agreement. She bent her head, blinking furiously. For all of Riel's talk around the campfire, he had not actually *asked* her if she would agree to be his Mary Magdalene. But Christ had not demanded Mary be his disciple, he had performed a ceremony to make her one. Josette felt the urge to run, and *would* if he spoke of Norbert hurting her, or the fallen angels. Faces were turned to him, the great Riel, whose only purpose here was to demonstrate his prophetic powers.

He looked down at her, his eyes hopeful and anxious. "God has told me," he said, "that Josette has suffered to become my disciple."

Father Moulin had taken the cross out of his belt, but remained silent, frowning. Several of the women's jaws dropped.

"Do you wish to truly know God?" Riel asked her. "To walk in the law of love, you must be delivered from darkness."

In the sudden, appalling quiet, only the sound of the creek, and a mutable wind that rose and whispered the grass. She reminded herself that this was a harmless ceremony, part of Riel's bid to gain respect, but Father Dubois' presence was there also with his admonition, "You do not yearn for reason, you yearn to love God."

There was a sudden, warm surge of blood, the cloth bunched between her legs soaked to overflowing. She had sought another name than "sin" for the battle she had waged since her earliest memory for the right to own her mind, her body, her life and feared herself strange to the world, perhaps no more than a deceiver, inhabiting the roles of wife and mother, a lone planet with moons and stars swinging in their arcs around her. *You must be delivered from darkness.* She could feel the women's expectant eyes, and a scalding ache spread from the centre of her chest, her entombed heart pouring out its solitude.

Riel waited, as though expecting her to kneel. He seemed to recognize her struggle and stepped nearer, placing his hand upon her head. "This woman now upholds the royal law," he said. "She is released from her prison of darkness."

She looked up to see Henriette Parenteau's face transformed by mystical wonder. And Marguerite Riel, who had just emerged from a tent where she had been tending her ill son, unaware of Louis' arrival. She had unbuttoned the top of her dress to nurse her sick boy and she drew it closed, eyes flickering in disbelief at the sight of her husband's hand on Josette's head, the women staring in rapt astonishment. The expression on Marguerite's face would stay with Josette, for she had seen it once in the eyes of a wounded buffalo that lay in the dust before the hunting knife was unsheathed.

At that moment, a scream came from among the gathered women. The heavily pregnant Elise Gladu clutched her belly and went to her knees.

Riel's face was flushed, his eyes bright with elation. "It is a sign— God answers by bringing forth new life. Just as Christ was born humbly to Mary she will have her child in the wilderness."

hunted like
an elk

MADELEINE EMERGED FROM the birthing tent and inhaled fresh air. It was now dark; a full moon partly obscured by cloud illuminated the meadow. She rolled down her sleeves, pausing when an agonized moan came from inside the tent. It was not going well for Elise Gladu, who had just given birth to her first child. The efforts of two midwives were frustrated by the refusal of the afterbirth to come. And the interference of Father Moulin. It was bad luck to hemorrhage in berry-picking camp with a man of God standing watch, forbidding Elise's relations to brew medicine teas to stop the bleeding.

Moulin lurked nearby, his eyes glittering when they caught the moon. Madeleine turned her back to him and cursed under her breath. She had liked this priest's humble ways, but now she wanted to kick some sense into him for thwarting the midwives' work.

Despite the heat of the day, a breeze had lifted off the creek and she tucked the collar of her dress tight around her neck. If wind touched her throat, she would fall into a fit of coughing that would make the women forget horrible birth stories or the wonder of Riel's new miracle. The smell of cooked meat and the familiar tang of black tea brewing drew her to the nearest fire. When she leaned to dip a cup into the billycan, she saw the silhouette of Riel, who stood on the creek bank with Josette and the white man from Prince Albert. A group of girls, including La Rose Ouellette and her sisters, surrounded them. There was no doubt they looked at Josette with a hero's worship. Today, the women had gossiped at how La Rose had become infatuated with *l'Anglais*. La Rose was only seventeen and the daughter of Riel's host, Moise Ouellette. It seemed like sin.

A long, terrible cry came from the birthing tent, but Josette was lively as if she hadn't heard, laughing at something that Riel had just said. Where were her children? Being minded by Cleophile, most likely, a *p'tite mère* at her young age. The travesty of Riel making Josette his Mary Magdalene. And with the wife, Marguerite, standing right there. She did not like to see Josette look so close to Riel when Gabriel was riding all over the South Saskatchewan with his brother Isidore, mustering support for Riel's petition. He would not be pleased to hear that his hero had staged a blessing in a woman's camp for what seemed like theatrical benefit. She would tell her husband of La Vieille, struggling within herself, receiving Riel's forgiveness. And Father Moulin. He had always considered Josette beyond saving and ignored her. Yet today he had followed her around as if she owed him something, the two of them arguing.

The young women had linked hands and began a hymn normally sung at the Feast of St. Mary Magdalene.

"Take my life, and let it be consecrated, Lord to Thee.
Take my moments and my days; let them flow in ceaseless praise."

Josette and *l'Anglais* had moved away from the others and had their heads together, as if their plans should not be known. Her eyes not leaving them, Madeleine threw what was left of her tea in the grass and walked purposefully toward the creek.

She could hear Josette say to *l'Anglais*, "I will teach you some French, too."

"Good luck," the white man said. "My accent is very bad." They seemed unaware of her approach or that Marguerite Riel stood miserably to one side, her youngest child drowsing on her shoulder, the other one ailing with summer fever in her tent. Madeleine threw a warning glance at Josette, but she did not look her way.

L'Anglais was a strange sight. Why was he here in a suit of clothes standing by a meadow stream in the dark, among Métis women? And now reciting verse in English to Josette, his head at an unnatural angle, moon sheen on his slicked hair. He offended her ear with his harsh language and yet Riel glanced to him with respect. *Now*, she thought, *do not think of him this way when he helps Riel write the petition, helps the Métis.* Unreasonable feelings had come to plague her more often. She was not one for emotion and idle thought, but at night her head was increasingly filled with fearful imaginings and she could not sleep.

Riel stood near his wife, enraptured by the girls' singing, but had finally noticed Madeleine. "William has taken to courting La Rose," he said to her. "Old man Ouellette insists that he convert. Josette has volunteered to instruct him in the catechism."

Madeleine could see Marguerite bristle. Why did Josette flaunt her learning? It was a slap in the face to any woman who could not read and write. And she was the last person who should teach the catechism. No wonder Moulin was in a state.

Riel looked to the birthing tent, where the priest still hovered. "Why was he in with the women?"

"The afterbirth remains in the womb," Madeleine said. "It is God's decision whether she will live or die."

Riel's eyes darted back to Moulin. "He is here to spy on me. I am watched all the time now. Hunted like an elk in my own country."

She squinted at Riel in the shadows, not sure she had heard him right. "Père Moulin is always with the women at berry-picking camp." The moon had come out from behind a drift of cloud and she could see Riel's face more clearly now. There was that look again, of uneasiness, that she'd glimpsed the day he'd arrived. Gabriel would have nothing to do with a man who said he was hunted like an elk, or feared he was spied on by an old priest. There was another long cry from Elise Gladu and then only the low keening of the girls:

"Take my will, and make it Thine; it shall be no longer mine.
Take my heart, it is Thine own; it shall be Thy royal throne."

Madeleine stared hard into the creek, for it seemed to her the shadow of grasses cast across the moonlit surface shuddered, and by some trick of reflection, she saw Gabriel's face, his hair loose around him, as if floating on snow, and it red with his blood.

supplication

A STORM HAD ROLLED in at dawn, drowning everything that the sun had not yet withered. Sheet lightning still flashed in the distance, followed by the low rumble of thunder. The sky was thick with every manner of cloud, black as night and each value of grey, brimming with moisture and the continued threat of storm.

Josette rode her horse up the trail through the Caron and Gareau farms. Their back fields emanated the heady fragrance of drought-stricken earth saturated by sudden rain. The oat stalks were still dry, almost devoid of life. Even if the Métis farmers managed to harvest the crops, these empty hulls would provide little value to their livestock.

Yesterday, Father Moulin had sent a message to her with Philippe Garnot, a *Canadien* who farmed land south of Gabriel and often passed by the house. The note was simple and abrupt: *Je veux te voir.* I want to see you.

She had resisted becoming Riel's Mary Magdalene. But a profound moment had occurred in the ceremony at berry picking camp that she still could not explain to herself, only that she had marked her sorrow, emerging somehow, with a lighter heart. And a kind of freedom she had not dreamed possible, going up to St. Laurent a few times a week to teach William Jackson his catechism, becoming involved in his and Riel's discussions as they drew up the petition. She brought her children, although Cleophile had complained that there was too much shouting, after the two men argued over a few specific clauses. Jackson became frustrated when Riel insisted on including Macdonald's various missteps in Red River and had yelled, "He needs reminding that he almost lost it to the Americans!"

William was appalled. "The Americans are a dangerous ally, Louis. Please tell me you aren't entertaining the thought of sending to them."

"Macdonald's worst fear is annexation," Riel said. "The North-West is not yet part of Confederation. If we remind him the Americans are waiting in the wings, he might listen to our demands." Thoroughly offended, William had closed his notebook and pushed back his chair, prompting Riel to add that he had never been serious about American involvement in Red River. Jackson agreed to stay only when Riel swore that he would never treat with them again.

Josette had considered ignoring Moulin's request to come up. She did not wish to face his scrutiny, but surely he would not continue to insist that Mary Magdalene spy on her Christ. Perhaps he wanted to question her absence at Mass, or he objected to her—the least competent woman in the South Branch to do so—helping William study the beliefs of the Catholic faithful. He could not speak French, and Moulin's English was not good. It had been left to her, a disbeliever, who'd had the catechism all but beaten into her at school in Red River.

On the trail to the church, she reined in her horse to see if anyone was about. Riel suspected the priests themselves of spying, and would not like to hear that she had visited Moulin. She tied up La Noire outside the rectory and shouldered a saddlebag that contained bannock and a bundle of recently harvested *salsepareille* roots. She opened the rectory door to find Moulin seated at the kitchen table, his hands in a tight grip before him, murmuring thanks to God for finally bringing rain.

He eagerly took the bannock, but as usual, he pretended not to see the *salsepareille* roots, and made a poor job of hiding them beneath a cloth on the table. He broke off a piece of the bread and bit into it. Chewing thoughtfully, he looked at her with an unreadable expression.

"William Jackson will be tested," Moulin said, "You must ensure he is properly catechized." He paused, as if reminding himself to stay calm. "Riel has been too much with him. Those two with their heads together. What is in the petition?"

Josette was careful to keep her voice neutral. "They haven't told me."

"That is not what I hear. There's talk the three of you speak only English together—is it true?"

He knew too much. Had Charles Nolin betrayed them? Riel said he was skulking around, asking too many questions. She would not admit to Moulin that being Louis Riel's disciple had brought its advantages. The women now treated her with greater respect, and William Jackson had been a surprise—both charming and impressively educated at a university in the east. He had brought books with him from Prince Albert and was lending them to her. With Norbert still away, working in Battleford, she often stayed up late reading by candlelight after the children went to bed. She had just finished the first novel she had ever read, *The Deerslayer*, which had been Jackson's favourite book as a boy.

Moulin heaved himself out of the chair. "You forget we had an arrangement. I offered you an indulgence in exchange for help with Riel."

"I did not think God made deals," she said, smiling to herself.

The priest placed his piece of bannock on the table. "The Law of Love. You do not even know what it means." He bent his head briefly, as if praying and raised it in a moment, with an ill-disguised expression of anger. "I confide in you because you are our only hope. When Riel went up to Prince Albert last week, he told Father André that the priests in Red River supported him when he formed a provisional government. He wanted the Church's blessing if he had to do the same here."

Josette eye's slid past Moulin's shoulder, her thoughts in confusion. She'd heard Riel and Jackson debate the points in the petition. Besides reminding Macdonald of his crimes in Red River, the demands were reasonable—the North-West should be brought into Confederation and title granted on their lands. If Riel already planned a provisional government in Batoche, why did he waste time with a petition? Because he feared it would be ignored by Ottawa and was preparing to advance his private agenda of a separate Métis and Indian nation. Riel had promised not to use the Americans as a threat, but she questioned his motives. Would they be interested in hearing from him again?

A louse crawled from a seam of Moulin's soutane and she knocked it off, stepping on it before it could scurry between the floorboards. The old priest had the gall to accuse both her and Riel when she could as easily accuse him. "You were not there when we brought Elise back from berry-picking camp," she said. "You did not see the trail of blood that dripped through the wagon slats."

"It was in God's hands."

"Did God direct you to stop the women who would give Elise herbs to check her bleeding?"

"Pagan brews!"

When Elise had been carried to the wagon, her skin almost blue, Josette had been shaken, sure that it was a bad sign to bear witness to death in childbed while suffering her own private agony. She had been handed the *bibi*, too, which was a curse of its own; she could still feel his small body in her arms.

Josette reached across the table and pulled the cloth away to expose the *salsepareille* roots. "Then you are going straight to hell," she said, matching Moulin's tone.

The priest began to pace, hands folded behind his back. "Of course, Father André refused to support a provisional government. Riel flew into a rage and Father André declared him the devil." Moulin paused in front of her. "We hear he now calls himself Louis 'David' Riel. Ask Cleophile to tell you of King David and Bathsheba, the woman he lusted after. He killed her husband to hide the sin from God then begged Him for redemption." He closed his eyes and breathed deeply to control himself. "Josette, he has chosen you from the Batoche Métis. You and Gabriel are his closest supporters. Yet he plans rebellion. If you both refuse him now, your people will not be dragged into this madness."

"You are the one who must beg God for redemption," she said, turning to go.

Moulin grabbed at her arm. "Riel is a false prophet." She pulled away from him and opened the door. "Your grandfather knows it," he said. "Why has he not come?" She hurried down the rectory steps and the priest shouted after her. "You think you walk in the Law of Love, when you have broken every one of His commandments? You do not love God. That is the requirement! You dwell in the law of *sin*."

One of the Old Crows had told her that the Law of Love was Biblical: *If ye fulfill the royal law according to the scripture, Thou shalt love thy neighbour as thyself.* She turned to look at him. "You speak to me of sin and let a woman die in childbirth. A priest who drinks root teas to rid himself of carbuncles. And nobody but La Vieille knows that you do."

His face had turned a mottled red. She got on her horse and urged it into a fast trot away, slowing only when she was out of sight over the rise past Caron's farmhouse. Gabriel had been riding all over the territory to muster support for the petition. She would talk to him as soon as he returned and find out what he knew.

Despite her getting in the last word, Moulin's vindictive remarks had stung. Only men were concerned with laws of sin and love. And judged women worthy or not to walk in them. Despair crept over her like a shadow. The memory of *P'tite Marie* remained, an aching hurt. She feared Moulin was right: Riel's ceremony had done nothing to erase the darkness in her own heart. There was no way to forget that she had cast three *bibis* into that same formless deep to save her own life.

i will have
that one

THE FIRST WEEK OF October it snowed, a slanting blizzard that kept the Métis in their cabins, wrapped in blankets by the fire. The temperature had since warmed and the snow melted, but they braced for winter, where only dances offered respite from the short cold days and long winter nights.

The oldest Ouellette girl had married Joseph Bremner on a day in mid-October. The parents of the bride and groom could not afford to host a community wedding, and the Métis of Batoche and St. Laurent had worked together, each family contributing something to the feast. Xavier Letendre had offered his fine house in the village for the celebration; his front room furniture had been taken out to the barn to make room for dancing.

After the meal, Madeleine Dumont dried dishes by lantern light in the kitchen, with Henriette Parenteau, Marguerite Dumas, and several other Old Crows. Some of the men had gathered around a large fire in the front pasture and shouts of laughter could be heard as they progressed from beer to Philippe Garnot's homebrew. Madeleine paused in the kitchen doorway to watch Louis Riel, who stood near the stove with the bride and groom. Like everyone in the South Branch, she looked forward to a wedding, the chance to enjoy good food and dancing, but tonight, Riel had done his best to ruin the fun. After Father Moulin had blessed the feast, Riel provided his own version, rebuking the people for loving too much the pleasures of the flesh.

"Look at your faces," he had said, like a scolding father. "They show the unmistakable signs of sensual overindulgence." The guests gazed regretfully at the feast laid out before them, the table piled high with roasted duck and *boulettes* made from deer meat that had been brought in from a recent hunt. Was he saying they could not eat their fill? Riel turned to Moise Ouellette and proclaimed, "At the wedding in Cana, our Lord Jesus was revealed as the Son of God, turning water into wine. He is not too busy to work miracles where He is needed. And so, He will bring about the miracle for the Métis to grant us our lands." Riel had drawn back a chair at the table. "This shall be His seat."

Even now, the empty chair was skirted by the guests. Did they still believe Jesus might show up there? When the feast table had been moved into the kitchen, the Old Crows did not dare help themselves to seconds after Riel's reprimand.

Gigitte Caron came up behind Madeleine, wiping her hands with a cloth. "We'll keep the table on all night," she said, with a glance at Riel. "He will leave soon enough."

"Good the children could eat," Judith Dumont said to the women's laughter. "They do not bear the signs of *sensual overindulgence*."

Madeleine was affronted by Riel's talk of miracles. Jesus had not arrived. And Josette was far from the Magdalene. Gabriel stood near Riel, drinking beer and laughing at something that Patrice Champagne had just said. She had described Riel's strange behaviour at berry picking camp, but Gabriel ignored her claims that the man was touched in the head, and told her to trust the method in his madness. Now she struggled to control her racing thoughts, unreasonable fear that following Riel would be the death of her husband.

Barthélémi Dumas began tuning his fiddle. Before long he was joined by three others with hand pump organ, mouth harp, and spoons. In years past, the sound of a fiddle would set Madeleine's hips moving, but the desire had gone out of her body. Her thoughts were often confused, her limbs tired as they had been after long days on the trap lines with Gabriel. At a celebration, only weeks ago, she had to leave the floor, coughing blood into her handkerchief. A lifetime of dancing and now she was forced to watch.

Henriette Parenteau followed her gaze to Josette, who was laughing at the edge of the dance floor. "She is beautiful tonight."

"*Oui*," admitted Madeleine, but she could not resist adding, "for the least among us."

Domatilde Gravelle said, "The Lord Himself has chosen her for Riel's disciple."

"And *we* were blind to her suffering," said Virginie Houle. "Her grandfather will help us now he has blood in Batoche."

The musicians had just launched into a tune when Norbert swung Josette out on the floor. He had recently returned from the North Saskatchewan. Earlier, Madeleine had noticed that Josette avoided him, but now she danced with her husband under the linked arms of other couples, as though nothing was wrong, skirts lifted to show the beaded garters at her knees. Her hair was done higher on the back of her head, and some pieces had come loose around her face.

The fiddler had struck up the tune for the Red River jig and Josette's movements became less Scottish reel and more Indian war dance, swaying to search the ground, her head moving as if she danced among her grandfather's people. When the fiddle hit a certain note, she bent and pretended to raise a spear to stab at the floor.

Norbert glanced at her sharply. Seeing Josette make fun, the spoons player mimicked the beat of a war drum, and Charles Nolin started a high, wailing Indian cry that was taken up by some of the guests. Josette pointed at Norbert as if she'd sighted a buffalo and went toward him with her imaginary spear, jerking her body like a warrior, skirts raised. He put up his hand to warn her off, but she made a quick motion, as if throwing the spear. The bride and groom clapped and Norbert smiled, deciding that he should go along with it. He grabbed his heart as though she'd hit him there. Everyone laughed, and the sound echoed in Madeleine's ears.

When the men had paused their conversation to watch Josette's antics, Gabriel turned too, a bottle of beer halfway to his lips. He stared at Josette the way Madeleine once saw him regard a band of wild horses on the plains. Among the herd had been a grey dappled mare who had stopped on a hill and looked back on them, her fine form stark against the sky.

"I will have that one," he had said to his wife.

Madeleine remembered laughing back at him. "You want her because she is the wildest."

The room spun as she looked hard at him. He had regained his composure before anyone saw what was in his mind, but Madeleine could read his face better than anyone. When had this begun?

To the great amusement of the guests, José Ouellette, who was ninety-three, began to jig at the edge of the dance floor. He was still able to give a good kick, but soon waved his hand and went back to his beer. Couple by couple got in and the fiddler played faster and faster until the bow began to fray.

There was a burst of laughter from another part of the room. Three men who had been on a wood-cutting trip with Norbert decided he should continue to be made fun of in front of the crowd. A story was told of him drinking his weight in rum in their camp. He listened with an expression of tolerance and crossed his arms, laughing too, but Madeleine was unconvinced. Josette had called open season on him, and it would not go well for her.

Maxime Lépine came in to the kitchen and said, "Eat, eat, Riel has gone upstairs."

Henriette threw a cloth in the air. "What is he doing there?"

Lépine went to the feast table and popped a *boulette* into his mouth. "Down on his knees, praying."

On the way home in the wagon, Madeleine drew the blanket around her head against a cold wind that had come up from the north and held a handkerchief to her mouth, suppressing a cough. Gabriel glanced at her, noticing, she thought, that her fingers were twitching, restless. It would not be long before she must tell him the truth, but she couldn't do it, not now.

"Josette looked beautiful," she said.

He frowned and snapped the reins. "Did I tell you I went to see Norbert? Said I'd kill him if he touched her again."

She was convinced that he would not be so outraged if he did not hunger for Josette. Or was it something else? It occurred to her that she had not fully understood her husband's losses of the past few years. He had been captain of the buffalo hunts for decades before the herds had disappeared. Gabriel did well with the saloon and their few crops, but it was in his blood to be out on the prairie, not powerless in a struggle with the Dominion over their lands. Riel's arrival had given him renewed purpose and Josette's need—the lovely vulnerable female—had only made his masculine heart beat stronger.

She finally succumbed to a cough. What would she do come winter? She had not been warm for months, and her handkerchiefs had come away with more blood. Gabriel had noticed her weight loss and said that she resembled the bony white women in Prince Albert. Suzanne Guernon had died of consumption last year and Madeleine nursed her through to the end, when nobody else would. Some feared it was catching, but she had laughed them off. If it were so, every one of them would have it. Surely it was not her fate to waste to a shadow and die choking on her own blood.

Madeleine glanced at her husband's hands on the reins. The sight of them still made her blood rise, remembering his touch on her body. She felt guilty for suspecting Gabriel of lusting after Josette. The poor girl lived in fear of her own husband. Although becoming Riel's Mary Magdalene had made Josette think too much of herself, Madeleine would let her enjoy a status that would not last. The girl had no idea that Riel needed her only for Big Bear's mark on a petition.

The lung disease had affected Madeleine's memory, but a fragment came to her, Josette admitting something years ago about her mother, something over a cup of tea in the kitchen. Madeleine struggled to recall the details. The story came to her in pieces, Josette telling of Big Bear and Little Pine in their youth, leading their Cree warriors on raids into Blackfoot territory, fighting for control over the Cypress Hills. Josette's mother orphaned on one such raid and adopted by Big Bear, taken in by the band.

Madeleine slipped her hand into Gabriel's. Josette was not the celebrated blood grandchild of the great chief Big Bear. She was of the Blackfoot Confederacy in the western territories, her ancestors nameless. It was on Madeleine's lips to tell her husband, but she would not. Josette's secret was safe with her, for she was Gabriel and Riel's only hope of getting Big Bear's mark on the petition.

the making of
a country

≈

ON AN OVERCAST DAY in early December, Lawrence Clarke, Chief Factor for the Hudson's Bay Company, stroked his exuberant moustaches and looked with polite suspicion at Riel, who sat across his desk. He had been told that the Métis leader had spent time in a madhouse, but Riel appeared exhausted, ashen, no more insane than he was himself. Clarke glanced at William Jackson, who had refused a seat and stood near the door. After months of reports from Nolin that the two of them had been holed up debating the finer points of constitutional law, Clarke finally had the Métis petition.

"Bravo," he said, looking down at the document. "This is quite an accomplishment." Riel did his best to look humble, but it was obvious he felt proud of the thing. Clarke was not being facetious. The petition had been a joy to read. Even better than he expected. He had in his hands the reward for all of the years he'd suffered in this wilderness building the Métis' trust as their government representative.

"And you'd like me to take it to Ottawa?" he said, perhaps a little too keen.

He was aware that his old rival Jackson had been watching him closely. What bad luck that he'd paired up with Riel. Jackson was a pasty-faced insurgent from the east, fancying himself a voice for the common folk of Prince Albert. But after time spent in St. Laurent with Riel, Jackson had become an honorary Indian with dark hair plastered to his head, a pair of moccasins, and one of their flamboyant red sashes tied around his waist. There had been rumours that, if he changed his religion, he would marry one of the Métis girls.

Clarke put his attention back to the petition. It was fair enough, asking Macdonald to uphold the rights he'd promised the breeds under the Manitoba Act and honour their land claims, but when the prime minister saw that Riel demanded provincial government, he'd throw it across the room. Surely even Jackson knew that Old Tomorrow's Canada would be unified by federal authority.

"We do not trust Father André," Riel was saying. "We think he sends letters to Ottawa, working against our cause. You know our land grievances as well as we do. And you are almost one of us."

Clarke winced. It was true that he had married an English half-breed, but she was worlds away from the French squaws of the South Branch. She possessed real elegance and dressed like a white woman. But Father André? There was a useful man. He'd met him for dinner last week, and the old priest had gone on at great length, saying that Riel had come to see him, demanding the Church's support, and flown into a rage when he had refused, saying he'd establish a provisional government if Macdonald ignored the petition. There was no sign of that temper now, as Riel sat holding his hat, expression gaunt and hopeful.

Clarke frowned over one clause in the petition. "Do you really think the Dominion will grant the Métis representation in Cabinet?"

"They will if you are the one to press our cause," said Riel.

And if you showed up in Ottawa, you would be shot, thought Clarke, with some amusement.

Jackson crossed his arms and regarded him with distrust. He had obviously told Riel about the land speculation going on in this agriculturally rich territory. Bringing European settlers here to farm wheat was key to settling the country. Macdonald had crushed the hopes of businessmen in Prince Albert by running his Canadian Pacific Railway to the south, but now the push was on to build a feeder line north. Riel and Jackson had included it in the petition when complaining "that no effective measures had been taken to put the people of the North-West in direct communication with the European Markets." But they were ignorant of one important detail: businessmen in the east had their eyes on land from Regina to Prince Albert by way of Saskatoon. Close to one million acres had already been earmarked for the line, cutting through sections in already settled districts. Acreage the breeds squatted on and farmed in French river lots.

Clarke humoured Riel because it benefitted him. He had not been in this territory for years without learning there was money to be made if you carefully played both sides. Charles Nolin had proven himself useful in Batoche, sending him dispatches on what Riel was plotting. Using government code that referred to Riel as "the lawyer," Clarke had contacted Macdonald's offices directly, and with the news of a threatened provisional government, had received a summons to Ottawa. He planned to present the petition, brief Macdonald on Riel's mindset, and how this could work in their favour.

"You'll see that we are concerned with the current state of the Indians," Jackson said rather smugly.

Clarke smiled and lowered his eyes to re-read the first point in the petition. Flowery language about how the Indians were so reduced that the settlers were compelled to furnish them with food to preserve the peace of the Territory. It might be coincidence that Big Bear was not done stirring up trouble, refusing to go to his reserve and a guess that Riel had promised the old chief that Ottawa would listen, but looking at him now—his face showing both strain and a shrewdness that could not be denied—Clarke felt that he'd hit the nail on the head. *He was on the verge of rebellion.*

The Indians were the wild card. The new agent at Frog Lake was starving-out Big Bear to get him on the damn reserve. But if the old chief came south with his warriors, then powerful men like Poundmaker and Little Poplar would leave their little patches of earth and join in. European settlers would not take kindly to the warrior societies beating drums and sharpening their tomahawks.

The breeds were a brutish lot. Savage Indian on one side and vulgar French on the other. The worst of two arrogant races, formidable men on the plains, and easy to manipulate. Only a few of them had proved that theory wrong. Gabriel Dumont for one. He'd locked horns with him ten years ago when Dumont had formed the St. Laurent Council to petition for land and govern the last buffalo hunts. Dumont got too big for his britches and Clarke had to rein him in. In revenge, Dumont started watching him closely and learned that he was trading rations to the area chiefs in exchange for their headdresses and regalia—selling them to the Smithsonian Museum in Washington. Dumont had issued a threat: *Best not find yourself alone on the trail at night if you value your scalp*.

Clarke ran a hand over his thinning hair and looked up at Riel. "Why not do what you did in Red River? That made Macdonald listen. You were a genius to take Fort Garry. And a provisional government? Ottawa needs politicians like you—willing to take risks."

Riel stood abruptly and put on his hat. Clarke worried that he'd gone too far.

"I trust you will do your best to explain to Macdonald that we are earnest in our desire to have all of these demands honoured," Riel said, his eyes now hard and unsettling. "We have the support of the Métis of Red River—Archbishop Taché is reading a copy of the petition as we speak."

After the men left his office, Clarke went to the window to watch them emerge in the busy street below. *They were in earnest*. His body thrilled with an almost childlike excitement. But one must be careful. All of the players were in place on the board of a complicated game. He had not heard of any meetings between Riel and the half-breeds in Red River. But he would find out.

The feeder railway line had already been started, and like Macdonald's own CPR, had run into financial troubles. The tracks now languished in swamp, unfinished near Qu'Appelle. Clarke considered it his life's purpose to get it finished. There might be a brief lull as immigrants refused to come in after savage Indians and breeds had staged an uprising, but when the last tie on that line was laid, they would come all right. The rebellion would long be forgotten and any remaining Métis stragglers would be serving time for treason, dispersed, or shamed out of the territory.

Clarke packed and lighted his pipe, savouring the first draw with closed eyes. He would ride out the next morning and be on a train from Regina to Ottawa in two days. He'd present the petition to Macdonald and offer his suggestions when the prime minister refused to honour it. Then return and enjoy a front-row seat to a rebellion that would be the making of a country.

beyond comfort
in this life

⟿

A SERIES OF PUNISHING blizzards during the first half of December had blocked them in with snow piled four feet high around the house. A week before Christmas, it warmed, and the drifts began to melt and soften.

Josette and her children had trudged through the snow to a stand of small poplar north of the house, on the bluff above the river. Her mother had taught her to harvest poplar buds before they opened in late January or February, but many large branches had come down in the storms, and Josette would not let them go to waste.

The sun hung like a still, dull orb behind a veil of cloud that drifted like smoke across the sky. A grey mist obscured the far horizon. Despite milder temperatures, the Saskatchewan was still frozen solid and riddled with snow-crusted pathways that had been cut by deer, wolves, and men. Because of the drought last summer, there had been no vegetables to put up from the gardens. The men were forced to find work in

Battleford, a day's ride north, where more white settlers had arrived, needing shelter. Norbert had taken his dogs and sled up there to work with other Métis, constructing a mill.

While her sons picked buds off the smaller downed branches, Josette and Cleophile shared the use of the hand axe to cut bigger fallen limbs to size. Later, in the warmth of the house, they would shave the bark for making tea to strengthen Eulalie's heart and lungs. Her second oldest was at the end of a persistent cough, but had come out bundled in a blanket to hold the tin pail for the buds, her hair smelling of woodsmoke from sleeping close to the stove. Josette stroked the girl's cheek and felt her forehead. Eulalie resembled her father, tall and with the strong chin, but was sweet and gentle in disposition—so different from Cleophile.

Overhead came the distinctive chucking call of *wîskipôs*, a whiskey jack. Eulalie peered up at it. "*Wîskipôs* does not like that we are stealing bark he needs for his nest."

"Offer tobacco," Cleophile said. Her normally guarded expression was now transformed by rapt attention to the task of stripping buds. They made a soft thudding sound as they went into the pail, releasing a strong resin scent, which was like perfume to Josette, and brought back memories of harvesting them with her mother on the banks of the Red River.

Patrice had wandered away to collect twigs from another tree. In a moment, he called out and showed them a place where a pack of stray dogs or wolves had recently killed and devoured a deer. The snow was stained red with the animal's blood. Even its bones had been eaten or dragged off, and only an antler was left among the scraps of bloody hide. If Norbert had been here, he would have seen the buck's tracks and hunted it down, providing them with fresh meat. But she would not trade a full stomach for his presence.

The month of the Cold Moon was her least favourite time of year, yet these had been the best days of her life, taking the children in the cutter to St. Laurent to teach William Jackson, enjoying the banter between him and Riel, and the secretive looks Riel would give her at times, over William's head: *only you and I know. Only we.*

Josette looked south in time to see Gabriel emerge from his house. He followed the packed snow footpath across his front pasture and glanced up toward her farm in a way he had never done in the past. He hesitated for a moment before disappearing into his barn.

She'd seen him at the Ouellette wedding, but they hadn't spoken since that day in the woods on the trail to Prince Albert. When she had raised her fears that Riel might very well cause them trouble, he had assured her, *I will not let him fail.* She would not forget how he had looked at her, a promise, but something else, too. It had seemed they would be close, disciples standing by their prophet. If Riel had asked the priests to bless the forming of a provisional government, he could not still be dreaming of his own church. Josette suspected that Gabriel avoided her because he was unable to deliver on his promise, and that he rode out even in the storms with his brother Isidore, assembling an army of Métis to back Riel if he must rebel against Ottawa.

Madeleine was nowhere in sight. Was it possible that she had gone up to Batoche? Josette went to the edge of the trees as Gabriel led his roan out of the barn and swung up into the saddle. His mare picked her way forward in the snow to find the Humboldt Trail in his back fields, then he looked over his shoulder and saw her, but did not slow his horse, only touched his hat with a gloved hand before settling into a canter south.

There was a movement of black in the yard, like a crow flapping against the snow, and there was Madeleine, who had come down from her porch and stood staring after him, hands on her hips. When she turned, she looked up at Josette, who raised her arm in a tentative wave. Madeleine nodded curtly before returning to the house. In the old days, she would beckon for her to come down and they would bake together, the children playing in the kitchen. Josette could not understand her behaviour. It was not like Madeleine to be possessive, but if she was going to resent anyone it should be Riel, who had thrown Gabriel and Josette together by making them his disciples.

As Gabriel's figure receded to the south, she thought of the last time she'd been in St. Laurent. Louis had been on edge, anticipating a response to his petition, which he hoped would come before the new year.

He told her that he had sent a scout to find her grandfather, but the scout had returned, saying that Big Bear had taken his band closer to the Frog Lake reserve. Riel had paced, unable to hide his disappointment that her grandfather was yielding to Ottawa in order to feed his starving band. She had felt guilty for not doing enough to persuade *Mosom*, but he had the survival of his people to think of, not putting his mark on a half-breed petition.

She went back to her children in the tree cover. Patrice was cleaning the antler he'd found in the snow, and singing an old Cree song about whiskey jacks. He mixed it up with another song about being stolen by a bear and soon had even Cleophile laughing. The sun broke through the clouds, and they returned to the house, playing a guessing game as they walked. As they neared the barn, a man on a horse came down the north Humboldt Trail from Batoche.

"It's *l'Anglais*," said Eulalie. "The one in love with La Rose."

"We're going up to St. Laurent tomorrow," Cleophile said with a scowl. "Why is he here?"

"Don't be selfish. William will soon be confirmed. He needs my help with the abjuration." It worried Josette that Cleophile was often stricken by black moods, yet she had seen other young girls close to their first blood acting this way.

After William had taken his horse to the barn, he climbed to the porch, removing his fringed buckskin gloves and fur hat. He wore a Hudson's Bay blanket over his coat, tied with a ceinture fléchée that La Rose Ouellette had woven him. His hair was now long, and he kept it parted in the middle and straight down the back of his neck. Some said he now thought of himself as a Métis. He held out his hand dramatically to Josette. "Turn your ear towards me and answer me quickly when I call," he said. "For my days are vanishing like smoke, my bones burn away like a fire."

She laughed. How fond she had become of him. "You've memorized your penitentiary psalm. Does it give you comfort?"

William's expression quickly changed. "I am beyond comfort in this life."

"You are meant to be joyful now that you are reformed to the true Church."

He shook his head. "If I'd known how involved this conversion would be, I would not have had the courage to undertake it. I confess the abjuration is knocking the stuffing out of me."

It had been a challenge for her, as well, to revisit the infallible dogmas of the Church. She understood why William might struggle with the abjuration, where he must renounce his Methodist religion as a "heretic cult," and "a preposterous contention in the supernatural order." Her eyes went to his saddlebag, seeking the telltale outline of a book. He had recently lent her a volume of poems by Ralph Waldo Emerson. She had not read anything like it—as if the man had taken Spinoza's thoughts and set them to verse. She had devoured the book in one sitting, fascinated by this poet who William told her had kept his own prodigious diaries. One poem in particular had captured her, which William later told her he'd written for his son, who had died at a young age:

"I am too much bereft
The world dishonored thou hast left."

It had stirred memories of *P'tite* Marie, but she was inspired to put her hand to his style, had even given the resulting poem to Louis, heart in her mouth to share this private grief.

Josette built up the kitchen fire and sat down at the table with William. He had brought his dog-eared copy of the abjuration, and she decided not to press him on why they were holding the lesson here and not in the house where he stayed with Riel and his family in St. Laurent. They went over the Profession of Faith, which he must understand and sign before Father Moulin.

William admitted to having trouble with a clause that demanded he promise true obedience to the pope in Rome. "Louis let me read a poem he wrote," he said. "He described the pope as a pasha—sly and dangerous as a cat. He wants the fiercest war waged to destroy the Roman Church."

She looked up at him, thinking for a moment, that she had misheard, but William would not meet her eye. "Riel told me he wanted to reform the Church," she said, with relief to finally speak of his secret. "But I thought it was a dream of his, harmless."

"Yes," he agreed. "A dream is all it is."

He glanced at her, his face drawn. She knew that he had the same questions in his mind: why had Riel bothered with the petition if he feared it would be ignored? Why ask for the priests' blessing to create a provisional government if he hated their church and meant to reform it?

William looked down at the abjuration, jiggling one foot in a repetitive, nervous gesture, and there was an unusual look in his eyes. He obviously did not find humour in the idea that he was converting to a religion Riel meant to throw down. That Riel was sponsoring his conversion and would act as godfather at his baptism had put William in an intolerable position.

She pulled the abjuration toward her on the table and made a half-hearted attempt to explain church hierarchy to him, but he drew in a breath and said, "After we gave that bastard Clarke the petition, Riel came to my sister's apartment for dinner. We had an argument over land rights. He was certain the food was poisoned and rushed out to throw up in the snow." William paused, his face now flushed in agitation. "I went after him and do you know what he said to me? Accused me of being among those who wish him dead."

Josette got up to put the kettle on for tea. She thought of Louis' bizarre actions at the Ouellette wedding. Now here were worries of being poisoned by William, of all people. He had fallen silent and she turned, not used to seeing him at a loss for words.

"I did not tell you," he said, low-voiced. "A delegation from Red River came last month to see Louis and Gabriel."

She fought resentment that she had been kept out of important matters. "Louis' old supporters?"

"Not the ones he wanted to see. His two war captains did not come."

"They are too old now."

"Ambroise Lépine is forty-five. André Nault, ten years older." William shook his head. "They sent their nephews and cousins. They wished to form a Union of the Métis to support our cause. Riel insisted they take back the petition to their Archbishop in Red River."

She looked at him with incomprehension. "What good will it do for a priest to have it first?"

"Taché intervened in the Red River troubles. Louis wanted Macdonald to get wind of it, fear we are collaborating. The threat is there: Manitoba is not glad of you—the North-West is not glad of you either."

"I should have known this. Why didn't you tell me sooner?" William said nothing, only fixed her with his doleful eyes. "What is it?" she said, thinking the worst. "Is Riel ill?"

"No," he said, sounding unconvinced. "He no longer wants you coming up to the house."

Although the fire was hot at her back, she stood transfixed, unable to speak.

"He thinks someone in our inner circle is spying for Father André and the priests." William eyed her cautiously. "He thinks that someone is you."

a viper poisons
the nest

FATHER MOULIN PUSHED back from the kitchen table and glanced around at the faces of Fathers André, Fourmond, and Vegreville. André had called an emergency meeting, and the priests of the South Branch had gathered at Fourmond's rectory in St. Laurent. Moulin thought of helping himself to more of the rabbit stew that had been made by one of their Métis parishioners, but stopped himself. It would not do to show greed when tension was so high.

His hands out of sight beneath the table, Moulin began to pick at his ragged cuticles, but with slow comprehension became aware that Father André had looked up from his bowl to fix him with an indignant stare. André was a stout country Frenchman who had, in his youth, held his own in the Métis canoes and on the trail. The old priest had dedicated the last twenty-five years of his life to ensure the breeds established a strong French community in the Saskatchewan, had even helped Gabriel Dumont petition for their lands. André had worked hard to earn their trust—built parishes and brought three priests here to minister. Now Riel threatened to undo it all.

"Lawrence Clarke tells me Riel left him with a threat of support from the half-breeds of Red River," André said to Moulin. "That they met with Riel and Dumont in *your* church."

The eyes of the other priests went to him, and Moulin felt the urge to scratch at the carbuncles on his back. He thought of that day last month, when Riel and Dumont had entered the church after Mass with a delegation from Manitoba. The Red River half-breeds had been respectable men, dressed in their best suits.

"Why did they come?" asked André.

"I thought the archbishop meant for me to bless them," Moulin said, disturbed at the irritation in the priest's voice. "They asked me to choose a patron saint as head of their society . . ." He trailed off, now realizing that any society formed with Riel and Dumont was of an evil nature.

"What society?"

"I believe they called it, *l'Union nationale métisse Saint-Joseph*," Moulin said in a small voice.

"And you did not tell me? You did you not realize these were the very men who supported Riel in the Red River troubles?"

"They had a letter . . . from Archbishop Taché."

"They also took back a draft of Riel's petition for him to read."

Moulin was mortified. He had warned Josette that Riel threatened to form a provisional government, and yet failed to notice sin taking place under his very nose. He had been too eager to see a letter addressed to him from such an important man of the Church. His fingers had shaken when opening it.

André went on, in a voice more peevish than before. "Riel knew what he was doing, the fiend. Give the petition to the Archbishop of St. Boniface before sending it to Ottawa. Trick Macdonald into thinking the North-West and Manitoba are aligned in their efforts."

Father Fourmond, a young priest and new to the region, had a pinched look to his face, as if remembering something distasteful. "If they truly meant to support him, they would have stayed."

"They know what evil Louis wreaked in Red River," said Father

Vegreville. "Evil they are not keen to visit twice."

Moulin cleared his throat, eager to get off this topic. "One of the women of Batoche let it slip in confession that her husband is one of Riel's inner circle," he said. "Riel told them at a meeting that he was a prophet from God. They fired their weapons in joy to hear it."

Father André had returned his attention to the bowl of stew before him. With a spoon halfway to his mouth, he said, "Charles Nolin has told me that Riel spent two years in an insane asylum."

The priests stared at him with incredulous expressions.

"Can you trust Nolin?" Moulin asked. "How does he know?" He could not imagine Riel in a straitjacket, although his actions at the Ouellette wedding made him worthy of one.

"The half-breeds should know the truth," said Fourmond.

"That their leader is insane?" André said, chewing thoughtfully. "It's too fantastic to believe. They will think we are spreading lies about him. Riel would discover that Nolin is our man here and we still need him. And it would give him reason to turn the people against us. *Non*, we must get rid of Riel."

He had hardly finished saying this when there was a stamping of feet outside the door and in a moment, it opened. Riel and William Jackson came in, shaking snow off their coats. Riel took off his hat and shot Father André an accusatory look. "We came to pray at the chapel. I asked God why we had not received an answer from Ottawa. When we left, I was shown your sleigh outside the rectory. I did not expect to find you here, plotting."

Moulin glared at him. "Now that you are finished the petition, you will leave the country, *non?*"

Riel raised his brows and regarded the pot of stew, a half-eaten bannock on the table. "The Métis survive on flour and water and save the meat for you." He looked meaningfully at Father André's prodigious stomach. "Do you forget Christ's frugal ways?"

Father André sent a warning glance to the other priests. "We have our divine mission directly from the apostles."

"The apostles supported themselves by the work of their hands," Riel said with a shake of his head. "It would do you good to return to sacred poverty."

André's blue eyes burned with indignation. "Twenty-five years I rode out with your people on the hunts." He thrust out his calloused hands. "Gabriel will tell you I have shouldered my share of buffalo meat to the wagons. And God knows I have damaged myself living in drafty tents on the plains."

Riel surveyed them with a long look, breath shallow in his chest. "You do not deserve to be called priests or fathers by my people. When I return to Batoche, I will insist they address you as 'servants of God.'"

Fourmond leaped out of his chair. "Show your respect, Louis."

"The Métis *have* a spiritual centre." Riel's eyes were wide, his voice louder. "It is not an overfed white priest, but a prophet chosen by God from their own people."

William Jackson chose this awkward moment to make his mark. "Do you not think," he said, "that priests put themselves too high above the people they serve? Christ himself did not wish to be worshipped."

Moulin noted that Jackson's French was improving, but like a typical *Anglais*, he still managed to butcher the most dignified language in the world.

Father André turned an outraged eye to Jackson. "Is it you, a Methodist, who whispers heresy in Riel's ear? Soon we will hear you say the Pope must be removed from his place in Rome."

"As he should," said Riel.

André reared up so fast, the dishes on the table rattled. "*Assez!*" He jerked his soutane down over his stomach. "Keep up this insanity and you will no longer be allowed to partake in the sacraments."

Riel covered his face. "Father, my passion to help the Métis is too great," he said from between his fingers. "It sometimes overwhelms me—I say things I regret."

The priests stared at Riel in horror. Moulin had to restrain himself from clapping. What a performance. Riel had spent two years in bedlam. His behaviour was erratic, *certainement*, but he was no rambling fool.

"The petition writing was very . . . *enervant*," Jackson said in his awful French. "Riel is exhausted. Please don't punish him."

Riel put on his hat, chastened, but André came out from behind the table. "You have sacrificed much for your people. Do you not think you should have a little something in exchange for all the work you have done?" Riel looked up with a guarded expression, and André hurried on. "I will write to the Territorial Council, get them to use their influence with Ottawa and win you an indemnity."

Riel took out a handkerchief and passed it over his face, straightened his coat. "Indemnity?"

"You have spent years of your life working to bring the Métis their rights. You were Governor of Red River and brought Manitoba into Confederation."

Riel seemed mildly surprised, as if he had not considered all these things together. "I lived as an outlaw, one step ahead of Macdonald's assassins. I did not benefit from scrip in Manitoba—my land was confiscated." He paused for a moment. "How much do you believe all that is worth? I would think many thousands of dollars."

André blanched. "Something to carry you. My thought was five thousand—"

Riel laughed. "What an amount. Five thousand was the bounty put on my head fifteen years ago. You do not know that Macdonald sent a party of men after me. I refused a purse of $35,000 dollars and the advice to take a trip over the water and the wide world."

"What of your wife and children, Louis?" said Father Moulin. "If we get you some money, you can go back to Montana and start a new life."

Riel was silent for a moment. "If the request comes from you with a convincing argument . . ." At this, he turned on his heel and was gone. William Jackson trailed out after him, leaving the door wide open.

After Father Fourmond had closed the door, André said, "Thirty-five thousand dollars. It would take much less than that."

"Macdonald has bribed him once to leave," Moulin said. "Will he do it again?" He laughed bitterly. "*Le pauvre fou.* Turning the people against us."

"Some of the French breeds in the South Branch speak quietly against him," said Moulin. "Charles Nolin says Xavier Letendre and Roger Goulet do not wish to be involved in insurrection."

"It's obvious that Jackson is affecting him," said Fourmond.

"He is converting to Catholicism," said Moulin. "Josette is teaching him the catechism."

André blinked. "Who?"

"Josette Lavoie, a woman in Batoche."

"Why her?"

Moulin hesitated. He had not bothered Father André with news of Riel's little ceremony at berry-picking camp, but now he regretted the decision. "Riel has made her his Mary Magdalene," he said, playing with a spoon on the table. "She has education from Red River—was meant to be a nun."

André frowned. "Then she would have only good influence on Riel."

"She's the granddaughter of Chief Big Bear. Closer to an Indian than any of the Métis women. She blasphemes regularly." Moulin was anxious to avoid a dressing down. He would not admit that Josette had somehow manipulated him into granting an indulgence. He chose one of her other transgressions. "She said one could trace the Virgin Mary's lineage back to Eve—and therefore Eve herself must be exempt from original sin."

André sat down heavily. "Do you see how a viper poisons the nest? Before too long we will have more of these women . . ." He glanced up at Moulin. "A pity you have allowed subversion of good order among your parishioners." He paused for a long moment, a hand across his eyes. "Let slip to some of your half-breed gossips that the great Louis Riel has requested money for services to his people, and that he's agreed to abandon them as soon as it's paid."

a dire blessing

$\backsim$

"*C'EST BEAU, MAMAN*," Patrice said, patting one of Norbert's sled dogs through its *tapis*.

Josette secured the knotted red ribbons that decorated the standing irons of their harnesses. Many an evening since Christmas, she had sat close by the fire, adding new beadwork to their *tapis*, copying a regal scroll design that she'd seen on one of Father Moulin's church vestments. All of this to please Norbert, who stood beside the sled, as grim-faced as she'd ever seen him.

Hundreds of Métis had gathered on the frozen surface of the Saskatchewan River for the annual New Year's Day dog race. A few inches of fresh snow had fallen last night and it looked like more coming, the sky heavy with cloud that hung close above the treeline. Norbert had the most impressive get up of dogs and sled in the South Branch, but last year he had come in second. Josette could tell by the set of his mouth that this year he would accept nothing but first place. She prayed he would win for two reasons: they were in desperate need of the bag of flour donated by Xavier Letendre as the prize, and she wished to avoid what seemed to be his looming punishment—for what, she did not know.

Since Norbert had returned from the north in mid-December, he slept turned from her on their straw pallet, his muscled back forming a silent rebuke. She had a crick in her neck from ranging as far as she could from him, listening as he drew tortured breath through his oft-broken nose and dreading a half-awake, scrabbling reach between her legs, but he had not touched her since the night before Riel had arrived. How long had it been? Six moons. All because Gabriel had warned him away—she heard it from one of the women—and the threat of crossing him had stayed her husband's hand.

A large fire had been built at the end of the Carlton Trail on the riverbank. Cleophile stood near it with other young people, a blanket around her shoulders. She laughed at something Alexandre Dumont was saying and Josette thought it was the first time in a long while she had seen her daughter happy. Norbert pulled on a pair of gloves and mounted his sled. As he whipped his dogs into the starting area, Cleophile stared after him with thinly veiled contempt. Josette feared that she had grown to hate her father after witnessing him beat her. It was a form of solidarity, but she did not know how to broach the subject with her daughter, who would surely disagree, just to be contrary.

Only Michel Dumas had a team that was as fast as Norbert's, but Dumas' dogs were not known for endurance and this was a ten-mile race—five miles down river and five back. As each team and its captain lined up, Dumas bragged of the new track he'd put on his sled, falling silent when Father Moulin came along, a hand lifted to bless the four teams taking part. The expression on the priest's face was sour. He did not approve of the Métis dog and horse races for the betting that went on, but believed much would be forgiven by God if he sanctified the activity. After he had blessed Norbert's team, he shook his hand and wished him and his family good health in the new year. He nodded to Josette and moved on, his eyes flicking over the dogs. Disapproval turned into astonishment.

"*Quoi*," he cried, pointing at the dogs' felt jackets.

Norbert presumed he had an issue with the bells. "When they hear them, they run faster," he explained.

"*Non*," Moulin roared. He charged forward, staring at Josette. "Did

you bead that design?" She took a step back, too stunned by this out-
burst to answer. Moulin lunged at the lead dog and pulled at its *tapis*,
but the dog snapped at him. "Get these off—it is desecration to put a
sacred symbol of the Church on a dog." He jerked his hand in a ges-
tural insult from the old country and went off up the trail, his thin boots
kicking up snow.

It was too late to do anything about the *tapis*, for Emmanuel Champagne had lifted his rifle to fire the starting shot. Beneath his fur hat,
Norbert's face was the same colour as the red sash around his waist.
The gun went off and the dogs sprang into a loping run, but Norbert's
team had already fallen behind Michel Dumas' as they raced down the
frozen river. When the last team disappeared out of sight around the
bend, the women went back to visiting and tending pots of stew that
had been set to cook over embers in a fire pit.

Riel was speaking to some Métis who had come across the river from
Duck Lake for the festivities. A few Batoche men were taking wagers
on who would win the race and others had struck up a game of cards on
a blanket, the betting already brisk. Like Moulin, Louis did not approve, but he made comments about the cards some men were holding,
laughing louder than anyone. He would not look at Josette, but she was
sure he had witnessed the volatile episode with Moulin. Hadn't it prov-
en that she was not his spy? She would not be so easily put aside, forgotten, or accused. Only she knew Louis' true purpose here, yet he had the
audacity to ignore her.

Eulalie brought Patrice and Wahsis to her skirts. The top buttons on
Wahsis' coat had come undone, exposing his chest to the cold, and
Josette drew him close to do them up again. She was surprised when
Domatilde Gravelle whisked the children away to play with others
their age. In a bid to make herself useful, Josette waded into knee-deep
snow, making for the bush to gather firewood, but another woman
shooed her from the task, and she could see the Old Crows eyeing her
and then Riel, expecting her to fulfill her role.

Go to him, Mary.

Henriette Parenteau had taken a bowl of bannock dough from the
back of a cart and carried it to the fire pit. She motioned for Josette to
kneel beside her in the packed snow. The two of them began to form

rounds, patting them into the hot cast iron fry pans that had been banked on the coals. Gabriel had just come down the trail with Damase Carrière, the two of them speaking in urgent, hushed tones. With Madeleine always hovering, she had not had the chance to go to him, to finally share the secret Riel had asked her to keep: that he intended to destroy the Roman Church and replace it with his own.

Despite concern from the women, Josette felt more like an outsider. And the threat of Norbert. He would think she had beaded the *tapis* to humiliate him and now had reason to discipline her. Gabriel had warned him; Riel had promised that God would save her. And yet neither of them, much less their punishing God, had looked her way. She wished that William Jackson was here, but he had gone to spend the Christmas season in Prince Albert with his family. The Métis laughed, drank, and gambled, trusting Riel, when he could not be trusted. Yet Father Moulin had insisted that she and Gabriel possessed the influence and power to turn them all.

Henriette tested the top of a bannock with her finger then flipped it in the pan, "My husband wishes to know if it is true," she said in a low voice. "I told him you would know."

"*What* is true?"

"That Riel has asked for money, a payment to make him go away."

"From who?" she said, then regretted it, for Henriette looked taken aback. Josette willed herself not to redden and said with authority, "It's an evil rumour—started by those who wish him gone." She looked up at Louis, silently daring him to glance at her. And he did, almost mournfully, his eyes drifting away again. He would surely not ask for payment to go away if he was close to realizing his dream.

Last night, the Batoche Métis had gathered in the church. When the moon had risen high, they shook hands, exchanged wishes: *good luck to you, we will get our lands, pray for rain on the crops this year—not too much, just enough.* There had been no word from Ottawa on the petition, and Riel had been assured again and again that it would be answered quickly. When the men went outside and discharged their rifles into the air after Mass, Josette had watched him kneel alone before the altar. And she *knew.* He did not mourn the passing of light, as she did, the Christmas season soon to be over with its fleeting joys, leaving them to face dark days and long nights. He prayed for guidance to create a new church while on his knees in the very one he wished to destroy.

As more people came up from the river to the fire, a horseman appeared on the west bank. His Appaloosa gelding came across, and she saw the rider was Louis Schmidt, Riel's old friend from Red River, who now lived in Prince Albert. Riel and Gabriel went down to meet him at the river's edge. Schmidt dismounted, handsome in a long coat and leather boots, like those the white men wore. He held the reins, face animated, sharing news.

Josette walked toward them with resolve, a woman, not invited, but determined that she would be. Gabriel had to know that the man he followed, despite her warnings, was on a path to destruction. The English half-breeds and white settlers were Protestant. They would withdraw support for Riel when they discovered he meant to use his political authority to stage a holy war and throw down the Catholic religion. And the Métis of Batoche? They would refuse to leave the Church.

When she drew near, Gabriel broke away to meet her. The cold had whitened a scar she had not noticed on the bridge of his nose, where it crooked to the side, slashed in some long-ago fight. He wore a troubled expression, his eyes dark and unwavering, and had on the old buffalo coat that Madeleine had made for him years ago. She remembered seeing him wear it, captain of one of the last hunts, standing with a hand to his horse just after the herds had been sighted on the plains, waiting for Moulin to finish Mass so he could mount and lead his hundreds of riders forward, horses reined in, advancing as one, ready to give chase.

"The petition has been received in Ottawa," Gabriel said.

It bothered her that his face remained grave, that he avoided her eyes. The man who had once looked into her soul and did not turn from what he had seen there was now brusque, his attitude dismissive. "Good," she said. "We will have news soon."

"No news that it has been read," he muttered, "only that it goes to the Queen."

"The Queen? What will she do with it?"

Gabriel said nothing and they watched as men gathered around Riel, clapping him on the back with congratulations, but he too seemed despondent. "Schmidt says a man is up there from the Dominion Lands Office," Gabriel said. "Registering any lot surveyed in the English square."

"Ottawa is listening. He will come here—"

"The Dominion man does not speak French."

"I could interpret for him—so could Riel."

Gabriel's eyebrow went up. "There is no way to translate our French river lots to an *Anglais*." He looked past her and she turned to see Madeleine up near the fire, staring at them. When she noticed them looking, she abruptly turned away. "What is wrong with *her*?" he said, cursing under his breath.

"Is she ill?" It still seemed strange to her that Madeleine resented Gabriel having anything to do with her.

He shook his head. "She says Riel is mad, that we will all soon be in hell."

"Perhaps she is right."

"Is that what you believe?" He looked at her briefly, with a flash of concern or distrust, as if he were now uncertain of her role in Riel's life.

She stepped closer so no one else would hear. "I have something to tell you—"

But she was cut off by sudden cheering; a group of older children waiting down the river bank had spotted the racers on their return leg. Dumas' team rounded the bend, alone on the last drive to the finish line, his arm held high in triumph. Two other teams straggled in after him. Norbert's was not in sight.

Riel had beckoned to Gabriel, and Josette watched, with escalating frustration, as he walked away. When Norbert's team finally came in, his face was a rigid mask. She hurried to find her children as darkness sank like fog over the river. After everyone had eaten, the party moved to Xavier Letendre's in the village. Outside his house, the young unmarried women had built a small fire and occupied themselves by dropping dough into a pot of hot oil. Young men loitered about, each waiting for a certain girl to grant him favour with a fresh *beignet*. The adults crowded into Letendre's large living room where the fiddler and mouth harp player were joined by another man from Duck Lake who was a legend with the hand organ. The musicians tuned their instruments for a moment and then launched into "The Reel of Eight."

Norbert came in, still holding his gloves, his coat wet with melted snow. She was thankful when a whoop went up as old Joseph Ouellette—who had ridden with the legendary buffalo hunter Cuthbert Grant at the Battle of Seven Oaks—began a song about the hunts, acting out the parts with tossing horns and pawing hoofs. He finished the last verse with arms raised and the crowd clapping him on.

> "Now old men and wives come you out with the carts
> There's meat against hunger and fur against cold
> Gather full store for the pemmican bags
> Garner the booty of warriors bold!"

When the song was over, the revellers encouraged Charles Nolin to deliver something from his large repertoire. His face seemed redder than usual, and his swagger made it obvious that he'd been into the rum. He did not glance at Riel, but it was apparent that he had him in mind, for he yelled to the crowd, "Louis, you should recognize another song composed at that time in Red River." He looked around, grinning. "Who can remember that February night in '70, when *les Anglais* came up the river to free the prisoners Louis kept at Fort Garry?" He put a hand at his ear and the people shouted, "Sing it, sing it."

Josette caught sight of Riel. He glanced up at Nolin as if he would like to kill him.

Nolin pretended to be bashful. "*Non, non,*" he said, waving his hand. "The Scots tongue is bitter in my mouth." Yet when the fiddle player sawed out a few bars, he launched into the song. Many in the crowd encouraged him, although members of Riel's inner circle, like the Nault brothers, Damase Carrière, Gabriel, and Michel Dumas, kept their arms crossed.

> "O Hey, Ri-el, are ye waking yet,
> Or are yer drums a-beating yet?
> If ye're nae waking we'll nae wait.
> For we'll take the fort this morning."

Only when the song ended, did Nolin dare look at Riel. "Louis, we were just having a wee bit o' fun at your expense," he said, still affecting a Scots accent. The crowd parted for a glimpse of a beaded purse he took from his coat pocket. "We of the South Branch have made a collection." Riel reached for the pouch reluctantly, but Nolin would not release his grip. "Sixty dollars raised for our great hero. You should have some of your own money, *non*? So, you can buy you and your family what you need instead of waiting for one of us to give it."

Marguerite had come out of the kitchen to stand beside her husband. Riel lowered his eyes. Josette could see that he was not so much touched by the generosity as he was by a deep sadness. Perhaps it was a bitter reminder of how poor they all were, and yet had sacrificed for the good of their hero. Or was it guilt for thinking those among him spies? The room went quiet as the people waited for one of his famous speeches, and in a moment, he told them that the petition had been received and was on its way to London. The rest of his words were drowned out by cheers.

Riel put up his hand. "Settlers want our lands *again*. Macdonald ignores us *again*. And what do we ask? Freedom. To own ourselves." He stared through the crowd, as if he were miles away. She could hear the naked vulnerability in his voice. Finally he meant to tell them his secret.

He rooted in one of his coat pockets. "I would like you to hear something," he said, and to Josette's horror, unfolded the poem she'd written in grief over her daughter and began to read:

"She walks with beauty in the rain
Aspen trunks gleam their disdain
Everything she touched gone cold
If I should find my heart has told
She lives on in birdsong, light, and grass
The days bore on, my grief won't pass
Her imp-eyed smile has left this earth
With it a mother's sad, lone worth."

There was an appalled silence, and Riel glanced up, tears in his eyes. "One of our women wrote this." He began to search her out, but she stepped behind Maxime Lépine's broad shoulder.

She stood still, her pulse racing. How had she ever trusted him? Those around her looked displeased to hear him praise a woman's mind. One among them had neglected her chores to write poems. What would she do next? Josette let out the breath she had been holding only to find Norbert watching her from across the room, a look of frank loathing in his eyes.

The crowd broke up and Riel and Gabriel went off with the Batoche men. Josette pushed her way outside. Cutters and sleighs had been drawn up near the barn and Josette found Alexandre and Cleophile there with her three youngest, gathered around Madeleine, who was climbing into the Dumont's cutter.

She prayed that Norbert would remain to drink, carouse, or fight with whatever man dared cross him, but he came up behind her. "Take the children," he said to Madeleine, who turned in her seat to look at him. Norbert offered only a blank stare in return. One of his headaches had come on, he'd lost the dog race, and his wife had embarrassed him by writing verse, reminding him of their dead daughter. His face remained expressionless, his mouth set like a man determined to get a job done. Josette climbed into his racing sled and waved Madeleine and the children on. She pulled a blanket over her, noticing that the dogs' *tapis* had been torn off their backs; only a few shreds of the offending material remained. Josette did not look at Madeleine as her cutter left, but she caught a glimpse of Cleophile's face framed in her blanket. Panic and worry, to the point of terror. What could she do? Refuse to go with Norbert and she risked his anger on the children. He was silent as he drove the dogs out of the yard, twitching the lines with brutal efficiency.

"You liked the beading I did on the dogs' *tapis*," she said. "You said so yourself." He flinched, as if she had reminded him of something he'd forgotten and he meant to add it to her faults. She drew off her glove and put her hand on his. "It's a lovely evening—look at the stars." She tilted her head back, could feel the tremor of muscle at his wrist. They passed the trail south along the river, and she thought she should work harder to placate him. "When we get home, I'll make you some tea with snakeroot," she said to his steel-jawed profile.

"You lost me the race with your sacrilege," he said. "My relations whisper behind my back—I am made to wear the skirts in my own family." He hauled on the dogs' lines and at the same time, brought up his elbow to hit her in the face. Josette reeled back as if she'd been shot. For a moment, there was only blackness and the far-off sound of the team slowing. Norbert steered them left and the dogs began to jump through the crusted snow of a cow trail. She could taste blood and wanted to touch her mouth, but would not give him the satisfaction.

He pulled the team up short in a clearing, the sleigh tipped at an angle. Josette's eyes swam, her head was spinning. In the silence, the dogs panted, their breath rising in vapour clouds. The only other sound was an echoing drip of snow melting off the trees. She waited for the next blow, but nothing came and she turned her head to look at Norbert. He sat with the reins in his hands, face like a statue. A full moon had risen in the sky—Midwinter Moon the Cree called it. The dogs still heaved with exertion, tired after the long race today. Moments passed and Josette had just begun to breathe again, when Norbert turned in his seat with lightning quickness, his hand out of the glove, the bare hard warmth of it at her neck.

"You think you can make a fool of me?" he said in her ear. "What have you been doing with him?" She could smell the rum, the food he had eaten. Madame Goulet's *boulettes*, she thought, and then a sweet tang of powdered sugar: *beignets*. He began to pull with increasing purpose at her clothes, which was not easy, for she was trussed up in her blanket. The way he pawed at her seemed pathetically comical and she laughed, hoping that he would see it too, come to his senses, but his hand tightened on her throat until she gasped to draw breath. She stared up at the stars, felt the bite of air at her legs, naked to the cold. Norbert kept pressure on her neck with one hand and with the other undid his pants. When he yanked open her legs, Josette felt herself slipping into unconsciousness.

There was a strange noise at the edge of her awareness, and Norbert was abruptly hauled off the sleigh by an unseen force. Josette could not move, only heard the thud of punches landing on bone and flesh.

bathsheba

IT WAS CLOSE TO midnight when Marguerite Riel knelt in front of Father Moulin in the second-floor chapel of the rectory. After Charles Nolin had humiliated her husband in front of everyone at the dance, Louis had handed her the money purse and left with Gabriel and some other men. The pouch was still in her pocket. *Sixty dollars*. But at what cost? Shame and humiliation. When Louis had read the poem, Marguerite had been conscious of Father Moulin's eyes on her. The priest had gone out in a huff afterwards. She had seen him on the snow-packed trail south of the village, and left her children with the Ouellette girls to follow him. It had been only a few days since her last confession, but she was desperate.

Now he sat facing her, a curious expression on his face. She crossed herself and lowered her head. "You saw that my husband is upset. I confess I may be to blame."

Moulin cleared his throat. "Do you . . . perform your wifely duties?"

"Louis comes to bed and turns to the wall," she said quietly. "He wakes at night with dreams that make him call out. Only then will he let me hold him. Nothing else." She looked up at Moulin. "It almost killed him to receive the donation. He does not wish us to be the poorest of the poor."

He sat back and crossed his hands over his belly. "Do not compare yourself to others who have more. You are living a humble life as Mary did, the divine mother."

The mention of Mary gave her a shock. Louis had insisted that he had acted on God's wishes by making Josette his Mary Magdalene, but she was still angry at him for shaming her at berry-picking camp.

"Do not liken me to Mary," she said to Moulin, "I am not worthy."

"You are always worthy in the eyes of God."

"I do not think even *He* finds me worthy."

Moulin gazed at her a long beat. "Yet you attracted the great Louis Riel. Do you think he suffers poor judgment?"

"It was only luck."

"You should not torment yourself thus." Moulin paused. "I hear that Josette Lavoie spends much time with you and Riel and William Jackson up at Ouellette's. What does she do?"

Marguerite avoided his eyes. Had he guessed that Josette was the one she envied or was it a coincidence that he mentioned her? "She teaches William his catechism." Or *had*. Louis had told her that he suspected she spied on him.

"And where is your husband during these sessions?"

"He is not often there. Now that the petition has been sent, he and Gabriel are . . ." She trailed off. Louis had warned her not to share details of his actions with the priests.

Moulin sat up straight and took the wooden cross out of his belt. "He and Gabriel are *what?*"

"My husband is no longer mine," she said to divert him. "I have committed the sin of envy, jealous of the time he spends with others. I am sorry for these and all of my sins."

He lifted his cross to her in benediction. "You may conquer this feeling with the help of God's grace. When the thoughts come upon you, say the rosary and feel them leave."

Hail Mary, full of grace. Marguerite sought solace from the words, but felt only a profound emptiness, as if air pumped through her heart instead of blood.

"It is Josette who should be kneeling here," Moulin burst out. "It was her poem he read just now."

The old voices were clamouring in her head. *Louis will take another woman to marry.* The Métis would not allow it. Or would they? This was the great Louis Riel, a prophet sent by God to save them. They would deny him nothing, even a second wife.

"What was this talk of trees and a mother's worth?" The priest slapped his knee. "It is not proper for a woman to read and write."

Marguerite lowered her eyes. She would not tell Moulin that *she* had lately learned to read, and Josette was not the only woman she envied. Louis had been gone for days at a time with William Jackson, meeting with Gabriel and the men, or up in Prince Albert. While he was away, La Rose Ouellette's younger sister, Mary-Jane, who had boarded with the Grey Nuns, had taught her to read. Marguerite had surprised herself and learned quickly, and on those dark nights alone, when the children were asleep, she had gone through the box of papers that Louis had brought from the Montana Territory.

She found his poems and progressed slowly from letters to words. Although she went to Mary-Jane for the meaning of the more difficult ones, she had managed to parse them out. One night, she happened upon a small bundle of letters addressed to him in a feminine hand. She had studied them until she understood they were from a woman named Evelina Barnabé, whom Louis had known and loved in the east.

I often go to sit under the lilacs, Evelina had written, *which are about to bloom. I enclose a few blossoms for you and am carried back to that time when we were so happy, both of us seated on the same bench.*

The thought of this woman and Louis' love for her had consumed her. She would fall asleep with the letters on the bed and wake the next morning to find them scattered around her. The one that interested her the most was Evelina's last correspondence, which conveyed a different tone.

I have read in the papers that you have married Miss Marguerite Monet.

I could not believe my eyes . . . incredible. How could you be so shameful?

And then her husband's response, explaining that he could not afford to buy Evelina a fine house and the comforts that she had grown accustomed to.

But he had not sent the letter.

Here were two sins she would not confess to Father Moulin: guilt for snooping through her husband's private papers, and an unhealthy obsession over his reluctance to reply. Both of which revealed an ugly truth—the great Louis Riel had settled for a simple Métisse, who did not expect more than a sod roof over her head.

"I will assign you a psalm as penitence," Moulin was saying, "so that you may grow in confidence of divine mercy."

"If anyone is above sin it is Louis," she said. "He prays constantly and is favoured by God."

Moulin's eyes rose to meet hers. "King David sinned most heinously with Bathsheba. He went about pretending penitence. Only after he was confronted by his sin did he admit to it."

She did not like this priest. Was he saying that Louis was a liar? She lacked the courage to ask, for fear of the answer.

The door opened downstairs and the familiar voice of Gabriel Dumont called for Moulin. The priest leaped to his feet and Marguerite followed him, heart in her mouth. If something had happened to Louis while she confessed her sin of jealousy, she would not forgive herself.

Gabriel stood in the kitchen with Josette in his arms. Marguerite stopped on the stairs, breathless as Moulin examined Josette, her head against Gabriel's shoulder. Her eyes were closed, and blood had congealed in a swollen gash on her lip. Even in an insensible state, she managed to look beautiful.

Moulin regarded Gabriel with suspicion. "Why don't you take her to your wife? She would sew it better than me."

Gabriel lowered Josette on a narrow bunk the priest kept in a small room off the kitchen. Father Moulin returned, muttering, with needle and thread fine enough to bind the cut, and Marguerite took Josette's hand while the priest stitched her lip. Bruises had already begun to form on her lovely, bare neck. Gabriel stood by the stove, snow caked in his buffalo hide coat and dripping on the floor. He looked their way again, his eyes lingering on Josette.

At that instant Marguerite knew why he hadn't taken her to his wife. He would rather answer Father Moulin's probing questions: how he had worried that Norbert might be trouble after the race and had left Riel and the men. Why he'd come back to Letendre's and—discovering that Norbert had taken Josette out alone—followed them on the trail to save her from a vicious beating.

Marguerite's jealousy dissolved and she felt that she could breathe again. Gabriel Dumont. Looking at Josette as if her pain was his own.

She was not the woman who should fear Josette's presence in her husband's life.

II

their blood is
water

ON A BRIGHT COLD day in early March, Riel strode past the rectory to the church, where Fathers Moulin, Fourmond, and Vegreville stood like dark gatekeepers. Gabriel was at his side and almost all of Batoche following at their heels, but the priests stared them down. Moulin stepped forward, barring Riel's path.

My soul is among lions, Riel thought, putting a hand in his pocket to feel for the telegram. He prayed for temperance, but here was the most important moment in his life and no priest would stop him. "Let us in."

"You will not use the church for meetings," Moulin said, loud enough for the crowd to hear. "Father André forbids it."

"*God* forbids it," Fourmond said from behind him. His eyes went to Gabriel's rifle. "And there will be no gun in a church!"

Riel showed him the telegram. "God directs *me*. The answer to our petition has come from Ottawa. If you do not wish to hear what Macdonald has to say, do not come in. You are no longer welcome." He and

Gabriel pushed past the priests, who could do nothing but allow the rest of the Métis to enter.

Riel stood at the altar rail and watched as his people packed the pews and aisles. A few of the young men had come with wood and tinder to build a fire in the stove. Before long, the room was warm, the air filled with the rising breath of hundreds of souls, waiting. Gabriel stood to the side, holding *le Petit* in front of him. From the moment they had received the telegram two days ago, he and Gabriel and his *capitaines* had had their heads together. Every diplomatic process had been undertaken in appeal to Ottawa, but rebellion was their only recourse. They had gone directly to Prince Albert and met the English half-breeds and white settlers. Riel had been furious at Macdonald's response and mentioned that it might be necessary to take up arms for the glory of God, the honour of religion, and their salvation. The men of Prince Albert had looked at him with frightened eyes.

The white settlers wanted their rights, but not if it meant fighting for it. And the English half-breeds? Their blood was water. They had shaken his hand at the end of the meeting and mumbled that rebellion against the Dominion should be avoided at all cost. Some of them had quietly been getting their land claims settled by Ottawa. How easily they forgot the petition they had signed, their wider rights. And the Manitoba Métis who had come to pledge their allegiance—where were they now? Where were his own brothers, or Ambroise Lépine, and André Nault, who had three sons living here? The French Métis of Batoche might face Macdonald with only God as their protector.

Riel looked down to where Josette sat with William Jackson. The cut on her lip had healed, leaving a tight scar where Father Moulin had made a clumsy attempt at stitching it. Mary Magdalene beaten by her husband and the Christ could not save her. Riel regretted thinking of her as a spy and letting his resentment show in spurning her these past three months. She was angry, he could see, and he must woo her back again, for he needed her now more than ever.

William wore the ceinture fléchée the Ouellette girl had made him tied like a scarf around his neck and he muttered to himself—probably the penitentiary prayer that he had learned for his conversion. Riel was thankful for William's help to draft the petition, but the man had changed, often quoting scripture to no one in particular, mixing Biblical verse with that of the romantic poets.

Riel tapped the telegram on the lectern. "We have our answer from Ottawa," he said. "Sir John A. Macdonald invites you to register your river lot claims at the Dominion Lands Office in Prince Albert. There is to be a commission formed to count your heads."

To his consternation, people turned in the pews, laughing, congratulating each other. "This is no cause for celebration. It is a delaying tactic, an insult." He scanned the crowd. Did they not remember that Macdonald had done the same thing in Red River?

Charles Nolin stood near the door with Xavier Letendre and Roger Goulet at either elbow, as if under his influence. Nolin held his hands up. "Wait! Ottawa is at least forming a commission. It is due process and we must follow it."

Riel considered telling the people that spies lived among them, but he marshalled his expression. When he and William had happened upon the priests' meeting in St. Laurent, Father André had used a very specific word that Riel did not like: *insanity*. Was it coincidence? He did not think so. Nolin, finally sharing his secret. Gabriel had banned him from their meetings, but how long before the news that Riel had spent two years in an insane asylum got out to the people? He could say the priests were spreading lies, but the damage would be done and the Métis would lose faith in him.

He let his eyes pass over Nolin, thumbs now hooked defiantly in his vest pockets. *Judas*. "Macdonald has ignored our rights under the Manitoba Act," Riel said. "Ignored our right to fair government. Ottawa will do the same thing here as it did in Red River. Do you remember it took them years to decide *how* to assess your claims there?" Too many of them still looked at him with baffled expressions.

Maxime Lépine stood in his pew. "I left for Batoche in '76, when Ottawa issued an order-in-council—said we were locking up large and valuable tracts of land—seriously retarding the settlement of the country. Said we'd only get scrip from then on."

With a grateful look to him, Riel said, "Macdonald ensured money scrip would be the only way to settle your land claims. A dollar an acre and speculators lurking at the Dominion Lands offices to buy it for less." Now he could see the light of recall in his people's eyes. He made the mistake of looking in Nolin's direction, only to find him holding up his hands again.

"You executed Thomas Scott," Nolin said. "Macdonald punished us by stealing away every right we had in Red River." He looked around like a politician, registering the impact of his words. "We lost our lands in Manitoba, and we will surely lose them here."

Thomas Scott again. It would always be Thomas Scott. But the crowd shifted, as if considering Nolin's words. "You were there when they brought in Norbert Parisien," Riel said, "murdered by Scott himself." The people were wide-eyed, some of them too young to remember, others had forgotten the details. To win them back, Riel pressed on. "What you have built here is beautiful. Sons farming beside their fathers, beside their brothers. Who is ready to crouch and submit? To sell your lands and community for nothing to speculators?"

Philippe Gariépy stood in his pew. "I did it in Red River. I will not here!"

Riel paused for a moment, allowing the people to turn to each other and quietly share their fears. With a finger pointed at Nolin, he said, "This man resists me in hopes he will be rewarded by government agents." He waited as the disquiet escalated. "And so, the Church! Father André has written his cronies in Ottawa, begging them to remove me. How do I know this? Just as Judas was paid by the priests to betray Christ, André offered me money, a bribe for me to leave you." The crowd erupted in anger, and he exchanged a glance with Gabriel. "Perhaps he is right and I should leave."

Again, there was chaos, calls of "Stay, stay!"

Riel looked around, meeting outraged stares. "What if Macdonald ignores the petition only because he still wants me dead?" There was more emphatic dissent and he took a deep breath, filling his lungs.

"They cannot make me leave. For I am as David who fled from King Saul into the wilderness. God has made a covenant with me. My kingdom is forever established in the North-West."

The crowd hushed, faces turned up to him with reverence. If this were his church, he would bid each of them to come forth; he would take up the bread, the cup and offer it to them. *This is my body, this is my blood* . . . Then he noticed Josette looking up at him, her eyes like those of some wrathful temptress. Almost beseeching, daring: tell them your new church will head this kingdom, *tell them*.

"These are rash words, Louis," said Nolin. "The Dominion will bring men to fight us."

Riel glared down at him. "We have God on our side. If Macdonald wishes to remove the prophet from his place at the head of his people, let him come."

The crowd erupted in cheers and Nolin patted the air with his hands to quiet them. "The feast of St. Joseph comes soon. If you wish to fight for the love of God, I propose we hold a novena—after nine days of prayerful reflection, the people will think more favourably upon your plan."

"The time for prayer is finished," Gabriel said. "We vote for action."

Riel was dismayed when the crowd's excitement grew at the promise of a religious festival. To refuse it would make him seem vindictive. He wanted to go straight to Nolin and wring his neck.

"Nine days is too long." As soon as Riel had said the words, it occurred to him that hundreds of Métis would come in to pray, and he smiled to himself. "A novena—yes," he said, avoiding Gabriel's angry look. He would speak to him later, and in nine days they would both watch the smug look on Nolin's face turn to disbelief when he understood that they meant to use the Feast of St. Joseph as a method of recruitment. And to finally tell the Métis why he had come.

the world will know

⁓

UNDER A WANING winter sun, Lawrence Clarke came up from Qu'Appelle in the south and passed along the Carlton Trail through Batoche. It was the kind of frigid March day he'd grown accustomed to in this country—oppressive grey and a chill damp that crept in at the joints.

Over the collar of his lynx coat, he surveyed the ramshackle buildings that made up what they called a village, if four stores, a blacksmithy, and a saloon could be considered such. It looked prosperous enough in summer with the trees in leaf, but in winter it was no more than a ghost town. A few half-breeds milled about in front of the blacksmith's on what represented a street—packed snow mixed with frozen mud—but Garnot's saloon was closed up tight. One of their squaws came out of Fisher's store, a bundle of cloth under her arm. He asked her where everyone had gone.

"The Feast of St. Joseph, on the Jolie Prairie."

He turned his horse to Fisher's Crossing. Just when he needed someone close to Riel, they were busy honouring one of their dead Catholic saints. It bothered him that Macdonald had sent an answer to the breeds: register your river lots! It was a political move, useless, as Riel would surely know, but it might give him time to bring the Indians on side. Clarke had an incendiary rumour to share, false, yet enough to ensure that Riel's famous temper was roused to action.

His horse stepped out onto the frozen river, following a packed snow trail used by those following the Carlton Trail between Duck Lake and Batoche. Three riders emerged from the trees on the far bank. Clarke studied the men and their fur-lined moccasins, rough woollen coats. Scouts by the look of them. The two parties met in the middle of the river, and after customary greetings, Clarke asked, "Where is everyone? What's happening?"

"We hoped you'd tell us something," Michel Dumas said with a frown. "You met with the men in Ottawa."

Clarke smiled. "There is talk in Qu'Appelle that since Riel received the telegram from Macdonald, he's held meetings every night—riling up the Indians."

Dumas exchanged a look with his men. "You hear wrong, *mon ami.* Riel is staying peacefully with us at Batoche. What is happening?"

"Plenty," replied Clarke. He could almost feel the railway feeder contract in his hand. "Police are mustering at Humboldt. I saw them with my own eyes."

"You speak of the police that went into Fort Carlton," said one of the scouts.

Clarke laughed. Not one gopher moved across the prairie that Gabriel Dumont and his scouts did not know about. "That was only Crozier moving a few men. I'm talking about Commissioner Irvine and five hundred of his police." He paused, enjoying the looks on their faces. "They'll be here in two days to arrest Riel and Dumont."

Dumas immediately spurred his horse. Without so much as a fare-thee-well, the others followed, trotting their horses across the river and up the trail toward the village. Clarke smiled to himself. Riel would hear this news within minutes. In case they decided to shoot the messenger, he urged his own mount in the other direction. As his horse scrambled up the west bank, Clarke thought of the moment when he'd walked into the office of the most powerful man in the Dominion. The prime minister had welcomed him with hand outstretched, impatient to hear from someone fresh from the half-breeds. Also in the office were some of his ministers and business cronies—men who had a vested interest in completing the Canadian Pacific Railway. When Macdonald had finished reading Riel's petition, he sighed deeply and rubbed his eyes.

"Riel demands a province with its own government," he said with a chuckle. "A lot of breeds running an agriculturally valuable twelve million acres." He threw the petition on his desk. "A rough band of them sitting in the House."

David McPherson, Minister of the Interior, picked up the petition. "White settlers in Prince Albert have signed it."

Macdonald stood and walked to the window, hands in his pant pockets. "Aye, but it's by Riel's hand sure enough."

Clarke relished the memory. He had expected Macdonald to rage with anger that Riel had been cocky enough to make such demands. Instead, he seemed almost pleased to have the petition finally in his hands.

"Riel has a temper," Clarke had ventured, testing his influence. "If he gets the Indians riled . . ."

But Macdonald did not respond, only stood looking out over the Rideau Canal. The men in the room seemed to take this in stride, talking amongst themselves as if the prime minister weren't present.

"How to send troops?" asked the minister of militia.

Cornelius Van Horne, who had been sprawled on a settee near the door, got up and sauntered into the middle of the room, a cigar held to his nose. He was the man who had managed the building of Macdonald's railroad before they'd run out of money to finish it. "What is this Batoche in miles?" he asked, lighting the cigar. "I would think a thousand at least." He took a long pull and blew a mouthful of smoke to the ceiling. "Can you see the headlines? Savage Indians and half-breeds threaten the North-West. Grit opposition endangers Dominion by refusing loan to finish railway. Volunteer troops struggle valiantly to put down savage rebellion."

The meeting had gone on for hours, with Van Horne standing over a map of the unfinished railway sections. "A few gaps in the line here and there—that'll pose a problem," he'd said, leaning his fists on the desk. "But we can get a couple thousand troops out there in ten days, eleven at a stretch."

Clarke had listened with fascination. He had missed his calling, for the halls of power in Ottawa were infinitely more interesting than dealing with dirty Indians and ignorant half-breeds in the far North-West.

His horse found the trail, and when he flicked the reins, it leaped forward. He was anxious to get safely to Fort Carlton by nightfall. This territory would soon be crawling with half-breeds, with their guns loaded for bear.

feast of the
novena

⁐

IN THE CENTRE OF THE Jolie Prairie, men circled an ox with spears and war axes. The animal stood with its four hooves planted in the packed snow, eyes rolling, and breath coming in defeated huffs. Josette was among a group of women who watched as Damase Carrière threw the first spear and struck the ox in the neck. It toppled and was hit by another and another in quick succession, in an old Biblical ritual meant to remind them how God had sacrificed his only son for their souls.

After the ox fell, the women pulled knives from their skirts and set to work. Josette knelt in the snow at its rump, first skinning the hide then slicing at the still-warm flesh, her coat sleeves stained with blood. In less than an hour, the animal had been gutted, the hide saved for curing, and large joints of meat hewn off, destined for a spit that had been built over the fire.

Josette wiped her hands and knife on the snow and searched for the familiar figure of William Jackson. He stood near a sleigh, exhausted and red-eyed, for he had been up all night praying before his baptism. Despite her estrangement from Riel, she had been moved during the ceremony earlier, watching him act as William's godfather and choosing his new Catholic name: Honoré Joseph Jaxon.

Hundreds of Métis from all over the South Branch had convened for the Feast of St. Joseph and the end of the nine-day novena. Norbert was still absent almost three months after attacking her. Gone north, his relations said. Josette hoped he would never return. Her eyes went to Gabriel, who was speaking to a crowd of men. When Riel had gathered them in the church to share Ottawa's answer to the petition, Josette had watched Gabriel standing at his side. That he'd brought *le Petit* into a house of worship had sent her a strong message: he would follow Riel regardless of anything he might do or say. Last summer among the birch trees, she had laid out her fear to him: Riel will make us suffer. *I will not let him fail*, Gabriel had told her, confident in his leader. Events had spiraled out of his control, and she would no longer hold him to a promise he could not keep. He was the only one to think that Norbert would be in a punishing mood after losing the dog race, following them to save her from rape or death.

The women tended the roasting meat and put bannock pans to the fire. Father Moulin stood among them with Father Fourmond. Moulin sidled up to Josette and nodded his head toward Riel.

"You would agree he has been acting prideful, *non?*" When she did not reply, he went on. "Does your Spinoza not say that extreme pride indicates infirmity of spirit?"

She should be grateful to the priest. Hadn't he sewn up her cut on New Year's? Her hand went self-consciously to her mouth, where, with a fingertip, she traced the scar on her upper lip. Spinoza's words seemed hollow coming from Moulin. Her eyes kept going back to Gabriel. *He is the one we should follow. Him.*

She thought back to New Year's. After Gabriel had rescued her from Norbert, he had stayed long enough to make sure she was all right, then had returned to a meeting with Riel and his men. Emmanuelle Champagne had taken her home to the children the next morning. Madeleine had noticed them arrive, and come up, stunned to find her nursing a black eye and cut lip. Josette, amazed that Gabriel had not told her he had saved their neighbour from rape or murder, muttered something about Norbert punishing her for losing the race. Since then, she had obsessed over why Gabriel had not taken her to his wife, especially when she was a master with the beading needle and would have left less of a scar than Moulin. She had decided that it had to do with Gabriel cursing when he discovered Madeleine watching them with their heads together earlier that day during the dog race. Gabriel was not a man to be controlled, and he resented being held accountable to his wife.

While she had been brooding, the priest had stepped closer to her. "Riel said he would accept an indemnity from Ottawa," he said. "You were not there when Father André extended it to him. Riel's interest would surprise you."

"But he did not take it." Josette kept her features composed. "If you cared for the Métis, you too would help us." She walked away purposefully. Why did she bother protecting Riel when he did not protect *her*? She thought of what he had said at the church meeting. *I am as David, who fled from King Saul into the wilderness. My kingdom, established in the North-West.* It was confirmation of his aim to create a separate state of Métis and Indians, but not quite an admission that he planned a new church at its head.

Several Métis men from Duck Lake walked past, rifles slung across their chests, and she could hear Father Fourmond say, "Come to the church and pray," but they ignored him. Father Moulin tried to corner another man from St. Laurent. "Do not join with these rebels," he said. "Be patient. History tells the story of peoples who suffered great hardship at the hands of those who governed. In time, the force of public opinion will inspire them to act."

Riel had heard this and pushed through the crowd to face Moulin. "History is full of oppressed peoples," he said, "who were annihilated by tyrant kings."

People gathered, curious, and Josette could see that Moulin had baited Riel with intent. "Trust in your government leaders," the priest said in a loud voice. "Trust in God, that He will provide a peaceful solution. He would be most displeased if his children rebelled. As much as the Church would—" he paused for dramatic effect "—by refusing sacraments to any who take up arms."

"Look at this Protestant," Riel said, his colour high. "You dare to refuse the sacraments to those who would take up arms in defence of their most sacred rights."

There was a murmur from the crowd. Three scouts had been spotted riding at speed across the plain towards them.

Moulin paused, obviously noticing them too, although he kept his attention on Riel. "The Bible says that God will strike sinners with *madness* as a curse."

A muscle in Riel's jaw twitched, but his face remained composed. "Surely oppression maketh a wise man mad," he said, "and a gift destroyeth the heart." From his pocket, he withdrew the letter from Bishop Bourget. At the sight of it, Moulin turned away, his arms crossed. "I am to fulfill my mission before God," Riel said. "*I*, to whom a bishop has written in official letters."

Moulin's lips worked in a struggle to control his anger. "The letter is old—you have misread it."

The three riders came thundering in, Michel Dumas at their head. He had spied Riel in the crowd before his horse slid to a stop in the snow. "I just saw Lawrence Clarke at the crossing," Dumas told him. "He claims five hundred police ride from Qu'Appelle to arrest you and Gabriel."

Gabriel and a number of other men ran for their horses. Riel turned to Emmanuel Champagne. "Get Father Moulin and Fourmond to the rectory and confine them there." Then to Damase Carrière. "Ride to St. Laurent for Father Vegreville and the nuns—bring them here."

"Riel is losing his mind," yelled Moulin as he was being led away. "He is insane!"

Gone were the lines of worry on Riel's face. Hundreds of people had assembled by now, and he straightened his coat, his eyes roving over them like a statesman about to deliver an acceptance speech. "It has commenced—the movement for the rights of our country."

Someone said, "Our priests will not give us the sacraments if we follow you."

Riel smiled broadly in the sudden quiet and held out his arms. "We will become our own priests—form our own church and rituals." He lifted his head and closed his eyes. *"Rome est tombée."*

There was an agonizing silence. *Rome is fallen.* Riel had just denied their Catholic religion and was on his way to creating his own government, with his church at its head. Josette held her breath, expecting open rebellion against this shocking pronouncement, but although Maxime Lépine and a few of the more pious men seemed taken aback, the others cheered. They had no idea that Riel had harboured this truth all along, only that he had written a petition that was ignored and his hand was forced.

Gabriel had come up on his horse, leading Riel's mare by the reins. His eyes were alive with anticipation. Did he think they could win a war against the Queen's government? Or was he eager to finally be in control of a situation as Riel's war chief?

After the men rode away, Honoré was left standing with the women, who seemed hesitant to question the great Riel, yet scandalized that their priests were now prisoners and had denied their men sacraments for taking up arms. Did it mean the wives, as well?

Honoré regarded Josette with a baffled expression. "In one day, the great Louis Riel became my godfather, granted me a new name, and welcomed me into the Roman Catholic Church. And not three hours later, he has denounced that church and formed his own."

Josette touched her lip once more, staring after the men, who were now halfway down the plain, their horses' hooves sending up a cloud of snow in their wake. Her eyes rested on the back of a man in a buffalo coat, one hand on the reins, the other on his rifle. Hands she could still feel on her body as he lifted her out of Norbert's sleigh.

pauvres misérables

TWO HOURS LATER, Gabriel pushed Antoine Marion and Daniel Boyer into a corner of the room, then tightened the rope around Charles Nolin's fat wrists.

"Traitor," Gabriel said near his ear.

Riel reclined in a chair at the head of Xavier Letendre's long kitchen table, a new Stetson hat on his head. He'd just formed a provisional government and elected a council made up of his closest friends and supporters, who crowded the room, loaded guns in their hands. The white owner of Walter & Baker's store and his clerk were locked upstairs under guard. Gabriel had sent men to cut the telegraph lines between Battleford and Clark's Crossing, and the Métis had broken into stores in both the east village and those across the river for supplies and ammunition. Antoine and Boyer had been caught deserting. Letendre had already disappeared like a thief in the night. His house and store were commandeered as their headquarters. It was discovered that Nolin had been busy during the novena, urging a group of men from Duck Lake to join him in overthrowing Riel.

"I hereby name the council *Exovedate*, for we are chosen from the flock," Riel was saying to the men. "All that is needed to govern our people, a nation of individuals, are a trustworthy few who use good sense and no other authority than that which exists by itself in the condition of our nature."

"Taking prisoners, eh, that's fine," said Moise Ouellette, who had just been voted to the council. "But, Louis, you must release the priests."

Riel glanced at him. "They have wilfully played into the hands of the government."

Maxime Lépine, who had also been voted to the council, was unnaturally agitated. "To say Rome has fallen . . ." He trailed off and could not meet Riel's eyes.

"It was necessary to formally separate from Rome," Riel said. "The Métis Nation wishes to leave behind the division between Catholics and Protestants."

Honoré Jaxon, who had been named secretary of the new council, stood near the kitchen door, looking stunned at the turn of events. When Gabriel had overheard Riel declare himself saviour to Josette last summer, he had felt this way too—a new church at the head of a separate state had been a crazy idea in Riel's mind. Gabriel had hoped that Macdonald would honour the petition, but on that day, he had reluctantly accepted Riel's religious vision along with his political one and committed to war. Riel had done all that he could to get Ottawa to listen: English half-breeds' and settlers' support, the threat of the Indians joining. Still Macdonald had ignored their demands.

Over the past few months, Gabriel had ridden through the territory with Isidore to gain support from the Métis, and had shared Riel's vision for a new church with his brother, who had objected, said the resistance was for their rights not religion. Gabriel knew that his old buffalo *capitaines* would follow him anywhere, but the English half-breeds and white settlers had already shown their true colours. Only time would tell if the devout Métis would accept a reformed church. He would have to twist the arms of peaceful farmers reluctant to go against the five hundred police that Macdonald had sent to put them down. Gabriel was not an orator like Riel, but the government had thrown down the gauntlet and it was now a fight.

"Macdonald did not honour the petition," he reminded them. "What do you think we must do?" The room went silent and he raised his voice. "Run away like these fine men before you?"

"We will not abide deserters," said Riel looking around at them. "And if you are caught going up to see the priests, you will be considered a traitor."

Gabriel nodded to Isidore and together they pushed forward Nolin, Marion, and Boyer.

Riel said, "Our first order of business as a provisional government will be to address the treason of these *pauvres misérables*."

"Where is Letendre?" Gabriel asked them.

Nolin ignored Gabriel and looked at Riel, his expression insolent. "Doing business in Fort-à-la-Corne. He knows better than to follow a lost cause."

Gabriel snorted. "He leaves his family here and hides up there like a coward."

Riel slammed his fist on the table. "Charles Nolin, sign an oath of allegiance or you are hereby sentenced to death for whispering evil into men's ears, even here, this day of St. Joseph."

"I am trying to save the Métis," replied Nolin. "What do you think Macdonald will do when he hears you have cut telegraph lines, made a provisional government, and talk of raising arms?"

"As he did in Red River. Do not underestimate my thinking. Sir John is trapped like a rat in a hole. He must now negotiate with me."

Nolin looked ready to spit. "A few police have set you off. Do you not think Macdonald has ready means to send more? His railroad is almost finished."

Gabriel hit him on the shoulder. "If they come we will kill them."

"There are more who do not support your call to arms," said Nolin, refusing to back down.

"We will find them and deal with them the same way," Riel said. "You each have ten minutes to decide if you will join us, or we will have to do something."

Isidore nudged Marion. "I have seen you kill four buffalo in as many minutes. You are the best of us—why won't you fight?"

Marion glowered at him. "I would rather face one thousand buffalo than one man on the plains. You and Gabriel have killed men in the Indian wars. We have not. Do you think it is easy asking us?"

Isidore grabbed him by the coat. "We *will* ask you." When Marion did not reply, Isidore threw him off. "*Le Pissou.*"

Gabriel watched Marion with growing unease. "They forced you from Red River," he said to him. "They *forced* you out. Do you think there is good land to plow in the great mountains? Will you move to the far reaches of this country and fall into the ocean at the other end?" Marion remained stubbornly silent, and Gabriel went on. "If a stranger comes to your house, demands you leave, will you quietly pack up your belongings, your children, your wife, and do so?"

Marion stared at a fixed spot on the floor. "*Non.*"

"That is what you are doing here," he said, his voice quieter now. "If a man will not stand by to watch a stranger take his house and family, he cannot stand and watch as police come up the river." He gestured to Nolin. "Macdonald wants your land. If we do not face him, he will destroy our families, our blood. Will we let him do that? Will we?"

The men answered with cheers. Marion, Boyer, and even Nolin nodded reluctantly.

"Good, good." Gabriel took a deep breath and lifted his gun. "Then we prepare ourselves as we did for the buffalo hunts."

the catholic apostolic and living church of the new world

A SECOND-FLOOR BEDROOM in Baptiste Boyer's house in Batoche village had been transformed into Riel's new chapel. Josette stood in the doorway regarding the strange scene before her. The bed had been moved out and Marguerite and a few of the St. Laurent women had created an altar on a low chest of drawers, propping up a picture of Saint Bernadette kneeling at the appearance of the Virgin Mary at Lourdes as its centrepiece. Someone had donated her own brooch to affix the letter that Riel had received from Bishop Bourget. Josette stared at it with single-minded purpose, for she had come here for one reason: to finally read the official words that had driven Riel to fulfill a mission from God.

Several young women were clustered around the altar in their long gingham dresses, holding hands and singing devotional hymns. The girls swayed, their eyes closed in rapture, unaware that they had an audience. When they launched into another hymn, Josette finally sent them away, and they filed past her whispering, "She is beautiful, the Magdalene . . . *Oui*, like her pictures in the Bible."

She wanted to laugh, but thought it would be unseemly in this recently blessed space, the beating heart of Riel's church. Three months had passed since he had read her poem at the New Year's dance. Her lip had healed, but not her pride. Riel had betrayed her secret life, and now she was determined to gain insight into his own. The council had been holed up for days. Josette suspected that Riel had allowed the prized letter out of his possession to prove to the Métis that a man of the Church, a bishop no less, had proclaimed him a prophet. And to show that he had good cause to imprison their priests and reform their beloved Catholic faith.

At the novena, Moulin had accused Riel of misreading the bishop's words and she meant to see if it was true. The chapel was finally empty and silent when she stepped close to the altar and reached for the letter. She had just touched it with the tips of her fingers when she heard a noise in the hall. Pulling her hand back, she turned to find Honoré Jaxon. He took a few tentative steps into the room. He was hatless, his face drawn, dark hair hanging in ratted pieces over his haunted eyes. The ceinture fléchée at his waist held up a pair of pants so wrinkled, she was sure he had slept in them.

"I thought the council was meeting," she said, unable to keep the spite out of her voice. Despite Riel's betrayal, despite the fact that he'd accused her of being a spy, she was outraged not to be nominated to his twenty-man council. Gabriel was there by right, as his adjutant general, and many others who deserved the honour, but Riel had made Charles Nolin the commissioner, a man who had been caught working against him in Batoche.

Honoré's eyes shifted to the altar and closed briefly, as if he could not bear the sight. "We should be praying in the church of St. Antoine de Padoue." He stared dumbly at the image of the Virgin. "What does he call this place?"

"The Catholic Apostolic and Living Church of the New World."

He shook his head. "Riel is a warrior saint, like the old prophets— David himself—but I pray to God for forgiveness in abandoning his new church."

Forgiveness. Norbert had returned the night before, walking in the door after darkness had fallen, expecting his dinner, as if the last time she had seen him was at church and not in the winter woods with rape and murder in his heart. There was still an angry scar—Gabriel's mark—upon his cheek, but he wore it as if it had been somehow earned. When he had eaten, and sent the children to bed, she feared the worst, but instead, he stared into his tea and asked her to forgive him. Said he had been drunk at New Year's, on the brink of a headache. She had granted it to him, for what choice did she have, forced to live with the devil?

Honoré shuffled closer to the altar. She had grown close to him during his conversion, enjoyed their talk of books and commiseration over Riel's unreasonable demands. He looked so miserable, she put a hand on his shoulder, but he jumped at her touch.

"I just walked out of a council meeting," he said, rubbing a hand over his face. "Riel shouted for me to come back. I . . . don't know if I can."

"Why?" She did not like to hear this. Abandoning Riel's church was one thing, but his council? Honoré would be considered a traitor.

"He had me write a letter to Superintendent Crozier," said Honoré, "demanding he surrender Fort Carlton or he will commence without delay a war of extermination upon those who are hostile to our rights."

When Josette expressed her astonishment at Riel's use of the word "extermination," Honoré told her that he had left when the council passed a motion to rename the days of the week. "Riel wants to make Saturday the Sabbath. Nothing is to remain from the pagan Romans," he said, his mouth twitching on the word "pagan."

Late winter sun shone through the window and caught at the brooch holding Riel's letter, sending a rainbow prism against the far wall. Josette felt as if she were unmoored, refracted and dispersed as the light. "If I were on the council, I would vote against this madness. Did Gabriel vote yes?"

"Of course. He does not love the priests for working against us, and his heart is on war."

War. Then it had come to that. Gabriel had visited Métis communities for hundreds of miles, ensuring Riel would have support in the event of rebellion. All of this had been sparked by Lawrence Clarke's claim that five hundred police were coming to arrest them. Métis scouts had been sent south, but not one police had left Qu'Appelle, much less five hundred.

No one in Batoche had remarked on why Clarke had spread a vicious rumour. There had been more consternation over Riel's new church and the name he had chosen for the members of his provisional government. *Exovedate*. Some of the councillors' wives had gossiped about the meaning of this Latin word, annoyed that Riel considered their men "sheep that had left the herd."

"The Old Crows," she said, trying to lighten the mood, "will die before allowing a Saturday Sabbath."

Honoré smiled, but a weak laugh died in his throat at the sound of footsteps in the hall. Riel stepped into the room, taking off his hat. "Ah, you've come to pray." He looked around with an admiring glance and knelt in front of the altar, beckoning for them to join him.

Honoré hesitated and turned slightly, as if ready to run, but in a moment, he sank slowly to his knees. Josette could not move or even look at Riel. Months had passed with no word between them, and now he acted as if all was well.

Riel crossed himself and fixed his eyes on the Blessed Virgin. "Mary Immaculate, Divine Mother," he prayed, "hasten to make everyone see, through the almighty grace of Jesus Christ, that God has sent me to redeem the honour of His people, to redeem the glory of the true faith. Make Superintendent Crozier surrender Fort Carlton to us. Change the obstinate mind of Moise Ouellette. In your mercy, make him freely and gracefully acknowledge that it is permissible to leave the Roman Church." He paused and waited for Honoré to finish a coughing fit. "May your power send the Indians quickly to us. Let them arrive very soon, provided with good weapons and a large supply of ammunition. Amen."

Incredibly, Riel reached up and found Josette's hand, tugged at it gently, as if encouraging her to kneel beside him. She resisted and he let it go. Did he think that she would so quickly trust him again? It was a travesty to think that his God would listen intently to all of these worries and work to grant his wishes.

He opened his eyes and looked up at her. "The council has agreed to send two emissaries to Big Bear," he said. "Ready yourself to leave with them tomorrow morning for Frog Lake with a letter for your grandfather."

"*We* will take it," Honoré said, his eyes intense. "Josette and I together."

Riel gave him a hard look. "You can sanctify the chapel on the west side of the river with your prayers." With a brief glance at Josette, Honoré scrambled to his feet and hurried out. She started to follow, fearing that he would cross the river and keep on going. She would never see him again.

Riel got up off his knees. "Why are you here, if not to help me?"

She stopped and let out the breath she'd been holding. "I am here wondering why I do not have a place among your exiled sheep," she said, turning to look at him. "Is it because I'm a spy? Or because I am a woman?"

He was careful not to meet her eyes. "I was mistaken," he said. "Honoré said you were heartbroken."

She stood in the centre of the room, her face hot. "You read my poem in front of everyone." She gestured to her lip. "And this because of it."

"The Spirit of God tells me you still have a role in this mission. He has told me the miracle I need to show the Métis I am a prophet is to bring the Indians to my side."

"No," she said. "What more must I do?" She thrust her arms out. "Give you my blood?"

He breathed in audibly, as if suffering her presence. "Scouts came in last night. Big Bear has finally been forced by his band to move on his reserve."

"He wants them to live."

"You are also his relation. Why does he not think of *your* right to live here, free on your own lands?"

She wanted to finally tell him that she had not a drop of Big Bear's blood in her veins, but something stopped her. After all Riel had done, did she still fear his judgement? "*Mosom* will not listen. You said it yourself."

Riel made for the door, as though he could no longer stand to be opposed. He turned in the hallway. "Ride north and I will know I was right in placing my trust in you." Josette stood still, a flush of indignation rising to her throat. How could he speak of trust after betraying her? He must have thought that she was considering the request, for in a moment he added, "Convince Big Bear and his warriors to return with you to Batoche."

He left as quickly as he had come and Josette went to the window then paced back toward the altar, her skirts dragging at the hem. Despite Gabriel's involvement, Riel took an impossible line, threatening to exterminate the police at Fort Carlton and sending her north at a time of war. She heard her grandfather's voice, *The spirit is not good with him.* If he hadn't supported Riel by now, he never would.

With purpose now, she put her fingers to the Bishop Bourget letter and turned it over. She read, "You have a mission, which you will have to accomplish in all respects," and dropped it as if she'd been burned.

god's ear

HOURS BEFORE DAWN, Josette bent over Honoré Jaxon, slumped on her kitchen floor. Earlier, she had come out to put more wood in the stove and was surprised by a noise on the porch. She found him sitting on the steps, gibbering like a madman. He told her that he had just walked from Batoche where he had been praying with Riel.

Josette had exclaimed at the sight of Honoré's bare feet, blue with cold. "You walked eight miles without moccasins? In the snow?"

She had brought him inside, her hair still unbound around her shoulders, and Honoré raised a hand to touch it, whispering, "The virgin bathed the feet of the lord with her own tears when he came off the cross—dried them with her hair." As his feet began to thaw near the fire, he moaned in pain. She had wrapped him in blankets, praying he would not wake Norbert and the children, and prepared a decoction of plantain leaves on the stove.

When she made him drink the tea, Honoré gripped her hand. "We must go to your grandfather. I did not tell you . . . a secret. I am the son of a Virginia father and French Indian mother—born in the Montana Territory."

"You are from the east," she said, keeping her voice low. "Born a Methodist, you told me yourself."

"No, no I was taken by my uncle, my uncle who hunted buffalo with the Métis in Montana . . . taken back to the east when just a child."

She looked away, shaken at his quick descent into madness.

"Listen," he said, pulling her close. "Whatever happens, remember Riel dances on the edge of the universe and has God's ear. He sent me his thoughts last night—I could read his mind because he wanted me to. You and I are the only ones who understand him."

His eyelids fluttered and he fell silent. She knew that he was wrong. Gabriel understood Riel more than any of them. Yesterday, he had stopped to see her before he left on a recruiting mission. She had gone out on the porch with him, while his men waited on their horses in the yard, and had caught his scent after days on the trail: the smell of sweat and horse and leather.

Although he had finally sought her out, he seemed uneasy.

"Norbert hasn't touched you?" Gabriel searched her face, as though looking for proof.

"*Namoyanitaw*," she said, there is nothing wrong.

"Maxime said Riel wanted to send you north. That you said no."

"I've seen his letter," she said, relieved to finally have Gabriel to herself. "This Bishop Bourget said Riel would have to accomplish the mission in all respects. You know he will die trying."

"He prays to the spirit of God for guidance." Gabriel raised his eyes to her. "I do not trust the spirit of God."

His hands were on the brim of his hat, rough and chapped from the cold, the fingernails pale, trimmed close with a knife, and oddly beautiful. "Riel suspected me of being a spy," she said. "Father Moulin was right, he is losing his mind."

"He believes God will protect us and he keeps things from me— what I need to know if we will win a war," Gabriel said. "I need you to remain his disciple."

She had absolved him of his promise. But she had closed her heart to

Riel. Now Gabriel, the one man she admired, the only one to save her from Norbert, was asking her to become the Magdalene again. She glanced up. His steady gaze faltered as it had in the birch grove last summer, and she glimpsed him for a moment, unguarded and questioning. "The Métis would follow *you*," she said, but he turned abruptly and put on his hat.

"I do not like Riel's new church, either," he said quietly. "This idea he has of being our saviour . . ." He shook his head. "Men are already running away. I can't have you turn from him, too." He went down the steps and got on his horse, spurring it into a full gallop, the other men following.

Josette checked the sleeping form of Honoré again and went to stoke the fire in the dark kitchen. Gabriel had made every effort to support Riel and now, with war imminent, the prophet would trust only his God to win it for them. Gabriel already faced Métis deserting. She had to help him.

She had just dipped a cup into the flour sack to make bannock when a voice said from behind her, "What is this?" Norbert had come out of the bedroom, tucking in his shirt. She explained how Honoré had been on the front steps, but Norbert walked slowly toward her, his eyes dark, a sign that one of his headaches was coming.

"I thought you went up to St. Laurent for Riel, but now I see it was for this worthless hound." He raised his hand to her, but winced in pain and grabbed at his head.

She rushed to stoke the fire to make more of the medicine tea. There was only a dipperful of water left in the pail by the door, but she poured it into the pot and quickly added a handful of herbs. Norbert doubled over, crying out, and she led him to a chair at the table. His headaches varied in intensity. Some would linger at a low ebb for days. Others came like the first crack of thunder in a storm.

When the decoction had boiled, she poured it into a cup and set it in front of him. He sipped at it, eager for relief. Wahsis broke into a high-pitched cry, and she went back to see that her two youngest were fighting among the blankets. Cleophile had just pulled a dress over her nightshift.

"Look after your brothers," Josette said.

Cleophile stared past her, sullen. "Who is in the kitchen?"

"A friend," Josette said, "Honoré Jaxon."

The girl's face was closed as she reached for her apron. "The one who makes you come alive."

Josette's temper flared. "He is a friend who brings books and speaks to me like an equal—*yes*, that makes me come alive." Cleophile would not look at her and Josette went on, relentless. "You are becoming an Old Crow."

Cleophile had been tying her apron and stopped for a long moment before continuing with a resolute defiance that made Josette's throat burn with shame. What kind of mother was only brought alive by books and the company of learned men? She went back to the kitchen and found Norbert drooling, eyes turned in his head. The empty cup had fallen to the floor. She ran to the stove. Leaves were stuck to the bottom of the pot. In her haste, she had added the same amount of herbs that she would have if she were making a full pot of the tea.

When she reached a hand toward him, he drew back, clawing at his hair. "It isn't working." He stood, sending his chair crashing against the wall and fell against the table, saliva bubbling at the corners of his mouth. The table skidded along the floor until it slammed against the stove and sent the pot clattering. She looked up to find all four of her children in the bedroom doorway.

"Go to the river and get water. He's drunk too much of the medicine tea."

Cleophile glanced at him, still bent over the table. She pulled a blanket close around her and went to the door. Lifting the bucket, she disappeared into the dark. Josette felt as if she were in a nightmare. Was everyone going mad? She enlisted Eulalie's help in restraining Norbert to keep him from harming himself. When Cleophile did not return, Josette went down the trail, a shawl around her shoulders against the cold. The moon hung above the trees in the west, a mass of cloud scudding across its white face. Twenty feet out on the ice, Cleophile stood with the pail in her hand near the hole that her father had cut to draw their water.

Josette ventured out, the cold striking upward through her thin moccasins and into the bones of her feet. "What's wrong," she cried. "What is it?"

Cleophile's eyes were fixed on the dim profile of the west bank. A far-off storm sent vivid lightning strikes across the sky, revealing her face. "Is he going to die?"

"Not if we get enough water into him."

Cleophile handed her the empty pail, and Josette was astounded to see angry tears on her daughter's face. "You are going to save him?" Cleophile's voice went up at the end of the sentence, like an accusation. She rushed past her and climbed the bank, stumbling in the crusted mud and snow. A gust of wind blew her hair straight out behind her. She screamed something over her shoulder that sounded like, "Why don't you just let him die?"

Josette's shawl flew off and she snatched it back. Why *didn't* she let him die? Give him more tea and it would all be over within minutes. She was stunned. Not because she hadn't thought of this, but that her own daughter had.

the law of love

AN HOUR BEFORE dawn broke in the east, Riel sat astride his buck-skin mare and sipped at a can of milk that had been taken from the Duck Lake stores. A fire burned in front of Hillyard Mitchell's estab-lishment. Both Gabriel's men and Indians from the area reserves milled about in the clearing. Lean Crow and his warriors were there, and the Crees from Muskeg Lake and One Arrow Reserve near Batoche. Little Ghost was painted up and bending over his gun to load it from a fresh box of cartridges. Various provisions were being examined and handed around—cans of beef and pork and other exotic items that only white settlers bought or traded.

Charles Nolin stood on Mitchell's porch, hands in his coat pockets, watching all of this with disapproval. When he noticed Riel, he made a mock bow, "Here is our King David." He gestured to a Métis, who had emerged with an armload of furs. "Your war booty, my liege."

Conscious of men looking their way, Riel lifted his hand in benedic-tion. "And the light shineth in the darkness; and the darkness compre-hended it not." He could not see Nolin's expression, but imagined he had turned red with humiliation. "Keep a list of all items taken," Riel added, giving him a job. "We are not thieves." Nolin turned and went into the store, and Riel let himself feel some brief satisfaction. Nolin had initially resisted the cause, but after he'd signed an oath to support the council, he was elected its commissioner by unanimous vote. His Exovedes trusted Nolin's history as leader in their community. Riel did not, yet even Judas had his role.

Riel made an attempt to count the men but soon gave up. He had sent Gabriel to Duck Lake with thirty Métis. Somehow that number had grown to over one hundred, and more were arriving. He had not slept all night, and a gnawing pain in his stomach had progressed to a burn that surged upward to his chest. He was unable to eat, yet hunger made it worse. It occurred to him that this was punishment from God for language he'd used in a letter sent to Superintendent Crozier, claiming the Métis were ready to wage a war of extermination if Fort Carlton was not handed over. *Extermination*. It was not a word he liked, but one that would get Macdonald's attention.

To offset this warning, Riel had insisted on diplomacy. The council was to be guided by God's commandments, and he had directed Nolin and Maxime Lépine to take the letter to Crozier, and in his presence, invoke the Law of Love.

Because I love my neighbour as myself, to prevent bloodshed and the war of extermination which threaten the country.

Riel pulled up his collar against the cold and silently prayed. Although he had made the threat, he was loath to carry it through. King David had sinned by waging war to subdue his enemies. David had gone to God for forgiveness with blood on his hands. But the sins of pride and lust for victory were punishable by death and the suffering of future generations. Only with sincere regret and fasting had David managed to repent. Riel would not make the same mistakes. He had laid his sins out before him.

Deliver me from bloodguiltiness, O God, thou God of my salvation.

At last night's council meeting, Gabriel had been outlining his plan to take Fort Carlton with the help of the English half-breeds, when Thomas McKay, an emissary from them, appeared at the door.

"Those of us in Prince Albert will not take up arms against the government," McKay had said in a voice so low and composed, it seemed a challenge. "We will remain neutral."

Neutral. The word had struck Riel's heart like an arrow and he rounded on McKay, accused the *Anglais* half-breeds of taking a bribe from Ottawa in the eleventh hour to keep them loyal. McKay had the temerity to laugh in his face, and Riel had lost all restraint.

"You don't know what we're after! It is blood, we want blood," he had shouted. "Yet a traitor has no blood." Riel picked up a spoon that was on the table and held it up. "There is not enough blood in your body to fill this spoon."

It was Gabriel who finally threw McKay out and requested permission to ride for Duck Lake with thirty men. "We'll take Mitchell's store," he said, "guard the trail if police come down from Carlton."

Riel had acquiesced, but only if Gabriel did nothing rash. Still shaking with rage, Riel had gone to his chapel with Honoré, praying for guidance. The Spirit of God spoke to him, promised that word would come from Macdonald with a message: *your claims will be settled, stand down.*

He decided that he would not stay in Jerusalem as David had, and in the early hours, he'd crossed the frozen Saskatchewan, bringing the prisoners with him from Batoche. The owner of Walter & Baker's store and his clerk huddled miserably in a cutter nearby. Honoré sat beside them, babbling to himself, delirious. Riel looked away. Those eyes reminded him too much of the men who had roamed the halls at Beauport Asylum, raving.

Gabriel had come out of the dark trees, riding his horse down through knee-deep snow. His quick eyes glinted in the firelight, took in the new men who had arrived. "Why is Honoré Jaxon in with the prisoners?"

Riel brought his horse closer, so the others would not hear and explained how he had been with Honoré in the chapel last night. Jaxon had slipped away while they were praying, and Riel had found his moccasins in the snow outside Boyer's. "I saddled my horse and followed, thinking I'd catch him, but he'd walked all the way to Josette's. Barefoot. Norbert and Josette woke to find him in their kitchen. Norbert did not take well to it." When Gabriel looked at him for the first time, Riel pressed on, told him that they had found her dousing her husband with water, and Honoré in a corner muttering that his mother was a Sioux princess. "His days in my council are finished."

Gabriel's brother Isidore was riding down from the Carlton Trail leading two white men astride horses, hands tied behind their backs. Riel pushed back his new Stetson hat to get a better look. One of the men was John Astley, a land surveyor who had attended a few of the Prince Albert meetings. Riel reached for the bridle of Gabriel's horse, and the can of milk slipped from his hand and fell in the snow. "What is this?" he asked, staring hard at Astley.

Gabriel's expression was watchful, eyes darting in every direction, as if he expected to see police at any moment on the trail. He turned in his saddle and said to Isidore, "Get them into Mitchell's store."

The first rays of sun had filtered over the western treeline and Gabriel noticed Norbert Lavoie on a horse across the clearing, looking almost as crazed as Honoré. Norbert stared back at him and his gaze slid away. Gabriel spat. "He should go in with the prisoners." He shot Riel a skeptical look. "If this was a buffalo hunt, I'd run him out of camp. Pray he will be killed this day and put Josette out of her misery."

Riel asked again about Astley, and Gabriel told him that he and Isidore had surprised the two men leading a small group of armed police sent by Crozier to protect the stores at Duck Lake.

Riel drew a long slow breath, *we want blood* ringing in his ears. "What happened to the police?"

Gabriel put his head back and raised his voice, "I told them to run back and tell Crozier he could fuck himself."

Men nearby had overheard this comment. They laughed, and Riel's stomach wrenched with a sudden pain. More Métis had arrived in rag tag groups while they talked, some on horses and others on snowshoes, carrying their guns. Riel's hands tightened on his mare's reins, and she stepped backwards, startled at the bit hard in her mouth.

Gabriel nudged his horse forward. "If Crozier comes, he will bring his thundering cannon," he shouted to the men. "It makes a big noise, but we will be down in the hollows where it can't touch us. Let him take the high ground, as *les Anglais* like to do. We will hem them in like rabbits."

Ignoring both the pain in his stomach and the threat of a fight, Riel rode up beside Gabriel. "If Crozier comes, I will parley with him," he said and noticed that the men seemed bewildered, even frightened when he spoke. He was confusing them, confusing himself. *I do not like war, Lord. Guide me.*

He was here, at an impending battle, without a gun because a prophet rode forth with the staff of God in his hands. He felt bereft of the wooden cross he'd been using to say the rosary. Charles Nolin had come out of the store and Riel got off his horse.

"Come," he said, "I need your help at the chapel."

Nolin looked unconvinced but followed without question. Riel led his horse as they passed Ambroise Wolfe, a head man from the Muskeg Lake Band, who was helping a blind elder from Okemasis' reserve open a tin of beef.

Nolin squared his chest and walked toward them. "It's time you were on your way back to your reserves."

The old Indian turned his sightless eyes to him, expressionless. "You are on our lands now, grandson. Maybe *you* should go." He and Wolfe laughed mirthlessly and packed their hide satchels with tea and sugar.

"That is not your property," Nolin continued, stubbornly.

"What is it to you?" Wolfe replied. He put on a pair of snowshoes and started off at a lope into the woods. The old Indian swung his satchel and turned to walk up the hard-packed trail.

Riel fought with himself. He had wanted to punish Nolin for spying, for spreading rumours of his insanity, but Christ had not renounced Judas. He had not quenched the small light in the flax that, by grace, might grow into a great flame. "Leave them," he said. "These men have more right to the stores than we do."

They arrived at the abandoned chapel and Nolin entered after him. Riel stepped over the communion rail to take the large wooden crucifix from the altar. He stared at it a moment, both in awe and sudden dismay at the bloody gash in the Christ figure's side, one of five holy wounds the Lord suffered during his Passion.

"This is sacrilege," Nolin cried in protest.

Napoléon Nault appeared at the door. "Crozier and his police are coming down the trail."

Riel turned, and the knot of his sash caught the altar cloth, knocking over the ciborium, the cup that held the wine.

Nolin gaped as it hit the floor. "You've defiled the altar."

Riel ran for the door. "Come," he yelled to Nolin. "It has begun." He mounted his horse, the crucifix held tight to his chest and failed to notice, as he rode away, that Nolin did not follow.

parley

LAWRENCE CLARKE CLIMBED out of the sleigh he'd been sharing with Police Superintendent Crozier. He took up his field glasses and trained it on a large fire that burned down near the Duck Lake stores. Shafts of early morning sun refracted through the tree branches on the other side of the clearing, and he could see the dim shapes of breeds and Indians scatter into the woods.

"We've interrupted them enjoying the spoils," he said to Crozier.

Clarke unbuttoned his fur coat and rested the glasses on the sleigh, studying the breeds closely so that he would know who to arrest if any escaped. They leaped through the snow like jackrabbits—testament to lives spent trapping and freighting in this country. But their faces looked too similar in the dawn light. There was no sign of Louis Riel, although Gabriel Dumont rose like an apparition on his roan mare not more than half a mile away.

Clarke lowered the glasses. Only days after he had delivered the threat to the Métis that police were coming to arrest Riel and Dumont, he'd left Fort Carlton. On the trail to Prince Albert, he had been startled by a noise behind him, and looking over his shoulder, saw a lone horseman in silhouette. None other than Dumont, who had sat motionless astride his horse until Clarke kicked his own into a gallop, like the devil was after him. It had put him on edge that Dumont had discovered in so short a time that he'd lied about the five hundred police. But not as much as it bothered him that a man who could shoot a buffalo from a galloping horse was now within firing distance.

He turned to look at Crozier's men and stepped off the narrow track, only to find himself up to his knees in snow. Scrambling back to the packed trail, he stamped his boots and convinced himself that the officers were finely turned out. But he did not like the way the Prince Albert volunteers, many of them young English or Scots immigrants from the east, had taken shelter behind their sleighs. They would be at a disadvantage in the deep drifts. The Métis would run at the first shell fired from the nine-pound cannon, mounted on its winter carriage. He was anxious to see it in action, and the look on Riel's face when he came in to surrender. Last night, with the letter from Riel in his hands, speaking of extermination, Clarke had worked to convince Crozier to ride south and put these rebels down.

"The Sioux who were at Custer's fight are with Riel," the Superintendent had offered as an excuse for not making his move. "I won't be pressured into decisions in isolation from my chain of command." His slow-witted eyes hardened into a suspicious glare. "These men have a legitimate claim for their lands. Do you not have reason of your own to fan the flames of revolt?"

Clarke was not surprised that an Irishman—his men secretly called him "Paddy"—would sympathize with the French, but he had been momentarily struck dumb that the dull, predictable creature had been poking his nose in his affairs. Surely, the police were not investigating his involvement in land speculation. To put him in his place, Clarke said, "Does a son wait for his father's permission to kill a rabid fox terrorizing the chickens?" It wasn't long before one of Crozier's men had arrived to say that Dumont and his breeds had looted the stores at Duck Lake and taken two volunteer scouts prisoner. When Crozier finally agreed that they must go, Clarke had insisted on tagging along, picturing himself hauling back the great Louis Riel in chains. But now he regretted his decision as he watched Crozier's second in command, Captain Morton, order the volunteers off the trail, many of them floundering in the snow.

"We'll put some daylight through these half-breed rebels," one yelled, brandishing his gun. "And send Louis Riel back where he came from."

Crozier had trained his own eyepiece on the Métis. "What's this?" he muttered. Clarke turned. About three hundred yards to the south, an old unarmed Indian meandered up the trail, as if on a pleasant walk in the woods. The man stopped and squinted at them, seemingly surprised to see such a large group in his way. Crozier lowered the glasses. "It looks as if they mean for us to parley with this Indian. I think it's a good idea—convince them to give up the provisions they've taken." He glanced at Clarke. "I'm glad you've come—you speak Cree like a native."

Clarke narrowed his eyes and made a mental note not to trust him in the future. Paddy was slow in appearance only. Clarke looked to the old Indian, who continued toward them in his shuffling, sure-footed gait. "It's a ploy—send an old man along to put our guard down." To his relief, Gentleman Joe McKay, one of Crozier's English half-breed scouts, said he would handle it. Clarke put a hand on his arm and said in a whisper, "Let *them* take the first shot." Macdonald had been adamant that it must seem obvious that the government was forced to react to Riel's actions, not manipulate them.

McKay went past them down the trail and Crozier followed him, adding, "Let's hurry things along. If we give Dumont too much time, he'll flank us."

Clarke's pulse began to race. Of course, Dumont would know this battle tactic after using it for years on the buffalo herds. At least Captain Morton had finally formed up the volunteers along the rail fence that skirted a short bluff. Clarke scanned the gully below the bluff and was astounded at the sight of half-breeds disappearing into an abandoned squatter's cabin. Others had crossed the clearing and hunkered down behind scrub brush and trees.

The sun was bright on the trail by the time Crozier and McKay approached the old Indian. Crozier stopped and McKay went on alone. The scout called out something in Cree. Clarke could hear the old Indian's response, "*Tesqua, tesqua.*" He knew from his years in the country that this meant "Hold on."

McKay said a few words to the Indian, who shook his head. McKay laid his rifle across the Indian's chest, but the old man stood his ground and the scout took a step back, his hand creeping toward the revolver hidden under his coat.

There was another exchange and McKay yelled back to Crozier. "He says we're on reserve land and should go back the way we came." He gave the Indian a shove with his rifle. The old man staggered to regain his balance, pushing the rifle off his chest. Crozier had already backed up the trail and gestured for McKay to follow, but the scout continued to exchange threats with the Indian. The two were grappling for possession of the rifle when a mounted half-breed burst onto the trail behind them, yelling, "Don't shoot," in Cree. Clarke recognized Isidore Dumont, Gabriel's brother, a rifle resting in the crook of his elbow.

Panicked at the half-breed's sudden appearance, McKay pulled out his revolver and shot Isidore full in the face. Clarke gasped as the Métis fell from his horse like a stone. McKay just as quickly turned to the old Indian and fired point blank.

Crozier sprinted back up the trail as fast as he could in his long boots. "Load the big gun!"

the red tide

SEEING HIS BROTHER cut down, Gabriel rode out from a copse of trees and gave an Indian war cry that sent the hairs up on his own neck. He spurred his horse and fired *le Petit*, not caring that guns were going off on both sides.

Isidore lay face down just off the trail, and Gabriel forced himself to look away from the widening sweep of blood in the snow. This was no time to weaken. He glanced over his shoulder to check the position of his men.

There was Riel, sitting on his mare, face upturned to the sky—one hand holding aloft a large wooden crucifix, other hand to his heart. "Fire in the name of God the Father," he shouted, "fire in the name of God the Son, fire in the name of the Holy Ghost."

Gabriel turned in his saddle in time to see Gentleman Joe McKay duck behind a tree, revolver still in his hand. Lawrence Clarke had torn off his fur coat and was running back up the trail ahead of Crozier. Gabriel sighted along the barrel of his gun and fired one round after another, the spent bullet casings flying so high, they skimmed the brim of his hat. The smoke hadn't cleared from his shots when the cannon on the trail went off, its first round just missing the cabin. Clarke had grabbed the reins of two horses and was dragging them along, using their bodies as a shield. Police were frantically reloading the cannon. It was fired again, but made an odd noise and bucked on its sleigh. The gunners had panicked, loading a shell before the powder charge.

Gabriel rode closer, but couldn't get a clear shot at McKay or Clarke. Turning his horse, he whistled and waved his arm for the Métis to come up. "Capture the gun," he yelled and threw the rifle to his shoulder again to pick off one of Crozier's volunteers, hiding behind a sleigh. The man went spinning backward, blood spraying the air. Gabriel's son Alexandre rode forward to throw him his own loaded gun. Without missing a beat, Gabriel targeted more volunteers that had jumped over the rail fence and were making a desperate charge, but they struggled through the snow and were cut down by Métis hiding in the cabin. As Alexandre reloaded *le Petit*, Gabriel quickly counted half a dozen enemy down, either dead or dying.

Rifle fire continued from the cabin, shots issued from windows and doors or between chinks in the walls. Baptiste Montour charged on his horse from around the back and poised with his gun to take a shot when a bullet slammed into his chest and he fell out of the saddle. Gabriel turned to see who had hit him. It was one of Crozier's police, who had braced himself behind a tree. Their eyes met for a moment before Gabriel whipped his horse forward and fired, bringing him down. Another policeman yelled a string of words in English, and the volunteers fell back in retreat. Gabriel urged his mare back onto the trail. The police had to get their horses hooked up to the sleighs, and he took his chance to search for Clarke and McKay, but neither could be seen.

To galvanize his men, Gabriel called out, "Look, I will make the red coats dance." He pulled the lever action of his rifle and was about to squeeze the trigger when a jolt to his head blew him off his horse. It plunged away and ran, leaving him in the snow.

"Gabriel's been hit," someone shouted from what seemed like far away.

With effort, he slowly lifted his hand and shuddered to feel a wet gash in his hair, blood pulsing against his fingers. The top of his head was ripped open, exposed to the cold. He closed his eyes and willed himself to get up. But he could not move.

Off to his left, a Métis yelled, "He's dead."

Gabriel opened his eyes and tried to speak, his tongue thick in his mouth.

"The police are getting away," said a voice he recognized—one of the Sioux. "Go after them."

Riel answered from the other direction, "*Non*, for the love of God— there's too much blood spilled already." He had come closer. "We have lost men, and Gabriel here . . . you will not take revenge."

A scream rose from the trees above the trail. *Isidore alive*, Gabriel thought in his delirium. With help from his younger brother Édouard and Riel, he propped himself up, and held a hand to his forehead to stop the stream of blood that ran down his face and into his eyes. Years ago, on a buffalo hunt, his horse had collided with an old bull he'd been riding alongside. Gabriel had broken ribs and wrenched his neck enough to see stars, but had managed to get back on his horse without help. This was different.

The scream came again. "Isidore," he whispered.

"It's the man that killed Montour," said Michel Dumas from somewhere out of his vision. "He's waiting to be finished off."

"Do it," Gabriel said from between clenched teeth. Within moments, he heard a single shot and the man's last cry echoed in the trees. He surveyed the field, his vision clouded by blood. Prince Albert men's bodies lay in attitudes of death or dying, great pools of red against the snow.

Riel stared down at Gabriel. "We must send a letter to Crozier," he said in a daze, "to come for his dead."

Gabriel wiped blood off his face and took note of the men who had fought and were still here with rifles in their hands—many that he had known would be courageous, and some he thought would run at the first shot. "Where is Nolin?" he asked with effort.

Theophile Caron said, "I saw him take a cutter heading north. I thought you sent him to Prince Albert."

"I saw him, too," said someone. "Whipping up the horse. If I'd known he was deserting, I would have smashed his head in."

When he tried to rise, Gabriel was shot through with a sudden, agonizing pain. "Go after him," he said. "Don't kill him—save it for me."

Édouard took off his ceinture fléchée and wrapped it around his head. Gabriel insisted that he be put on his own horse and taken to Isidore. With difficulty, they got his foot into the stirrup, and he shouted with pain as they hoisted him to the saddle. Michel Dumas took up the reins, leading his horse slowly forward. Riel and the remaining Métis fighters followed behind quietly as if they were in a funeral procession.

There was movement in the trees; one of the Prince Albert volunteers had been hit in the leg and was hauling himself toward the trail, using his gun as a crutch. Little Ghost and another one of Lean Crow's men set off at a run, plunging toward him through the drifts; a few Métis followed after them. The volunteer was halfway to the trail when he seemed to realize that he had been left behind. He reeled and almost fell, but when he spotted the Sioux warriors, he went to his knees and cried, "Don't let the black devils get my hair."

When Little Ghost lifted his gun to club him in the head, one of the Métis rushed to stop him. The Sioux war chief stared around at the half-breeds. "Why do you not finish him off? A man left alive after battle will return in revenge."

"He will go in with the other prisoners," Riel called to him.

In their hasty retreat, the police had left behind three sleighs and half a dozen good horses. Abandoned rifles were scattered about, and Métis claimed them as they came up the trail. Michel Dumas had found Clarke's lynx coat. He held it out to Riel. "Look at what *le bâtard* left us. He wore this when he said the police were coming to arrest you."

Gabriel's eyes had not left the familiar shape that lay motionless in the snow. With Alexandre's help, he got off his horse and approached what was left of his older brother. The world was devoid of sound. His own breathing echoed in his head as he drew closer. Any minute now, Isidore would get up and brush himself off, laugh. Or it wasn't Isidore at all. It couldn't be. How often had they been charged by angry bulls on the hunt? Or almost had a tree fall on them when cutting wood in the bush? Too many times to cheat death and find it now. He stood over his brother's body. Isidore was smaller than he remembered. The wide shoulders that could carry three hundred pounds on a portage, his feet now skewed, the ruined head. How would he tell Judith, his wife . . . their eleven children?

He wanted to fall to his knees, but too many eyes were on him. The old Indian who had found himself in the middle of the whole affair was not far down the trail, moaning from his gut wound. Pierre Gariépy knelt beside him, but it was obvious from his expression that the man was dying. Another body lay near—not a red-coated police—a Prince Albert volunteer. One who looked too much like Crozier's scout, Joe McKay. Gabriel swung himself forward, his eyes hazed with sweat and blood. This one he could turn over. The volunteer had been shot through the heart, probably dying before he hit the ground. Gabriel pulled out his knife and went down on one knee, grabbing the dead man's hair.

He had never taken a scalp, but had seen it done and heard the war songs of the Cree who told of those they had won in battle. Gabriel had just begun to slice into the delicate skin of the white man's forehead when he found himself staring into blue eyes gazing lifelessly into the void. He dropped him in the snow, staggered and fell.

Alexandre and Édouard carried him back to the horses. Frightened whispers, "Look at his head . . . Will he die? . . . *Non, merte*, it's his brother. Can't you see?"

Gabriel drifted into a fog and when he came to, found himself on the front steps of Mitchell's store. He lunged through the door and up the stairs. On the landing, two Métis stood guard with rifles in their hands, astonished to see him, confused and feverish, pushing his way into the room. Here were the prisoners, including Honoré Jaxon, who stood almost paralyzed with fear at the sight of him.

The sash that held the top of Gabriel's head together had soaked through. Blood flowed from his hairline along the side of his nose, dripping off his chin and down the front of his coat. He pointed at Crozier's two scouts—Astley and another one—that he'd taken prisoner earlier in the day. "Get them into the yard." He turned, expecting the guards to obey him immediately, but they stared at him, wide-eyed. "Get them out and shoot them!" If he could not kill McKay or Clarke, someone else would take their place.

Napoléon Nault put a hand on his arm. "Come, I'll take you to your wife."

Gabriel wrestled with one of the guards for his rifle. "I'll do it here," he said, but slumped sideways. Someone caught him before he hit the doorframe.

Before he lost consciousness, he heard Nault say to the prisoners, "God must be with you."

rababou

A WEEK AFTER THE battle at Duck Lake, Riel's council was meeting in Xavier Letendre's house, and Josette went with a few of the women to bring them food. Strict rules had come down from the Exovedate—rules for "Kitchen Service"—and what times of the day each meal should be served, because too many women had been coming in, curious to hear news of a British general who had arrived on a train from Ottawa and already marched north with a contingent of soldiers as far as the Touchwood Hills. Josette had not been on the list of "acceptable persons having special business with the council without seeking to impede their work," but earlier, at the cooking fire, she had inserted herself in the preparation of the food and the women had relented for Riel's Magdalene. They did not guess that she insisted on going only to see Honoré Jaxon, who was being held with other prisoners on the second floor.

When she stepped through the door of Letendre's house, the room went silent and every man turned to look at her except for Riel, at the head of the table, brooding over a handful of papers. She narrowed her eyes at Philippe Garnot, sitting beside him. The short French Canadian had his pen raised over a minute book, an expression of shame upon his weaselly face. Riel had said the Spirit of God claimed she still had a role to play in his mission, yet he'd chosen a white saloon owner over her, to replace Honoré as secretary of the council.

When Riel continued to ignore Josette's arrival, Maxime Lépine tentatively reached to take a bannock from her, his eyes downturned. She hesitated. Was it possible they'd just been speaking about her? *Non.* The women had simply interrupted talk of strategy.

Gabriel sat on a rocking chair by the stove. He placed his hands on his knees, as if to get up, but decided against it and regarded her with a conflicted expression she found puzzling. A cloth wrapped around his head had bled through to a patch of dark red over his wound, which the women had said was an angry gash that pulsed blood and refused to heal.

At dawn on the morning of the battle, Riel had come to Josette's house and taken both Honoré and Norbert. She had bundled the children in the cutter and gone up to Batoche, waiting all morning with the women by a fire near Fisher's Crossing for news of their men. And then a long, unbearable hour listening to the sound of distant shooting from the west. Riel eventually sent back an Indian from One Arrow's reserve wearing a fine lynx coat.

"Police crawled through the trees," he said in Cree, "afraid of the scalping knife."

After he told them that four Métis had been killed, the women surrounded him, asking him to name the dead. Cries and screams rose out of wives, children and extended relations of Augustin Laframboise, Isidore Dumont, Baptiste and Joseph Montour. He added that Gabriel had been wounded and Madeleine pulled at the Indian's saddle demanding to know how badly, but he shrugged and kicked his horse into a trot away from them.

By late afternoon, dark shapes began to show at the line of trees and bush on the west bank. As their men crossed the frozen river in silent groups, the women whispered among themselves. "It was our victory, *non?*" and strained their eyes, desperate to identify a certain horse, a specific slouch hat or coat that meant their husbands had returned without harm. When Gabriel finally appeared, tears sprang into Josette's eyes, but her relief was short-lived when she saw that he was tied to his horse.

She glanced at him now, seated by Letendre's stove, staring as if he could see inward to the fire itself. He lifted his eyes and held hers for a moment before looking away. With her knife, Josette cut slices of bannock and meat for the men, indignant that she was not sitting among them, privy to the council's secrets instead of in servitude to its needs. But Riel punished her with silence, shamed her for refusing to go north to her grandfather.

Some of the council members were discussing an enemy scout, who had been captured by Gabriel's men down at Clark's Crossing, as he mapped the path his general planned to take north to Batoche.

Moise Ouellette scraped his chair back and stood. "What will we do with him?"

"Send word to Macdonald," said Riel, his eyes still on the papers. "Title for our lands in return for his release."

Gabriel stared at his right hand, splaying his fingers and then flexing them into a fist. "Macdonald did not send this General Middleton to parley."

Riel shook his head. "The *Anglais* general cannot move an army until spring." He waited while the men muttered their concerns about the weather. The first of April had brought a thaw and melted most of the snow, but the river ice had not yet gone out. "His English half-breed scouts have already told him *l'eau surie* in the sloughs will give his horses the scours," Riel went on. "And he must wait another month for grass to come up on the prairie. By then, Poundmaker will have come to us."

Josette's hand slipped on the knife. She glanced at Riel. He had talked so much about her grandfather coming, she was taken aback to hear him speak of Chief Poundmaker instead.

"Poundmaker will come only if we have a decisive victory," said Gabriel, his voice suddenly loud in the room.

"We had one at Duck Lake," Riel insisted.

"Did we?" Gabriel winced, as though mention of the battle had caused him pain.

"We will defeat Middleton here," Riel said. "Who is this Philistine that he should defy the army of the living God? Let Goliath advance in his ignorance."

Gabriel listened with a deepening frown. "David went out to Goliath. And there are many good places for ambush in the Touchwood Hills." He sat forward in the chair. "Let me go down there with a few good men before more soldiers arrive to strengthen the general's camp."

A shadow seemed to pass over Riel's face, but before Josette could ask why her grandfather was now out of the picture, he finally looked directly at Gabriel. "The Lord delivered me from the paw of the lion, the paw of the bear. He will deliver us from the hand of this Philistine."

There was a profound silence in the room, the strain between Riel and his adjutant general, palpable. Josette folded some meat inside a slice of bannock, determined to take it to Riel and force him to acknowledge her presence.

One of the women stopped her. "*Non*," she whispered. "He only eats milk and broth since the battle."

Josette went to him anyway. "Let me take food to the prisoners," she said, gesturing at the stairs.

Riel had returned his attention to the sheaf of papers he held on his lap. What was the look on his face? A confusing mix of aloofness and regret. "Go up and give it to Fleury. He will take it in to them."

"I want to see Honoré." When he did not answer, she felt the sudden urge to push him off the chair. "He walked eight miles to see me. You saw it yourself."

"There was a motion made yesterday," Riel said, "that no person have permission to see the prisoners without an order from the council." He turned his head to address Garnot. "Was it not carried unanimously?" His secretary flipped through the minute book and found the entry. Without looking up, he nodded.

"Let her see him," Gabriel said angrily. "You owe her that much."

Riel's stare was fixed, as if he thought he hadn't heard right. "*Tell* her, why don't you," he said. "She will know soon enough—"

He was cut off by the sound of arriving horsemen. Whoops and yells came from the yard, then the voice of the Sioux war chief, Little Ghost. "We will shoot the white dog!"

Riel went outside with the men. When the women gathered at the door, Josette took two rounds of bannock from the table and went up the stairs. She would know soon enough about . . . *what?* On the second floor, Patrice Fleury stood with his gun outside a locked door in the hall, and she showed him the bannocks.

"For the prisoners," she said. "Riel says I am to give them."

Fleury unlocked the door. Four of the men were at one of the windows, anxious to see what was going on outside. The room was in disarray. She knew the owner and clerk from Walter & Baker's store across the river, and had heard that the other two white men were from Prince Albert, but she did not recognize a prisoner who leaned against the wall, his arms folded. He glanced up briefly to give her an insolent stare. *The army scout*, she thought, setting the bannocks on a table.

Honoré crouched in a corner, listening to what was happening in the yard. "*Rababou, rababou,*" he stuttered, as though he were proud to have remembered the French word the Métis used for a great noise.

She put a hand on his arm and glanced out the other window. The Sioux still galloped around the house, their rifles held high. Lean Crow slowed his horse, mud splashed all the way up to its flanks, and let Little Ghost take charge.

Riel grabbed at the reins of his horse, and lifted his hand, as if trying to calm him. "No," the young war chief shouted in reply to something Riel had said. He pulled back on the reins, and his horse reared. "If Big Bear can kill whites, we can kill whites."

A flurry of high-pitched yips and Sioux war cries ensued, and Josette leaned closer to the window. Had she just heard her grandfather's name in the company of the words "kill" and "whites?"

One of the men from Prince Albert said to the others, "I told Riel myself—told him he'd burn in hell for riling the Indians. He can't control these bloodthirsty dogs. They'll have us for dinner."

The clerk from Walter & Baker's had seen her and nudged him. "Quiet, Astley, here's Big Bear's granddaughter."

Astley turned. Now she remembered him from an encounter last summer in Batoche. He had been getting his horse shod and thought she was an Indian from One Arrow's band. He'd looked her up and down as she passed and made a few lewd remarks to the blacksmith as to her availability. When told who she was, he had immediately shut his mouth, but now his blue eyes sparked with both fear and a curious bravado.

"Are you here to deliver us to these hounds?"

The army scout had unfolded his arms. "You should run with your tail between your legs," he said, and when she looked around at him, confused, he laughed. "If General Middleton don't catch your grand-daddy, he might catch *you*."

She struggled to absorb what he was saying, but misunderstanding must have been writ large on her face, for Astley now regarded her in the way a cat plays with a cornered mouse. "She doesn't know Big Bear's been out murdering. Shooting white men—priests—in the back."

"Careful," said the owner of Walter & Baker's, "she's Riel's woman."

Astley inclined his head toward the window. "The irony is you fol-low that crazy bastard who riled him up. Sending his letters—inciting the Indians to do his dirty work."

She stood there, numb, as he told her of letters that Riel had rushed to the Métis in Fort Pitt and Battleford. Letters that recounted the vic-tory at Duck Lake and urged them to take the forts. Her grandfather's warriors had worked themselves into a frenzy and killed Thomas Quinn, the Indian agent at their reserve, who had withheld rations. Big Bear was unable to stop them from killing eight other white men.

Josette's eyes were fixed on a spot somewhere over Astley's shoulder. Her mind was spinning, trying to make sense of this unbelievable news. What had Riel said not one week ago, as he knelt in the chapel? "The council has agreed to send two emissaries to Big Bear—ready yourself to leave with them tomorrow morning for Frog Lake with a letter for your grandfather." *The council has agreed.* All minutes and correspon-dence were transcribed by the secretary and dictated by Riel. *He* had been the one to send the letter. Josette could not see Riel now and went to the other window. The prisoners parted to make way, as if she, too, were capable of violence.

Below in the yard, Little Ghost now gestured at the house with his rifle. "Give us the White Queen's man—we will knock his head in."

Riel was asking the women to bring out food, his face flushed with the effort of placating the Sioux war chief. "The White Queen's scout is valuable to the half-breeds," he said. "And will be used to trade with his people."

Little Ghost said, "It is not our way to take prisoners for bait," but he had already begun to pass the bannocks and meat among them.

Riel stepped back out of the mud, a relieved smile on his face. He glanced up at the prisoner's windows, as if to convince himself that his tools of barter were safe. When he saw her, his features settled into an expression of alarm. Their eyes met for a long, impossible moment, before Josette turned away.

the confessor

THREE DAYS LATER, Josette woke at dawn, quietly closing the back-room door to avoid waking Norbert and the children. After starting a fire in the stove and mixing bannock dough, she went out to milk the cow. A fine misted rain fell, melting the last remaining patches of snow in the pastures. The river ice had begun to break up and shift, its surface roiling with slush and great frozen sheets, the jagged edges pitched against each other in the current.

When she emerged from the barn fifteen minutes later, the sky had lightened, and the air was fragrant with wood smoke. She slowly walked toward the house to avoid spilling milk from the pail and, as she did each morning, looked south to Gabriel's. He had gone scouting, but smoke rose from their chimney. Josette glanced up at his back fields and stopped in her tracks at the sight of many tipis standing shock white in the pale morning air.

She recognized their standards: Chief White Cap's Dakota Sioux and Charles Trottier's Métis band from the south. The day after the incident with Little Ghost, Josette had gone to speak with Maxime Lépine. He admitted that some of the *Exovedes* were doubting Riel and spoke privately of their outrage at the changes he wished to make. Lépine had turned to pace in front of the fire, his dark eyes unsettled. "Riel was serious when he said, 'Rome has fallen.' He's taken us back to the old Mosaic laws."

"He goes too far," she said. "You should vote against it." Tall, gentle Maxime had moved heaven and earth to help Riel in Red River, and then to bring him here. He had expected a politician, not a prophet who meant to reform the Roman Catholic Church.

When she asked him about the letters, he admitted that upon returning to Batoche after the battle, the council had met, Riel dictated the letters, and scouts had left immediately to take them to the Métis communities near Fort Pitt and Battleford. He told her that Riel had beseeched them to "gather from every side, murmur, growl, and threaten. Stir up the Indians. Take Battleford – destroy it."

When she went to the door, Maxime added, "He sent others too, asking the Métis and Indians to take the forts and ammunition, but not to kill anyone."

Staring back at him, she said, "Would the whites give up arms and their forts without a fight?" She had gone away furious, more disturbed than before. Now White Cap's band was here, Dakota Sioux who had escaped the States twenty years past and had intermarried with Métis in Trottier's band. It did not surprise her that Trottier had come, a friend of Gabriel's from the hunts. But she suspected that Chief White Cap shared her grandfather's reluctance to fight the Métis battles, regardless of their relations.

Cleophile came out on the porch, looking tired and older than her years. When she saw the tipis, her face brightened. "Is it *Nicapan*'s band?" she asked, using the Cree word for both grandfather and grandchild.

News of the massacre at Frog Lake was spreading through Batoche, but Josette could not bring herself to tell Cleophile that her great-grandfather's warriors had killed whites—nine men, two of them priests.

She blamed herself for the whole affair. If she had delivered the letter, as Riel had wanted her to, this would not have happened. With the opportunity to read it beforehand, she would have thrown it into the fire. Other Métis had gone up instead and read the French letters to her illiterate grandfather. Wandering Spirit had finally set up a soldier's lodge and embarked on a murderous rampage. Word had come that Big Bear had prevented him from shooting two wives of the victims, but his war chief had taken the women prisoner. The English general had dispatched a field force from Fort Edmonton to hunt them like wolves. It was the end of Big Bear's dream to change the treaties. Because of Wandering Spirit and other braves in the band, her *Mosom* was now a fugitive.

Cleophile had been braiding her hair in one long plait, and Josette stepped behind her to finish it, quickly weaving the thick pieces, and tying the braid with a leather thong her daughter handed back. They stood silently, watching the camp. Two of White Cap's women were coming down the Dumonts' porch stairs and stared up at them for a moment before they started across the pasture.

Cleophile hugged her thin chest. "Why did you stop going up to St. Laurent?" she asked, shivering.

"Riel spoke to me only because he needed your grandfather." To admit it made her feel like a fool. Josette regarded her for a moment. "Have you had your first blood, *Nicânis*, my daughter?"

Cleophile's face clouded. "If I did, why would I tell you?" She turned and went into the house. Josette followed, hurt, and intent on reprimanding her, but could hear the children and Norbert stirring in the backroom. Wordlessly, she and Cleophile set about frying the bannocks. Josette had just cracked eggs into another pan when there was a soft bump at the door. Cleophile opened it to the Indian women, wrapped in blankets against the cold. Josette spoke quietly in Cree, inviting them to come in and sit, but they remained standing just inside the door.

Norbert came out from the bedroom, his face still flushed with sleep. "What's this?" he said, taking in the scene. "You will not give these dogs our flour."

The other children emerged behind him and Norbert turned to them. "Get out to the barn and clean the stalls. I want the horses rubbed down too," he said, his eyes hard on Cleophile. She went without a word, taking the younger ones with her.

"Riel has brought their men to fight his war," Josette said to her husband. "We can share what we have."

"If Riel wants the Indians close," Norbert said, "he can feed them."

"I can feed who?" said a familiar voice. Riel appeared in silhouette at the door wearing his grey Stetson.

Josette spooned the eggs out of the pan and slid them between two hot bannocks, pointedly ignoring Riel. As she gave the food to the women, he put his hand on her arm and she took a step back. They both looked up to find Norbert's eyes on them.

When the women had gone, Riel sat down at the kitchen table, too excited to realize that she was angry. "It is a good day," he exclaimed. "White Cap and Trottier have come to join us, and I have been to Madame Tourond's. The Spirit of God has spoken to me directly about her sons. I have seen them as seven glorious stars around me. To have them in our army will bring more men to our side."

Norbert, overwhelmed at the presence of Riel in his house, offered him tea, which he refused, saying that his stomach bothered him, and he had been fasting for days.

Riel regarded him carefully. "Whose company do you belong to?"

"Patrice Fleury."

"A good man."

As if he were a boy asking his father for his first rifle, Norbert pleaded to be sent scouting. Riel took off his hat and placed it on the table. When he said that there were already enough of their men on the trails, her husband tried to conceal his disappointment and went to the stove to scoop a cup of tea from the open kettle.

"What news of *les Anglais*?" he asked. "Do they sit like scared rabbits in the bush?"

"Scouts tell me that Macdonald's general is a fat old man," Riel said, looking at his hands. "I have been shown by the Spirit of God that he wishes to make me prisoner."

Norbert lowered his cup. "We will not let him close enough to take you."

"If I had more men like you, Norbert . . ." He paused and looked searchingly at Josette, who had taken up the broom and begun sweeping. "I have come to speak to your wife of a private matter."

Norbert drew a long breath. "*Bien sûr.*" His eyes rose to briefly meet hers and then he took his cup of tea outside. In a moment, she heard him near the barn, directing the children at their chores. She stood with her back to Riel, her throat burning. It was only for Gabriel that she kept her tongue, only for Gabriel that she let him stay.

Riel was silent for a long while before he spoke. "The priests deny us the sacraments, but I have heard some of the women are secretly going to them, saying their husbands will not follow me."

"I too have heard," she said, hands tense on the broom handle, "that you have declared all deserters will have their cattle shot."

He paused, either uncertain of her mood or how to form his next thoughts. "Gabriel is obsessed with scouting. Marguerite has a look of terror on her face when I speak to her of matters. It is only you who understands what I am trying to do here. I have prayed to God that I do not jeopardize the cause—or do anything rash—but my thoughts are like the wind and I cannot direct myself."

Josette swept at the floor with a vengeance. "Your letters drove my grandfather's warriors to violence."

He watched her for a moment then squeezed his eyes shut. "I asked them to take the fort, not kill people and capture prisoners," he said, in a voice weary with regret. "I cannot live without a confessor." When he turned in the chair to face her, elbows on his knees, she understood that he meant for her to fulfill the role. "I have sinned," he began, "by praying that the general be wounded and carried from the field."

Josette walked slowly to the table, the broom still in her hand. "You ask forgiveness because you prayed a bullet might find the man who comes to kill you?" Aware that he watched her, she would not give him the satisfaction of meeting his eyes. Yet some part of her was curious how it would feel to absolve the great Riel. Taking her hand off the broom, she placed it on his head and felt him soften.

"Say four Aves and four Paters and you will be forgiven this sin."

There was no sound except for a gust of wind rattling a loose plank on the porch. She stood motionless, realizing that it was the first time she had ever touched him. It startled her when an unexpected, pulsating wave of anguish came up through her fingertips. Breathless and a little shaken, she withdrew her hand.

Josette had thought him impassioned, fanatically religious but now was certain that his coming back to the North-West to suffer Macdonald's continual denial had harmed his health. Gabriel had not liked it when she agreed with Father Moulin: Riel was losing his mind. Yet how had it been possible for a man who had lost his reason to write that petition? It was brilliant. She had read it herself.

She left Riel earnestly repeating his rosary and went to the pail near the door. A memory came at her as she ladled water into an open kettle, something she had said the day Riel had arrived last summer. *Macdonald will punish us for his sins in Red River.* She had said it out of frustration at Madeleine's hero worship, but now it seemed like a forewarning. Her arm weakened, the kettle heavy in her hand as she lifted it to the stove. Would Macdonald have answered a petition written by any of them? *Non.* His refusal to honour it was an excuse to get rid of Riel once and for all. She stared into the kettle water, at the small flecks of bark and detritus that had come out of the river. Rebellion had been inevitable.

She glanced over her shoulder at Riel, who still muttered his rosary, his head downcast in contrition. He seemed weighted with anxiety, a profound loneliness. She thought of Spinoza's idea, that sorrow was a man's passage from a greater to a lesser perfection. And then of a Cree word, *kiskwesew*, which meant doesn't think straight.

Riel had concluded the last phrase of his rosary. Although she kept her back to him, she could tell that he had not finished sharing his fears.

"Red Pheasant and Little Pine have both died in the last month," he said. "Their bands have joined Poundmaker's."

"Have the young men put up a soldier's lodge?"

"They looted Fort Battleford, but have not the courage to go against the great Poundmaker."

A suspicion began to form in her mind. "How do you know this?"

Riel hesitated a moment before answering. "He wrote to me, asking to hear the progress of God's work."

"He cannot read or write," she said, "and he does not believe in your God—it was one of your own men."

"Poundmaker is camped at Cut Knife waiting for Big Bear. Police are coming from Swift Current to disperse them. Soldiers that Middleton has sent."

"But *Mosom* has run north from the police." She was both trying to contain her anger and determined to expose his mistaken logic. "My grandfather would not sign your petition, so you force his braves to murder. Now they are no longer useful, you bully White Cap and Poundmaker here."

"White Cap has come of his own accord."

"*Calisse*," she said and took up the broom again.

"Over one thousand are in Poundmaker's camp now," Riel said, ignoring her curse. "To have one like him . . . every other chief in the Territories would leave their reserves and join us. He will come only if we arrange for the Americans to capture Macdonald's railway."

Josette felt bumps rise on her arms. She thought of when Riel had argued with Honoré when writing the petition, claiming it was threat of the Americans that had scared Macdonald into listening to their demands in Red River. "You told Honoré you never trusted the Americans, that you'd never treat with them again."

"Yes," he admitted, "they are foul dogs . . . jackals. But the council has voted three times to send a letter to them. I have refused them until now."

She turned her back, continuing to sweep. "The council?"

"I want you to take it south with Michel Dumas," he said quickly.

She wanted to say that she would not be his errand girl but was too curious to hear what scheme he was working. "Why me?"

"You speak English, are smart—the perfect emissary." She swept close to the table, and Riel stood and began to pace. "You will deliver it to a friend in Helena. He operates a newspaper there."

Josette had decided that it was fascinating to watch him fight with himself. What was it like inside that beautiful mind of his? He knew that it was a mistake to involve the Americans, yet he had dictated a letter, had put it before council with these very same arguments. And he had refused their decision to send it, not once, not twice, but three times.

Riel turned in the middle of the kitchen and looked at her expectantly. "We are in a desperate situation—an *Anglais* general and troops so soon across the country." He tilted his face upward, eyes closed. "I humble myself to the ground before you, Lord. Open to me Yourself the route I need to send Josette to the United States."

"I won't go," she said, trying to make him see reason. "The Americans have massacred our people. You can't trust them."

Riel groaned in pain and clutched his stomach.

"Fasting does not help you," she said and brought him a little bannock soaked in milk. He sat down and reluctantly ate a little but when recovered, said nothing more about the letter, only that he must be at a council meeting in Batoche before noon. They went out on the porch. Norbert and the children were nowhere to be seen. Riel mounted his horse and took up the reins, looking down at her.

"I did not trust the Americans in Red River—it's true I refused them—I will not do so now." He eyed her with speculation. "A letter to them will bring Macdonald to my feet. He will call off Middleton, Poundmaker will join our cause. We will have the power again."

He had taken off his hat and held it in one hand, reins in the other. His hair, too long now for pomade, was messed and unwashed, his moccasins caked with mud. It was useless to argue with a man who had already made up his mind, brilliant and troubled as it might be. Unlike Red River fifteen years ago, the Dominion had control here, was on the verge of bringing the North-West into Confederation with a railway built almost to the western shores. The Americans would not take the risk. And Macdonald knew it.

Riel was now regarding her solemnly. "God has shown me that the United States are destined to inherit all the power and prosperity which Great Britain now possesses," he said. "God in His mercy will give us a pure French-Canadian-Métis colony, a New Italy, a new Bavaria, a New Poland in the North-West to the Rocky Mountains. This land will be open to all of the oppressed peoples of the world."

He swung his horse north. She watched him ride away, thinking that Gabriel would soon return from scouting, and she would go to him with news of Riel's latest obsession. And her worries that he had lost his mind. But Gabriel was on the council. Had he voted "Aye" when the vote came to send the letters? It was time to convince him that they must stop Riel.

city of god

~

THE NEXT MORNING, Josette poured cream into the churn in her kitchen. As she made butter, she looked out the front window, keeping her eye on the Dumont's house. Finally, Gabriel crossed his yard and disappeared into the saloon. She'd learned that he had returned from scouting when Pierre Garnot had passed by on his way from a council meeting in Batoche. Madeleine had come out too and went into the barn. A few minutes later, she drove out their horse and wagon, heading north on the trail. As soon as Madeleine was out of sight, Josette left the churn to Cleophile and hurried across the front pasture, a tin of brewed willow bark tea in her hands. She did not like going behind Madeleine's back to see Gabriel. But she wanted to avoid the look they'd been given at the New Year's dog race.

She paused in the doorway of the saloon where he had so often welcomed freighters on the trail in the days before Riel had come. Gabriel stood with his back to her, both hands on the pool table, a crude map spread out before him. It wasn't often she got a chance to observe him

unnoticed. He had on a checked flannel sh
were held up by an old leather belt and his f
under his knees were the pair of beaded gar
was off, a freshly tied cloth wound around

If the bullet had found him a fraction c
be here, intent on a map of the South B
haustion and pain. He pulled one of his hands on
fist against his leg. In a moment, his shoulders relaxed. Madeleine
that a stabbing pain often struck him without warning, sometimes
sending him to his knees. He sensed that he was not alone and turned,
as though expecting to see someone else, maybe even Riel. When he realized that it was her, some mysterious emotion passed over his face.

"*Kiya*," he exhaled in Cree, *You*. He shut his eyes briefly and when he
opened them again, looked directly at her.

She struggled to bring her thoughts together, then saw a bottle of
rum open on the bar behind him. It was a combination of alcohol and
pain talking. The torture of his wound—an injury that would have
killed a lesser man—had changed him, made him more vulnerable. She
should not feel roused by regard from the great Gabriel Dumont. But
she was sure that other women had been on the receiving end of his
penetrating looks and wondered how it would feel to be touched by the
best man in the South Branch with a horse and a gun.

Josette slipped behind the pool table across from him and lifted the
tea tin like an offering. "I have something for your head."

His eyes shifted to it, a dubious expression. "It makes me want to
sleep. I would rather feel this damn head and think straight."

"You *should* sleep."

He glanced at the map. "I have a man in Middleton's camp, Jérôme
Henry—he escaped to bring me their marching plan. The general spent
three days ferrying half his force across the river in an old scow. He's
ready to break camp tomorrow."

"How did they come north so quickly?"

"The Hudson's Bay Company made teamsters and wagons available—for a price of course."

He told her how Henry had heard soldiers bragging about their

a master of frontier warfare. In the British colonies, Middleton fought rebellious "natives" and knew how to "put them down."

Gabriel laughed bitterly. "If he knows bush fighting why carry a book
about Custer? Henry says the old man has a lamp going in his tent at
night, studying it. He doesn't want to make the same mistakes as the
long hair. Henry made sure to spread the story that Little Ghost is in
Batoche, son of Inkpaduta and brother of the warrior that killed
Custer." Gabriel cocked an eyebrow in her direction. "Now Middleton
will not go anywhere without a bodyguard."

She tried to focus on the map. In Batoche, news had come that Middleton's men had struggled north from Qu'Appelle over the frozen
sloughs, suffering with frostbite and dysentery. Many said that God was
working His miracles.

Gabriel rubbed his eyes. "Henry says there's a Lieutenant Hugh John
Macdonald there. Says he's Sir John's *only* son. A fucking officer in
charge of his own men." His face was dark with contained anger. "Riel
has heard there are *Canadiens* with Middleton. He does not want them
harmed." He met her eyes. "Scouts have brought news of your grandfather. Wandering Spirit leads the pillaging as they run north. They
took Fort Pitt. Burned it to the ground. The traders and families were
spared only because your grandfather warned them."

She could almost see Big Bear pleading with his war chief and remembered who was responsible. "Riel's God will punish him for sending letters to the Cree."

Gabriel frowned. "Macdonald will burn in hell for refusing them
rations. Why do you think Wandering Spirit shot the agent Quinn
first?" He suddenly bent over, hands on his knees. When the episode
passed, he said, "The men are deserting after the Duck Lake battle.
How can I make them stand with us without the need for threats?" In
his eyes was a mix of hopelessness and determination, as if in asking the
question he had already answered it. A good enough moment to tell
him.

"Riel has asked me to go to the Montana Territory with a letter—
Poundmaker won't come south unless he knows the Americans have
taken the railway."

Gabriel punched his open palm and winced at the resulting pain he'd caused in his head. "Riel, *nisakahpitik*—he has tied my hands. He will not let me take forty good men to attack Middleton's camp at night, but sends you across the line, through country thick with Dominion soldiers. You will remain here."

"Riel is *kiskwesew*."

Gabriel walked away from the pool table. She had said it as a simple statement of fact and waited for him to disagree, but he stopped and appeared to think. "We have petitioned for years and did not get results. Riel knew the words to make Ottawa listen, did he not?"

She saw that he wished to be reminded only of Riel's decisive actions in Red River. But she could not resist pressing him with the truth. "Macdonald has answered Riel," she said. "With guns and soldiers—an English general."

"You were too young to remember when the Queen sold Red River to Ottawa. Surveyors came and marked off the lands of your relations," he said, his voice now heavy with fatigue. "Riel stepped on their measuring chains and told them, 'you go no further.' Did your father have the courage?" He took a deep breath and let it out slowly. "Ask yourself why we should not follow that man today. He is the only Métis smart enough to take on Macdonald. We asked him here. It is our duty to support him."

Disturbing rumours had circulated: how Ottawa had sent salesmen to Europe, advertising 160 acres free to "real farmers" in the vast North-West, land already cleared and ready to till. They had received confirmation of those rumours last week when news came that Métis near Fort Edmonton had returned from hunting to find their farms taken by white settlers. Squatting rights they called it. A cabin on cleared land was now an invitation to steal. Gabriel did not care that Riel was *kiskwesew*. He admired his politics, his history, and through the force of his own will, would try to win this rebellion despite what Riel had brought to their doorstep.

"Take your men regardless of what he thinks. Attack this *Anglais* general."

Gabriel stared at the wall, logs that he had cut and squared with his brother years ago. "A group of Métis men—ones I didn't think were traitors—came to me in secret last week, said they don't like Riel. They want me to take over, run him out of the territory."

"Wandering Spirit set up his soldier's lodge in my grandfather's camp," she reminded him. "Fine Day will soon do the same in Pound-maker's—young warriors taking power from the great chiefs. You are Riel's war chief. Do the same and he must listen to *you*."

Gabriel leaned against the pool table, watching her. She wanted to look away, but couldn't. "God owes me two lives—one for the man who killed my brother and one for Clarke, whose rumour started this war."

"Go at night, like the ancestors," she urged him. "Count coup."

"Little Ghost and his warriors have been making medicine for a raid. It is all I can do to stop them going down there." His deep-set eyes were on her face, almost dazed, as though weathering his pain or re-membering the days he'd ridden against the Blackfoot, striking his enemy and escaping unharmed to tell the tale. Gabriel closed his eyes. "Fuck *les Canadiens*. If they fight with *les Anglais*, they deserve what comes to them. It's Middleton I want."

"God has told Riel we will be victorious at Batoche—the City of God." She paused. "Do not let them get that far. Run them like buffalo through the pounds."

"*Eh bien*." He looked up at her, his eyes blazing. "I will bring the goddamn City of God to Middleton."

river of blood

LATER THAT SAME EVENING, Madeleine Dumont stood in front of the stove, her eyes on a bannock that browned in the pan. Gabriel sat at the table with his rifle and cleaning supplies laid out before him, handling *le Petit* like a mother with a newborn *bibi*. He had just come back from Batoche, where he'd convinced Riel to allow an ambush of Middleton on the Humboldt Trail. She had sent Alexandre to the barn, for she wanted a word with Gabriel, who had taken the boy to the Duck Lake fight without her permission.

"Alex will remain here," she insisted. "He is only sixteen."

Gabriel looked up at her, distracted. "He will be out of the line of fire. I need someone to keep a gun loaded."

"Was he out of the fire when you got that?" She pointed at his head wound, her voice rising. She had given Gabriel a draught of one of Josette's medicine teas for his pain. The effects would wear off in a few hours, but her husband seemed almost giddy or reckless.

"Riel only agreed to the ambush," he said, "if he is allowed to stop every few miles to say the rosary."

She pulled the bannock out of the pan and flapped a towel to cool it for his saddlebags. "Don't go," she said. "I have seen a vision of your death."

"Some say we should run them like buffalo through the pounds." He pulled a box of bullets out of his coat pocket and threw them on the table. "Riel will be here in a few hours with two hundred men. Who do you think I listen to?"

"*Some say?* You mean Josette." He looked away and she closed her eyes, trying to keep her temper. Every time he came or went, Josette was up there on her porch with a blank stare, finger tracing the scar at her lip. Before Duck Lake, Madeleine had seen him stop at her house and had watched, knowing they spoke of Riel, but seething that they had to stand so close to do it. This blind jealousy was eating at her heart. It was ridiculous to envy Josette Lavoie, a woman beaten by her own husband. The premonition she'd had at berry-picking camp floated behind her eyelids, of Gabriel lying on the snow, red with his blood. "God showed me you would die in the snows."

His gun in one hand, he took up the cleaning rod and threaded a small patch through the slot. "The snows have melted," he said with a twitch at his mouth. "The river is breaking up, you saw yourself."

She was livid that he considered her visions a joke. "You forget that your own brother's blood was the first to be shed."

Her words hung in the air like knives. He paused with the rod down the inside of the gun's bore. The stillness of his eyes and a certain rigid quality in his posture made her regret mentioning Isidore's death. In the early years of their marriage, Gabriel had often said, "I love you, even if you like to break my balls." *Oui*, she was hard on him at times, for a man could not often see he was headed to disaster, even when it stared him in the face.

She turned away, pulled a handkerchief from her skirt pocket, and smothered a cough. It was getting more difficult to hide her worsening condition from him. For almost a year now she had made excuses: drafts, dust, a chill in the air. She did not want him to think her less than she already was—barren and now dying. He would have suspected something else by now if he were not preoccupied. Last week, she had thought him gone scouting and boiled water to wash her handkerchiefs, but he had come back for some reason or another. Her heart had been in her mouth the entire time he was in the house, praying he would not lift the lid of the pot and find them floating in a broth of blood.

He had brought out a tin of precious buffalo fat, saved from the last hunts, and she watched as he dabbed a bit of it on a cloth and greased the gun's mechanism. His calm intent angered her. Not even a moment of indecision showed on his face.

"Riel told you he did not want bloodshed," she said, "and in the next minute he wanted to exterminate the police." Gabriel lifted the lever to close the breech of his gun with a decisive click, his expression dark, as though he regretted telling her about the letter Riel had written to Crozier. "*Rome est tombée*," she said with a snort. "Rome is still alive and well in Batoche. I saw Louise Gravelle sneak to the rectory the other day and beg for the sacraments. I hear she told Moulin her husband only follows Riel because he does not want his cattle shot."

Gabriel carefully placed his gun on the table and took cartridges from the box. He would not look at her. "Jérôme Henry tells me Middleton flew into a rage," he said, pressing fourteen bullets, one after the other into the magazine, "to discover so many of his men have never fired a gun. He forces them into daily rifle practice, shouting, 'You're going against an enemy of crack shots.'"

The mocking bitterness in his voice and his insistence on changing the subject infuriated her. "They have more courage than the men who desert you each day—"

"—Not one of my old *capitaines* has deserted."

"There is an army of Métis through the Territories, in Red River. These men will cry at Riel's funeral, say they are patriots, that it was their war too, yet they do not come to help you now." Madeleine had seen the posted council motion outside of Letendre's: that they had declared, "Louis David Riel a prophet in the service of Jesus Christ and the Son of God and only Redeemer of the world." It had pained her to see Gabriel's mark under those voting in favour. She heard that Albert Monkman, a member of the council, had refused to vote and when Riel asked him to relent, Monkman declared that if he was forced to speak on it again, he would have to desert. "At least Monkman was strong enough to go against this madness."

"He has since examined his conscience," Gabriel said without looking up. "Yesterday he signed a sworn oath in front of the Exovedate— that he had a false idea."

"A false idea! He was afraid of his own neck. Did Riel tell you on the long trip up from the Montana Territory that he was a prophet at the feet of Mary Immaculate?" Gabriel would not respond and pulled the lever upward to cycle a cartridge into the chamber, setting the hammer in the half-cock position. Madeleine felt desperate enough to add, "I would like to know if he confided it to his own Mary Magdalene."

Gabriel's back stiffened, but he still refused to glance her way. She could see that he was in one of his rare, quiet rages.

"You will not speak against Riel in Batoche," he said, an uncharacteristic warning in his voice.

"Why would I speak against him when Father Moulin said it best at the novena." She looked to the ceiling in mock drama. "What was it? Riel is misguided, delusional, even insane." Gabriel lifted his gun and sighted down the barrel, and she, furious at his silence, continued. "I could not fail to notice when Riel said our church had fallen, that Josette was relieved to hear it." Gabriel set his gun carefully on the table and emptied the box of cartridges, counting the remaining bullets before they went into his pockets. "Josette will be to blame for our destruction," she said, "if she did not tell everyone, months ago, that Riel had other reasons for being here."

"*Other* reasons?" He stood slowly, his face turned ashen with pain. He reached for his saddlebags, and said through his teeth, "Can you not see what he means to do?"

"I am the *only* one to see." She clumsily wrapped the bannock in a towel and tossed it on the table in front of him. "If Macdonald has not honoured our claim to this land, he never will. And you stand behind Riel, a madman who is locked in a fight to the death with him. Dead and landless. That is your dream?"

Gabriel took up the wrapped bannock and looked at it for a moment before stowing it in the saddlebag, and she could tell by the set of his shoulders that he did not agree with her. Or he did, and was too stubborn to admit it.

"There is no other way than to finish the job," he said. "I need you to trust me."

She was silent, feeling her face flushed, her breathing shallow. Always she had trusted him, but she wavered now before a man she no longer knew, a man who followed Louis Riel.

tourond's coulee

GABRIEL LOOKED SIDEWAYS in the dark. Riel was about to do it again. The Métis leader lifted the wooden cross he had kept from the Duck Lake chapel and called a halt. Behind them, two hundred men paused in the deep shadow of a stand of cottonwoods, their horses snorting in the cold night air.

Riel began to say the Lord's prayer. "Our Father Who Art in Heaven . . ."

He had insisted they beseech God in the most dangerous spots, including the bald prairie, where they could have been picked off easily if Middleton's scouts had dared come that far north. Gabriel would rather pray as they had on the winter buffalo hunts. Riding with the men to find the herds, he would close his eyes and ask the Great Bull,

Lead your cows out of the woods and onto the shifting snow of the great plains.

Gabriel studied the sky, stars hidden behind a haze of cloud. It was midnight or close to it. He was impatient to ride if they were to find Middleton's camp before dawn. It was nearing the end of April yet sudden gusts of icy wind went through the old buffalo robe coat that Madeleine had made for him years ago. There were patches of underlying hide showing through at the sleeves and collar, but he would not part with it. The effects of Josette's medicine tea had worn off, and now he keenly felt the wound at the top of his head. Madeleine had packed it with a poultice, but the simple act of getting on his horse had made it pulse and throb.

Madeleine's anger at Riel had only served to bolster his resolve. If they were to lose their lands, regardless, he would rather go down fighting. He surveyed the Métis and Indians who had come down to ambush *les Anglais*. Farmers, blacksmiths, freighters, trappers—men he'd known for decades, their eyes glinting in the dark like spooked horses. Lean Crow's and White Cap's men had some Springfield single-shot carbines, but a few of the Métis were armed only with potato tillers. Young Modeste Ladouceur carried one of Riel's religious flags. Most, like Gabriel's nephew, St. Pierre, had old muzzleloaders, the powder horns slung across their chests, as they had worn them in the buffalo hunts.

Gabriel's friend and ally Charles Trottier was there, his broad-shouldered form in the saddle distinct from that of Maxime Lépine's, who sat hunched and miserable upon his horse. Earlier, Riel had removed the Christ figure from the Duck Lake chapel crucifix and given it to Maxime in a ceremony meant to show the men that he would not suffer the same fate as the Lord. Gabriel could see the Christ in Maxime's hands, its alabaster arms outstretched and gleaming.

In preparation for battle, the Sioux had painted their faces and freshly braided their hair. They held their horses' reins tight, impatient to ride. One of them, a man named Scarlet Bear, sidestepped his pony toward Gabriel's.

"I will be the first to touch the white chief with this." He held up his coup stick and shook it until the beads rattled.

Gabriel met his eyes. If they did not find Middleton's camp soon, the Sioux would leave. They did not take unnecessary risk in battle and preferred night raids to lining up in pretty rows before an enemy in the light of day.

Not to be outdone, another Sioux with the name of Black Bull said,

"I will eat the white chief's heart. He will go to the Great Spirit without courage."

Riel faltered in his prayer and held the bare wooden cross higher, its metal embellishments shining dully in the dim light of the grove. "And lead us not into temptation," he said with a raised voice. "But deliver us from evil."

Gabriel did not look forward to keeping Riel—a man who said he would fight Middleton only in the City of God—safe in a night skirmish. It was not the *Anglais* bullets he worried about, but those from his own men. He didn't put it past a few of them—who had sought him out last week with talk of mutiny—to "accidentally" take out Riel during the fight. Gabriel watched them now, their heads turning, flinty looks passed in silent dialogue.

He drove his horse forward and into the shoulder of Little Ghost's pinto pony—so close he could smell the charcoal the boy had used in his face paint. "Send two of your fastest riders," he said under his breath. "Find the white chief's camp."

Little Ghost turned and spoke to his men. In a moment, a few of them broke off in a gallop to the south.

As Riel finished his prayer, a rider approached through the trees behind them. It was Emmanuel Champagne, who had ridden hard from Batoche. In a rush, he told Gabriel that one of the scouts on the trail to Prince Albert had seen police coming south. Gabriel and Riel trotted a short way off, and after a hurried discussion, Riel reluctantly agreed to return to Batoche with fifty men to supplement those they had left behind to protect the women and children.

Gabriel hand-picked men to return who he knew did not want to fight and arranged for his younger brother to lead the group back. Then he edged his horse away, eager to be off. He did not want to seem too grateful to have Riel go, but it would be a relief to finally operate the ambush *his* way.

"I will pray for you in Batoche," Riel said, "as Sitting Bull made medicine for his warriors at the Little Bighorn." Gabriel nodded but before Riel went to join the return party, he added, "You will not harm *les Canadiens*."

It was more of a warning than a statement, Gabriel thought as he wheeled his horse.

"Have faith," Riel called after him, "that God will deliver the Philistines to your hands. You will return in victory."

But Gabriel had already given his horse free rein, and it broke into a gallop to clear the trees.

"Now we will make progress," he said to the men who followed.

⚊⚊

At five in the morning, they skirted a slough in the Touronds' back pasture. Rain water had pooled in the field rows. The army of silent riders spread out across the plain, the horses' hooves thick in the wet ground and their underbellies spattered black with mud. A lamp burned in the window of the farmhouse. As they passed, seven men rode out to join them. Riel had made much of recruiting the Tourond boys, for their late father—dead these past two years—had been with him in Red River when he had stepped on the surveyor's chains. Gabriel could see that the brothers' arrival emboldened the men. For the second time that night, he gave thanks that Riel was not present; he would most likely stop their march again and say a prayer to the Spirit of God.

The dawn sky had lightened as Gabriel, Michel Dumas, and Jérôme Henry left the main group and skirted the northern edge of a nearby coulee. A prairie chicken flew up before them from the newly sprouted grass in a burst of wings and frantic calls.

Michel Dumas studied the terrain. "*Les Anglais* are on the trail by now."

Gabriel nodded. "*Oui*, but how far?" When Little Ghost's men had not returned, Gabriel presumed they'd deserted, so he'd sent Patrice Bréland down there with a good horse. But he worried that Middleton had heard of their plans for ambush and captured the scouts he had sent to find the camp. There was another possibility. The Sioux had found Middleton's column, and the sheer size of it had brought back memories of being hunted and driven from their lands for daring to raise arms against the whites. He looked back at Lean Crow and Little Ghost, who were circling their horses with the rest of the Sioux, singing war songs. At least they had remained. For how long? Revenge was one thing, but this was not their fight.

A faint crescent of Frog Moon hung low on the horizon. The Humboldt Trail twisted down the south side of the coulee between leafless trees and thickets and disappeared behind six-foot-high banks of scrub willow and small poplar. Gabriel could almost hear Fish Creek running in the dark, covered by a small bridge the Métis called Tourond's Crossing. The trail then reappeared, climbing a gradual slope to where they stood. Gabriel directed his horse into the wind that brought a powerful musk scent of wet ground and rotting leaves from last year's fall.

Word came that a rider approached and Bréland rode in, his horse in a lather. "Middleton's column is on the trail."

"How far?"

"Two miles."

Gabriel turned to spit, and to hide his frustration. He spurred his horse down the north bank and through the creek. Tourond's Crossing. It would happen here then. No better place for an ambush than a great depression in the earth, the southwest and southeast faces pitched wide. Middleton's column would march down the trail, and the Métis would lie in wait among the bushes and the trees and a low bluff on the east face. The north lip of the coulee opened to prairie where the Tourond farmhouse and stables were placed to provide cover or retreat.

Run them like buffalo through the pounds.

Jérôme Henry gestured at the coulee with his chin. "The ground is good, *non*? Half of Middleton's army across the river and his 'crack shots' over here."

The ground was not just *good*, it was perfect. The coulee was a natural buffalo pound—one way to come in, one way to get out. Long ago, before the arrival of horse and gun, the Indians drove herds toward a cliff or butte, where the jump would kill the buffalo or they could easily be shot with bow, arrow and spear. But sometimes you found a herd on land that offered a narrow passageway through trees or rock, a pound to trap as many animals as possible with the least effort. You could steer them to that natural chute and assemble them for the kill.

The sun was not yet visible, but the sky above the eastern horizon was streaked with clouds the colour of fire. Gabriel rose in his stirrups, calling to the Métis. Within minutes, they had left their horses tied to the small poplars in the north edge of the coulee and began to dig rifle pits in the bush along the creek, using their knives to burrow holes beside trees and then hacking at branches to form a shooting screen.

As they worked, Gabriel rode up the south bank and yelled down. "The soldiers will descend toward us on the trail. Do not fire until they have gone past you."

Daniel Charette stood in the creek, where he'd rolled a few boulders to create a barricade. "We will squeeze down here then," he said with a laugh. "Like pigs in a ditch."

"*Oui*," Gabriel cried. "The strongest at the bottom."

Sioux warriors thought it beneath them to hide in holes and had positioned themselves above the low bluff. The Métis found perfect spots to rest the barrels of their rifles. Nobody spoke. The only sound was the swollen gurgle of the creek and the odd wakening bird. Gabriel and his twenty *capitaines* rode out through the trees that skirted the trail. Without warning, Alexandre appeared beside him. The boy had sneaked away despite Madeleine's worry, but it was too late to send him back. The men took off their coats, as they would before riding out on a buffalo hunt, and draped them over their saddles, the horses blowing and pulling at their bits for enough rein to crop grass.

Gabriel turned his mare, intending to make for the top of the ridge when his quick eye caught the movement of brush four hundred yards to the west. A lone rider came along the creek, the green and red and yellow stripes of his Hudson's Bay capote visible through the trees. Gabriel regarded him with bile rising in his throat. An *Anglais* half-breed working for the enemy. The scout held his reins in one hand, rifle cocked in the other. The sky rapidly darkened as great clouds banked over their position. Gabriel had devised a code of bird calls to direct the men, and he gave one short whistle, the signal not to fire.

But behind them, another *Anglais* scout emerged from down the creek, and an Indian on the bluff could not resist a shot at him. The first scout wheeled and galloped, not seeing Gabriel and his men until too late. Several of them fired to take him down as quickly as possible.

Clearly hit, he fell forward over the saddle horn, but kept his horse on a run, bursting past them up the bank and over the south lip of the coulee. Gabriel and his men thundered after him, riding through the criss-crossed tracing of smoke from their rifles.

Gabriel reined in his horse and stuck his head over the edge of the coulee. A confused first line of Middleton's column had drawn up two hundred yards along the trail. The scout who had been shot rode toward them and his horse stopped so suddenly, the man fell out of his saddle in front of one of Middleton's officers, who looked up with outrage. Within seconds, Gabriel had registered the might of the *Anglais* army, winding back for over a mile. And across the river, the other half of Middleton's field force, already called to a halt.

"*Ah-hai*," he shouted and jerked his reins, sending his horse careening down the bank. His cry was taken up by the Indians and Métis. Blankets and coats flew out of the rifle pits. He had forgotten his head wound and now ran on pure instinct. He glanced back. Mounted soldiers had advanced to the edge of the coulee and looked down on them. A horn sounded and the soldiers lifted their rifles, but they did not bring the stocks tight against their shoulders and the guns bucked as they fired, throwing them off balance in their saddles. Gabriel rode like a fury, yelling at his men to get down.

Jean Caron junior's black mare had been shot out from under him. After a panicked struggle, Caron freed himself from beneath the horse's motionless body and rushed headlong down the hill. A young Sioux warrior foolishly got up in full view on the bluff and danced, singing his war songs. His brothers added their yips and cries, but soon pleaded with him to take cover. As he jumped down, he was shot in the back by a soldier on the ridge and fell with blood pouring from his mouth. Charles Trottier ran out to grab the Indian's gun, horn, and shot bag and sprinted back to cover.

Gabriel looked around for Alexandre, and signalling him to keep close, headed toward the creek rifle pits. They dismounted, whipped their horses away, and ran, bent double, along the creek bed. Another horn went off up on the plain. The mounted men had withdrawn and foot soldiers rushed forward. They stood, some in red uniforms, some in dark green, like a herd of deer, silhouetted against the dawn sky.

"Hit them in the bunch," Gabriel yelled in Cree. A deafening volley was let off from the bush around the creek. Several soldiers fell on the ridge, and the trumpet sounded again. More ran forward to replace those who had been shot, then cowered when faced with immediate fire. One soldier had been hit and pitched head first into the coulee. Gabriel lifted his rifle and waited for the horn to go off again. But the soldiers were no longer presenting themselves as targets, and he whistled twice, a signal for his men to conserve their ammunition and only shoot at a sure mark.

Baptiste Sansregret pulled both him and Alexandre into a rifle pit, just as a small group of soldiers were sent over the east side of the ravine under the cover of relentless sniper fire. The soldiers ran from tree to tree, the first few making it to the scrub thickets near the creek. The Métis who were in those rifle pits abandoned them in a hurry, running low in the creek bed and attracting fire from the ridge. Isidore Dumas jumped into Gabriel's pit and knelt in the mud, four bullets arrayed in his mouth, loading and shooting as soldiers ran between the trees, a few spinning backward when bullets hit their mark. Isidore told him that Jérôme Henry had already been wounded up on the bluff, taking a shot in the back of his shoulder.

After the echo of the last barrage faded away, Gabriel would have liked to raise his head and see how many soldiers had made it down, but did not want what was left of his head blown off.

A voice yelled from somewhere in the thickets, "Is there lots of people?" Gabriel recognized it as Tom Hourie, another *Anglais* half-breed, who he had heard was Middleton's Cree interpreter. "Don't shoot," Hourie said. "I will come to you." Quiet again. "Why do you not answer?"

The men in Gabriel's pit smirked at each other. "Hourie, *bâtard*," they muttered under their breaths. A few aimed at the bushes, waiting for his face to appear. Gabriel thought of Bloody Knife, one of Custer's Sioux scouts, and the first to die at the Little Bighorn. Hourie had balls coming down. If he was caught in the open, it would not go well for him.

More soldiers appeared on the east ridge, and a small group of Sioux warriors, forced to seek cover in the next pit, fired with precision, reloading with enviable speed. Gabriel levelled *le Petit* on his shoulder and joined them. After each shot, he threw himself down to earth, avoiding the savage fire in his direction, and when that fire had cooled, he ventured up again. His gun was soon empty, and he threw it to Alexandre, who handed him a freshly loaded repeater.

It began to rain. Gabriel's head wound had opened up—he could feel the blood seeping through his bandage. "Cover your guns with blankets," he called, cursing the old muzzleloaders. Now only those who owned single shot or repeater rifles could fire. He squinted through the downpour, shivering now and regretting the loss of his buffalo coat in the charge up the coulee.

From above came a sudden barrage of bullets fired with such intensity, the men around him dove into creek mud to escape the fusillade. A tree near him had its bark stripped in seconds, bullets ricocheting off the trunk. An officer on a white horse surged over the lip of the ravine and drove down the embankment, a look of terror on his face. He was closely followed by twenty soldiers yelling a foreign battle cry. Gabriel raised his rifle to shoot him out of the saddle, but the officer dismounted in a hurry and Gabriel missed, hitting the man behind him.

The army's big cannon had been rolled to the southern lip of the coulee and was fired. But its aim was too high, and the shell hit the trees behind Gabriel's pit. He emptied his rifle at those loading and reloading the cannon, aware that Métis to his left and right were crawling out of the pits. The soldiers tried to lower the barrel of the cannon. One grew frustrated and exposed himself in the task and a Métis sniper took him out. The next man was not so eager to replace him and the cannon was wheeled back.

Gabriel went hoarse from whistling. He looked around to find too many of his men running up the north end of the coulee. Some could be seen disappearing inside the Tourond farmhouse. How could he hope to win the battle with less than half his force in the creek, and maybe a dozen sniping in the bluffs? He cursed again, wishing that he had the extra men that had gone back with Riel. If Middleton hadn't sent half his army across the river, he might launch a full-blown assault and discover there weren't many Métis down here. Jérôme Henry had said the old man had taken three days to ferry his soldiers to the other side. He'd need at least the same amount of time to haul them back. Until then, it was five hundred to fifty.

Hourie again shouted from somewhere in the bushes. "Your relations are running away—you should surrender." The soldiers and their officer were still hidden in the coulee. From within the bush, Gabriel sighted a few running through the trees, but could not get a clear shot. Where were the rest? He cursed when he realized that Hourie and the soldiers had dropped into the same east rifle pits his men had just abandoned.

He sent Basile Primeau to find a horse and ride to Batoche for reinforcements. "Send back any of our men that have run away," he told him. Primeau left as another shell burst near them, shattering a boulder to dust and chunks of flying rock. A gunshot echoing too close to his head sent Gabriel diving for cover in a tangle of willow bush. Dozens of Métis rifles went off, and as he twisted sideways, he saw three soldiers fall.

An officer yelled, "Goddamnit move," to one of his soldiers, who could be heard whimpering like a child. A Métis down the creek fired at the officer, and missed. Little Ghost charged out from the bluff yelling something in Sioux that the wind carried away. He ran from tree to tree, his rifle held close to his chest. Gabriel fumbled in his pocket for bullets and pressed a few into his gun's magazine, looking up in time to spot the officer rise out of a rifle pit and aim a pistol directly at him. Little Ghost came up behind him and the man shouted, "My God, my God," as both he and the Sioux fell back out of sight. A strangled cry and then nothing.

He heard one of the Métis yell, "Good, good, back down to earth, back down to earth."

True what Jérôme had said: Middleton's men were cowards, although Gabriel thought some were better shots than he'd been told. Judging their rifle pit too exposed, he and Alexandre retreated deeper into the bush. They listened as some of the soldiers spoke French in a strange accent.

"These dogs, can't we kill any of them?" one said from somewhere in the trees. Another replied, "We should rush them with our bayonets—" At that instant his voice was cut off, and a war whoop issued from Little Ghost.

There was a barked order from one of the officers that Gabriel did not understand, and a Métis yelled, "They're going to run." Soldiers bolted in a panic up the east slope of the ravine, flushed out like rabbits. A flurry of Métis rifle shots found them as they scrabbled and clutched at any rock or tree that would get them back sooner. One of them, wearing a red uniform, was carrying a buffalo coat that Gabriel recognized as his own. He sighted carefully and shot the man, whose body fell backward, letting go of the coat.

"Do not tell Riel we are harming his *Canadiens*," he said to Alexandre.

After the last soldier had disappeared, the Métis cheered and someone began to sing Pierre Falcon's song from Red River.

"They could not move those horseless cavaliers
You should have seen those Englishmen—
Bois-Brûlé chasing them, chasing them!"

A few war cries followed from the Sioux and then an ominous quiet. Ignace Poitras and a dozen other Métis who had deserted, straggled back down through the trees at the north side of the coulee. When they were close, Ignace yelled over to him. "We thought the ambush was *rien*, nothing, and that we should go back to Batoche."

Gabriel refused to look at him. The sky had blackened and rain turned to sleet. He powered backward through the willow scrags and found himself alone in a small clearing near the creek. He propped his gun against his knee, thought of removing his slouch hat. It protected his wound, but was now sodden and heavy.

His eyes focused on a large white skull that was embedded in the creek bank, not ten yards away. Years ago, a buffalo had come here to die. A bullet, either Middleton's or Métis, had pierced the skull's planed forehead. Gabriel looked away. To find such a thing seemed a bad omen. After a moment, it occurred to him that someone could use the bullet, and he crawled over on his elbows. He tried to work it free from the bone, but it was in too deep, and he gave up, his head pounding from the effort. From this angle, he could see up through the trees to the north coulee, and a multi-coloured image came to his addled brain—black, white, grey, piebald. He sat up quickly. His heart almost stopped when it came to him that he was looking at the dead and bloodied bodies of their horses.

He prayed that his own horse had not run up to find the others and been killed. She was a good mare that had been with him for years. If Middleton sent soldiers down in numbers, how would they escape? The sleet ended as quickly as it began and a thick fog rolled into the coulee, tracking the ground like a snake. He struggled to get himself together, but when he closed his eyes, Josette swam into his inner vision, how she had looked coming into the saloon yesterday, a shawl pulled around her thin shoulders, and carrying the medicine tea.

Count coup, like the ancestors.

It seemed like a lifetime ago. And Madeleine—jealous for no reason. His wife with her hoarse voice, always coughing, yelling at him to stay home. He shut his eyes tighter.

She is ill—ill with the lung disease. How did you not notice?

Another cannon had been drawn to the edge of the bluff, and Madame Tourond's house was hit up on the plain behind them. Her rooster crowed once then fell silent. The Métis who'd taken refuge there ran out, some crawling away on all fours through the back field. Gabriel sprang up and found a cow trail, not caring if he was exposed. He went down on one knee and drew a bead on the gunner, dispatching him with a single shot, leaving the horses rearing in terror in the gun carriage harnesses.

"I will not be like you, *Anglais*," he whispered as another gunner come up from the ranks to replace the one he had hit, "and kill a good horse when I can kill a man."

James Short had come up the creek bed and thrown himself behind a large boulder. Taking off his hat, he placed it on top of the rock and pressed himself to the ground behind a screen of bush. As shots rained down on his hat, Short took aim at the cannon operators as coolly if he were sighting buffalo. Pierre Laverdure joined him and managed to nail one of them, blowing the top of his head off. Gabriel took heart when one after another of the soldiers were hit—he counted at least a dozen down.

"Don't expose yourselves too much," he shouted to Short and Laverdure, but they took no heed and kept firing.

An officer in a grand uniform had appeared on the bluff, riding his horse back and forth, his arm raised and shouting commands. With the realization that this was General Middleton himself, Gabriel took careful aim, but was too far away and missed. But it gave him pleasure to see the old general look upset to find so many of his men wounded or dead. Gabriel began to think of retreating toward Tourond's house, when there was a sudden crack of a sniper's rifle. He turned to see his nephew St. Pierre Parenteau fall straight back, blood pouring from a hole just under his eye. His arms had caught in the willow bushes and he was held fast, suspended like a bird in flight. Men in the pits made themselves smaller, afraid of exposing one inch of their bodies to this skilled a marksman. Gabriel ducked behind a boulder, the image of his nephew's ruined face a nightmare vision in his head.

Maxime Lépine chose this moment to walk out of the bush near the creek as if he were in Batoche village, not visiting rifle pits to pray with the men. His old muzzleloader dangled from one hand, and in the other he held the Christ figure that Riel had given him.

"Stay down," Gabriel shouted.

Maxime looked dazed, in a kind of rapture. "Say the rosary," he said, turning his head to men in the pits on either side of him. "We have a religion that is losing us—let us ask for the grace of a perfect contrition so that we will be saved."

Someone said, "Save yourself!"

Maxime began to head toward the trail. Gabriel yelled at him again to stay down, but he did not hear. A shell was launched from the ridge and exploded behind him. He disappeared in a spray of blown mud. Gabriel was sure that they'd lost one of the best men in the South Branch, but Lépine reappeared without a scratch.

The cannon was rolled away again and in the impending silence,

Gabriel stared up at the ridge, avoiding the sight of his nephew's bloody face. Sorrow. Perfect contrition. Madeleine often prayed for such a thing. And why? Out of fear of punishment from God. The Métis in this ravine would not be saved by repentance or shame.

Middleton had also pulled back his sniper from the ridge. Why didn't he order a large company to charge and rout them out? It was either too muddy now or he was discouraged to see so many of his soldiers wounded or dead. The old man respected the fighters he was up against and would wait for the other half of his army to arrive.

Gabriel was cold, colder than he had ever been on the winter hunts. To count coup with honour, one must take the enemy by surprise, face death, deliver an insulting blow. And live to tell the tale. The Métis were trapped like buffalo in a pound and had very little time to escape unharmed. Riel was in Batoche, praying, making medicine as Sitting Bull had for his warriors at the Little Bighorn.

Did he not hear the guns?

and the people
stood beholding

ON MISSION RIDGE at the bluff above the river, Josette stood with a scattered group of women and some of the men who had come back with Riel. It had just rained and they were soaked through, yet remained there, compelled by the distant booming of cannon fire twenty miles to the south. And by the spectacle of their leader, who knelt before them in the damp new grass.

"God, I beg You," Riel prayed, "for the love of Jesus Christ, in the name of Your Immaculate Virgin, in the name of Your Saint Joseph, keep Middleton's cannon broken in three. Separate the carriage and barrel—separate them forever."

Josette watched him with a hollow feeling in her stomach. Riel's arms were outstretched as Christ's had been on the cross, hands turned upward in solicitation. She shifted her eyes to Madeleine standing behind him, who met her look with a pitiless gaze. The question seemed to be on her lips, too.

Why has he not gone back to the fight?

Last night Josette had watched from her porch as hundreds of Métis led by Gabriel and Riel had passed, riding south to ambush Middleton. Then, an hour later, Riel had ridden back in the opposite direction with fifty men. He told her that police had been spotted on the trail from Prince Albert and asked if she would come up with him to help encourage the people, who were losing faith in his leadership. She had agreed, only because Gabriel was out there, facing Middleton and his soldiers with less firepower than he'd planned. Shortly after they had arrived, the rumour that police were on their way had proved unfounded. Yet Riel thought himself more valuable here than at the fight.

Riel had opened his eyes to regard them. "As Moses watched the Israelites and Amalekites do battle," he said, pausing for their murmurs of approval, "I will kneel on this bluff with the staff of God in my hand."

The ground beneath them seemed to shake with another thump of the distant guns. Josette envisioned Gabriel hit and lying mortally wounded. She'd heard that after the Little Bighorn battle, the Sioux women had gone up the hill with clubs to dispatch the dying American soldiers, crushing their heads and meting out punishment for the deaths of their men. Her hands itched for such a club and the opportunity to use it. But fifty men had come back with Riel and did not seem to share the same impulse. Gabriel's younger brother Édouard was there, looking agitated, and Pierre Parenteau, chairman of the council, who was too old to fight.

She caught Pierre's eye. *Send the men south*, she said in one look, *save Gabriel*. He glanced away toward Madeleine, whose head was bowed, her body in the black dress so rigid, she seemed as though she were witnessing a funeral rather than a hopeful entreaty to God. Josette struggled for composure. The wives of men who fought with Gabriel were grouped together, watching those around Riel too closely, almost waiting for someone to speak against this madness. But if she did, if Madeleine or Pierre said anything, the wives might lose faith in Riel and wait for their men to return from the battle, gather their possessions and be gone. Gabriel would be left with an army of stragglers.

She did not want to lose him. Not now.

Something had begun last summer in the birch forest, escalating over the past few months when she often awoke from dreams of him after he had rescued her from Norbert. How he had stood on the porch before Duck Lake, asking if she would open her heart again to Riel. And his face when he had turned from the pool table in his saloon to find her there. "*Kiya*," You.

Remembering the look in his eyes when he had said it put her into a mute panic. *You* could mean so many things. A challenge or claim, even an appeal. Or simply a statement when nothing else could be said. Because it was impossible.

She stole a glance at Riel and saw that he had held his arms out for so long, his muscles had begun to shake. He looked meaningfully at Édouard and Pierre. "As Aaron and Hur held up Moses' arms during the battle with the Amalekites, assist your leader's arms and show your faith in his power." He nodded as Édouard came tentatively to his side. "My hand grows heavy, God—hold it up as you hold the Métis' hands steady on their rifles, their hearts steady on the field."

There was movement up near the rectory, and Josette could see Marguerite Caron, the wife of Jean Caron senior and the sister of Michel Dumas, with her extended brood of children. The Carons had the first farm south of the church. Her husband and her three oldest boys were at the fight with Gabriel. She was one of the stalwart and pious Métis women who had been cooking for the men, despite being eight months pregnant with her ninth child. Marguerite had spied the crowd on the bluff and she headed that way, curious to see what was happening.

She approached as Riel began to relate another vision and stood with hands on her hips, regarding him with disapproval. "What are you doing here when our men are fighting?"

"Asking God to help Gabriel."

There was an increase in rifle shots from the direction of Tourond's Coulee. "Do you have news?" Marguerite demanded. "They aren't all dead since we can hear them firing. Aren't you going to see?"

A rider had appeared on the crest of the hill, and left the trail, running his horse straight toward them through the prairie grass. As he came closer, they saw it was Basile Primeau, who did not slow until he was almost upon them. He reined up his mount and gasped out to Riel, "Gabriel sent me for reinforcements."

Josette drew a long breath. At least he was still alive.

"Send them men," said Marguerite, "and ammunition."

Riel looked at Josette for help, but she avoided his eyes and silently applauded Marguerite's courage in going against Riel. If anyone could get away with confronting him without harming Gabriel's efforts, it was one of the Batoche matriarchs.

He got up off his knees. "Gigitte," he said, using her nickname, "pray the rosary—"

Marguerite shook her head. "This is no time for Paters and Aves. Why aren't you going to see?" She stared meaningfully at Édouard and Pierre. "What are you all doing here? A gang who passes their time looking around." She nudged Gabriel's brother. "You would do better to go yelling on the other side—you would get strength."

Riel jumped at a sudden pounding of cannon from the south. "Gigitte," he said. "Don't get angry without reason—come with me to my church and pray."

"I am not angry without reason. And I don't want to pray." She glared at Édouard. "You were more ready to charge ahead and loot stores than going to help our people that are in risk there." She regarded the assembled crowd. "If you don't want to go, tell me, I will go to see if they are alive. Yes or no?"

Madeleine stepped forward, as did Josette and a dozen other women. "We will go in our wagons," Madeleine said, "and take supplies."

Exasperated, Pierre said, "Is the battle here or there? Go home, I will go see, me."

we whipped them

GABRIEL OPENED HIS eyes in a cloud of pain and delirium. A single candle burned at his bedside. He had a vague memory of Madeleine leaning over him to peel the bloodied cloth from his head, change the poultice, and dribble medicine tea down his throat. After hours spent cold and shivering in the creek bed, he was now consumed by fever. Every muscle in his body ached, but the pain in his head—it almost made him want to pray.

He heard Madeleine's voice in the hall. "Men on the buffalo hunts have died of wounds less than this." Disoriented, he was convinced that Isidore was there and Madeleine prevented him from entering. Her murmured voice again, low with disapproval. "*You* are rested, I see."

And Isidore, answering. "I must get his report."

"He's asleep. It can wait until tomorrow."

Isidore spoke louder now. "*Non*, it cannot."

Gabriel lifted his head, sure that he'd glimpsed a figure at the door—a shadowy form that stood there, watching him.

"Brother," he called out before falling back.

It was Riel who came into the room and looked down at him, the big Stetson hat on his head. "I have been told what happened, but I want to hear it from you."

"We whipped them and got four rifles . . ." Gabriel broke off when an agonizing pain hit his head like a hammer.

"God was on our side." Riel removed his hat and crossed himself before sitting on the bed. "How many dead, and wounded?"

"Didn't you see the bodies that came in the wagons?" Gabriel dug a fist into his thigh to stop himself from groaning. "Michel Desjarlais shot in the head just before your men came—the blood poured out. He screamed all the way back." Gabriel searched his confused mind for the names of the seven dead and twelve wounded, including St. Pierre and Joseph Vermette, more relations he had lost that day.

Had they whipped them? It was an ugly fight. The *Anglais* soldiers, desperate to take them, and the Métis saved only by the good ground. But other battles had been won by position. Gabriel had already begun to think of the land between Batoche and Tourond's Coulee, deeper ravines and dense copses of trees, where he would plan other, better ambushes.

"I would like to know if anyone prayed the rosary," Riel said, looking down at his hat.

Gabriel gazed at the ceiling. "Maxime Lépine went about with the Christ you gave him . . . asked for the grace of perfect contrition to be saved." Riel bowed his head, muttering a prayer and Gabriel added, "While you are talking to God, ask Him to keep the men from deserting."

"Exactly as it was during the last days in Red River," Riel said in a monotone. "Men in my council lost their courage and disappeared one by one. First it is Charles Nolin and then Albert Monkman."

"Monkman?"

"He was caught escaping south. I had him arrested."

Gabriel looked at Riel from between half-closed lids. Monkman had commanded the men on the west side of the river. His desertion was a low blow. "Each man for himself," he said, "as it was when we ran the buffalo, *non?*"

"We must keep men in Batoche where we can see them," Riel said stubbornly. "Bring their families too. We'll issue a proclamation that anyone who deserts will be shot."

Gabriel lifted a hand in protest. "We must hit *les Anglais*—hit them in the bunch as they lick their wounds"

"They won't march to Batoche tomorrow."

The left side of Riel's face was illuminated by the candle flame. Gabriel tried to read his expression, but the act of focusing his eyes shot pain through his head. Not only had he taken on the job of defending the Métis against Middleton, he also found himself struggling to convince everyone to remain loyal to Riel. He had never worked this hard at anything in his life.

"What kind of war are you fighting?" he asked Riel.

"There will be no more ambushes."

Gabriel could feel the medicine tea take effect; his heart beat slower now, pain easing away. He opened his mouth and said with effort. "We must ambush Middleton . . . before he comes . . ." But he drifted, dimly aware that Riel had taken his hand. The herbs Madeleine had given him sent his spirit out of the room and the house, over his lands and the river, in à haze of euphoria.

And Riel's words floating after him, "There will be no more blood spilled on the sacred soil of the Métis."

consumption

AT DAWN, TWO DAYS after the battle, Josette stood on the porch of her house and watched Gabriel ride north to Batoche. He had been in bed for days with a fever, and she almost expected him to drop from the saddle. When he had been brought in from the fight, she had taken down more willow tea and birch bark that she had steamed and softened for making bandages. Madeleine had refused her offer to help, saying that she had just thrown out Riel and nobody else could see her husband.

Gabriel should not be exerting himself, but he was Riel's war chief. Who else would organize the Métis and fortify Batoche against an invasion? Although he did not look up at her house, some part of her thrilled to see his stalwart figure ride away.

Métis scouts had reported that Middleton was still encamped near Tourond's Coulee burying ten of his dead and operating a field hospital for over fifty wounded. Already, soldiers seeking revenge had looted and burned Métis houses in that area, and it was only a matter of time before the army regrouped and marched north on the Humboldt Trail. Riel had issued an order for all families within thirty miles of Batoche "to move in without distinction."

Josette turned and went into the house. Norbert had been sent scouting, so it was left to her and the children to move anything they did not want to lose to *les Anglais*. All of them were helping except for young Wahsis, who stood in the doorway of the backroom, clutching the blanket he'd had since he was a *bibi*.

"When the soldiers come," he said, "will they burn our house?"

Josette wanted to believe that Middleton's men would be too intent on reaching Batoche to burn houses on their march north. "*Non, mon p'tit*," she said, "it will be here when we get back."

"What of this?" Eulalie asked, holding up the old lead tea case they used to hold beads and thread. Josette nodded. Anything made of tin or lead was reserved for the pile that would be melted down to cast buckshot for their men.

It was the end of April, spring, but the trees would not break into leaf for a few weeks yet. The temperature could fluctuate wildly in a day, the morning cold until sun broke through cloud cover to warm the air. Small sloughs still glistened out on the pastures, melted snow that had not yet sunk into the wet ground. Josette wanted to be in her garden; it was time to seed potatoes and carrots, but they were missing the chance. The men should be in the fields plowing the soil for oats and hay and barley. Instead, they were scouting or going in to Batoche, feverishly digging rifle pits to fight an army that outnumbered them five to one.

She saw Cleophile carrying a pile of blankets from the house out to the wagon in the front yard. Josette turned and went out to the barn to find the tipi canvas that Norbert used when freighting. *Eulalie will catch the lung disease*, she thought as she shook it out, *sleeping on the ground in this weather*. When she headed back, the sound of a familiar unsettling cough made her look up. Madeleine stood on the front porch, holding her shawl close around her throat. Josette slowly climbed the steps.

"Gabriel's wound has festered," Madeleine admitted. Josette was suddenly mortified, ashamed, that her neighbour had come to beg herbs from a woman she suspected was attracted to her husband. Madeleine had been right to begrudge Gabriel's attention to her. Their marriage was not unhappy. And yet Josette continued to violate that bond by caring for a man she had no right to think of as anything but a fellow disciple of Riel, a trusted friend.

"What do you have to stop the bleeding?"

"Yarrow," Madeleine said, not meeting her eyes. "I packed the wound and made a poultice. He falls into a tormented sleep and wakes shouting with pain. Only another poultice and draught of tea will drug him back to rest."

Josette thought of Gabriel in Batoche, taking charge of his men, ordering them to dig rifle pits. All with an infected head wound and burning with fever. "He should rest."

"You know as well as I do that he cannot. It is like nothing you have ever seen—a riven strip along the top of his head—too far apart to stitch closed—and almost an inch deep. It still pulses blood."

She told her that she would bring down what she had, and Madeleine left without another word. Josette went down to her root cellar in the summer kitchen, remembering Moulin's words to her after the berry picking ceremony.

"You think you walk in the Law of Love, when you have broken every one of His commandments? You do not love God. That is the requirement! You dwell in the law of *sin*."

When she had taken herbs to abort her own child, she had not believed it a sin, but she was sinning now. Twenty-seven years Gabriel and Madeleine had been married. Josette sank down on the lowest step of the ladder and closed her eyes. Despite the healing power in the hanging rows of herbs and roots, her lungs were filled with the bitter scent of death. She thought of her talk with Gabriel last summer on the way to Prince Albert to see her grandfather. How he had avoided her afterward, only coming around when he needed more help with Riel. It struck her that she had misread his expression in that birch forest, the heat of his gaze when he had made the promise, *I will not let him fail.* The great Gabriel Dumont had glimpsed her sorrow, her secrets and doubts and her relentless grief. His gaze had not been one of appreciation. It had been dismay. She had misread every one of Gabriel's looks, mistaking them for something meaningful. Now she heard "*Kiya*," You, as an expression of his frustration at her appearing again, adding to his burdens.

The small underground cellar seemed like a dark womb to her or a prison, the crushing stillness and cold seeping into her bones. She stood slowly and pulled down the last of her devil's club roots and stalks of a dried spiked flower, which she knew only the Cree word for: *kipôh-kâskan*. She ground the root and flower into powder and by the time she had crossed the pasture that afternoon with the blend in a cloth under her arm, she had persuaded herself to stop this foolish obsession. For that's what it was—a dream she had made up in her own desperate heart.

She found Madeleine in her kitchen. "Make a poultice," she said, unwrapping the bundle. "It will draw out the infection."

Madeleine nodded in thanks and turned to sort through her cast iron frying pans. Henriette Nolin and Gabriel's sister Isabel Ouellette had been helping her and came in from loading her sewing machine onto the cart in the front yard.

Isabel started to take down the framed photographs of Jesus and the saints from the kitchen walls, when Henriette cried, "*Non*," startling her. "Father Moulin says keep them up. It will save the house."

Madeleine frowned. "That priest is a prisoner in the rectory and has refused us the sacraments—refused our dead a Catholic burial. Why are you talking with him?"

Henriette coloured and began to speak of the uproar caused when Joseph Pilon and his family had been caught packing up their possessions to make off for their relations in the States.

Madeleine folded a blanket in half, her work-hardened hands smoothing it flat on the kitchen table. "Gabriel told me that at Tourond's Coulee, Pilon rode down with the men, took a few shots at the English, then slunk off when the fire got too hot. Riel had a talk with him the next day, and he crawled like a child to the priests."

"If a man does not want to fight, he should not fight," said Henriette.

Madeleine, Isabel, and Josette exchanged looks. News had come that Henriette's husband, Charles Nolin, had been captured in Prince Albert and was being held by the police. How could she still defend a man who had deserted, leaving her and their children to face a government attack? It was no wonder she went to the priests.

"It is unlucky to live in Batoche," Henriette continued. "Métis in other places are not forced to fight."

"Forced?" Madeleine cried. "They are cowards not to come help us. We are all in this mess together. Some *Anglais* will move in and set his ass in their houses, too. They are nothing but old buffalo bulls the herd has cut away to be taken by wolves." She snatched up a pile of blankets for the cart.

"*Oui*," Henriette agreed. "Weak animals die, strong animals live."

Josette went quietly out the back door, and up through the side pasture to her barn, intending to saddle La Noire and ride to fetch the *Spinoza* from its hiding place on the bluff. She peered into the stalls. To prepare for the chickens, Mimoux, and La Noire to move with them to Batoche, Josette had asked Cleophile to bring down some hay from the loft. But the horse and cow greeted her with hopeful anticipation of having their feed troughs filled. Muffled laughter drifted down to her from the hayloft, and Josette looked up to find Cleophile and Alexandre sitting up there with their heads together, giggling.

"What are you doing?" she said, her voice shrill.

Alexandre stood. "Nothing, just talking."

Josette could feel the blood rise in her cheeks. "A man is not interested in *talking* to a woman." She stared at Cleophile. "And you are a woman now, is that right? Eager to lift your skirt for any man that comes along?"

Cleophile's face was made of stone. "Look at you, off to your hiding place—don't be surprised. Do you think I did not know what you have been doing all this time?"

"Why have you grown to hate me?"

"I do not hate you. Only what you've become since you fell in love with Riel."

"I am not in love with him. And your father is not the first man to take a woman at One Arrow's. You know I will die if I become pregnant again." She threw Alexandre an accusing look. "And you must learn that a man can make you pregnant in seconds—that is how romantic love is."

Alexandre frowned and shook his head. "I am courting Mary-Jane Ouellette. Cleophile and I are *amis*."

Josette stormed out of the barn and across the pasture. Henriette and Isabel were out at the cart, but she found Madeleine standing in her kitchen, with every available pot in her arms.

"We cannot get the washing machine out of the root cellar in the summer kitchen," Madeleine said. "But what would *les Anglais* want with a thing like that?"

"Your son has been messing with my daughter," Josette cried. "She is only twelve."

Madeleine turned and glared at her. "Alexandre would not do such a thing."

"He is sixteen and a man."

"He would not—"

"How do you know? He is your adopted son, come to you already grown." She immediately regretted her words.

"You are a fine one," Madeleine said from between her teeth. "Alexandre helps Cleophile when you are away—she is *la p'tite mère*, making sure Norbert is fed. Lying for you, so he will not beat you when you come home from fucking another woman's husband."

Isabel and Henriette had come up the porch steps in time to see Madeleine dissolve into a racking cough and cover her mouth as she bent over, choking. She reached into her skirt pocket for a handkerchief but did not get it out in time.

Josette was close enough to see the blood that specked her hand.

an embarrassing but
novel position

GABRIEL HAD BEEN bothered all night in the tent he shared with Madeleine on the riverbank in Batoche. Lying still made him feel every throbbing pain in his head, as though God Himself had placed a belt around his skull and took joy in tightening it slowly. Hours before dawn, he had managed to slip away without Madeleine waking and rode south, compelled to see if Middleton's soldiers had looted his farm.

He sat on his horse in the trees for half an hour, watching his deserted house and barn to make sure the enemy was not about and finally went down to look around. Madeleine's washing machine was in the root cellar, his pool table still in the saloon. There were signs that enemy scouts had been in. At least they had not burned the place, but one or more of them had pissed in a corner.

Dawn had not yet lightened the sky when Gabriel came out of the house. He could smell another man's horse and ducked back in the door, but a familiar whistle made him release his finger from the trigger

of his gun. One of his own scouts. Damase Carrière rode out from behind the barn. He had been riding to Batoche to make a morning report
to the council that Middleton still remained camped only miles from
the battlefield.

"Ten days since the fight," Gabriel mused. "What is he waiting for?"

Damase, who had been watching the camp since yesterday, said that
the general was putting his men through rifle practice. Gabriel jumped
on his horse, turning it south. He had relied thus far on Jérôme Henry's
reports of Middleton, but he wanted to see for himself. When he had
been the captain of the hunt, he and his men had scouted out for days,
looking for the herds. *Anglais* soldiers were just a different kind of
animal.

Half a mile north of the camp, he and Damase tied their horses in a
dense copse of willow on the riverbank, evading Middleton's two lines
of guards. Gabriel could have picked them off to take revenge for his
brother's death, but the sentries were young, naïve men who had been
eating and talking, unaware that the enemy was within shooting distance.

Dawn was breaking over the South Saskatchewan when the two
Métis crouched behind a boulder above Middleton's camp. Gabriel had
taken out his field glasses and surveyed the many tents when one flap
opened and a portly figure emerged, clad in a grey, formal uniform and
long leather boots. The same man he had seen commanding his soldiers
at the coulee.

"Eh," whispered Damase. "There he is."

Middleton fixed a fur cap on his head and walked briskly through
camp, his cane swinging. He went to the river's edge and briefly looked
into the water, studied the far bank, and then squinted at the sky, as if
taking note of the weather. One of his men came out of another tent
and swung a great coat across his shoulders, keeping an eye on his commanding officer. It was true then—the general was on guard against a
sudden attack from the Sioux and their scalping knives.

Gabriel studied Middleton. This *môniyâw*, white man, was soft and
weak, smoking his pipe and stroking his white mustaches. If he were a
buffalo, Gabriel would ride past, judging him unworthy of killing. But

perhaps he had underestimated the strength of this prey—it might look like a bloated buffalo cow, yet it behaved more like a trapped fox.

Teamsters were up, tending to their oxen. Gabriel regarded the wagonloads of supplies and ammunition with proprietary envy. And anger. If the damn Hudson's Bay Company hadn't rushed in to save the army with water, feed for their horses, and good pay for two hundred teamsters—many of them English half-breeds—they would still be stuck in Qu'Appelle.

Near the riverbank, a large wooden cross had been thrust into a pile of stones, marking the site where they had buried their dead. The general paced on the bank, looking up the river with an expectant expression. Several other officers were coming out of their tents.

Years ago, Gabriel had seen a photograph of the prime minister, and now he searched for one with a resemblance to Sir John. "Show me this Lieutenant Hugh Macdonald," he whispered to himself, moving the field glasses from one face to another. "*Show me.*" The Dominion leader would listen if his only son was held captive by the Métis.

Middleton would soon march north. There were twenty miles between the army and Batoche. It was said that before the general went to bed, he visited each sentry on his *piquet* lines, and his commanding officers checked on them every few hours until dawn. *Les Anglais* were vigilant, but this did not stop Gabriel from playing a scene over and over in his head: lead fifty of his best men in the night, set a fire around these tents, hem them in, and it would all be over. But Riel would not allow it.

There will be no more ambushes . . . no more blood spilled on the sacred soil of the Métis.

Forced to meet the army in Riel's City of God, Gabriel had been doing everything he could to make it difficult for Middleton. Rifle pits were being dug everywhere around the village. No *Anglais* general would outflank him. News had come that Poundmaker had been forced to surrender his power to the Rattler Society—warriors headed up by Fine Day, who now controlled his band—and Riel's council had agreed to send four men up there to bring them to Batoche. Two days ago, the Indian camp had been attacked by one of Middleton's officers and his troops up near Battleford. The Rattler Society had driven off the soldiers, but there had been reports of a new kind of gun used against them, one they had described as issuing so many bullets at once, it was like a swarming host of wasps. Hearing of this gun made Gabriel nervous. If Poundmaker didn't arrive before Middleton did in Batoche and bring the area chiefs, the Métis would surely lose this war.

Riel had put much importance on the Indians, but Madeleine was right: what of the Métis throughout the Territories, Battle River and Qu-Appelle? Their relations in Red River? He and Isidore had visited half-breed communities from Prairie Ronde, Fort à la Corne, and into the Cypress Hills. The council had also sent letters beseeching them for help. *Without delay come this way, as many as possible. Send us news.*

Some had trickled in—old buffalo hunters that Gabriel had known on the plains. But the majority had not. If all Métis men in the Territories stood behind them, Macdonald would have listened to the petition, and they would not have been forced to take up arms. Riel had never admitted it, but Gabriel and others thought these men knew better: they did not wish to be involved in a war that would end badly.

Damase nudged him. One of the old Hudson's Bay steamers had come into view around a bend in the river. They watched as the ship threw anchor and soldiers came up from the hold. A strange thing was wheeled up from below. The first rays of sun flashed behind it, revealing a hulking monster. Soldiers backed against the railings as it crept across the deck, the long snout with many nostrils, a dragon with a long crest atop its head. It crawled down the gangplank, creaking.

"*C'est le Rababou*," said Damase. "The one they used on Poundmaker."

"*Rababou*." Years ago, Gabriel had fought the Blackfoot and bands of Sioux warriors over buffalo hunting territory. But this thing struck fear into him.

The sun rose over the trees on the west bank, sending long shafts of golden light across the river. Soldiers massed around *le Rababou* and pushed it, squelching through the mud. Gabriel saw it now in the shadow cast by the boat. A wheeled carriage linked by an axle. A dozen gun barrels joined as one, and a long handle on top for the one who would wield its power.

i will raise up evil

MOSQUITOES AND MAY flies rose out of the wolf willow scrub as Josette and young Virginie Tourond climbed the riverbank trail the next morning. In her apron, Josette carried half a dozen still-warm bannocks that had come off the cooking fires. Virginie, who was heavily pregnant, held several roasted ducks wrapped in a blanket under her arm. The cutbank below the cemetery sloped gradually to the river and was now camp to many of the families that had come in on the council's order. A series of shallow dugouts had been made on either side of the trail among the willow scrag, each shielded by an overturned cart or tipi cloth.

A small herd of their dairy cows grazed contentedly in the meadow near the cemetery, kept close to provide them milk. The stock cattle and horses were pastured in the fields north of the village. After the horse massacre at Tourond's Coulee, Riel and Gabriel would not let the English slaughter their only means of survival. As the two women passed the church, the sound of children singing drifted from an open window.

"It is good of our council to think of the young ones," said Virginie.

Josette remained silent. It had seemed a noble effort to bring in a French-Canadian schoolteacher from St. Louis de Langevin settlement near Prince Albert, but she knew the real objective was to prevent families from deserting the riverbank camp by keeping their children in the church all day.

The air was still except for the sound of shovels and picks hacking at the earth in rhythmic chinks. Riel had lectured them over the fifty-five horses that had been killed by Middleton's big guns. He declared that God had long been offended by the Métis' gambling on horse racing, and He would be appeased only if they all fasted for four days. But Riel was in a council meeting, and the working men would eat.

After delivering food to those digging in the woods behind the church and rectory, the two women headed to the Jolie Prairie pits. Virginie was close to her time and pestered Josette with questions to do with the mysteries of labour, and her wish to keep the baby from coming until the men finished their warring. As they passed a stand of poplar, a flock of black-throated sparrows rose from the bare branches and turned as one into the sky. To encourage her, Josette said birth was as natural a process as a flower coming to bud or a bird taking wing.

She glanced back, thinking that her own children's births had been nothing but studies in pain and torture. Riel's white flag, the symbol of his Catholic Apostolic Church, fluttered outside the rectory. The figure of the Mother Mary appeared to be walking forward, but was trapped forever on that white patch of cloth. There was a flash of movement to the left of the church, and Josette was surprised to see Cleophile running across to the rectory. The front door opened and her eldest daughter disappeared inside. Josette faltered. Why had she left the church school? And why had the priests allowed her in the rectory when her father and mother were aligned to Riel?

She wanted to go back, but would not leave Virginie to carry the food alone. The sun had climbed higher in the sky by the time Josette arrived at the rectory. Moulin, the Fathers Vegreville, Fourmond, and four Irish nuns from St. Laurent had been confined there for the past month. She found Moulin cooking a thin gruel of last year's oats on the stove. The kitchen was a mess, for the structure had been built to house one or two people, not seven. Cleophile was nowhere to be seen.

The priest raised one of his overgrown brows at the sight of her. "What will Riel think if you are seen consorting with the enemy? You don't expect that I will hear your confession."

Josette did not meet his eye. "I do not wish to confess."

"But you need it more than anyone." He gestured at the state of the kitchen. "You see we are under house arrest," he said, and added in a sarcastic tone, "for our safety." He showed her a piece of paper. "Riel made us sign this, promising to remain neutral and not leave this place without the consent of his sham government. He declares he will now act as *our* spiritual advisor—priests of God! And the flag of his *hérétique* church flying outside our door. There is nothing left but to beat us and put us to death."

Josette did not tell him that everyone was watched. Each Métis arriving in Batoche had been ordered to take an oath of faith to the movement and the provisional government's laws. Even the scouts required permission from their *capitaines* to leave. She looked toward the stairs, expecting Cleophile to come down. "You are free to bring the prisoners their meals."

Moulin's face was rigid. "I would rather not see those *pauvres misérables*. Each time we open the door, they are desperate to be set free." She asked after Honoré Jaxon, and Moulin said he seemed not quite as mad after his brother Eastwood had come down from Prince Albert to visit him, but Riel had imprisoned him, too. "Honoré is wasting in that room," he said. "He lets others take his share of food."

"I saw my daughter come here," she said. "Did you offer her the sacraments?"

"Cleophile's piety should not be questioned by you." He watched her for a moment, one hand inching unconsciously toward his mouth before he caught himself and placed it decisively in his pocket. "You doubt Riel. And yet you help him with his church."

"I ask you again—did you offer Cleophile the sacraments? Her father fights with the *evil* Louis Riel."

"Would you control her relationship with God?"

"Children do not need to confess. They are without sin."

He shook his head in frustration. "But sin might be done to them."

She was startled, both hurt and concerned that Cleophile had chosen to trust this priest. But he could not violate the sanctity of the confessional by telling Josette of her own daughter's fears.

Moulin regarded her with growing impatience. "You are her mother," he said, lifting a finger to his lips to chew at the nail. "Can you not see that she is unhappy?"

"Cleophile has become a stranger to me."

"Thus saith the Lord," he thundered, resorting to scripture to make his point. "Behold, I will raise up evil against thee out of thine own house." He pointed his finger at her. "You have neglected your children with your poems and Riel."

He came toward her, and she flinched in spite of herself.

"Do you not think *Riel est fou?*" He looked at her keenly, as if expecting an answer. When she did not give one, he said, "You have displeased the Lord and are being punished. Repent as David did. Lie all night upon the earth. Fast—"

"All the Métis are fasting. It means nothing."

"You fast for Riel's church, his sins. Not your own." He reached around her and opened the door. "Go and find your daughter then. Beg forgiveness for neglecting her. And ask Riel to tell you of the two years he spent locked in an insane asylum!"

the blood of
christ

THAT AFTERNOON, Riel stood on the west bank of the river in his outdoor chapel, eyes closed and head bowed.

"God, in Your mercy," he prayed to his congregation, "touch these women's hearts so that they will devote themselves entirely to overcoming all the deficiencies which Rome has inculcated in the peoples of the earth."

He opened his eyes and was met by the welcome sight of his wife, Marguerite. The attentive expression on her sweet, obliging face almost broke his heart. But the sixty or so Métis women crowding the clearing were looking everywhere else but at him. Some even glanced to St. Antoine de Padoue, which was visible across the river, its whitewashed steeple stark against the sky.

He lifted his worn leather Bible. "The Roman Church," he reminded them, "is opulent and tarnished by greed, compared to your new one, humble in its sacred poverty."

A flock of ducks roused themselves from the reeds, fluttering over the surface of the water in a blur of wings. The clearing in the woods was an idyllic setting where the Métis with farms on the west bank could worship. He had not bargained for it to give the women a perfect view of their old church. Two days ago, icy rain had fallen, yet now it was warm as an early summer day, and poplar trees were beginning to send out their buds. The natural beauty of the grove should have buoyed his spirits, but his heart was filled with foreboding.

Sun shone down through the branches, almost directly upon the altar, which was only a rough plank nailed between two trees. A photograph of Jesus—his sacred heart aflame—had been attached to one of the trunks with a few tin tags from a plug tobacco container. Upon the altar, Marguerite had placed a jar of milk and a bannock wrapped in cloth. The cross that Riel had taken from the Duck Lake church was braced precariously behind these items, and he stared hard at it, praying, *do not let it fall, Lord.*

Riel swayed in a trance brought on by hunger. Clouds passed over the sun and mosquitoes found them, rising in a fog from the damp earth. The women wrapped shawls and blankets closer around their necks and murmured amongst themselves. Henriette Parenteau and Gigitte Caron regarded him with particular wariness, and he was convinced it was women like these who were behind their men resisting a Saturday Sabbath and leaving the Roman Church. Gigitte, it was said, supplied the priests and nuns with milk from her cows.

There was a bad taste in Riel's mouth. Either the sour bile that came from fasting, or the memory of the council meeting this morning, when Moise Ouellette had refused to vote on a decision that—with God's and Christ's help—a miracle would save the Métis from General Middleton. Rushing out in a temper, Riel had gone to the riverbank camp to find his wife. As he approached the cooking fires, he overheard the women express fear that their men would face battle again without a priest to give them communion and hear their confessions.

He had immediately herded them onto the ferry and to the chapel to receive the Eucharist, but he regretted the decision. A rifle pit was being dug nearby—the noise of trees being cut, shovels hitting rock—and many of the women strained to keep their attention on his service. The warning pressure began to build in Riel's chest, and he gazed at the sky to beseech God.

Send down all the charitable gifts of the priesthood, the solemn and consoling services of the true religion, edifying Your people in grace.

He slipped the Bible in the pocket of his coat and assumed the regal bearing of a priest. Milk instead of wine. Bannock instead of the host. His mouth watered dangerously. Marguerite handed him the bread, and he could feel the women's eyes upon him. He was painfully aware of the state of his wrinkled and filthy clothes, his untrimmed beard.

"You would like me to have a fine soutane and a linen surplice," he said, "but God has saved me from the decadence of the Catholic priesthood, saved me for the day when I will deliver to you the Promised Land."

Superstitious women and an obstinate council were the least of his worries. Riel desperately needed Poundmaker. Four Métis in the chief's camp were working with the Rattler Society to bring the band south, but scouts had come in with news that the chief had been caught trying to escape. The Rattler Society had brought him back in and put him under guard. They would be here in a matter of days, but Riel was on edge.

He had suffered a worrying dream last night, finding himself at the edge of a chasm. On the far side, Poundmaker had ridden up on a white horse, the sun behind him, eclipsing his face in shadow. Riel's ears had been filled with an ominous rustling sound and he looked down in time to see a large grass snake coiled at his feet. He awoke shouting.

To erase the memory of his dream and drown out the clang of the shovels, he lifted the bannock skyward. "Spirit of God, our Father, mercifully bless this bread." He handed it back to Marguerite and held up the jar of milk. "Infuse this drink with your essence."

A few of the women had their heads together, whispering. He caught one of them saying, "An ordained priest must bless the sacrament, *non?*"

"God does not require a priest to make a blessing," he warned. "Priests are not religion."

Through the trees came a sudden jarring ring of shovel hitting rock, followed by a shouted oath.

"*Crisse de câlice de tabarnak!*"

Riel flushed with anger. "Thou shalt not take the name of the Lord thy God in vain," he bellowed. All was still, and then voices floated through the trees, "Is that Riel?" "What is he doing on this side of the river?" "Consecrating the host, can't you hear?"

The women had begun to file forward, crossing themselves. It did his heart good to witness their fervour. Or were they simply anxious to have something to break their fast, if only a mouthful of bread and a sip of milk? Caroline Arcand knelt before him. Riel broke off a piece of bannock. "The body of Christ," he murmured, placing it on her extended tongue.

Her crude features transformed as she took the bread and mouthed her amen. She did not look at him as she rose, brushed off her skirts and turned away, her hands clasped in prayer. He was grateful when she began to sing in a quavering voice.

"Let all mortal flesh keep silence,
And with fear and trembling stand;
Ponder nothing earthly minded,
For with blessing in His hand,
Christ our God to earth descendeth,
Our full homage to demand."

One by one, each woman took the host and joined her in the psalm. Riel was ebullient. *A success*, he thought, as Marguerite knelt before him to receive the sacrament. When he bent to let her sip from the jar of milk, her dark eyes flicked up at him. Was it his imagination or did she also seem to regard him with distrust?

O God, hasten to help me. Do not delay. Make the Métis vigilant, obedient, and ready for whatever happens.

He could feel Christ's love course through him. God would bring the Indians in time, and he would not have to send the letter he had agonized over writing to his friend in Helena, who would take it to certain men he knew in Montana, men of power. The council had agreed with him: the Hudson's Bay Company and Dominion of Canada had no right to claim these lands, and the Indians, English, and French inhabitants should seek annexation to the U.S. But to send the letter would tempt the same fate King David had suffered, and for which God had punished him.

Riel lifted his eyes and noticed the ferry swinging out from Fisher's Crossing, a man on the bank pulling the cable to bring it across the river. The women's faces turned *en masse* to watch its slow progress toward them.

"The ferry comes bearing a sign from God," he said. "There is someone on it who will bring news." The women seemed confused and then doubtful. Some, like Domatilde Boucher, frowned and looked away.

He launched into another hymn and soon they were singing along and swaying shoulder to shoulder, their voices a mix of off-key sopranos and a vibrating alto from Henriette Parenteau. The ferry had docked by the time they had finished the last verse, and soon there appeared on the path—which was no more than an old game trail—the resigned figures of Pierre Fleury and Bazile Godon. Unaware that they were the objects of attention, the two men walked past them toward the rifle pits, shovels pitched over their shoulders and guns in the crooks of their arms.

Riel regarded Pierre Fleury in consternation. *Why him, God?* Since Tourond's Coulee, Pierre had flagrantly ignored him. While the rest of them fasted, Pierre had brought in a rabbit he'd snared. He skinned and cleaned it, then roasted it on the riverbank campfire, gorging himself in front of everyone. But Riel had promised the women a messenger, and one such as this could only be a challenge issued from God to his prophet.

Riel called out to him. "Pierre Fleury! You do not wish to face the enemy without God's blessing."

"That's good." Pierre said, walking back toward them, his arm out, finger pointing across the river. "Come to the cemetery with me. There are the dead from the coulee. You will make them resurrect and I will believe in your God."

He walked quickly away and the women began to whisper, shaking their heads. To recapture their attention, Riel launched into his version of the sacrament of penance.

"Come to each woman here, Lord," he said. "Live in the very centre of their souls, take possession of their beings so they may receive from You the power to forgive the sins of those who confess to them." He looked at them with expectation and they turned to each other reluctantly, murmuring their confessions.

The sun was sinking behind the trees, and one last ray penetrated a bank of orange cloud. Josette was hurrying up the trail from the ferry, a look of distress on her face. Riel had never been so grateful to see his Mary Magdalene. Here was the messenger he'd been promised. But when she arrived in the clearing, she ignored him and stared around at the women with hopeful expectation.

"Have you seen Cleophile?" she asked one of them. "Someone in Batoche said she was here with you."

Someone else was coming up the trail. An Indian on a horse. Riel breathed out in relief. It was Mad Bull, one of White Cap's men, come back from Battleford. He handed a letter to Riel, who was aware of Josette's reproving stare as he unfolded it. He tried to keep his features solemn, but as he read the letter and its damning contents, he could not help but let his devastation show.

Marguerite put her hand on his arm. "What is it?"

Riel re-read the letter, gutted. God had promised him. *Poundmaker* had promised him. "It's . . . from one of my men riding south with Poundmaker's band." A shadow fell over him and Riel glanced up, but it was only a hawk swinging over the window of sky above the clearing. "He will not let his warriors leave the women and children without protection. They are travelling south as a band and won't be here for another week. He delays on purpose."

"He wants to save his people." Josette was now regarding him with outright defiance and an appraising curiosity, as if she were seeing him for the first time. Why did he still need this impossible woman? Because his Magdalene knew better than anyone how important it was to have Poundmaker here. His wife would not like it, but Josette was the miracle he had been waiting for.

He turned, raising his voice. "Josette's arrival is a sign. She will go to the United States with a letter. Fifteen thousand will ride to save us from the *Anglais* horde." He lifted his arms. "Spirit of God, open the route I need to send Josette south. Guide her there with Your hand."

Josette gathered her skirts and walked purposefully up the trail where Godon and Fleury had just disappeared.

Riel went after her and grabbed her arm. "Would you desert me too—"

She turned quickly and cut him off. "I must find my daughter."

Riel released her and looked with desperation across the river. "Let the United States protect us spontaneously," he whispered, "through an act of Your Holy Providence." He was weary and suddenly famished. Despite four days of fasting, God had brought nothing but bad news. And he saw something stupendous coming: a great blow. He closed his eyes to the fading light and prayed.

Let us be ready.

discovery

AT MIDNIGHT, JOSETTE left her three children asleep in a dugout on the riverbank. Behind a diffuse screen of cloud, the Leaves-Appear Moon shed ghostly light upon the water. She had been kept awake, sure that Alexandre was out there, taking advantage of Cleophile. When she had discovered the two of them in the hay loft last week, he had claimed to be courting Mary-Jane Ouellette, yet Josette could see Mary-Jane at one of the fires, helping Marguerite Riel with her little son, Jean, who was up and fretting with a chest cold.

Scouts had come in with news that the English army was only eight miles to the south and would arrive at dawn. But the Métis campfires still burned and Baptiste Arcand played his fiddle for a few men who had been drinking and dancing with feverish bravado, as they had in the old days before a buffalo hunt. Some women were occupied with melting down tins and pots for ammunition at a large kettle. On the west bank, the fires of Lean Crow's band flickered, their war drums beating out a steady rhythm.

A cool wind had come up and blew patterns of shadow across the surface of the river. Josette put her back to it and went quickly up the trail, meaning to act on her suspicions—catch Cleophile and Alexandre in the act. Earlier, Riel had allowed two steers to be killed and the Métis had eaten well. The smell of roasting meat must have carried a mile in every direction. If anyone would be drawn to camp for a meal, it would have been Cleophile, who had bitterly complained during the fast.

Near the cemetery, a few young men were taking the hobbles off the dairy cows. Josette found Mimoux and passed a hand along her wide flank. The cow seemed content in the company of those of her kind, trotting off happily when the boys switched at their backsides to herd them north.

The moon revealed itself and poured light on the meadow. Josette whispered a prayer to it. "*Nohkô*, lead me to my daughter."

Napoleon Arcand had been following behind the cows with a shovel. When she asked if he'd seen Cleophile and Alexandre, he shook his head and continued with the task of scooping manure.

Only a day had passed since her daughter had confessed to Moulin. Initially, Josette had blamed herself for neglecting Cleophile, but then she reasoned what must have happened during that confession. Her daughter had been desperate to share with someone that Alexandre had been messing around with her. Out of shame, she had been unable to admit it, and Moulin, in his usual manner, had tried to get it out of her. Cleophile, pressured to reveal *something*, had panicked and told him what he would already have suspected: she had felt Josette's distraction the past few months—helping Riel and Jackson—as profound neglect. A sin. Despite the soundness of this explanation, the priest's admonition that God had raised up evil against her out of her own house lingered like a curse.

What he had said about Riel spending two years in an insane asylum was too specific to be vindictive spite. She had been right: Riel was *kiskwesew*. Did Gabriel know that their leader had been so deranged that the only safe place for him had been an institution? Somehow, she feared that he did.

Dew was on the prairie grass, wetting the hem of Josette's skirts as she went up the sloping meadow toward the church. Her mind ranged to the first moment when she sensed something might be wrong with her daughter. Had it been before Riel arrived in the South Branch, or after?

She followed one of the cow trails that criss-crossed the bush behind the church and rectory, and soon passed lanterns flashing between the trees, where men were at work fortifying the rifle pits. The south meadow between the church and the village was full of tents, the canvas peaks like the backs of white pelicans fishing on the river in spring. Men were still up, smoking and talking around a few small fires.

When Josette passed through the village of Batoche, she paused in front of Letendre's house, where she knew the council was meeting. She would have liked to know if Gabriel was there or down with his scouts, watching the *Anglais* army. Other men might eventually sleep tonight, but he would not. Why did she continue to think of him, worried that he was tired or in pain?

She went up the stairs of Boyer's house. Riel's chapel on the second floor was deserted. Moonlight shone through a window, flooding the altar with light. The image of Saint Bernadette had fallen to the side and she straightened it, noticing as she did that the letter from Bishop Bourget had been removed. With the English army so close to Batoche, Riel would not be without his mentor's blessing.

When she turned to leave, she heard a bump from the room at the end of the hall, where Boyer and his wife had slept before deserting last week. Josette turned her head to listen. Another bump and the murmur of a male voice. She almost ran toward the door, sure that she had caught them in the act, and pulled it open. Cleophile was kneeling, facing away from her. The man she thought to be Alexandre lay on the bed, his pants down around his ankles and his head back, face hidden behind a clutched blanket.

Josette gave a cry and stepped into the room. "Alexandre—Cleophile." Her daughter on the floor, arms now flung over her head. She would not turn. The man on the bed sat straight up, pulling at his pants.

Josette stood there a long moment. It was not Alexandre, or any other boy in the village.

It was Norbert.

he hears god

AT TWO IN THE MORNING, Father Moulin tiptoed down the stairs of the rectory, a rosary still in his hands. He had used it many times in the last few hours, and the night was far from over. The priests and nuns were imprisoned here like animals, with hardly a wink of sleep between them. He hesitated, listening to the nuns' muffled prayers in the upstairs chapel.

Hail Mary, full of grace, the Lord is with thee.

The kitchen and front hall were thankfully empty of half-breed women who had visited after dark, sneaking in with a jar of milk, or a stolen piece of beef. After they had stopped coming, the priests heard the impossible scrapings of a fiddle and hesitant laughter from the riverbank camp. He and Father Fourmond had crept like thieves to look over the bluff, amazed to find campfires still burning. Men dancing, women hovering over a cauldron, and the awful black stench of melting tin and lead. All of it to the ominous noise of drumming from *les sauvages* across the river. From their hiding place, Moulin and Fourmond had looked at each other. Had these people not heard the news?

After weeks of anticipation and waiting, the *Anglais* army marched one thousand-strong upon Batoche.

The priests had returned to the rectory, hoping for a few hours of rest, when Moulin had woken to find Cleophile Lavoie standing at the foot of his bed. He had sat up so fast, his head whirled. Why had she come in, crouched over and hardly breathing, like a wounded rabbit in the bush? His exclamation of surprise had brought the nuns and priests. They had found nothing physically wrong with the girl, but despite their questions, she refused to speak. It was as if she had witnessed a great calamity and remained haunted by it. She steadfastly refused to leave, and was soothed only when the nuns had invited her to pray the rosary. Moulin had just left them in the second-floor chapel.

He opened the door and sniffed at the air. No more drumming from across the river or frantic fiddling from the half-breed camp. Only the meadow and long shadows of trees cast by a moon, almost to full. Closing the door, he bent his head.

I pray not that thou shouldest take them out of the world, but that thou shouldest keep them from evil.

He wove the rosary around his fingers and thought back to Cleophile's confession. Was it only yesterday? She had been visibly upset, but when Moulin encouraged her to share her sins, she had admitted guilt at scorning her mother for spending too much time in St. Laurent with Riel and William Jackson.

Josette should have come with the women tonight, begging forgiveness for the sin of neglecting her daughter. The priests had remained steadfast in their promise to refuse sacraments to the families of those who took up arms. But when the women had arrived with food, Moulin, Fourmond, and Vegreville had agreed to unburden them in exchange for some news. They listened patiently to their rushed confessions, each one merging with the next. "I fear the soldiers will burn my house . . . My children are sick, hungry . . . We are doomed."

Charlotte Gervais had been there with a *bibi* in a beaded cradleboard upon her back. She begged them to pray for her husband, who they learned was in Poundmaker's camp near Duck Lake. "He will hang if the English catch him," she cried. "How will I feed our children?"

"I am surprised to find you here," Moulin had said to her. "We saw you today across the river, accepting the body of Christ from Riel."

Her mouth dropped open in surprise and Moulin laughed. "Do you not think we can see his blasphemous outdoor chapel from here? Even in the midst of hell, one must keep track of the devil."

"You will not speak of him in such a manner," Charlotte said. "He is guided by the Spirit of God. The council has voted that God will use a miracle to save us."

Moulin had regarded her with compassion, and, because there was no longer reason to keep it from them, he said, "*Ma p'tite*, what kind of man tables a motion to his governing council asking them to vote on a miracle from God? A crazy one! Your leader has spent two years in an insane asylum—he endangers your people." Of course, she and the other women ran, as if they had just discovered that he and the priests carried the pox. The poor Métis were so easily led, so easily overcome. But rumours that Poundmaker was on the trail worried him. In a matter of hours, there would be a clash of titans here, and the priests and nuns caught in the crossfire. The man commanding *les Anglais* was a British gentleman. He would immediately recognize the white steeple of the church, yet the Indians could not be trusted.

Moulin chewed at a ragged thumbnail. Desperate for some contemplative time of his own, he went into the kitchen to put on a pot of water for tea, when the door was flung open and he turned to find Josette, long black hair flying around her head.

Her eyes were wide with accusation. "Where is she?"

Moulin stared at her angrily. "She is safe—with the nuns." Josette bolted for the stairs and he managed to get there before she did, blocking her way. "She is praying."

"Let me see her." Her hands were surprisingly strong on his arm, her thin body trembling with emotion. She repeated over and over, "Let me see her," and when he finally shoved her backward, "How could you let this happen?"

"*What* has happened?" he asked, frustrated at the mystery. "She will not speak."

Her eyes widened. "You don't know!"

"I know enough," he said. "You are a neglectful mother . . ."

But she had already run out the door.

god of war

RIEL'S COUNCIL HAD gathered in Letendre's house. Charles Trottier squatted on his haunches near the door. David Tourond and Philip Gariépy leaned against the wall, looking grimly at the other eight Exovedes seated around the table, their faces thrown into shadow by a single candle, the only light in the room.

Gabriel straddled an empty rum keg that had been in Letendre's storehouse, watching Riel at the head of the table. Moise Ouellette had just asked a question that should have been simple enough to answer: "When is Poundmaker coming in?"

But Riel was taking his time about it. He remained silent, the stem of his pipe—long gone out—held between his teeth. Gabriel waited to hear the explanation that he and Riel had agreed upon earlier. When Riel had visited him privately with the letter from Poundmaker, Gabriel had fought a rising sense of doom. He knew the chief. If he hadn't come in by now, he never would. But to avoid more Métis desertions, he and Riel had decided to feed the rumours that Poundmaker was in Duck Lake.

Riel set his pipe aside and looked at it a moment. "I cannot lie to my Exovedes," he said. "Poundmaker will not be here for another week."

Philippe Garnot glanced up at Riel, his pen hovering over the minute book.

Moise threw up his hands. "Then we cannot win."

A sudden pain streaked across the top of Gabriel's head. This was not the time for Riel to suffer an attack of conscience. He had just destroyed his councillors' hopes that God would work His miracle by bringing the Indians. And on the eve of the battle of their lives. Middleton didn't know the truth, and Gabriel wanted to use his fear of a Custer situation to his best advantage. Poundmaker's presence would be useful as both encouragement and threat, even seven days' ride from Batoche.

Maxime Lépine said quietly, but with an undercurrent of intimidation, "Let the women and children go."

"Our men will not stay," Gabriel said, "if their families aren't here."

Lépine slapped his palm on the table in outrage. "We endanger women and children so their men can fight and die?"

Riel cleared his throat, silencing the room. "God will punish Middleton for attacking us here on sacred land—attacking us on the Lord's day of rest."

Lépine and Ouellette exchanged looks. They still could not accept that Riel's church had honoured the old testament and declared Saturday their Sabbath.

"If your brother Ambroise had come from Red River the men would not desert," Riel said. "If *my* brothers and André Nault had been here too." His Bible and diary were stacked on the table in front of him. He had been carrying them everywhere the past few days. Placing one hand on his Bible, he looked with purpose into the eyes of each man. "God has told me that Gabriel will hold off Middleton for three days," he said. "When the army invades, we will send a scout north to find Poundmaker's camp. If the Rattler Society hears we are winning, they will convince him to ride south."

Heads turned to Gabriel, who tried not to appear stunned. *Hold off Middleton for three days?* Riel had frustrated him one too many times. And it was impossible. They would be lucky to hold off Middleton for a day, at best.

The men were falling for it, though. Renewed hope shone in their eyes. They would believe anything Riel said if it came from God. Of course Poundmaker *would* consider it a decisive victory if they held the English off that long. Although Gabriel had allowed a messenger through to give Middleton a report of Poundmaker's victory at Cut Knife, the telegraph wires between Battleford and Clark's Crossing were still down. Despite English efforts to repair them, Middleton could not get news. But if rumours were spread that the chief and his warriors were in Duck Lake, only a few hours' ride west, the old general might make tactical errors that Gabriel could use against him.

The Indian commissioner, one of Macdonald's men in the Territories, had issued a proclamation ordering, "all good Indians to stay quietly on their reserves." Middleton had sent soldiers out to put up notices on trees along the Humboldt Trail. Gabriel's scouts had torn them down, but it was proof the old general still feared losing his hair.

Gabriel shifted restlessly on the keg. His plan of defence for Batoche was complicated, and he only had so many men to make it work. He was anxious to get out there and direct their efforts against the army's attack at dawn.

After making his proclamation, Riel had lapsed into a reflective mood and Garnot called the meeting to a close. The council members were filing out, claiming their rifles at the door. Gabriel picked up his own gun, but Riel rose from his chair.

"The Spirit that is good enough to guide me has said, 'By dint of hard blows strive to defend every inch of ground.'"

Gabriel looked around. "Tell your Spirit I need more men—ammunition." He regretted his cutting tone, but Riel had put him on the spot.

Riel's dark eyes were intent, his expression guarded. "How many do we have?"

"Two hundred and fifty. At most."

"Soon you will have thousands of Cree warriors. Until then, how do we hold off Middleton?"

"Ravages," Gabriel said without hesitation. "Strike hard and kill enough men that he does the same thing he did in Tourond's Coulee—retreat to avoid losing more."

Riel shook his head. "I have fears you will expose yourself too much in battle, and there are not enough rifle pits."

For a man who claimed they would be saved by divine intervention, Riel was not leaving anything to chance. "The men have been digging for weeks." Gabriel shouldered his rifle as a signal that he must go, but Riel opened his diary; he ripped a piece of paper from the binding and offered him a pencil.

"Show me how you will defend the City of God."

Gabriel's head was throbbing and he did not have time for this, but he took the pencil in his hand, the feel of it strange to him. He could speak six languages, yet had never felt the need to read or write and had only used a pen when his mark was needed on a petition to the government.

With ham-fisted strokes, he drew a few stick buildings at the top of the paper to represent the village, a large circle for the meadow just south of it, a thick stand of trees and bush separating that and the church and rectory. He managed a curved pass of river and bluff to the left, then the open plateau that was Mission Ridge, slightly behind and between the bluff and the rectory.

"The army will march along the trail," he said, making two X marks for the houses on Caron's and Gareau's river lots, and a line to show the low crest of hill where the Humboldt Trail came up from the south. Gabriel scratched his beard and studied the map, calculating yardage and shooting range. "Roughly half a mile from the church and rectory to the hill . . . same distance back to the village. We'll use these houses in the middle as our main defence."

Riel was surveying the map with a skeptical expression. "Middleton will shell the pits."

"I saw how he positioned his cannon at Tourond's Coulee. They must be on level ground. He will have to place them here." He pointed to the low hill. "My best shots with Winchester repeaters are across the river to kill the *Rababou* man. Then we capture the gun."

Riel did not seem convinced. "If it was a month later, the leaves would be on the trees."

"It is *not* a month later. It is not a lot of things we want." Gabriel added a few jagged crosses to show the cemetery on the bluff by the river. *The thought of Isidore, buried under a mound of dirt.* He forced the image out of his mind and made slash marks for the gradual slope from the cemetery to the church and rectory, circles for every small draw and gully. "We've dug pits in here," he said, indicating the trees lining the meadow and around the church and rectory. "The small aspen and willow underbrush will hide our rifle pits from Middleton's gunners."

"He won't split his force and come up the west bank?"

"Not after Tourond's Coulee." Gabriel stood back and regarded the snake line of river. It was their strength *and* their weakness. When he'd first seen the Hudson's Bay boat, he thought it would follow Middleton as a supply ship. Scouts had shadowed the army on its march north from Tourond's Coulee. Soldiers were sent to loot and burn Métis houses. When Gabriel asked about his farm, the scouts were reluctant to share that soldiers had hauled the pool table from his saloon and dragged everything, including the kitchen table and mattresses, out of his house before torching it. He had still not told Madeleine they had lost everything. He had been more concerned to hear that his barn had been torn down and the boards nailed along the railings of the ship. Middleton had armed the *Northcote* for war.

"While the old man comes up from the south," he said to Riel, "he'll send the damn Hudson's Bay boat to attack us from the river. If they surround us, it's all over."

A frank look of astonishment spread across Riel's features. "The riverbank camp won't be safe. We'll put the women and children in the village."

"The only place for the boat to moor is at the crossing. Middleton means to take the village. Our families will be safest on the bank." He made an X at Fisher's Crossing. "I'll have most of my men hidden in the bush here." With a decisive stroke, he drew a line across the river. "We'll move the ferry cables south—stop it dead as it sails in to dock. Kill the helmsman, capture the supplies, and take more prisoners."

"If Middleton sets up his guns on the hill, he'll overwhelm the few you have here," Riel said, indicating the pits Gabriel had drawn in the bush along the ridge. "And get to the village."

This worried Gabriel, too, but capturing the *Northcote* was his priority. Seize it and they might have a chance. "We'll come up after we've taken the boat." He turned the paper and dotted the bush and trees surrounding the ridge. "Fend off Middleton from here."

Riel surveyed him with a dubious look. "What of the priests and nuns?"

"You said yourself Middleton is a gentleman. He will see the cross and steeple." Gabriel did not have many strategies in his pocket, but he was counting on the priests and nuns remaining in the rectory. If Riel wanted his prophecy, he would not rob him of this advantage.

"*Non*," Riel said finally. "I won't endanger them."

"Middleton will not shoot. They are safe."

Riel glanced up at him and must have decided not to test him further, for he closed his eyes briefly, muttering a prayer. In a moment, he said, "How do you know Middleton won't come from the east? Attack the village?"

Gabriel was anxious to get away but grudgingly drew a wide circle to show the Jolie Prairie. "My scouts will watch them advance. An army that size can't move without us knowing." He pencilled in a few crude arcs to represent a line of bush separating the Jolie Prairie from the village, his frustrated strokes almost tearing through the paper. "We've dug pits all along here."

"Our cattle and horses," Riel said. "We can't lose them."

"We've already moved them farther north." Gabriel's patience was at its limit. "In Pierre Parenteau's back fields. Posted guards." He threw down the pencil. "If I don't get out there and organize the men, this will mean nothing." When he turned at the door, Riel had lowered himself into a chair. In the guttering flame of the candle, his face was that of an old man, his hair uncombed, a far-off look in his eyes, as though he were receiving another missive from the Spirit that guided him.

Gabriel faltered. Over the past year, Riel had more than once shaken his confidence, had been too reliant on God. But this man, on the eve of the attack, had shown he was willing to fight to the death for their lands.

"You should not be here alone."

Riel looked up, as though surprised to still find him there. "I wish to write in my diary and pray."

"What will you do if we can't hold off the English—if Poundmaker doesn't come?"

Riel's eyes were now fixed on the candle. When he did not answer, Gabriel went out, closing the door behind him. He would fight forever. But he feared what Riel might do if God abandoned him.

may god so
keep me

JOSETTE RAN THROUGH the small aspen behind the church, retracing her steps in a kind of madness, through the tents in the south meadow camp, through the village. It was still dark, but people were up, women starting fires to boil tea, men saddling horses or cleaning their guns.

A light flickered in the bush ringing the Jolie Prairie and she moved toward it, hand on the skinning knife in her pocket. The cool night wind on her face, tears there too. Norbert would be in that pit, his back turned, and she would leap down on him, thrust her knife in him again and again, not stopping until they dragged her away.

It seemed like a lifetime had passed since she had come across her husband and daughter in Boyer's room. The unbearable image. She had stopped dead in the doorway, hardly noticing when Cleophile sprang to her feet and rushed past her down the hall. Norbert had been unable to move, and then rose from the bed, fumbling with his pants. He looked at her with a horrified expression, and she launched herself at him, almost flying across the room.

"I'll kill you—*kill* you."

He let her beat him on the chest for a moment then threw her off and strode out, swearing. Josette had sunk to her knees on the floor, in the same place Cleophile had just been. Staring at the wall, she had pulled her hair out of the knot at the back of her head until it fell around her face, and she knelt there, hardly breathing. She knew that her daughter would seek the church, but Moulin had refused to let her up the stairs. Refused.

Josette approached the light on the prairie to find three men in the pit, their labour aided only by the dim radiance of a coal oil lamp and the distant rising sun. Slowly she edged the knife from her pocket, but *he* was not among them.

"Where is my husband?" she said into the dark, unable to speak his name.

Philippe Vandal leaned on his shovel to look up at her. "He just rode out—took the trail south."

Her mind worked desperately. *Find a horse, go after him.* But she had missed her chance. He was most likely on his way to Red River, where he still had relations. A place to hide and wait her out.

She stumbled out onto the Jolie Prairie, and Vandal called after her, "Josette—have you heard God speak to Riel?"

Hands over her ears, hair blowing around her shoulders. The men dug rifle pits for Riel's war with questions on their lips, in their hearts. The sun, still hidden, had tinged the clouds pink, a shelf of sky above it, grey as river ice. She took longer and longer strides toward it, running far enough to drop on her knees, her mouth open in a silent scream.

She coiled her fingers in the bent and broken stalks of last year's grass, the damp rot under her nails. Each warning from the past year rose before her, signs she should have recognized but ignored: Cleophile running from the summer kitchen last summer, after Norbert had gone in there. Cleophile on the bank of the river the night before the Duck Lake battle, afire with her poisonous secret.

You are going to save him? And perhaps the most damning: *Why don't you just let him die?*

The sun was rising and spilling light over the prairie grass, like a vast sea falling off the horizon. Only the far-off sound of digging and the rasping call of a burrowing owl, his body small and dark, as he swept down over the prairie, and the death cry of a mouse when he found his mark.

She closed her eyes. Riel's face swam into her mind, how he had looked yesterday in the outdoor chapel, offering the women Christ's body and His blood. The women and Vandal just now, believing him a prophet sent by God. If Spinoza were here in Batoche, he would not follow Riel. Father Dubois had told her that Spinoza believed God was like the Great Spirit and did not require a prophet or priest for explanation. She thought of her beloved book, hidden for so long in the birch grove above the river and now under some clothes in their dugout on the riverbank. There had been tears in Father Dubois' eyes when he gave it to her.

"I cannot take Spinoza's *Ethics* where I am going," he had said. "They will think I am a heretic." He had recovered himself and smiled as he liked to do, teasing, but his gaze hard, with a glint of threat that had always confused her. "You are a heretic aren't you, Josette? A natural-born unbeliever." He took up his pen and opened the book, reaching out as he did and drawing her tight to his side. "I like to think I have put you back in God's grace." He had inscribed this in the book, his fingers on her arm narrowing with each word that went on the page.

It began to rain, and she stared at the drops that freckled her apron and the back of her hands. Her anger had ebbed to a terrible vacant impassiveness, like the dimming of light.

"Josette."

She turned her head, beyond caring who had found her in such a state. Sitting on their horses on the Carlton Trail were Gabriel and Pierre Gariépy. Pierre rode off toward the village, and Josette held Gabriel's eyes for a moment then looked away across the Jolie Prairie, seeing nothing.

He got off his horse and came toward her. "What is it?"

In halting words, she told him what Norbert had done. "I should have killed him at New Year's," Gabriel said. "We must go. Middleton's men are on the march."

When she didn't move, he leaned down to look into her face. "Norbert is gone," he said. "You and the children are safe."

that dark one

⁓

AS DAWN BROKE, Marguerite Riel emerged from a dugout on the riverbank with her daughter on one hip and Jean at her skirts. Her son had kept her up with a cough in his chest, and she shivered, exhausted, drawing a blanket around her and Angélique's frail body. Marguerite was troubled by the progression of her own cough. Lying on the ground the last ten days had made it worse, with damp coming up through the buffalo hide she had been given by the other women to keep it out.

Several fires would normally be burning at this time of day for cooking and warmth, but Gabriel had forbidden it. Most of the men had already left camp and were hidden in the bush along both banks, waiting for the Hudson's Bay steamship. Scouts had ridden in before first light to report that Middleton and his troops were only miles from the village. The camp was in a panic, the women muttering anxiously at the thought of their men out there with an army coming. And complaining that they did not want to go up the trail when Gabriel had insisted they remain in the riverbank camp. But Riel had just asked every woman and child to meet him on Mission Ridge to hear a message from the Spirit of God.

Marguerite followed them on the trail to the bluff, their shoulders draped in blankets against the chill morning air. She carried Angélique and held Jean's hand to hurry him along, praying that he would not beg for her to pick him up. She was pregnant, three months by her calculations. Louis had not guessed and she would tell him only when all of this was over. Jean stopped dead on the trail, snivelling. As she pulled her sleeve over her wrist to wipe his runny nose, she could hear other women coming up behind her. The trail turned at that point and they had not seen her yet.

She recognized Henriette Parenteau's voice, alive with indignation. "Why go up there just to come back down again? My knees."

Charlotte Gervais answered her. "You heard what Père Moulin said—he is *fou*, crazy."

Another woman joined in. "Why must we do what a crazy man says?"

They were excited now, speaking over each other.

"Your husband and son are in the fight. Who knows what Riel will do if we don't obey."

"I knew all along he was crazy. But two years in an insane asylum? He should be ashamed to hide it from us!"

"You would not tell someone you were in a crazy house."

"I would not be put in one!"

Marguerite shifted Angélique on her hip and urged her son forward with a frantic whisper, "*Vite vite*," but he pulled at her apron, demanding to be carried, too. She looked up in defeat as the women rounded the corner. They slowed at the sight of her, mortified expressions on their faces.

When she had met him four years ago, Louis admitted that he had suffered from brain fever after the Red River troubles, and had explained that his friends and family insisted he go to a sanatorium. She had not asked about it further, presuming it simply to be a place where he had recovered his health. Why hadn't he told her it was an insane asylum? For the same reason he had not told women like Henriette

Parenteau, who filed past her on the trail with a look of fearful apprehension.

Thankfully, Gabriel's sister Isabelle Ouellette came along with her girls, and La Rose scooped up Jean in her arms. Marguerite followed along behind, her head down. *Insanity*. She should have felt outrage, but her heart was numb with shock and unexpected relief. Finally she had an explanation for her husband's melancholy and tortured intensity.

When she arrived at the top of the bluff, Louis was standing on the ridge with his arms out. As the women and children gathered around, he said, "The Dominion army rides against us today. They will fail, for God is on our side—the side of right. They do not know that reinforcements ride to us from the north and will arrive within the hour. God will use our ferry cable to overturn Middleton's steamboat. We will gain possession of all the weapons and ammunition."

Marguerite pushed forward to see him better. What reinforcements? He had been up late praying for the Indians to come. He began to name the men and their families who had deserted in the night. "As the *Anglais* army comes to the City of God, they abandon you!" he said. "I beg you to consider your own blood here. You do not want your husband to end up like Charles Nolin, chained to the wall of a police dungeon in Prince Albert. That is the fate of those who desert the sacred cause."

Louis' eyes were dark with passion, but when he looked her way she could see his shoulders relax. The mere sight of her appeased him. She thought of the women in Sun River. They would be surprised to see that the girl they had judged as too plain for the great Riel, the small dark Marguerite, had grown into the only one who kept him from going insane. It was not Josette in his bed, holding him close when he awoke with the night terrors. Evelina Barnabé did not stand where he could see her and draw strength. His pampered French fiancée would never have survived sleepless nights in a tent on a riverbank, coughing blood into the sleeve of her dress.

The last of the women had come up and Louis raised his voice. "Here we are," he said. "Squarely arrived at the time God has marked in the order of things to come with all the signs that are to accompany it, just as we are told in the scriptures."

A child began to cry, and his mother bent to hush him. Late last night, Louis had not returned from a council meeting, and Marguerite had gone to find him at Letendre's kitchen table, furiously writing in his diary by the light of a candle. Thinking her still illiterate, ignorant, he made no effort to hide the entry from her, nor the pressed flower that he used to keep his place—the dried bit of lilac that Evelina had sent him to remember her by. Marguerite caught one phrase before he closed the diary.

Do not let England get the better of me.

Now, as the English army advanced, Louis sought her out over all the other women, who stood silently and seemed to gaze at him with reluctant admiration. Most or all of them had learned that he had been in an insane asylum, yet they were hypnotized by Louis' power, his vision.

"I am protected by God," her husband said. "But if I should be killed, know that I will be resurrected on the third day." He gestured in her direction. "My wife will be the one who will deliver the news of my resurrection to you, as Mary Magdalene did for Christ."

She hugged Angélique to her and managed a grateful smile, but the dried lilac came back to her, the way he had closed his diary on it to mark the page. Why do you need this token from another woman? She wanted to shout at him. Why did you not tell me?

Gabriel appeared on his horse over the bluff near the cemetery. "The English are on the trail," he yelled. "They're firing the houses along the river."

Blood drained from Louis' face. "How far?"

"Three miles."

Gabriel waved his arm. "The government boat is coming. Get to the dugouts."

Louis took Jean from La Rose's arms and headed for the trail. Marguerite ran to keep up, their daughter still on her hip. She watched her dear husband's back and then the top of his head disappear below the rise. He was no Christ. She was no Mary, but soon he would be finished with his mission here and she would have him back to herself. *Soon.*

the worst
possible place

SUN BROKE THROUGH the clouds, its first rays warming the riverbank. Madeleine huddled in their dugout, a handkerchief to her face in
fear of a coughing fit. The boat had not yet appeared around the bend
in the river, and the women were still quieting their children behind the
tent canvases or upturned carts.

The camp felt very exposed. Gabriel had assured her that it was the
only safe place for them, that the fight for the boat would be at the
crossing. Yet it had just occurred to her that soldiers might—as the ship
passed by—decide Métis fighters were hiding there instead of women
and children. Riel had promised that God would not allow the English
into Batoche, but Madeleine trusted more in her husband's efforts than
she did in the Saviour's.

"Get back," she said to Alexandre who had rested his elbow on the
cart outside their hole. He watched the river, opening and closing his
fingers, as if they itched for a gun. Madeleine would not let him sneak

away to join Gabriel again, as he had at Tourond's Coulee. She glanced around at Riel and his family in another hole nearby, and Josette in Isabelle Ouellette's dugout, arms around her three children. Madeleine's sharp eyes noticed that one was missing.

"Where is Cleophile?" she said to Alexandre. He had obviously heard her question, but did not respond. Madeleine asked if she was safe and he nodded, but his expression was so grave, she leaned out and grabbed his arm. "Why won't you tell me?"

With reluctance, he whispered in her ear that Gabriel had found Josette that morning on the Jolie Prairie. He had asked Alex not to tell anyone that Cleophile had been poorly used by her own father, and that she was in the rectory with the priests. Madeleine sat back on her heels, digesting this news, then looked back at the Ouellette's dugout. She could just see Josette's profile, afflicted, yet also resigned, her skin luminous as a saint's.

Alexandre had sighted the steamer and crawled in to join her. From between the cart wheels, Madeleine stared hard down the river. She had seen the *Northcote* pass many times on its way north to Prince Albert with Hudson's Bay cargo. But as it sailed around the south bend, she noticed that its decks and pilothouse had been fortified with an odd number of looted goods, including the pool table from Gabriel's saloon. She frowned at the sight of several mattresses lashed to the railing.

There was only the sound of birds in the trees as the ship sailed toward them, pulling two barges of supplies in its wake. It motored past the camp and angled in toward the crossing. The engine slowed as it drew closer to the ferry cables high on the banks and she held her breath, waiting for them to drop. But a sudden, piercing whistle came from the pilothouse, and a few Métis on the other side of the river started shooting. Soldiers came out on the deck and dove behind the mattresses, returning fire. Men in the pits on the west bank and those on the bluff above made the ship a target, and bullets whizzed over the dugouts. Madeleine exchanged a defeated glance with Alexandre. Gabriel's first plan of defence had failed.

She craned her neck to see him ride along the stony lower bank on their side of the river. He shouted for his men not to waste ammunition but could not be heard over the *Northcote*'s frantic whistle as it swung into the current again.

"You will not die before I do," she muttered, watching her husband gesture vigorously to his men. In the past few days, his head wound had begun to close, but these efforts would have it bleeding again. A few nights ago, he had come into their dugout and lay down next to her. She had expected him to fall into immediate sleep, but in a moment, he placed his hand on her shoulder.

"You are ill, *ma p'tite*," he had said. "Promise to tell me if you suffer."

When she had laughed bitterly, saying she did not have long to keep that promise, he broke down. He was in pain from his wound, spent, but she had closed her eyes, arms around his heaving shoulders, beyond caring if he wept out of guilt or grief.

A bullet flew past and hit the dirt above their dugout, and women screamed, shielding children with their bodies. The ferry cables were still strung too high across the river. Men operating them seemed to be pulling when they should let them go slack. The boat sailed underneath the cables, and Madeleine could hear Gabriel yelling to lower them, lower them, *lower* them. Finally one dropped and caught the smokestack, tearing it off. Flames immediately burst out of the wreckage strewn across the deck and the ship twisted until it faced backwards in the current, its engine now useless. Cheers erupted from the Métis and whoops of celebration from the Indians, but the steamer soon drifted around the north bend. Gabriel was shouting for the men to get to the church and rectory rifle pits, and Alexandre ran out of the dugout.

"You will not go to the fight," Madeleine called after him but was distracted by a fragment of prayer that floated to her on the wind. She stalked to Riel's dugout, finding him on his knees in the dirt with his wife and children, saying the rosary.

"You said God would not let *les Anglais* into Batoche," she cried, "and they are here!"

Riel frowned, opened his eyes. "Kneel," he said. "You will help Gabriel more with prayer."

Napoléon Nault appeared above them on the bluff. "The English are setting up their cannon," he shouted. "Stay down."

smoke and
mirrors

～

FATHER MOULIN PEERED out from behind the curtain at the front
window of the rectory. Heavy firing had come only a moment ago from
the river, but now it was quiet. Gun smoke settled in the basin like mist
or low-lying cloud, and he thought it looked almost beautiful. The
priests and nuns had listened to the Métis attacking the *Anglais* boat and
watched the prairie, anticipating an army approaching from the south.
At last they had come, red-coated soldiers moving into battle formation
on the small hill above Caron's house.

"Nous sommes sauvés," he said to Fathers Fourmond and Vegreville.
We are saved. Soldiers were unhitching horses from a gun carriage and
manoeuvring the cannon into position. Before Moulin had time to react, the echo drifted down, an officer shouting in English, "Common
shell, percussion fuse—load!"

A sudden explosion shook the earth. Two more blasts were followed
by the sound of wood splintering and glass breaking. Caron's and

Gareau's houses were hit, four hundred yards away. Half-breed fighters streamed out and ran back toward the church. Powder in the cannon balls ignited and the houses burst into flames. Some rebel sharpshooters on the opposite bank of the river were targeting the artillery men, who dropped back as a smaller gun was rolled up, its menacing barrels aimed straight at the church.

"*Alors*," exclaimed Moulin. "What evil is this?"

A man with elaborate moustaches had settled himself behind the gun and cranked its handle, sending quick fire across the river. After silencing the half-breed snipers, he swung it around and raked the entire meadow, tearing up bushes on either side of the church.

Father Vegreville opened the door, grabbed Riel's white flag and frantically waved it. The priests rushed out behind him, only to face a line of soldiers that had risen out of a small gully behind the burning houses. At the sight of guns pointed directly at them, Moulin crossed himself, praying that their black cassocks were obvious against the white outer walls of the rectory. But the machine gun went off again, bullets ripping into the paneling above their heads. Moulin ducked and covered his head as slivers of wood rained down on them.

A shout had come from the direction of the hill, and when he dared look up, an officer on a black horse had appeared, yelling for a ceasefire. From his fine dress uniform and bearing, Moulin presumed that it was General Middleton. A few of his men rallied around him and the group rode warily toward the rectory, watching the surrounding bushes. The nuns had come out, their heads down, blinking against the sun. Moulin was keenly aware of Métis running through the trees and jumping into the rifle pits to the west of the rectory. Would Dumont respect the white flag?

General Middleton kept his head turned to the river as his horse approached. He took an unlit cigar from between his teeth, and said to one of his officers, "Get some men down there, Boulton—find the damn *ship*!"

When they had brought their horses to the rectory steps, the general removed his Astrakhan fur cap and introduced himself as commander of the Dominion Army. Moulin cringed to hear both the English language and a cultured British accent. Although stout and long in the tooth, the general cut an impressive figure. Drooping moustaches as white as his hair had been masterfully curved at each end to draw attention away from a weak chin. His bloated *Anglais* face was animated by indignant blue eyes.

Father Vegreville spoke in halting English. "You are at Batoche. The half-breeds . . . they are in rifle pits all around."

General Middleton looked off to the river again and then away. He took a matchbook from his breast pocket and struck one, lighting his cigar.

"Riel said you will . . ." Moulin broke off, trying to remember his English. "He said you will let your men at these nuns."

Middleton took a deep draw on his cigar and exhaled a pall of smoke. "Outrageous," he said with a cough.

"Monsieur, my church is at the middle of your fight," said Moulin. "It was built only a few years ago. Save it and bring your protection."

"If you are not with the rebels," the general said irritably, "of course you shall have it." He glanced over his shoulder to the big guns on the hill. "How many men does Riel have fighting here?"

"*Quoi?* Not as much as he would like you to think. Many run away. Two hundred or less will fight. Those are stubborn mules," Moulin said with a shrug. "And good shots, eh?"

Instead of answering directly, Middleton tilted his cigar and studied the lighted end, as if he were at home in his study. Another puff and he levelled his gaze at Moulin. "Guns and ammunition?"

"The women melt kettles for bullets," volunteered Vegreville. "They are poor people but proud. They will put on a show—make you think their numbers are many."

"Do not be fooled," said Moulin. "They are *enfants*, like children— peace-loving and fight under protest."

The general told them that his doctors would commandeer the church as a field hospital, claim it as neutral ground on the battlefield. He managed a gentlemanly bow from the saddle and before turning his horse, regarded the priests with a long, curious look. "Why on earth are you still here if you knew we would attack the village?"

The priests and nuns looked at each other. How to say it in English? "Riel holds us against our will," said Moulin. "*C'est impossible* to escape. We fear *les sauvages* on the trail. They do not love the church as much as the half-breeds."

Middleton had gone white as death. "We posted proclamations," he said, "ordering Indians quietly to their reserves."

"Gabriel sent men to tear them down," Fourmond said. "The women say Riel waits for Chief Poundmaker and his Cree *guerriers*. His people are under command of the Rattler Society—"

The general's hand dropped to the sabre hilt at his waist. "Poundmaker? Do you know where he is?"

"A few hours' ride—at Duck Lake," Father Fourmond offered helpfully. "He waits to hear how well you do this day."

"We shall do very well indeed," Middleton said archly, but the news appeared to have unsettled him. "These rebels have not been on the business end of a Gatling gun!" He wheeled his horse and spurred it back toward the hill.

Moulin thought he did not look as tall in the saddle as he had when riding down.

ravages

IN A RIFLE PIT MIDPOINT between the church and Mission Ridge, Gabriel centred his gun sight on General Middleton's broad back as he rode away from the rectory.

"The priests said something to work him up," he said to Salomon Boucher, who knelt beside him.

Boucher spit in the dirt. "He is angry we attacked his steamship."

"Take a shot at him," said Michel Dumas, at his other elbow. "Finish it here."

Even if Middleton were in range, Gabriel could not be made to pull the trigger while Father Moulin still stood on the rectory porch with Riel's white flag in his hand. As Middleton's group went up the hill, two wagons came down, teamsters whipping and yelling at their mules. Gabriel watched as the wagons careened to a stop in front of the church and soldiers spilled out to unload stretchers and supplies.

"This is good," he said. "*Le général* plans for us to hit some of his men."

He repositioned his rifle in an opening in the log barricade along the front of the pit and sighted Moulin. The priest strutted like a rooster now that *les Anglais* were setting up a field hospital in his church. His eyes not leaving the priest's face, Gabriel swore to himself that he would find Moulin later, even if he had to steal into the church and kill these soldiers to do it.

He tried to get his breath under control, still winded after his pursuit of the steamship. The Métis had disabled the *Northcote*, but its ammunition and supplies were still protected by soldiers on board. Gabriel had come up the bank to find that the general had already advanced a troop of his men past the cemetery. Under cover of cannon and *Rababou* fire, a line of redcoats had swarmed up the slope and thrown themselves into a small draw at the edge of Mission Ridge, not two hundred yards to the southwest. Too close. Too soon.

When the priests had finally disappeared into the rectory and closed the door, Gabriel said to Boucher, "Go up the river and check on the government ship. Make certain it still founders—and that White Cap's Sioux come back." He had last seen them galloping along the bank after the boat, and was afraid they would not return. He needed every man.

When Boucher ran for his horse, Gabriel glanced down at his right hand. An *Anglais* bullet had bloodied his knuckles during the steamship fight, but had not penetrated deep enough to affect his aim. He had not had time to take medicine tea since last night, and now his head roared with a pain that sparked sudden flashes of light in his eyes.

A fine powdered ash still fell from the sky, all that was left of Caron's and Gareau's houses, which had almost burned to the ground. Gabriel pulled out his field glasses to scan the small draw near the ridge. The redcoats were out of the range of Métis guns, but they were not taking a chance by showing their heads. He moved the glasses back to the hill, where an officer was yelling an order for gunners to load more shells into the cannons. He adjusted his focus on the man who operated the *Rababou* gun, leaning over the long barrels in his blue uniform, to examine some part of its mechanism.

Gabriel blinked to clear his vision. "We'll get down the riverbank," he said to Dumas, "come up close to the *Rababou* gun and capture it."

The words had hardly left his mouth when both cannon went off together, the shells soaring over their heads into the trees and the meadow south of the village. *Le Rababou* began its rapid, stuttering attack to cover one of Middleton's officers, who rode down past the burning houses, his fine horse goose-stepping at tight rein. He yelled something in English to the soldiers lying in the draw. They stared at him for a moment and then, in a chaotic jumble, fixed long knives to the ends of their rifles. Shoulder to shoulder, they shuffled into line and angled forward. Gabriel levelled his gun, determined that the Métis would not be flanked or the women's riverbank dugouts discovered.

"This is where we do ravages," he said to the men in the surrounding pits and let out a war cry as the signal for them to fire in one continuous volley. The sound of so many guns going off at once was deafening. The redcoats dropped so quickly, Gabriel was sure they had all been killed, but when the *Rababou* man turned his barrel and aimed it in the direction of the pits, the soldiers cautiously raised themselves and advanced under its protective fire. Gabriel cursed. Still out of range. He would not misjudge distance again and waste their precious ammunition.

The powerful barrage of Métis weaponry had sent the *Anglais* cannon horses rearing in their limbers. Patrice Fleury's snipers across the river let loose some carefully aimed shots at Middleton's gunners, who trampled each other, leaving the guns unmanned.

Gabriel could hear an officer shout at them, "Goddamn, get back here, or I'll shoot you myself."

When the smoke cleared, one of the gunners lay on the ground, half his head blown away, the front of his uniform a mess of brains and blood. Gabriel's eyes had not left *le Rababou*, placed strategically between the abandoned cannon, the man behind it swinging the barrel, determined to stop the marksmen on the west bank. Redcoats had crept closer to the ridge, and Gabriel whistled again for the Métis to fire another volley. He wedged the stock of his rifle against his shoulder and—in an effort to replicate the devil gun's intensity—unloaded ten shots, hitting several soldiers, who fell back, screaming. Others went down on their stomachs in a panic and crawled along on elbows and knees, cowering under the blast. A few soldiers came out of the church with stretchers, and Gabriel whistled to hold fire while they picked up their wounded and ran back again.

Another deliberately placed shot echoed from one of Fleury's snipers across the river, and a second later, the *Rababou* gunman grabbed his shoulder. Gabriel ran with Dumas to a rifle pit farther east in the trees. After throwing himself in, he held his breath, hoping his prayers had been answered. When he cautiously lifted his head to look, the man remained at the gun, turning the crank with one hand, spent cartridges flying from the central shaft like pellets of hail.

"*Calisse*," Gabriel swore. Only a flesh wound.

He realized with a start that during the last barrage, another battalion of soldiers had stolen along the bluff near the cemetery and others had managed to find cover out of shooting distance in bushes to the left of the church. He whistled to his men to hold until they had a clear shot, but the troops did not advance further. Although his rifle pits denied the enemy a target, Gabriel did not like his position.

Just then, a large number of Sioux came in from the north, moving among the dense poplar and willow as if they were converging on a Blackfoot village, intent on stealing horses. And without warning, the impossible sight of Norbert Lavoie, who had arrived with Little Ghost and a few of Lean Crow's men. Why had he come back? Gabriel stared hard at Norbert, willing him to turn, then whistled, ordering his men to go up and shoot as they advanced. Norbert ran ahead, firing with the accuracy that Gabriel had seen him use years ago, during the buffalo hunts. Soon there was confusion down near the cemetery, with a few more redcoats hit and clutching at their wounds. Gabriel and Dumas threw themselves into a pit in the trees closer to the rectory. Norbert was only thirty yards away from them now, on one knee, quickly reloading his gun. Gabriel pushed a few more bullets into his own magazine. In the next barrage, would he have the nerve to shoot him?

Someone in the pit closest to him shouted at Norbert to get down or behind a tree, but he disregarded the warning and cocked his rifle again. As though he had felt himself watched, he turned to look directly at Gabriel, his handsome features distorted in a grimace. Then he burst into a run toward the cemetery.

He was here to die.

Gabriel fought a begrudging respect for him. Norbert had preyed upon his own daughter. He was a monster. But if he killed a few *Anglais* on his way to hell, Gabriel would not stop him.

goliath

WOODEN CRUCIFIX IN HAND, Riel ran through the bush behind the church, bullets from the *Rababou* gun flying past him, tearing bark off the trees. He slowed at the edge of a rifle pit and slid into it with as much dignity as he could muster.

Immaculate Mary, in Your great mercy, ward off sin, death, and any wound . . .

He looked out from a hole in the log barricade, appalled at the sight of too many red-coated soldiers scattered from Mission Ridge to the small hill, where Middleton and his officers had gathered. It was sunny, still cool in the bush, but sweat had broken out on the back of his neck. He clutched the wooden crucifix, his knees weak and stomach achingly empty.

"Where is Gabriel?" he asked the men in the pit. They didn't know any more than he did, and he prayed to bring them strength, his hand on old Joseph Ouellette's shoulder. "They who seek our lives will be destroyed," he said. "They will go down to the depths of the earth."

Joseph nodded his head after saying his amen. He was ninety-three years old, but had insisted on joining the fight with his old muzzle-loader. He seemed to remember that Riel had urged them to provide each other the sacraments and mumbled, "I wish to confess that I have killed an English—" He broke off as the shadowed figures of Sioux warriors ran silently past them through the trees.

"It's a sign," Riel told the men. "Poundmaker will soon be here."

He had hoped that God would grant His first miracle with the *Northcote*, but they had not succeeded in capturing it. When Riel had been overseeing the relocation of the women and children from the riverbank to the village, Baptiste Gervais had arrived with news that the boat lay up on a shoal downstream and could not come back against the current without engine power. He had dispatched Gervais on a fast horse north to find Poundmaker, with a message that they had their first victory over *les Anglais* and were defending Batoche. As Gervais spurred his horse, Riel called after him, "Do not mention that we failed to seize the ship." Now he was desperate to find Gabriel and remind the men that there was still plenty of time for God to bring his miracle.

He turned his attention to the hill, where Middleton surveyed the ground with field glasses and the air of a man who would not take chances. The general spoke to one of his aides, and a few shouted orders came down. Riel waited, but the soldiers did not move from their positions.

Salomon Boucher ran past and Riel followed on impulse. In a pit behind the church, they found Michel Dumas, four other men, and Gabriel down on his haunches against the earthen wall. Riel jumped down beside his war lieutenant. "The devil walks about on the hill like a roaring lion," he said, "seeking whom he may devour." Gabriel would not look at him or respond. "What did the priests say to Middleton?" Riel asked.

Gabriel spat through his teeth. "Our secrets."

"How did *les Anglais* get this far?"

"The *Rababou* gun."

Riel stared out at it from between the logs. "Custer refused to take one of these to the Little Bighorn," he said. "He thought it was useless against the Sioux."

"Do you see it useless here?" Gabriel said.

"Break the *Anglais* cannon," Riel said, closing his eyes in prayer. "Break them in two—"

Gabriel stood and gestured toward the hill. "Here is Goliath. In the City of God. Will we hold him off for three days?"

Riel opened one eye. He had prayed long and hard before making his announcement to council last night, a strategy to bring Poundmaker, but Gabriel was obviously in pain and unable to conceal his disappointment over failing to take the boat. Riel turned, raising his voice so that others could hear in the nearby pits. "Did you see the *Rababou* attack the church? God told the English to fire at the priests. You must remember we have the right to this land. Your claims are not false. They are just! *Les Anglais* are trespassers!"

Some of the men had taken out their rosaries and were mumbling the Apostles' Creed, "I believe in God, the Father Almighty, Creator of Heaven and earth . . ."

Gabriel's eyes moved like those of a hawk, watching Mission Ridge, but the troops did not advance. There was a flash of movement up on the hill as three men rode out to the east, spurring their horses into a gallop. Among them was an older officer with handlebar moustaches and a white pith helmet, his long sabre flashing in the sun. Gabriel followed their progress with his field glasses.

"Where are they going?" Riel asked.

"To a working telegraph," he said bluntly, "for reinforcements."

Riel turned to the men and shouted, "*Les Anglais* are already afraid of our bullets. God is here."

The Métis were cheering, taking this as proof of weakness, but Gabriel still had his attention on General Middleton, who paced on the crest of the hill, hands clasped behind his back.

"What is it?" Riel asked, watching him closely.

Gabriel's reply was cryptic. "The old man is planning something."

"Take the *Rababou* gun," Riel urged him. "Capture the ammunition and supplies. God will protect you."

Gabriel looked at him for the first time, frustration raw on his face. "You think I should walk across and no *Anglais* will shoot me?"

Riel prayed for peace, for relief from the constant tide of refusal and dissent that had thwarted every effort of his life. He spotted Moise Ouellette in a far pit and raised his voice to get his attention. "Spirit of God," he shouted, "I beg you, through Jesus, Mary, Joseph, and Saint John the Baptist, grant us Your Holy spirit of courage and strength so that we may complete all Your good works." Moise looked back at him and nodded, crossing himself. Riel took it as a sign and allowed himself a moment of reprieve.

A lone officer rode down to the soldiers near the cemetery. Gabriel sighted with his gun, but he was out of range. Then God brought His miracle. Within seconds, the company started to leave its position. Riel waited for them to advance again, yet they kept moving back. The company to their right began its retreat. A few soldiers broke into a run, but their officers shouted at them and the men slowed to a reluctant walk. Soon they were disappearing over the hill and into Caron's plowed fields. The Métis watched with disbelief as two uniformed doctors issued from the rectory, their aprons covered in blood, followed close behind by soldiers carrying stretchers with the *Anglais* wounded.

"God is with us," Riel cried, turning to the men, aware that they still had not lowered their guns. "Gabriel has succeeded in holding off an army of thousands. Three cheers for our hero."

But Gabriel looked over his shoulder and behind him, as if he expected Middleton to charge from another direction.

"God has intervened on our behalf." Riel raised his hands in supplication.

Gabriel suddenly leapt from the pit, whistling for the men around him to start a prairie fire.

"Goliath is running," he yelled, surging forward. "Capture the *Rababou* gun!"

the visit

LONG AFTER DARKNESS had fallen, Moulin sat on the bottom stair of the rectory, listening to Fathers Fourmond and Vegreville in the upstairs chapel, praying for the souls of their misguided parishioners. From across the river came the steady throb of Sioux war drums, broken only by the periodic crack of rifle shots, from at least a mile away.

The nuns were in the rectory kitchen, scrubbing the table, determined to remove bloodstains from the wood. *Anglais* doctors had worked on their wounded and dying soldiers until late afternoon when their commanders had mysteriously and without warning ordered a retreat. Cleophile was upstairs in one of the nuns' beds, trying to rest. The poor girl had cried today as the big guns boomed over their heads. Despite his encouragement, she still refused to speak.

Moulin had just been pondering Josette's visit last night, attempting to reconcile her question, "How could you let this happen?" with, her curious admonition, "You don't know!" when there was a rap at the door.

He cautiously got up off the step. A visit at this time of night could bring only bad news. His hand hovered over the door handle. It was a possibility that one of the women had come up from the riverbank camp with food, and he was too hungry to refuse. He opened the door to the familiar face of Madame Dumont.

She held out four eggs nestled in a cloth, her eyes wide with anxiety. "Give Gabriel absolution."

Moulin gazed at the eggs, his mouth watering. They hadn't had any for a week. Was he desperate enough to forgive the man who followed Riel into certain death? "*Non,*" he said. "I cannot."

"You owe me this much."

He gnawed at his thumbnail. *Did* he owe her? She had been one of his supporters since the early days, and had often brought him food, but if he let her in, every woman would think the priests had forgiven them for following Riel.

"It pains me," he said, "that the best man in the South Branch has become a lunatic's henchman." Outrage spread across her blunt features, and in an effort to calm her, he hastened to add, "I would like to remember Gabriel as the good man who brought Josette in on New Year's, after Norbert beat her."

Madeleine backed away. "Josette?" she said, livid or crying, he couldn't decide which. "Even *you* think she is a saint. She is more like the Magdalene than anyone guesses." She coughed uncontrollably, and he tried to get her indoors, but she disappeared into the darkness, off toward their sad riverbank camp.

Moulin had gone in to speak with the nuns, when the rectory door opened again. He looked up, expecting to find Madame Dumont with an apology on her lips, but a man stood there, hat brim pulled down over his face, rifle held in big hands crusted with dirt and blood.

"I will not give sacraments to any of you." He walked toward the man to show that he would not be trifled with. But Norbert Lavoie refused to budge out of the doorway. His gun was now all too near, and the priest's irritation gave way to alarm.

Norbert looked over his shoulder into the night. "Grant me absolution."

"You fight for Riel's new church. Ask *him* to bless you."

Norbert lifted his head, and Moulin could see that his eyes were unfocused, the pupils dark. "I have seen my death," he said, "I dreamed it, on the trail."

"You all will die from the *Anglais* rifles if you do not surrender."

"I would rather die with honour than at the hands of my wife."

Moulin knew the half-breeds were superstitious, but this was going too far. "*Maintenant tu rêves en couleurs*," he said. "Now you are dreaming."

Norbert laughed humourlessly, and the nuns came to the kitchen door to see what was going on. "Josette wishes to see me in the ground." He grabbed at the sleeve of Moulin's soutane, the smell of rum on his breath. "I want the last rites."

The priest threw off his hand. "Surrender. The general would receive you."

"Give me the sacraments," Norbert demanded. "I wish to die with Christ."

Moulin remembered Cleophile. "Your daughter is upstairs. You can take her back—"

He was not able to finish, for Norbert started violently. "Do not believe what she tells you!"

Father Fourmond had heard the commotion. He charged down the stairs to help Moulin push Norbert back. Together they managed to slam the door and held it closed, hardly daring to breathe.

Norbert's voice came loud from the other side. "You don't know her. She has killed to save her own life."

The priests looked at each other. When they were assured that he had gone, Moulin told Fourmond that Norbert had dreamed his own death and demanded the last rites.

Fourmond tutted. "What did he say of his wife?"

"That she wanted to kill him."

"Impossible!"

Unnerved, Moulin thought of Josette's confession last summer. What was her sin?

I refused my husband.

And why? Fear of death in childbirth. She had been visibly ill then and worse in berry-picking camp only days later. Josette with her herbs and potions. *La Vieille. More like the Magdalene than anyone guesses.* Sudden understanding made the bile rise in his throat at the thought of her, on her knees in his chapel, begging God for forgiveness.

Murderess.

Cleophile had crept down the stairs, pale as a ghost. "He is gone?" she said, as though she were terrified of her own father.

Moulin forced a smile to calm her. The beautiful young girl, innocent, yet born to an evil woman. And the father no better. Gone mad, begging for absolution. Why would Josette want to kill him?

Cleophile stared back at him, her eyes red with crying.

Do not believe what she tells you.

Moulin's smile quickly faded. Heat flushed his neck and bloomed into his face as comprehension slowly dawned on him.

nikâwiy

⌒

JOSETTE HAD BEEN WITH her three children in the village all day, out of range of enemy cannon balls that had exploded in the south meadow, destroying tents and leaving gaping craters in the earth. When *les Anglais* retreated, the women went back to the riverbank camp to start cooking for the men who filed down before dusk. Some told of Gabriel's failed bid to capture the *Rababou* gun, and how he had led the Sioux in chasing Middleton's retreating troops to their encampment in the Carons' back fields. But most of them were silent, disturbed. When Josette overheard that General Middleton had ridden down to talk with the priests after attacking the rectory, she stole away, leaving Eulalie with the boys.

On the bluff, she put her hand to the cemetery fence and listened. Stars wheeling and the smell of earth, the newly dug mass grave of those who had died at Duck Lake and Tourond's Coulee. Smoke still rose from the burned houses on the meadow. She had thought Cleophile was safe in the rectory, but to find that it had come under fire and the *Anglais* general at its door. Unbearable. The rectory would be in the middle of the fight tomorrow. And Moulin did not know what kind of sin had been done to her.

Erratic gunfire came from the army encampment, followed by whoops and shouted insults in Sioux and Cree. Her fingers closed over the handle of the skinning knife in her pocket. Where was Norbert now? Her first thought had been that he'd go to Red River, but even his relations there would not forgive his sin. Out of shame and fear, he would ride across the line into the States. There was a chance he might return, placing her daughter in danger again. When this war was over, she would find him and kill him.

Josette broke into a run up the slope toward the church, stumbling once or twice over ruts left in the grass where English soldiers had been that day. In the shadow of the rectory, she made an attempt to tie her hair into a knot, compose herself. It had not worked earlier to enter as a harridan, fighting Moulin to get up the stairs. If she acted reasonably, would he let Cleophile go? She knocked and when there was no answer, opened the door to find the priests and nuns standing around the kitchen table. They turned their heads at the same moment and saw her, their expressions ripe with condemnation, perhaps even revulsion.

"I've come for my daughter," she said, painfully aware that she had interrupted a heated discussion.

Moulin managed to look both appalled and guarded in equal measure. "Cleophile has gone back to sleep after a long day of upset."

"Her father has sinned against her," Josette said, expecting Moulin to be confused at her meaning, but he did not flinch. She glared at him. "You know that Cleophile has been misused and do nothing?"

"I *will* do something," he shouted, then looked to the ceiling. When he spoke again, his voice had dropped to a heated whisper. "As soon as this war is over, you will be excommunicated from the Holy Roman Church."

She blinked hard, struggling to understand. "You have already refused the sacraments to me and every Métis who follows Riel."

"Sacraments are one thing," he said. "Excommunication is the only answer to mortal sin."

Somehow the priests had discovered what she had tried so hard to hide from them. From everyone. "Norbert will never return to receive his punishment," she cried. "*His* is the mortal sin."

Moulin's eyes blazed with righteous anger. "Norbert was just here begging for the last rites. He told us he would rather die with honour at the hands of the English than have you kill him."

Norbert here. *In Batoche.* He knew her too well, that she would not let him live. But he would not go to his God with honour. He would die an ugly death at her own hand. And these priests would not keep her daughter a moment longer.

Moulin had come closer, his breath rank in her face. "It is you who are possessed of the devil here, Josette—*you* who have murdered an innocent to save your own life."

"What proof do you have to accuse me?" She waited for his answer with a kind of fatalistic relief, that she would soon be finished with a religion that failed to honour a woman's life.

"We have certain proof."

Josette leapt toward the stairs, taking them two at a time, her skirts hiked up around her knees. The priests and nuns jostled with each other, trying to follow, but she was up on the second-floor landing before they had started on the first step.

And there was Cleophile, standing in the doorway of one of the rooms, her face swollen from crying, eyes red-rimmed with grief. A girl who had become a woman too soon. Josette forced herself not to look away, to register the ruin of neglect, her failure. Relieved that Norbert had left her alone, she had become blind to where he turned his attentions. Obsessed with staying alive, she had died to herself, to her own daughter.

Cleophile's lower lip trembled and Josette waited for her to speak, but Moulin had come up the steps and rushed at her, his face purple with outrage. Caught off guard by the intensity of his attack, she tried to pull away from him, but he held her arm fast. Panicked, she began to flail, and the two other priests grabbed her.

Moulin's breath came in gasps. "You must leave."

"Excommunicate me now," she said, as the priests and nuns tried to wrestle her toward the stairs. "Before you lose your hatred and anger."

"We will do it when this war is done." Moulin looked at Cleophile, who shrank back in the doorway.

"She is no longer innocent." Josette's voice was hoarse. "But you know that, don't you?"

The nuns had come up and stood with eyes wide in astonishment at the scene. One of them said, "Surely the girl knows her mother's sins."

Moulin appeared to think for a moment then let go of Josette's arm and took a step back. "You are formerly accused of committing the mortal sin of abortion, and are hereby excommunicated from the Holy Roman Church."

"Include the reason I wilfully aborted a child," she said. "Was it out of spite or evil intent?" The priests exchanged looks. "To save my own life, wasn't it? That my children would not be left with a man like Norbert." She held Moulin's angry gaze. "You cannot hurt me with excommunication. I have never loved your God."

At this, Moulin and the priests turned their backs on her in a symbolic gesture, meant to signal her banishment from both church and community. The nuns shifted on their feet and avoided her glance. Cleophile had disappeared into the bedroom, unable to bear the sight of her either. Josette went down the stairs as if in a trance, ignoring the nuns' murmurs of disapproval.

Behind the church, she almost stumbled into an abandoned rifle pit, hidden but for a blanket or two left by the men. Wind roared in the trees, clouds drawn across the moon like a funeral shroud. Norbert had been there today. She pressed fingers to her temples in an effort to keep herself from screaming; the sounds of gunfire and war cries in the distance reverberated like the pulse beat of her heart.

"*Nikâwiy.*"

She turned to find Cleophile there in sudden moonlight, a child's body, frail arms hanging powerless at her sides. Her daughter had not called her the Cree name for "mother" in years.

Cleophile stood in quiet horror, almost struggling for breath. Gone was the open rage, that feral longing to be seen. Had Josette ever truly seen her? *La p'tite mère*, who had taken up her mother's obligations as they were discarded, one by one. The final duty an enormous betrayal. Her daughter had kept more than a secret and had been, quite possibly, broken by her father's sin.

Nikâwiy. It was a dare to trust, one that she had not earned. Her arms went around Cleophile's trembling shoulders and they held onto each other at the edge of the rifle pit, the still bare branches of the trees lifting in the wind, like skeletons against the starred sky, summoning flesh to their bones.

more to eat yet

SHORTLY AFTER MIDNIGHT, Gabriel crouched in a thicket of willow, pouring gunpowder into an old packing tin. Pierre Parenteau had
found an unexploded cannon shell south of the village, and had brought
it out to him with the idea of using the powder to make a bomb. Thirty
of Gabriel's core fighters and some of the Sioux knelt in the grass, several of them giving Michel Dumas advice on how to fashion a fuse from
a strip of his ceinture fléchée.

The shadow of Middleton's encampment spread across the Carons'
hayfield. The general's teamsters had pulled hundreds of wagons into a
circle until a barricade had formed, three wagons deep to the outside.
Scores of horses were in there, almost a thousand soldiers, too, attempting to sleep. Middleton had positioned several officers and their men
outside the wagons to prevent an attack from the Métis.

Dumas carefully wound his piece of sash around the tin. "Enough
gunpowder here," he said, "to blow us to kingdom come."

Charles Trottier and Little Ghost carried the bomb closer to the camp, the two of them bent so low to the ground, they almost seemed to melt into the dark field. Gabriel watched with nervous anticipation. This was their chance to stampede Middleton's horses and oxen and capture the *Rababou* gun, turn it on the soldiers fleeing in chaos. If it worked, the war would soon be over.

Out on the prairie, Trottier and Little Ghost had stopped and leaned over their package. The others followed one by one and Gabriel crept after them, his muscles aching, and the bandage under his hat wet with blood. He should be the one to throw the bomb, but he had passed out an hour ago, overcome by fatigue and the pain in his head. He had regained consciousness, disoriented, to find his men standing over him, agonizing over his ability to continue.

There was a sudden flash on the prairie when Trottier sparked the fuse, his face briefly lit up as he stood to hurl the bomb into the enclosure. Middleton's sentries had seen it too, and shot at him, but Trottier had thrown himself down the moment the bomb left his hand. A moment of trepidation and then an intense bang and shower of sparks just inside the corral were followed by shouts from soldiers and the sound of horses screaming and kicking at the sides of wagons. The Indians and Métis yipped and howled. Gabriel was emboldened at the confusion among the sentries, who were running about like chickens, but an officer shouted orders and within a minute, control had been restored.

Dumas took off the handkerchief around his neck. "*Les Anglais* here like fucking rats in a trap," he said, mopping his face with it. "And we can't get at them." He looked at his commander as if to say, "What next?"

Gabriel sank to one knee. Riel was somewhere, celebrating the fulfillment of his prophecy. But Middleton's retreat was far from a miracle. The Métis had foiled the general's every move and killed enough soldiers that he had withdrawn to avoid losing more men. Gabriel would like to rest easy on this thought, but he could not ignore one truth: the old man had sent for reinforcements, and with supplies to wait them out, the Métis were again at a disadvantage. Tomorrow they must capture the *Rababou* gun or pray that Poundmaker would arrive in time to save them.

Little Ghost was far from disheartened. Hidden in the willow bush, he kept up a string of insults to the sentries around the camp. "I am Little Ghost," he yelled. "I have eaten many whites. I think I have more to eat yet."

Another warrior, not to be outdone, shouted, "White Faces—are you women that you must hide under your skirts? Don't sleep—tomorrow you will sleep soundly."

Gabriel clasped Lean Crow's hand. "Keep the *Rababou* man awake," he said, "and afraid of his hair."

He and Dumas pulled back from the encampment and went to the rectory, where they found Madeleine and Marguerite in the kitchen with Pierre Parenteau and the nuns. Two men who had been wounded earlier were stretched out on straw pallets in the hall. They had been bandaged and given some herbal decoction, but groaned in fitful sleep. Gabriel asked one of the nuns if she'd also tended the injured government troops. With a bowed head, she said that she had.

"Why?"

She did not look up at him. "He maketh His sun to rise on the evil and on the good."

Gabriel turned away before he said something disrespectful to a bride of Christ. Riel had come in to find him. He was in a strange mood: his eyes darting about and muttering one of his prayers. Gabriel climbed the stairs of the rectory, followed by Riel and Dumas. They found Moulin, Fourmond, and Vegreville, kneeling in the small chapel.

"What did you tell Middleton?" Gabriel demanded.

Moulin did not look up, but Fourmond regarded them with defiance. "That you are a formidable foe and they should be careful."

"Lies," said Dumas. "You betrayed us."

Father Moulin blinked and crossed himself, but Fourmond remained confident, unwavering. "It does not look like they are winning. What do you care if we tell them you are making these poor people fight against their will?"

To Gabriel's relief, Riel had gone to the altar on the far side of the room, distracted at the image of Christ on the cross. He knelt, took out his rosary, and began to pray.

Fourmond eyed him suspiciously and said to Gabriel, "We are trying to save you with our mediation."

"You think your talk helps us?" he said. "It helps the other side."

"Today we learned what evil lurks in the Métis Nation," Moulin said. "We have been praying for one of your own, who was excommunicated from the Church for committing a mortal sin."

Gabriel looked up at him. "*Quoi?*"

"Josette," said Moulin with satisfaction. "She has wilfully ended the life of her unborn child."

Gabriel shook his head. Why would she have done such a thing? Then he remembered the women's gossip over Josette, almost bleeding to death in childbed. "Men are dying," he said. "And you excommunicate a woman who would save herself from that fate?"

"Her husband has also sinned." Moulin straightened his soutane. "He must be brought to us."

Riel had not moved from his place, kneeling at the crucifix, but now he made the sign of the cross, his back set in a hard line. "Norbert?" he asked. "What has he done?"

Moulin snorted. "He shall be excommunicated for offending the dignity of a child."

Riel got to his feet and walked slowly toward him. "You have refused the sacraments from all who follow me. Yet God has shown Himself to the Métis this day." He raised his hand and the priests shrank back. "I hereby excommunicate *you* from the Catholic Apostolic Church of the New World."

Colour had risen in Father Moulin's face. "Insanity and sin runs rampant in your people—it is like Sodom and Gomorrah. Josette should have left her pregnancy in God's hands. It is a mortal sin—just below murder—"

"It is murder going on out there," Gabriel shouted. A wave of nausea overtook him, and he went down the stairs and out into the night, leaving Riel and the priests to trade insults. He paced near the cemetery, trying to clear his head. Josette was still in his mind, and he forced himself to think of strategies he could use tomorrow against Middleton. A group of Métis had come up from the riverbank, plates of stew in their hands. Gabriel said to Emmanuel Champagne, "Get some men and start digging pits south of the burnt houses."

"Why?" Champagne said, his mouth crammed with food. "There are pits all over here."

"Not that far out. Middleton thinks he'll come down here in the morning and stand on the land he did today. We won't let him." Despite the pain in his head, Gabriel seized a potato shovel and hacked at the hard ground. Soon, out of guilt, a dozen Métis were digging alongside him. He decided that he would order them to sleep in the pits. If they spent the night with their wives and children in the riverbank camp, they might be persuaded to desert.

A movement in the shadow of the poplars caught his eye, and Gabriel turned quickly. *Josette*. He handed his shovel to one of the young men and, saying he meant to find something to eat, walked under the trees.

"Norbert is back in Batoche," he said when he was near to her.

"You said he was gone." She did not look at him. "You said Cleophile was safe."

Her voice was flat, emotionless and Gabriel stared through the dark. That face, tragic, yet beautiful. Or it was the tragedy that made him love her. He shook his head. Not love. What had war done to him that he thought of another woman and excused a man for hurting his own child because he needed him to fight? But Josette did not wish for him to kill Norbert. She wanted to do it herself.

"Can you wait?"

She didn't answer, and he watched her for a moment, felt the odd stirring in his chest. When he had discovered that Madeleine was dying, he resolved to put Josette out of his thoughts. But the bullet had done more than addle his brain. Constant pain and lack of sleep made him weak, made him need her. He had kept up a brave front to the men, to his wife, who spoke of her worries in their dugout on the riverbank. Gabriel had listened when she said Riel was mad and could not be trusted. Madeleine, asking the impossible.

Leave him.

Gabriel wanted to tell Josette what he had not admitted to anyone else: Poundmaker wouldn't come and the Métis would lose this war.

But she knew it too, knew he could not turn from the man who had helped them in Red River. She stood with him under the trees, her fine features settled in the grave look she had in the old days as an outcast among the women.

Finally, she said, "Have you been down to the farm?"

He nodded.

"Were the houses burned?"

"*Oui*," he said. "Everything."

Her expression didn't change. Middleton would soon capture Batoche and either kill the men or take them prisoner. Families would be torn apart, their lands lost. Josette had aborted a child to save herself and faced shunning from the women. If her husband didn't die in this war, she would kill him. She could not go to her grandfather's people, fugitives from the government. Big Bear's camp was in ruins, his only future—death or imprisonment.

Don't think these things, he told himself. *Get back to the business of war. Encourage the men digging, even now whispering, planning to desert.*

"Moulin tells me that Riel spent two years in a mental hospital," she said. He glanced at her briefly but did not answer. "You knew," she went on, "and would not tell me, even after I tried to convince you he was losing his mind."

She looked hurt, as if he had betrayed her. Maybe he had. "You did not tell me of his vision to create a separate state with his church at its head," Gabriel said. "We are even."

He could see that she was crying and he reached to her, his hand careful, detached, brushing the coarse wool of the shawl over her thin shoulder. He had not bargained for the feel of her, and his heart beat wildly in his chest. Lifting his hand, he let it drop, fingers hesitating at the fringe of her shawl. It was quiet among the trees, only the sound of digging out on the meadow, the men talking amongst themselves. He should have pulled his hand away, but let it slip beneath the fringe, a quiver at the tips of his fingers as they traced the line of her back, followed the curve of her waist. The top of her head was only inches away. She had become very still, almost not breathing, a slight resistance then turning into him, the smell of her, like woodsmoke and the river when the ice broke up in spring. She looked up at him, a strand of her black hair caught in a sudden lift of wind. The moon had come out and rained light through the bare branches, onto those eyes, dark and unfathomable. He touched her cheek, still wet with tears.

"*Wâwâc*," he said in Cree. Even now.

He released her before it went any further and looked away, feeling strangely bereft, and more shaken than he would have thought possible.

a gathering
of souls

BEFORE NOON THE next day, Riel left the village for the church and rectory pits, armed only with his Bible. With him were Baptiste Gladu and Alexandre Dumont, who had helped kill and butcher two steers that morning and carried meat the women had cooked for their men. The camp south of the village was in ruins after the previous day's attack. Meadowlarks were hunting bugs, swooping to search the holes left by exploding shells then flying to the trees, breaking into celebratory song. The sun was almost overhead, the cloudless sky a dome of light.

Les Anglais had been shelling the rifle pits around the church and cemetery at intervals since dawn. Gabriel had not let Middleton's troops advance beyond the small hill. For safety, Métis families had moved out of range of the cannon to abandoned houses north of the Carlton Trail. Lean Crow had sent his women and children away, but White Cap's and Trottier's clans were still there. Now that they were fully engaged in battle, Riel found himself acting as his war general's aide-de-camp.

The council had not met in two days, and it was left to him and Pierre Parenteau to run an army of two hundred men and their prodigious families.

Yesterday, Riel had been dismayed to find that, despite God's protection, a bullet had grazed his coat sleeve, leaving a slash mark that no one seemed to have noticed. Yet it was necessary to go back out and efface the sins of Gabriel's army. Last night, he had allowed himself a moment to celebrate God's miracle, only to be told by Moulin that Josette had wilfully ended the life of her unborn child and Norbert had offended the dignity of his own daughter. He had panicked when Moulin mentioned Sodom and Gomorrah. Riel had fasted, prayed, and laid his own sins before God to work miracles, so that the Métis would not be consumed by His wrath.

When Gabriel had stormed out after the priest's accusations, Riel was sure that Norbert was halfway to Battleford by now, suffering another one of Gabriel's acts of retribution. There was still the matter of Josette's sin. Riel had not been able to find her this morning, but he could at least remind the Métis who had slept in the pits, that they would win this battle only if they repented before God.

Riel found the bush trail, Baptiste and Alexandre following. At the sound of another pounding fusillade from the south, they picked up their pace. A few high-powered rifle shots answered from across the river then a period of silence followed, and with caution, the birds began to sing again.

In Riel's prayers this morning, the Spirit of God had told him that he should foresee a mutiny. Always he had faced this threat, even in Red River. He could still not accept that the English half-breeds had betrayed the cause. He thought of the letter that Gabriel had brought last June. *Who is not ready to defend you to the last drop of his blood? The whole race is calling for you!*

The "whole race." If the English half-breeds came in, if every Métis and Indian in the Territories rose up against Ottawa, against the treaties, they would win all of their rights. Yet he struggled to keep even the French Métis free of sin and remind them of their promise to defend him.

In the bush close to the church, they passed a line of rifle pits. As Alexandre and Baptiste handed out the meat, Riel held up his Bible. "Lord, bless these men who seek redemption before you." He paused and regarded them expectantly. One after another, they knelt in the dirt and took out their rosaries. "They are vigilant, obedient," he continued. "Their penitence will bring the conqueror to his knees."

Riel flinched at a sudden, earth-shaking blast, as the two cannon went off to the south. The men barely registered the sound and looked up at him with dispassionate eyes, many of them coughing, their faces streaked with dirt. Riel urged them to confess to each other, but they were more anxious to tell him that soldiers had been reinforcing the *Anglais* encampment all morning and making vain attempts to recapture ground they had held yesterday.

"Middleton is building a fortress," Riel said. "He knows his army will be here a long time—long enough for Poundmaker to come. We will be victorious."

"We killed one of his soldiers when they charged," said Elzéar Gervais. "The whole company was called back."

"Who did it?" Riel asked, meaning to praise the man.

"Me," a familiar voice said from two pits over.

Riel looked up to find Norbert Lavoie gazing at him with a peculiar, unsettling expression. He took a step back. Norbert. In Batoche. With no sign of having received a beating. Obviously, the men had not heard of his crime, and Norbert did not realize that the priests meant to excommunicate him. *But God knew*.

Riel turned blindly and went off the trail through the small aspen undergrowth in search of Gabriel. Norbert had to be brought in before he defiled the sacred cause. Through the trees, he could now see up to the crest of the small hill, where the cannon were positioned, their barrels still smoking. Middleton was up there stalking about and then disappeared over the rise. No soldiers on the plateau. Riel found Gabriel in a pit behind the rectory, huddled with Édouard Dumont and Daniel Larance, discussing strategy. Édouard had seen Riel and stood with respect, but Larance remained in a squat, his eyes to the ground, listening to his war chief.

"Get up to where that officer has his men to the east," Gabriel told

Larance. "Hold them off with sparse fire." When he was about to leave the pit, he added, "Whistle three times if they try to rush you."

Gabriel glanced up at his brother, Édouard. "Go down to the cemetery pits. Tell them no shooting wild. We need every bullet."

When they were finally alone, Riel said, "I do not like the look I got from Daniel Larance."

Gabriel stared straight ahead, his face drawn. "He came to me yesterday—said the priests told his wife you'd been in a crazy house."

Riel felt his stomach cramp, as if from a blow. "I suspected that Nolin told Father André."

"We should not have imprisoned them."

Riel knew he was right. The priests had done more damage inside the rectory than out and would continue to use every means at their disposal to discredit him. "Norbert Lavoie is here," he said. "Have him brought to the village. I will banish him—"

"Three more men deserted in the night." Without warning, Gabriel leaped from the pit. "And he is one of our best shots."

Riel climbed out after him. He wanted to say that he would not allow a sinner here opposed to the Holy Spirit of truth, only because Gabriel valued his marksmanship. But his war general was already out of earshot, running along the west trail.

A plan began to form in Riel's head: move the prisoners from Garnot's saloon to Baptiste Boyer's root cellar. Wedge a pole between ceiling and trap door to free up the two guards, then Gabriel could no longer object to Norbert leaving the fight. He headed back to the village and was about to enter Garnot's, when Damase Carrière and Élie Nault rode in from the northeast.

"Has there been news?" Riel asked.

The men reined in their horses. "Riders are coming south on the trail," said Carrière, "from Prince Albert."

Riel raised his hands, smiling. *Thank you, Lord.* "Poundmaker already," he said and when he saw the looks on their faces, ". . . or Métis coming to join us."

"*Non,*" said Carrière. "Fifty *Anglais* scouts—hard men that look like they know how to use their guns."

"Reinforcements?" Riel could hear the cold terror in his voice.

Carrière turned his horse. "I must tell Gabriel," he said, following Nault in a gallop toward the church pits.

A woman's guttural scream issued from the direction of Emmanuel Champagne's house. Horrified, Riel turned to find Josette coming down the trail. "Virginie Tourond is in labour," she said. "Would you have her remain silent?"

Women had come out of Fisher's store to hear what was going on but seemed more concerned with watching him than her. Riel turned to avoid their accusing stares. If Larance's wife knew that he had spent two years in an insane asylum, they *all* knew.

Another scream from Virginie jarred Riel's memory of the Beauport asylum. At night—every hour—the night-watchers would walk the floors to ensure the suicidal had not killed themselves. They had keys for their rooms, charged with protecting the poor souls, but sodomized them instead, and he had been forced to listen to their cries, powerless to help.

The women's stares, memories of other screams. Riel felt his thoughts unravelling. Marguerite appeared, and he settled at the touch of her hand. He turned to give the guards orders to move the prisoners to Boyer's cellar and some of the older boys to find a lomg pole for the trap door. Within minutes, the prisoners filed out of Garnot's. The white store owners and surveyors from Duck Lake, Middleton's scout, and Honoré Jaxon being helped to walk. His pants were stained with urine. Riel could smell him from yards away. He watched his old friend with morose fascination. How close he had been to him, this Methodist who had so keenly dedicated himself to helping the Métis.

Josette ran to Honoré, but he did not seem to recognize her. "He's dying," she said to Riel, who now regretted that he had not moved the prisoners at night.

Honoré had finally got him in his sights. "Louis," he cried, his voice gruff from disuse. "Have you gathered enough souls to your isolation and despair?"

"Get them to Boyer's," Riel cried. And to himself: "Oh God, I beg You through Jesus, Mary, Joseph and Saint John the Baptist, have the charity to send me Your providential help. Please make it arrive soon."

Josette was now at his elbow. "He's harmless—let him go."

"Would you keep him with your children?" he said, startled to find her suddenly close. "In the night, he would go to the other side."

"He would be safer there."

"I am ordering your husband in," he said, "for excommunication."

He thought she would welcome the news, but she stared him down. "Good," she said, "bring him in. Release him from your God. Then I will kill him."

Virginie's screams were coming closer together, and Josette ran back up the trail.

Riel watched her go. Would God forgive a woman who had aborted her child, and yet helped birth them into the world? The Lord had allowed fifty scouts to come to the side of evil, of tyranny. And the Métis, the children of Israel, were deserting the cause or threatening mutiny. Riel would fast until he had effaced their sins. He would confess, but the woman he had chosen as his confessor had broken a covenant with God.

"Lord," he whispered in a prayer, "speed the Indians to us as if on wings."

death may
come today

⤳

JOSETTE WENT DOWN the riverbank with a pail. Alone, only the sound of a whippoorwill in the trees. The water looked unnaturally dark with sediment or spring run-off—too dark, even in the predawn light. She reached to dip the pail and recoiled at the odd metallic smell. The water was sticky, viscous, the colour of blood. When she peered closer, she saw that it *was* blood, seeping from cuts on her body, streaming down into the river, turning it red. She tried to staunch its course from her veins, but it only flowed faster, the river rising on the bank until she felt it lap at her feet.

She awoke with a start. It was still night, and for a moment she panicked, unsure of where she was. Reaching to touch a shadowed object not inches in front of her face, she remembered that she lay on the floor behind the stove in Xavier Letendre's house, the children in blankets beside her. One of the wounded men groaned in the corner, and she pulled Wahsis to her. His small body curled against hers in sleep, and she lay there awhile longer to orient herself, moonlight glancing through the window above her head.

Riel's prophecy had come true. It was the third day of the *Anglais* assault on Batoche. She could hear a hoarse cough from a room on the floor above, where the Riel family slept. Weeks camped on the riverbank had worsened Marguerite's condition—one that Josette recognized well enough. Louis Riel's wife would be dead within a year.

Josette's dream was receding, but she could not ignore its dire message. Last night, she had anticipated the excommunication and banishment of her husband that Riel had promised, but a council meeting was hastily called and his plans forgotten. Gabriel had asked her if she could wait. It had seemed that she could, but now, the thought of Norbert so near . . . and the ancestors had warned her in the dream—*kill him or pay with your own life's blood.*

She got up quietly and tiptoed to the kitchen, stooping to a wounded Sioux warrior who had been carried in yesterday with a bullet wound in his upper leg. The women had set his shattered bone as best they could. Now the herbs he'd been given were wearing off and he drifted up out of sleep. Josette lifted his head to give him some medicine tea, then picked up a knife from the sideboard, slipping it inside her dress sleeve. It had a shorter blade than her skinning knife, more suited to her purpose. She pulled her shawl close and stole out into the night. Across the face of the waxing moon, wisps of cloud drifted like steam from a boiling kettle. Her foot had just left the bottom porch step, when a voice whispered in the dark.

"Be careful."

Josette turned quickly. While she had been in the kitchen, Marguerite Riel had left the house to wait for her. She could clearly see her round face in the moonlight.

Marguerite drew closer. "Gabriel Dumont is a dangerous man to love."

Josette looked up to meet her eyes. Not that long ago, she had convinced herself of the same truth. And had it dispelled the other night when she had seen him leave the rectory, waited in the trees to confront him. *Riel spent two years in an insane asylum and you did not tell me.* She had not planned to break down, to be so startled by Gabriel's touch. She could still feel the path his fingers had taken across her back, the heat of his hand at her waist.

"The first day I came to Batoche, you asked me if I had read the books that Louis brought," Marguerite said, watching her.

"Yes," she said, remembering. "Women do not read."

Marguerite smiled at this. "I once feared that Louis would take you as a second wife." Her tone was unconcerned, as if this was no longer one of her fears. "I learned to read my husband's poems. I am not the tender creature, always attentive to her duty."

Josette could not believe what she was hearing. *Second wife?* "Two days ago he chose you as his Mary Magdalene."

"I wanted to tell him that he is no Christ, I am no Mary," she said, muffling a cough. "But he chose the perfect woman. One who will ease his fears—strong enough to survive him and weak enough not to speak against him."

"You aren't weak."

Marguerite shrugged. "In any other place, we would have been friends." She held out her hand and Josette took it for a moment, then Marguerite turned to go.

"You love him," Josette said. Riel's wife had stopped on the stairs but did not look around. "That is all he asks."

"Is it?" Marguerite said quietly, then continued up the stairs and into the house, closing the door behind her.

Josette walked south across the meadow, over the rutted ground, past the damaged tents. Riel's City of God. A heavy dew was on the grass, the air damp with mist. Dawn was coming, an echo of darkness undoing itself. By the time she arrived at the line of trees everything was cast in blue-grey shadow, birds rousing themselves to wakefulness in the trackless light.

Her mind was in confusion. Riel wanting a second wife, and Gabriel —a dangerous man to love. The only man who had been a danger was not another woman's husband, but her own. She found the trail, and it occurred to her that she should not be too quiet. What if one of the men mistook her for the enemy? When she had the rectory pits in her sight, the men's hats appeared, silhouetted in the growing light. Some still slept, while others stood looking out over the barricades, watching the terrain in front of the church and down into the cemetery. A few had left the pits to do their business.

One stood a little farther from the rest, and even in the half dark, she recognized Norbert. Most Métis men were tall and broad shouldered, but he had always been taller, his neck thicker than the others. He walked to a bush and undid his pants. In a moment, he was relieving himself. If she were closer, she would have heard the sigh he always gave out when the stream began to flow. She crept near, knowing that he would not hear her approach over the sound of his own piss. As she tried to get the knife out from her sleeve, a round of fire from the *Rababou* gun ripped through the bushes, accompanied by a screeching shell that exploded only yards from the front line of pits.

Élie Nault emerged from the small aspens to the east, yelling, "*Les Anglais* are on the Jolie Prairie."

divide and
conquer

GABRIEL LEFT HIS RIFLE PIT behind the church at a dead run, and shouted for men to follow him, leaving Michel Dumas and a dozen of White Cap's Sioux to watch for any movement in the south. As he led the way down the east trail, he berated himself for another tactical mistake: he'd been watching Middleton's troop movements on the small hill over the past two days, and failed to send enough men to watch what forces might ride on their east flank.

When he arrived at the Jolie Prairie, a barrage of gunfire erupted from the direction of the church, and he closed his eyes. *Tricked*. He turned to go back, not sure from what direction the assault was coming.

Michel Dumas came charging through the trees as if someone chased him. "The old man is trying to surround us—he's got the cemetery . . . and put his cannon in position to stop our snipers across the river."

Gabriel brooded over the strategy used. Middleton had drawn him away from the church pits so that his men could recapture the cemetery.

Stupid to think a full attack would come from the Jolie Prairie. The general might soon outflank them, but it wouldn't be today. He ran back with Dumas, swearing *les Anglais* would not take the ground around the church and rectory. The *Rababou* gun had opened up to spray the rifle pits. Gabriel dove into one as the bushes above were cut to pieces. The Métis returned fire and there was a sudden yell from the church. Gabriel looked out of a crack between two logs in the barricade.

It was light enough now that he could see Father Fourmond on the rectory steps with Riel's white flag in his hand. "What are the priests up to now?" He whistled to stop the fire and watched as Middleton's soldiers ran down to speak with Fourmond and then immediately returned to their position on the hill. Presently more of them appeared, flying their own white flag with its red cross stitched upon it. Two men carried a stretcher.

Those in pits closer to the action passed back the message, "Father Moulin was hit by one of the *Anglais* bullets—he is crying like a baby."

pompous old fool

LATER THAT NIGHT, Father Moulin lay in a tent in Middleton's camp. The doctor had given him something for pain, and he had dozed in and out as the day passed. When he had been brought in, he clutched at his lower leg, moaning to the surgeon who knelt beside him. "Do you think I will lose it?"

"The bones are not broken," the doctor said as he worked to stop the blood flow at the wound's entry and exit points. "The bullet went clean through the muscle."

That morning he had been up in the attic looking for more blankets for the nuns when a vicious firefight had broken out between *les Anglais* and the half-breeds, his church and rectory in the middle of it. He had gone to the window to see what was going on when he felt a stabbing pain in his leg and had collapsed against a cedar box, shocked to see a small hole in his soutane. At least his belly was now full of beef, and what they called "hard tack," a dry biscuit that did not come close to bannock. He drowsed in a medicated haze and was jarred to wakefulness by men who had come back from the fighting. Two of them—officers by the sound of it—passed close to his tent.

"Three days fighting on the same ground," a voice said. "Are we managing to kill any of these miserable half-breeds?"

"Get down to the cemetery at daybreak," said the other officer. "When you hear cannon and Gatling fire on the prairie, test the rifle pits in the bush along that ridge. If you aren't challenged, move the men up and capture the church and rectory."

"The general can't try the same feint he did today," complained the other man. "Riel won't fall for it twice."

"Gabriel Dumont's afraid of the Gatling. He'll go wherever it does." The officer paused. "I'll personally drag Riel to his death if I catch him, but Dumont—I hope he gets away."

The younger officer snorted in displeasure. "I'm getting tired of Middleton fucking around. My men won't be happy—why not just keep pushing and take the village? The pompous old fool would be surprised if we dashed right on and ended it all at the point of the bayonet."

"You'd be court-martialled for going against his orders," the older officer said. "Advance to the church and rectory. No further."

The voices passed the tent and receded. Moulin got up on his elbows, straining to hear the last of their conversation. He fell back and patted the blanket close around him. Asking Middleton to move the priests and nuns out of the rectory was pointless. The general would refuse to do something that might warn the Métis of his battle plans. The rectory would be in the middle of the fight tomorrow, the clergy in danger after serving the Métis for years. How had it come to this?

He fished under the blanket for his rosary and prayed. "God, save the priests and nuns. Save your innocent children," he whispered. "If you must take anyone, let it be Louis Riel."

a child

AT DAWN ON THE fourth day, Gabriel climbed out of a rifle pit near the church and rubbed his eyes. He had tried to stay awake last night to prevent more men from deserting, but had finally succumbed to sleep in the early hours of the morning. He ignored a blazing headache as he gave orders for more men to the pits down near the ridge, sure that the first attack would come from there. Yesterday, he had resisted Middleton's attempts to overrun them, but only because the old man had retreated in fear of losing soldiers. Three days he had held him off. *Three*. And God had yet to deliver Poundmaker and his one thousand braves.

Napoléon Nault came running through the trees. "*Les Anglais* are marching up to the Jolie Prairie again—with the two cannon, and the *Rababou* gun."

Gabriel took off his hat and ran a hand over his face. Yesterday, he had lost ground around the cemetery. He refused to be drawn away again and risk the church and rectory. But if not enough men were in the pits along the Jolie Prairie, Middleton would take the village with his big guns.

As the sun came over the trees and far bank of the river, he could see soldiers moving down toward the cemetery in a neat line. From what direction did the worst threat lie? Men were stirring in their pits, and he made a rough count, only to find that at least a dozen more had slipped away while he'd been asleep. Together with the ones manning the Jolie Prairie pits and those across the river, there were only sixty Métis left to fight the *Anglais* army.

Another problem was ammunition. He was down to his last twelve cartridges, and other men had been picking up nails or rocks, whatever would fit into their musket barrels. Gabriel decided he was needed where the cannon and the general had gone. He took some of his best men and returned with Nault in time to throw himself into a pit and watch Middleton ride at the head of his mounted scouts on the Jolie Prairie.

"Come closer," he whispered, but the general reined in his horse just out of range.

The old man took a pair of field glasses from his satchel. Every pit along the treeline was manned by Métis and Sioux Indians. Gabriel gave two short whistles, telling them to keep their heads down. When Middleton waved *le Rababou* into position, his horse trotted forward, and into range. Gabriel set his rifle on the log in front of the pit.

Kill him now and end the war.

But shooting from bush to open prairie was difficult. A full-on wind had come up and was blowing the tail of the general's horse sideways. Gabriel sighted in. The headache impaired his vision, but he squeezed the trigger and was surprised when Middleton's horse jumped—the shot had come close enough. He adjusted his aim. This time the bullet whizzed past the general's shoulder. When his horse charged back, the Sioux whooped. Gabriel drew a bead on one of the mounted soldiers closer in range, and the man fell instantly out of his saddle, dead before he hit the ground. The Métis cheered but quickly ducked their heads under the edge of their rifle pits as *le Rababou* and both cannon shelled their positions.

At that instant, all fire ceased and Gabriel raised his head. Middleton's officers appeared to be in conflict over where to move *le Rababou*. Finally, it was taken one hundred yards north, jostling on its gun carriage. Instead of following, the general immediately steered his horse south at an angry trot while an officer sounded retreat. One man dead and Middleton was running.

Gabriel turned and was brought up short by the sight of a horse approaching at full gallop from the village. One of the prisoners, William Astley, was astride Riel's buckskin mare, a white handkerchief flying from his jacket. The horse's hindquarters bunched to jump the line of pits. Thinking that Astley had escaped, Gabriel lifted his rifle, but Riel approached at a run, his hands held high.

"He's taking a note to Middleton."

The Sioux had also raised their guns, and Gabriel whistled to hold fire. Riel came into his pit. Everyone watched Astley chase after Middleton and hand him the letter. The general read it and spoke at length with him as he waved his arms about, obviously telling him they were low on ammunition, and other damning information.

Gabriel was incensed. "What is in this note?"

Riel hunched in the pit beside him, his eyes not leaving Astley and the general. With his shabby clothes and overgrown beard, he looked more like a poor farmer than a rebel leader. "*Le Rababou* killed one of White Cap's girls in the village," he said. "*A child*. I told Middleton if he continues to fire on the houses, killing women and children, I will massacre the prisoners."

Gabriel glanced down the line of men in the rifle pits on either side of him. They were uneasy. "It does not help them to see you sending letters to the English—one you have not told me about." He watched Astley turn and point in the direction of the village. The general's officers patted their coat pockets and soon a pencil was produced. Middleton bent over Riel's paper and jotted a brief note.

Isidore Dumas was now sitting on the edge of his pit. "Is it peace?"

"Riel is only trying to save the women and children," Gabriel said. Other men had a look of relief on their faces, as if they thought the battle was over. Some began to gather their blankets and glanced over their shoulders toward the village. After they had witnessed this spectacle, he would never get them back. Middleton's trumpeter again blew his retreat song, and the soldiers marched away south. The Métis were climbing out of their pits, the Sioux muttering amongst themselves.

Astley returned in a cloud of dust and Gabriel caught the reins on his horse. "What were you telling Middleton?"

"I might have mentioned that Big Bear and Poundmaker were on their way," Astley said brazenly. "Just to scare him."

Riel took the letter and read the general's reply aloud, "We do not wish harm to come to your women and children. Place them together in one spot, and let me know where they are, and I will take care that no shot be fired in that direction. I trust in your honour that no men will be placed with them."

Astley, now full of his own importance, said, "I asked Middleton how you could safely surrender."

Gabriel raged forward, almost unseating Astley from the horse. "Riel will never surrender."

god is not here

⁓

THE SUN WAS AT its zenith when Josette went up with her children and Alexandre Dumont to Champagne's farm. She had brought a dress for Virginie Tourond to replace the one the girl had bled through after giving birth to her baby. Families of the fighting men had sought shelter in abandoned houses north of the trail. Blankets littered the floor of Champagne's front room, and his wife's kitchen was cluttered with the detritus of many people living in one space.

Josette had just helped Virginie into the dress, when the sudden report of three spaced sniper shots came from the Jolie Prairie, followed by the rattle of the *Rababou* gun and cannon fire that seemed alarmingly close. The chickens in Champagne's fenced yard squawked at every loud bang and sputtering line of fire.

The door was open to Cleophile and Alexandre out front, watching the younger ones, when a woman passed by on her way north, five of her children carrying their belongings. She stopped with news that a Sioux girl had been killed in front of Boyer's store, and Riel had just sent one of the prisoners with a note to Middleton, threatening retribution. Josette ran back to the village, picturing Gabriel in the pits, desperate to keep the men from deserting.

When she arrived, White Cap's women were tearing at their hair in grief over the bloodied body of a young girl lying in the dirt. Firing had ceased on the Jolie Prairie, and Riel was returning from that direction, his face red and in a fit of anxiety.

"Everyone in one place," he shouted. "Women and children to the houses north of the trail." A dozen fighters had followed him, and he rounded on them. "Go back! Didn't you hear? The general trusts in my honour not to put you with the women and children."

The men hesitated, but did not turn to go, despite his orders. Riel took off his hat and paced in front of Garnot's saloon, holding a piece of paper that he took care not to crumple. His wife stood near him with their children and exchanged a look with Josette.

Riel scanned the assembled women and finally found Pierre Parenteau standing with his wife, Marie. "Get the council papers," he said, and with a side glance at Alexandre Dumont. "Help him bury them on the riverbank."

Pierre headed toward Letendre's where the council had been meeting. Madeleine stood in the doorway, holding a handkerchief to her mouth in an attempt to control a coughing fit. She moved aside to let Pierre and her son into the house but would not meet Josette's eye and blatantly ignored Riel.

William Astley rode up on Riel's horse and waited a little way off, watching them.

Riel had stopped pacing and took a small notebook from his pocket, no longer caring that the deserters had gathered their families and were already moving toward the north trail. He tore a page from the notebook, took out a pencil and began to write.

Josette drew closer, as if circling a trapped animal. Gabriel had asked her not to speak against him, yet she had to know what he meant to reply to Middleton. But when she asked what he was writing, he glanced at her and away, his eyes dark and plagued by doubt. He seemed to float above his body, witness to disaster, a scene where God had failed to bring His miracle.

He stared down, pencil paused over the note. "*Humanité,*" he muttered, then hurriedly finished the sentence and handed it to her. While he fumbled in his pocket for an envelope, Josette glanced down to read.

General—Your prompt answer to my note shows that I was right mentioning to you the cause of humanity. We will gather our families in one place and as soon as it is done we will let you know. Louis "David" Riel.

He whirled at a barrage of fire from the direction of the church and rectory.

Astley had brought up Riel's horse. "Your men are under attack," he said to him. "What's your reply to Middleton?"

Shouts rose over the trees from the direction of the cemetery. English voices and cheers. Alexandre and Pierre Parenteau came out of Letendre's clutching armfuls of council papers. Riel watched them run off in the direction of the riverbank, his expression unreadable. He turned to look north, as if Poundmaker might appear on the trail. His hands were shaking as he slid the note into the envelope. Josette watched him write something on the back.

I do not like war, and if you do not retreat, and refuse an interview, the question remains the same concerning the prisoners.

Astley took the note and rode away. Watching him leave, Josette shook her head and said to Riel, "The general will not retreat. He is winning."

They watched Astley make a mad dash across the south meadow, zigzagging among the ruined tents. His horse stepped into a hole, almost throwing him. Farther south, rifle shots were building in intensity on both sides. Riel stole a glance at her, eyes stark in his face. "The Lord will vindicate His people and have compassion on his servants," he said, "when he sees that their power is gone and there is none remaining, bond or free."

Josette felt her face flush with anger. "If you are so sure our power is gone—surrender."

"You know the men I have," he said. "I cannot go among them and tell them to stop firing."

Madeleine had recovered from her coughing fit and charged toward Riel. "Gabriel will not be taken prisoner or die in those pits."

A shell burst on the south meadow, sending clods of earth and fragments of tent canvas flying through the air. Riel closed his eyes. "My God, stop those people," he said. "Crush them."

"God is not here," shouted Josette. "Save your men by ending this now."

running away
like rabbits

IN A PIT BEHIND the church, Gabriel stared in desperation toward the river bluff. While two cannon pounded shells at Métis snipers on the west bank, a long line of both red- and black-coated soldiers advanced toward him from the cemetery, shoulder to shoulder, bayonets fixed to the ends of their rifles.

Beside him in the pit, old Joseph Ouellette was stuffing nails into the barrel of his ancient shotgun. "*Mort à les Anglais*," he yelled, shooting as the line came into range. He whooped when one went down. The line faltered. A stretcher was sent to retrieve their man, but a desperate Métis from another pit shot at them. One of the officers charged forward with his sabre, howling a foreign battle cry. The column soon followed and Gabriel took hold of Joseph's coat, trying to drag him out.

"You go," the old man said, throwing him off. "I want to kill another Englishman."

Astley had reappeared on Riel's horse from the direction of the village. Gabriel lunged to stop him, but the prisoner veered his mount and galloped past, breaking out of the trees and heading south to find Middleton. Métis were running up from the pits flanking the cemetery. They'd seen Astley, and presumed that Riel had made a truce.

Isidore Boyer cried, "It's peace—peace," but a bullet caught him and he fell, grabbing his shoulder. Pierre Henry went back to drag him away to the west as the soldiers overwhelmed the pits along the treeline. Ambroise Jobin had been shot through the chest and fell without a cry. A soldier bayoneted him with a triumphant shout, then pressed on again with the others. Gabriel broke into a run north, weaving in and out of the trees where some of the Sioux were still making a stand.

"Get out," he yelled. "Save yourselves." In the woods, he caught up to his brother Édouard, Jean Caron junior, Pierre Henry, and two Trottier brothers running for their lives. They burst out of the trees and onto the south meadow. Within minutes they were back in the village, finding Riel there in front of Letendre's store with Josette and Madeleine.

"What are you still doing here?" When Gabriel turned, he could see the first flash of black- and red-coated soldiers in the far trees.

Madeleine clung to him. "Give yourself up."

He shrugged her off. "Take Josette and the children—I'll come for you after dark."

Riel laid a hand on his arm. "Escape with me."

"I will not leave the men. You go."

Uncertainty flashed across Riel's face. His wife made the decision for him, handing him their son and starting away with Angélique in her arms. He followed close after her. Gabriel looked over his shoulder. Joseph Vandal and Donald Ross had appeared from the direction of the riverbank. Seeing the first line of soldiers emerge from the trees, Vandal discharged his old muzzleloader and reloaded it with enviable speed. Ross had a Winchester and fired round after round. When they were joined by two Tourond brothers, the soldiers flung themselves into the craters that their own shells had made in the earth, others crawling in after them, seeking cover.

Gabriel turned to see Madeleine and Josette fleeing with her children up the trail toward Champagne's farm. Where was Alexandre? Riel and his family had disappeared. Gabriel and the men sprinted for a copse of willow in the gully behind Garnot's saloon. They threw themselves down into the bushes and watched an officer wearing a buckskin jacket lead his men into Letendre's house. In a few moments, the officer leaned out of the second-floor window, yelling something to his soldiers. Gabriel sighted him but was too far away to get a clean shot. Vandal and Ross had come up around the side of the house. Ross aimed straight up, hitting the officer in the chest. The body fell back out of sight and immediately his men advanced, screaming in anger. They cornered Ross, shooting him a dozen times. Vandal tried to escape across the south meadow and took a bullet to the shoulder that spun him around.

The men in the gully were loading their shotguns with rocks then frantically working with their powder horns and ramrods. Gabriel's hand went in his pocket to check his own supply. Nine rounds.

Make them count.

Hundreds of soldiers came out of the trees and charged headlong through the south meadow, the *Rababou* gun bumping along behind them on its horse carriage. By the time Gabriel had pressed his remaining bullets into the magazine, the gun operator positioned *le Rababou* and had the crank going, cutting down the Tourond brothers in his first pass. Three soldiers ran toward Champagne's barn. Gabriel raised his gun and dispatched one of them and Édouard wounded another. The third ran back as fast as he'd come.

Gabriel jumped out of the gully and crashed through the bush east of the Carlton Trail, where it intersected the old road to St. Laurent. He was acting on a hunch that Riel had not taken his family with Madeleine and Josette. Or had he run to the ferry, meaning to get across the river? Gabriel hesitated. Another volley of shots and battle cries came from the village. Turning to run back, he looked again and spotted Riel carrying his young son out of the bush beside the road about three hundred yards north. He still wore the Stetson he'd taken as booty at Walter & Baker's store a month ago—the distinctive grey hat with the curved brim. Gabriel wouldn't call Riel's name, for fear that an enemy sniper might be near enough to take out the great rebel leader and his lieutenant.

He ran as hard as he could, finally gaining on them. "Where are you going?"

Riel stared around at Gabriel, then to the north, as though he were expecting someone. His face was pale, in a kind of languid shock. The top of one of his moccasins had been torn away, exposing his bare toes. "Who is guarding the road?"

Gabriel was momentarily taken aback. "François Tourond."

Riel's expression changed at the mention of this name. "The Tourond boys—are they . . . ?"

"I saw two of them fall to *le Rababou*."

Jean began to cry noiselessly in his father's arms. Riel closed his eyes. "I will tell François to run for it."

There was a loud cheer and bugling from the village. "There are still English to kill."

"Promise me you'll escape."

"We'll go together."

Marguerite had come around the bend of the road with their youngest daughter on her hip, and Riel looked back at her. The skin around his eyes twitched. "Gabriel, you will be pardoned by both God and men."

Gabriel's fingers felt numb on his gun stock. Riel meant to surrender. Alone. "Did you know we would lose?" Riel didn't answer. He had already retreated to some dark place, and in a moment he turned and walked quickly away. Gabriel called after him. "Do not let that be the last words I say to you."

Riel paused to adjust the hold on his son and lifted his hand in a strange kind of salute before continuing up the old road. He caught up to his wife and they disappeared out of sight.

Gabriel choked back his rage and disbelief. When all this was over, he'd find Riel, convince him to escape. Shots still came from the direction of the village, and he forced himself into a loping run. He wanted to hold the English off a little longer so the women and Riel could get away. In the small aspens bordering Champagne's hayfields, he came across Moise Ouellette and Charles Thomas. Moise had a rosary in one hand, gun in the other.

"We thought you were dead," Thomas cried. "Where is Riel? Did he say that we're going to win?"

"What are you talking about?" said Ouellette. "Haven't you noticed we're running away like rabbits?"

They told him that soldiers had swarmed the village, and the men left in the gully had escaped. Riel was right. What good would it do for more to die?

"I just saw him," Gabriel said. "He wants us to run."

The men stared at him, confounded. The looks on their faces were what he would remember months later when he heard that Riel had been hanged for treason.

an attack of resolute whites, properly led

⁐

NEAR THE FERRY CROSSING, twenty women crouched with their children in the willow bushes beside an old cow trail. Smoke still hung in the air over the river, acrid and stinging their nostrils. The children did not have to be told to remain quiet and disclose their presence to soldiers in the village, who were celebrating the English victory with shouts and short bursts of gunfire.

Josette was on her knees, holding Wahsis in one arm, the other around Eulalie. Cleophile huddled close by with Patrice. After leaving the village, Madeleine had suffered a debilitating coughing fit and Josette would not abandon her. Many of the women had disappeared along the trail, but those with sick children—and Virginie Tourond, a new *bibi* in her arms—had also lagged behind. A few, like Marguerite Caron, were among them, slowed by age or advanced states of pregnancy. Several of the younger mothers were whimpering their fears that the English would rape them. Eulalie buried her head in Josette's shoulder.

"Hush," Henriette Parenteau said from somewhere behind them. "The soldiers are up there getting drunk on our whiskey."

"They won't think to look down here," said Josette to her children. "And find us so close."

Cleophile whispered, "Did Alexandre bury the council papers?"

Madeleine, who had been in a bush across from them, scrambled out onto the cow trail, as if she meant to look for him, when a loud cheer came from the village.

"Men, you are to be congratulated," a man shouted over the din, his English accent distinctly cultured. "Indeed, you are to be celebrated."

More cheers went up following this pronouncement, and women whispered from close by. "Josette. What does he say?"

"It's Middleton," she told them, "praising his troops."

"You have made me the happiest man in Canada to be at your head," the general continued. "Your gallantry will be remembered. This day's victory proves the correctness of my opinion that these great hunters, like the Boers of South Africa, are only formidable when you play their games—bush fighting—to which they are accustomed. They cannot stand a determined charge."

When Josette related this as best she could to the women, a few of them began to mutter with worry over their men. Had they been killed, or taken prisoner? Josette looked dazedly across the river. Gabriel had said he would not let himself be taken. Despite putting himself in the heat of battle, hoping to die, Norbert had surely managed to escape while other men stood to the last in the pits.

The general was speaking again, and Josette closed her eyes to hear better.

"There is Prince Albert to secure then we must catch these trouble-some Indians," he cried. "Big Bear and Poundmaker, who have doubt-less heard already of Riel's defeat and pointed themselves in another direction entirely. What say we give them a good drubbing?"

Josette was saved from translating this disturbing message when a single shot went over their heads and into the village—sniper fire from the direction of the west bank of the river. Several of the women stood to see if it was one of their men.

Josette could hear the general add something in a blustering tone, as if to prove that he was undaunted to remain a target of rebel guns.

"What is it?" Madeleine asked her.

Josette hesitated a moment before answering. "He says Gabriel and Riel are already across the river."

There was a commotion above on the bluff. Alexandre and Pierre Parenteau leapt bushes straight down the bank toward them, a group of soldiers following close behind. Alex and Pierre were only yards from the women when the soldiers caught them. Parenteau let go of the council papers and an officer chased around the bushes, snatching them up. Expressions on the soldiers' faces changed from surprise to resentful curiosity to find families of the men they'd just been fighting hiding so close to the village.

The priests and nuns had ventured out from the rectory and stood in a tight group, peering over the bluff. They seemed unsure whether they should join the victors or the defeated.

Madeleine tore forward, screaming in French that her son had not been in the fight. She stopped only when one of the soldiers warned her away with his rifle, the knife fixed to its end hovering dangerously close to her face. He turned to shove Pierre hard with the butt of the gun, and the old man fell backward, his hat falling off. Wahsis had begun to cry. Josette picked him up to shield him from the sight.

Breaking away from the priests, Father Vegreville came down the riverbank trail, shouting in his bad English, "The boy was not with Riel—and that man is old. He cannot be held."

The officer motioned for Alexandre to be let go, but said to Pierre, "Too old to fight, but not too old to bury the evidence. You are under arrest for high treason."

When Pierre was led away, Judith Dumont muttered, *"Bon Dieu va vous écraser."*

The officer turned to his men with a smile. "Doesn't sound like any kind of French I've heard. Anyone know what she said?"

"God will crush you," Josette replied in English.

The officer received the threat with a derisive laugh. "If God wished to crush us, Madame, He would already have done so."

"Des beaux bonhommes," added Marguerite Caron. Fine men you are. But even she was cowed by a group of soldiers from the same regiment, who were coming along the riverbank from the south, blood smeared on their uniform jackets.

One approached La Rose and Mary-Jane Ouellette. "The women are better looking than their men," he said, grinning around at his friends. "A pity we can't take the soldier's reward."

"Dusky things," said another, "pretty in their way." He reached behind La Rose, yanking at the tightly wound knot at the back of her head. It finally released and her long black hair fell down to her waist. "It's said they're like animals in bed. I'd like a go at this one."

The officer overheard this and ordered the men back to their unit. He turned to Josette and told her the women had to remain in camp until their men came in. He started up the trail, and the women filed back to their dugouts on the riverbank to salvage what they could from the camp. Josette followed behind Madeleine, who was suffering another bout of coughing. When Middleton had said that Gabriel and Riel were already across the river, he'd added something that she did not think Madeleine needed to know.

"Tomorrow we will hunt them out."

spoils of war

MADELEINE BENT TO THE ashes of a cooking fire in the riverbank camp to retrieve a small pan that had not been melted down for ammunition. Alexandre, still shaken by his ordeal with the soldiers, stood looking around at the damage done during the last four days, the tents in disarray, half of them down. At least she still had him. She scanned the trees along the west bank. Storm clouds had gathered and it was raining far to the east, a dark haze that poured veiled mist to the earth. Gabriel, across the river. She could feel his eyes on them.

Madeleine eyed Josette, grubbing with her children in the remains of their dugout, gathering blankets and clothes. She seemed to desperately search for something and fell upon what looked like a book, tucking it quickly into a saddlebag.

When Gabriel had wept in Madeleine's arms on the eve of the battle, she suspected that some of it had been guilt for daring—with an ill wife—to look at another woman. But she could not forget Father Moulin when she'd gone to seek Gabriel's absolution, the priest wishing to remember him as the good man who had brought Josette in, broken from Norbert's beating. Josette had told her a story of how she had received the cut on her lip, a black eye. Norbert had punished her and she had managed to escape. Both she and Gabriel had neglected to mention that it was he who had saved her. Madeleine could understand Josette lying, but not Gabriel. Why hadn't he told her?

Because his rescue of Josette had been an act of love.

It was no wonder the girl kept looking at the other bank, even now, yearning for a glimpse of him. The great Métis buffalo hunter had charged in like a knight on a white horse to protect her from harm. What woman could resist? There was the issue, the impending certainty of her own death within the year. Maybe sooner. She would not begrudge Gabriel marrying again. But she was not dead yet.

Another group of soldiers appeared on the bluff above and descended the trail, their tall boots kicking up mud. One of them, an officer by the looks of his uniform, had noticed Josette's saddlebag and shouted, "All supplies are to be requisitioned." There followed a brief scuffle as one of his men decided he would take the bag, but she held on to it, scratching and kicking.

"Let her have it," said the officer. "The squaws are harmless. It's their husbands we want." He took her chin in his gloved hand. "You are pretty enough to be the wife of Louis Riel."

Josette said nothing, only stared insolently into his face. When the other women ranged away, trying not to attract attention, Madeleine glanced across the river.

Gabriel, do not be reckless.

The officer laughed. "What of Gabriel Dumont's wife? Is she here? If any of you give up the wives of these two men, you will receive provisions for a year." When he got no answer, he released his hold on Josette.

Sudden screams came from Marie Boyer, who had found her husband Isidore lying face down under their tipi cloth. A soldier drew his revolver and another lifted Boyer by his arms. But he was dead, blood staining his shirt and coat. Sometime during the last charge, another Métis had brought him down here, wounded, out of the line of fire. Boyer had staggered to the dugout his family had shared, almost tearing down the cloth in an attempt to crawl inside. He had died with his hand twisted in the fur of an old buffalo hide.

Marie had drawn his head up on her lap, stroking his hair back from his forehead. Her young children stood around, staring dumbly, not yet understanding that their father was dead. Madeleine turned away, appalled. The soldiers rooted in the dugouts for a few minutes, decided there was nothing of value there, and trudged back up the trail. Josette, still clinging to the saddlebag with one hand, gave Wahsis into Cleophile's arms. The girl was pale, devastated by the death and dying all around her and by her mother's neglect, yet Josette continued to use her as a *p'tite mère*. With her luck, Norbert had survived this war when better men had not. *That was how Riel's God worked.*

It had begun to rain. Madeleine went up the riverbank with Alexandre, only to find that some of the women had followed the priests back to the rectory. Mounted soldiers had chased down a herd of the Métis cattle and were shooting them for sport. Alexandre took a step forward, as though he might stop them. Madeleine put a hand on his arm, urging him to search for provisions in a wagon that had been left near the rectory gate. When he looked inside, he shook his head and turned away.

Heart in her mouth, she glanced in, only to find the body of old Joseph Ouellette, the front of his coat soaked red with blood. Rain was falling on his ancient face, which still wore an expression of surprise and regret. "Ninety-three years on this earth," she said. "And he ends like this."

Alex had just covered Joseph with one of their blankets and said a prayer over his body, when Father Fourmond came away from the ruins of the Caron and Gareau houses on the ridge. He broke into a trot when he saw them, holding up the length of his soutane. "Two more of your men have been found," he said, gesturing behind him. "Their wives must claim the bodies, so they can be buried with the others."

A group of officers had set up a table near the church, behind which Father Vegreville sat in an officious manner. Josette had come up from the riverbank camp. "What goes on there?" she demanded of Fourmond. "Métis lie around us dead, and the priests are all at once thick with *les Anglais*."

"Riel's council documents are being checked," he said. "When your men come in to surrender, any whose name is on those lists will be brought to justice." He noticed the Ouellette girls crying near the wagon and patted Mary-Jane on the back. "Your grandfather will have his own coffin—he will receive the last rites."

"And the others?" asked Josette. "What will they receive?"

Fourmond's eyes rose to meet hers. "They will be buried together."

"In a hole!"

"They were excommunicated for following Riel."

She pointed at him, an accusing finger. "Your throat is an open grave," she said. "The venom of asps is under your lips."

Fourmond stalked away. Madeleine expected the women to rail against Josette for using scripture to accuse their priests, but even a few of the Old Crows seemed to have attached themselves to her, as if she were the only one with courage to say what was on their own minds. Madeleine overheard them talk among themselves, of how they might escape along the river after dark.

Other women had gone out on the meadow between the church and Jean Caron's burned-out house and stood around the dead bodies that had been found. A few of them wept and turned away, as if they could not stand the sight. Alexandre, in the way of boys, was curious and Madeleine let him go.

Domatilde Gravelle had just come from there, a handkerchief over her mouth. She whispered to Madeleine, "Keep Marie Carrière and her children away."

Marie was Damase Carrière's wife, one of Gabriel and Riel's finest scouts. Madeleine could not resist venturing out to see. The rain had stopped by the time she arrived, and as the women parted to give way for her, she saw the two bodies on the ground. Damase lay on his back, head at an unnatural angle, a rope buried tight in the flesh of his neck. The other man had come to rest face down, rope still tied around broad shoulders, which were dislocated forward in a kind of supplication. Prairie grass had been trampled all around, the mud thick here, as though a herd of horses had passed.

Both men's clothes had been ripped in places, the skin showing through almost raw, as if burned by fire. Flies had already collected on the wounds. Madeleine pitied the woman who must find her husband like this.

The women did not have the courage to move the other body, so Alexandre and one of the boys pulled it from the mud. When they turned it over, Madeleine stared down in horror at a face she had seen a million times, and knew by heart.

Norbert.

those who are eaten

THE NEXT EVENING at dusk, Louis Riel searched the barn for eggs that he could bring to his family. He had come out from a day of hiding in the root cellar under the abandoned house of an *Anglais* half-breed near St. Laurent. It had finally dawned on him that Marguerite's persistent cough had a more disturbing cause than drafts or dust. Both children were ill, as well—Angélique was anemic, too weak to cry and Jean sat staring at nothing, saying only that he was hungry, could they get more to eat. Riel felt through a haystack, his fingers finally closing around an egg, smooth and warm in his palm. He held it up to the last light filtering in the door. *Now the earth was formless and empty, darkness was over the surface of the deep.*

Moise Ouellette had found him this morning with a letter from Middleton. Riel had almost memorized the words, but he took it from his pocket again to read in the fading light.

I am ready to receive you and your council and protect you until your case has been decided upon by the Dominion Government.

Riel had sent Moise back with a note of his own, telling the general that his council was dispersed, and that he wished the government would let them go quiet and free. But no answer had come. Middleton would not leave until he had captured Louis Riel and Gabriel Dumont.

Moise had said the Métis were angry with him for destroying their lives and families. The same men who had invited him here, pledging to fight to their last drop of blood. Moise had admitted that Gabriel was searching the woods, trying to find him. "Do not tell him I am here," Riel said, remembering the look on his war chief's face on the trail yesterday, begging him not to surrender. Gabriel had asked a question that might have been on his lips since the first day of battle: *Did you know we would lose?*

Riel hesitated in the doorway of the barn. Last night, he had been haunted by a dream where the angel of divine mercy had chanted, "Riel! Thirty years of Purgatory." Desperate to mortify himself, he had come out in the dark to kneel in a horse stall, praying, weeping, the chalice of his spirit drained. But anger had slowly replaced his despair and he had emerged an hour later, convinced that by surrendering and standing trial in Quebec, with good lawyers, he could win the case for the Métis and Indians of the North-West.

Dense clouds drifted over the moon. The great shadow of the barn, a sensation of standing on the edge of the universe, and the name of a ruthless God issuing from that mystery, overwhelming his senses. King David had murdered Uriah, the husband of Bathsheba. Finally admitting his sin had been the only way to win God's forgiveness. Riel had weighed every sin he himself might have overlooked. Had God abandoned him because he had failed to stop Thomas Scott's execution? He refused to admit guilt for a murder he did not commit.

You struck down Uriah, killed him with the sword of the Ammonites. Now, therefore, the sword will never depart from your house.

God had already struck him and his family. Marguerite was pregnant and ill with consumption, dying. Jean and Angélique were surely cursed, as God had visited the iniquity of the father on the children. He wanted to confess, unburden all of these worries and be clean again.

He went back toward the house, the egg in his pocket. He was fasting to rid himself of the last vestiges of pride, but his wife and children would eat. He froze at a sudden movement in the trees, the shadow of a horse and rider. In a moment, he was able to see by the shawl and long drift of skirt that it was a woman. She turned in the saddle. *His confessor.*

"What are you doing here?" he said, as Josette dismounted. "Who is with you?"

She told him that she had made Moise tell her where he was hiding. Riel listened as she spoke of the chaos in Batoche, how Middleton would not let the women and children leave. "We slipped away this morning," she said, "while they held funerals for their dead." She took a wrapped bundle from her saddlebag and handed it to him.

Grease had leaked through the cloth; it smelled like cooked meat. Despite the coming dark, he could see that her hair was unbound around her neck from the ride, and she was distant—removed as she had been when he had first tried to win her to his side.

"The soldiers have killed all the cattle," she said. "We butchered and roasted what we could. Your wife and the children should keep up their strength."

It did not escape his notice that she had failed to mention *him* needing strength. He found it difficult to read her expression. She seemed distracted, agitated, turned inward to herself.

"Has Norbert surrendered?"

"He's dead." Her voice was flat, emotionless.

Riel dropped the bundle on the grass and looked back at the house. He had told Marguerite and the children to stay in the root cellar no matter what they heard.

"We found Norbert on the prairie," she said, almost ruthlessly. "Both he and Damase Carrière had been shot in the pits by the church."

Riel passed a hand over his eyes. Moise had failed to tell him this.

"They did not have mortal wounds when the soldiers dragged them out," she said. "A rope was tied around Damase's neck."

Riel shook his head. "I don't—"

"They dragged him from the back of a horse." Although a low moan escaped him at this news, she did not pause. "When the women found his body, his hands were still clenched upon the rope."

The memory of Damase's face came to him, laughing at a joke one of the men had told at the council table. Damase, riding out in the dusk alone so many times over the past month to scout Middleton's camp. When Riel could trust his voice, he asked what had happened to Norbert.

She was very still, her face controlled, without expression. "The soldiers dragged him, too."

"*Non*." God had truly abandoned them if the best of their men had suffered the same fate as their worst.

"The bones in his hands were broken, the nails black with blood where he'd clawed the ground."

Riel was appalled to hear her speak in such a voice. And why the need to tell him these unbearable details? "You can be at peace now," he said to placate her.

"I will never be at peace."

Riel was thankful to have the meat for his family, but now wished she hadn't come. He took the letter out of his pocket. "Middleton has asked me to surrender. I will go in the morning." He hoped, perhaps expected, that she would try to dissuade him, but she continued to give him that dark, resolute look. He lowered his eyes. "My mission is not over. The world cannot ignore our morality, our humanity. All our good actions will be rewarded in heaven. And Macdonald, by his actions, will be punished in hell."

"What of my *Mosom*?" she said. "How will he be rewarded?"

Now he knew why she had come. God had sent her as He had sent Nathan to David. "Mary Magdalene was with the Lord until his very end," he reminded her. She seemed rooted to the earth, great waves of indignation rising off her like heat from a stove.

"Mary Magdalene did not have to bear enemy soldiers making an effigy of her grandfather," she said. "The Magdalene did not watch them take turns stabbing it with their long knives as they did on the Jolie Prairie yesterday."

The faded moon had risen over the trees, the features of its stippled face arranged, it seemed to him, in accusation. He took off his hat and dragged a hand through his hair. "What of your relations in his camp?"

"They have fled to the north country," she said, her voice bitter.

"Did Parenteau bury my papers?" She shook her head. He did not bother to ask her why, just accepted the answer. "After I surrender, I will be taken to Montreal—there will be a Supreme Court trial."

"Perhaps you will be put in a cell with Honoré Jaxon."

The little resolve he possessed had worn thin. It was a struggle to stand upright, facing her. "I heard that Honoré was taken."

"I saw him when they were loading the prisoners on the steamship. I tried to tell the guards that he was harmless, insane . . ."

She was turned now and he studied her face. He had admired her mind and liked her very much. He had not—as some had accused him —used her only to get Big Bear to his side. He had chosen her as his Mary Magdalene, his confessor. Now, in the moon's light and in her ragged coat, she looked both aggrieved and impossibly beautiful.

"I will tell you what Honoré said to me as they led him on the boat," she said. "'Do you see there are only two kinds of people? Those who eat and those who are eaten.'"

Riel fought the desire to fall on his knees, humble himself before her and God. But she had already gathered her skirts and swung up into the saddle. She looked down at him, long dark hair falling across her face.

He laid a hand on her horse's neck. "I have been mistaken all this time, waiting for God . . ." He paused, telling himself that he would not break down. "I did not know that God has been waiting for *me*."

i will not fall into
their hands

IT WAS DARK WHEN Gabriel jerked awake, his back against a tree, senses alert to any movement. A full day had passed since they had lost the war, and the top of his head hurt more than at the moment he had taken the wound. Cold had got to his lungs. When he coughed, he almost passed out from the pain. He had slept for a few hours, a luxury, but it now felt that he was closer to death than he had been during the battles.

The moon stood bright in the sky overhead, shedding light upon the path as he unhobbled his two horses and brought them to a creek that wound down through a shallow coulee. He knelt where a pool eddied and cupped his hands to drink, then leaned back, closing his eyes. A dark smell rose out of the mud, the smell of rot and life shifting on the wind that brought it like an unfound ghost.

That morning, Gabriel had roamed the bluffs north of the Jolie Prairie, trying to find his younger brother, Édouard. Many of the fighters had turned themselves in, but some were holding out in the bush, too worried about their families to run, yet fearful of poor treatment from *les Anglais* if they surrendered.

When he had come across Métis horses running loose in the trees, he told the men to take them or the English would. He had found Josette's horse, La Noire, grazing below a small bluff and caught her. It was more difficult to hide with two horses, but he would not let her be stolen by *Anglais* patrols. Shortly before sunset, he had found James Short hiding to the north of the Jolie Prairie and listened to him tell of seeing Joseph Vandal's dead body bayoneted so many times, that the *Anglais* soldier who tried to get his powder horn off as a prize had to wash the blood off his hands. Of André Letendre killed in the shadow of his own brother's house. Michel Trottier and John Swain—shot in the back. And two girls who had died, caught in the crossfire. When James said that he'd heard that some of the women and children were seen that morning on the riverbank trail north, escaping Batoche, Gabriel had given up on trying to find Édouard.

He rose from the creek bed and held his breath to quiet the beat of blood in his ears. If he found Madeleine, he might find Riel. He stood for a moment to get his bearings before leading the horses down the creek to the river. When he thought of his wife and then Josette, a vicious ache bore into the centre of his skull, blurring his vision.

He had not gone far on an old cow trail north when he heard movement in the bush ahead. Gabriel dropped into a squat and quietly flicked the knife sheath at his waist. The call of a prairie chicken in the night air, a bird that lived out on the plains, not here, so close to the river. He whistled back and watched the trees. The shape of a man formed up on the other side of the trail near a low run of willow. *Michel Dumas.*

"Your wife sent me to find you," Dumas said, after they'd clapped each other on the back.

"You've seen her?"

"The women are up at Fayant's."

They walked the horses along the bank, and Dumas told him of evading *Anglais* patrols to watch some of the Métis straggle in to Batoche. "You should have seen Maxime Lépine turn himself in. He was broken down—didn't want to speak to anyone." Dumas said that more than seventy of their men had surrendered or been caught and charged with treason. They were held aboard the *Northcote*, which had been repaired after the battle and was docked at the ferry crossing.

"Why hasn't it sailed?"

Dumas punched him lightly on the shoulder. "The general is waiting for the big prizes." He glanced at Gabriel. "I will never put myself in *Anglais* hands. We will ride for the border, *oui*?"

"We must find Riel, before they do."

"Moise Ouellette found him today—"

Gabriel stopped in the track. "Where?"

But Dumas was uncharacteristically evasive. "He said Riel made him promise not to tell us."

Gabriel spit into the mud. "Do you have any food?"

"The women have some beef."

Yesterday, after the battle, Gabriel had watched soldiers run down their cattle on the prairie, shooting them one after another. Was he hungry enough to eat his own beef slaughtered at the hands of *les Anglais*?

Within an hour, they were climbing Fayant's cutbank trail, and Gabriel heard Madeleine before he saw her. A coughing fit that ended in wet gagging. *Blood.* The floor of Fayant's house was crowded with the bodies of women and children wrapped in their blankets.

Madeleine got up at the sight of him and kissed the rosary around her neck. It was dark in the room, but she used her hands to feel up and down his arms for wounds, and finally his neck. He winced when she touched his head, her fingers light upon the wet bandage. "I will fix this," she said, and he could hear the trembling in her voice. "You will eat. Then you will ride for the boundary line."

He pulled away from her. "I won't let him surrender. I'll find him first, Madeleine."

She took firm hold of his shoulder and steered him out to the porch. Dumas' own wife Veronique had gone to him in the yard where he stood with the horses.

"Leave the black one in the barn," Madeleine called, "and give the other two oats for the ride south." She put a hand to her throat and faced Gabriel. "You have found *her* horse, I see."

He shrugged. "Why let the English take her?" The porch was dark, but he could imagine her deep-set eyes, staring him down.

"Riel will surrender, and you are going to run."

His wife only wanted to save him. Yesterday, Riel had asked him to do the same. *You will be pardoned by both God and men.*

"Riel will hang for this," she said, "and you too, if you are caught with him."

Women were coming out onto the porch, as if to convince themselves that Gabriel Dumont was still alive; the older children were awake now too and pushing past the door to gather around him. Alexandre was there and Isidore's children with Patrice, Josette's oldest boy. Gabriel glanced up before he could catch himself.

"She took off on one of Fayant's ponies," Madeleine said from behind him, "right after we cooked the meat."

One of his nephews clung to his leg. Gabriel patted the boy's head. "And you let her?"

Madeleine's voice had grown cold. "Who can stop her doing anything."

Gabriel knew that Josette had gone after Riel. To convince him to surrender? *Non.* To face him one last time.

The women seemed to realize that Madeleine and her husband were in the middle of an intimate conversation, and they herded Alexandre and the children back inside. The door had not closed when his wife's voice took on an undertone of hurt.

"Is it because I was barren?"

He did not think it was possible to feel more physical pain, but she had managed to deliver a blow that almost sent him to his knees. When he had discovered that Madeleine was ill and dying, he had pushed Josette away from him, prayed to love his wife the way she deserved. He *did* love her.

He was about to turn when she added, "Or is it because she does not break your balls?"

"She breaks them too," he said bitterly. "They are broken—are you satisfied?"

"Ah then," she said, "you are no use to either of us."

He pulled Madeleine into his arms, but she pushed him away in another coughing fit, got the handkerchief to her mouth in time to catch the blood. "If you love me," she finally managed, "escape."

Too tired to argue, he nodded. "*Oui*, I will go."

She drew him indoors, where his brother's widow, Judith Dumont, had already started a fire in the stove to heat water. He sat on the edge of the kitchen table while the women bound his head with a piece of cloth torn from someone's coat lining. They told him of finding Norbert Lavoie's body with Damase Carrière's, dragged behind horses until they were dead. Gabriel listened with his head down, hand clenched upon his knee. Norbert's death did not move him, but to think of Damase, suffering this low form of torture and murder . . . When Riel heard, it would devastate him.

The women had a leg of beef they had cooked on embers to avoid revealing their location to *les Anglais*. The meat was mostly raw inside, yet Gabriel and Dumas ate and accepted more for the trail. Dumas went out to bring their horses to the gate and tighten the cinches, swing up the saddlebags.

The moon washed the tops of the bare trees and the slanted roof of Fayant's house. By Madeleine's formal and hesitant manner, Gabriel knew that she was not done speaking of Josette.

His wife followed him to his horse. "After the first day of battle," she said, "I went to the rectory." He faltered, one foot in the stirrup, unable to look at her. "I asked Père Moulin to grant you absolution. Do you know what he told me? How you came to him with Josette the night of the New Year's dance, after Norbert beat her." He took his foot out of the stirrup, knew that he deserved this. "Why did you keep it from me?" she asked. A coughing fit overtook her, and she almost choked on her next words, "I am not an old buffalo cow to be left on the prairie."

"I never thought you were." A feeling of desolation came over him, and he thought of taking her with him. She was dying. He did not want this scene to be their last. But he and Dumas must stay off the trails, places a wagon couldn't go. "I will send for you when I get to Montana," he said, the words heavy on his tongue. He grabbed her around the waist, buried his face in her neck, as he had done almost every day for the past twenty-seven years.

She had never been one for emotion and patted his shoulder, even held out the stirrup for his foot. After he mounted and turned his horse, she put her hand to his leg, to the garter that she had beaded for him by their kitchen fire long ago. He told her that he would surrender to the authorities as soon they reached the States, ask for amnesty, and she nodded, gave his horse a slap on the rump. He and Dumas rode away with Gabriel looking back at her solitary figure until they had gone into the trees and she was lost to him.

As soon as they had found the trail at the edge of the Jolie Prairie, he turned his horse north.

Dumas called after him, "What are you doing?"

Gabriel would no longer listen to detractors. He would give it one last chance. "We will go as far as the bend in the river," he told Dumas, "to Calixte Lafontaine's. If we don't find Riel there, we'll give up and ride south."

she spoke his name

HOURS BEFORE DAWN, Josette rode past the abandoned houses—Napoléon Nault's farm, Gervais' and Laplante's. The trail she had taken so often when visiting Riel and Jackson in St. Laurent. Would Middleton burn these houses too, as his army moved north? When she had come to Lafontaine's farm, an indistinct murmur of voices drifted to her on the wind, and she turned her pony into a stand of young poplar trees behind the barn. The moon glowed white within a ring of cloud, lighting up the trail like a lantern held high. She dismounted and listened carefully, her ears searching for any sound through the bare branches. Nothing but a hush of river in the near distance. There it was again—a man talking in low tones, another answering. She led her mount further into the trees and before long, two riders appeared on the trail. One of them reined in his horse, which almost reared, champing at the bit. Soldiers this far north? After Riel.

One of the riders turned his head and she almost cried with relief.

The moon showed Gabriel's face. He got off his horse and she watched him walk into the trees. To see him again was like a gift, but as he drew closer, she could feel the burden of his grief, and another, unspeakable emotion. She was confused and elated at having him suddenly near. *Gabriel*. Not ridden to the south. Alive. The clothes he had worn for the past few weeks were caked with dried mud. Somewhere along the line he had lost both his sash and the belt that held up his pants, replacing it with an old rope. They stared at each other for a long moment, standing so close, their foreheads almost touched.

Finally, he said, "Madeleine told me what they did to Norbert—it is finished, *non?*" When she couldn't speak, his hands went to her shoulders, lingered there, as if he were calming a frightened horse. "Did you find Riel?"

She could smell sweat on him and the fresh blood from his wound. "I left him just after dark."

"What did he say?"

"He wants to stand trial—show the world what the government has done to us."

"Take me back to him."

To say yes would mean she would have him to herself a while longer, but she took his arm. "Ride south, get across the line."

"You too?" He looked north, as if he could somehow conjure Riel.

"He said God is waiting for him."

Gabriel glanced up at the moon. "When Riel came here, I thought he was the stronger bull and we were in the right. Macdonald would lose the challenge. But the Métis never had a chance, regardless of who led us."

She studied his face with a sick fear that she would forget the way he looked at that moment. Gabriel would start a new life with Madeleine in the States, and after her death, remain exiled as Riel had been, from the land he had loved and fought for, never to return to Batoche, just as surely as she was trapped there. But he did not want to hear that she loved him.

Gabriel placed his hand on the side of the barn. "What will become of this? What we have built?" He lapsed into anxious silence, as though he had more to say, but could not start.

"You've seen Madeleine."

He nodded. "She asked me if it was because she was barren." Josette could not read his face in the shadows. "She learned of that night," he went on, "when you were beaten by Norbert, when I brought you to the rectory. She knew . . ." He didn't finish or would not say aloud what she had questioned for so long, what she had hoped.

"It will soon be light," Josette said, to save him from saying something he might regret later.

He nodded, almost imperceptibly. The moon had slipped behind a bank of cloud by the time he had mounted his horse and settled in the saddle, the leather creaking with his weight, *le Petit* under his arm again. Within a few hours, the sun would come up, and this night would be only a dream in her mind. She fought the impulse to jump up behind him. A man could do what he pleased. Her husband was dead, but she had children, a farm. And the only man she loved was married to another woman.

When he picked up the reins, his body softened. He touched the ends of her fingers then his horse pulled away, and she was left with only the smell of him still on her.

epilogue

HELENA, MONTANA
AUGUST, 1887

JOSETTE HAD NOT BEEN among so many white people in her life—the ladies in tightly corsetted dresses and matching hats and parasols. Men who wore fine suits and polished boots, despite the dust. From her seat in the grandstand, she could see the town of Helena in the valley, the great Missouri river behind it and mountains rising in the near distance, their summits and the clouds that ranged above them touched pink in the late afternoon sun.

Wahsis had his head on her shoulder, his eyes closed in sleep. Patrice sat next to her, eating popped corn out of a waxed paper bag. Hungry, and eager to explore after the five-day wagon trip south, Eulalie and Cleophile had gone off to discover the fair.

The farmer's field below had been turned into a showground. Members of the crowd waited impatiently, staring with expectation at a man in top hat and long black jacket who strode around a fenced arena. Off to one side, a large white tent had been erected; other, smaller tents and enclosures dotted the pasture to the trees.

Eager applause broke out when the man raised a bullhorn and began to speak. "Ladies and Gentlemen, I present to you, Buffalo Bill's Wild West and Congress of Rough Riders of the World! Sit back and enjoy lurid western blood and thunder drama—the rugged life of primitive man." He swept his arm in a flamboyant gesture. "Here you will see heroes of the dugout, the cabin, the ranch, and the trail, whose lives have been passed in reality eclipsing romance."

The flaps were drawn back on the large tent and a grand parade of performers poured out of it and into the arena. Most were Indians in the traditional war paint of the Sioux, chiefs among them in full regalia, feathers flying. From enclosures in the pasture, cowboys drove a stampede composed of every manner of beast: a dozen buffalo, deer, cows with long curved horns, mules, donkeys, oxen, and absurdly, a few wild elk, one with a set of impressive antlers, the tips of which had been broken off in a fight. Josette could not take her eyes from the buffalo that galloped around the ring, snorting and tossing their heads. It had been over ten years since she'd seen them on the plains.

The program booklet had dedicated an entire page to a description of the methods for tracking buffalo, how the Indians and half-breeds had done it. She read of hunters that howled and made their war cries, the great beasts, bleeding from arrows and shotgun blasts, skidding to their death in the dust. There was no mention of the women who came after to make the first cuts, or of skinning and dressing, saving the kidneys, hump, and liver. Her own memories as a child, kneeling in the prairie grass, waiting for her mother to slice a piece of liver and hand it to her, still warm.

All animals but the buffalo had been herded out of the arena, and a group of Indians remained. They whipped up their horses; some of the younger braves picked out a few of the buffalo and chased them around the ring, pulling their bows back with exaggerated might. Wahsis was awake now, wide-eyed with amazement. He hadn't seen Indians painted up since the fight in Batoche two years ago and seemed confused, unsettled by the spectacle. It was an astounding sight even to Josette's eyes, who, as a child, had known men like these among the Cree, her own grandfather riding to war.

After the buffalo were driven out, the announcer raised his bullhorn. "I give you the bloodthirsty savage of the plains, the man responsible for sending General Custer to an early grave—the indomitable Chief Sitting Bull."

Josette sat forward with anticipation. Father Moulin had once shown her a photograph of Sitting Bull in the *Saskatchewan Herald*, sacred pipe on his lap, confident, level eyes almost staring down the camera. She had expected an Indian dressed up to look like the great chief, but Sitting Bull himself entered the ring on a mustang pony, the eagle feathers in his headdress arrayed like a crown on his head.

Soldiers in blue U.S. Army uniforms galloped their horses in, chasing half a dozen Indians who whooped and pretended to shoot at them with bows and arrows and shotguns. Sitting Bull kicked his horse to a trot and brandished his long spear, as if giving orders. It all looked real, to the red flannel handkerchiefs that had been produced to mimic blood bursting from the chests of Custer's men.

As Sitting Bull inspected the soldiers' bodies, a white man with curling blonde hair under his hat entered the ring on a high stepping horse. He wore a light buckskin coat decorated with fringe. His white mustaches were so long, they curved upward, like a sleigh runner.

"Ladies and Gentlemen," cried the announcer, "I present to you the Pony Express Rider, serving the Union in the Great War, recipient of the Medal of Honor—Buffalo Bill Cody!"

His horse cantered a slow circle as Buffalo Bill pretended shock at the discovery of his dead comrades. Most of the Indians, including Sitting Bull, had since exited the ring, except for one bare-chested brave who rode directly at Buffalo Bill. Bill's horse reared and sprang into a gallop. Patrice gripped Josette's hand as the two riders careened toward each other at breakneck speed. Buffalo Bill swerved at the last minute and raised his rifle. There was a loud crack, puffs of smoke, and the Indian flew out of the saddle. Bill dismounted and ran to where he lay on the ground, bending with his long knife drawn over the Indian's head. The audience gasped when he rose quickly, waving a scalp, which proved later to be a black braid wig with red flannel attached underneath.

"I'll not leave a Redskin to skim the prairie," he declared loudly and paraded around the centre of the arena with his trophy.

The crowd erupted into rowdy applause when the announcer yelled, "The first scalp taken by Buffalo Bill Cody, Indian fighter responsible for capturing and killing Chief Yellow Hair in retaliation for murdering Custer."

Buffalo Bill gallantly tipped his hat. He made it look like the Indians were out for blood, that they needed taming, and it was luck, or pure providence, that the whites had come along when they did. Josette looked around her at the jeering faces. She wanted to tell them the Bighorn battle had been fought by Sioux refusing to let whites push them off their lands. But she remained silent. Over the past two years in Batoche, she had learned to keep her mouth shut when more settlers arrived with hatred and fear of "Riel's half-breed rebels." Many of the Métis told government surveyors that they were French. None of them had jigged at a wedding since before the war. Their men no longer wore the ceinture fléchée. Children playing in the fields brought back spent rifle shells, which mothers confiscated, saying, "We had nothing to do with Riel and those bad Métis."

When Buffalo Bill vaulted back on his horse and had ridden it out of the arena, the announcer waited for the "dead" Indian to be dragged off before turning to the crowd. He held out his hand. "And now—what you've all been waiting for—a fine demonstration of the great might of the firing arm."

Two people entered the ring on horseback. The first one Josette took to be a small man, but as the rider passed before their seats, she saw it was a woman, whom the program pamphlet had described as Annie Oakley. On the other side of the arena a man sat astride a chestnut roan mare that he kept at a canter. As his hand went to the horse's withers, tears burned in Josette's eyes.

A week ago, she had gone up to the rectory, where Father Moulin now ran a postal outlet on the second floor. The mail packet had come, and Josette watched the old priest untie the bundle. She had waited anxiously as he sorted the letters, his mouth moving as he read the familiar names. Periodically since the war, she had received an envelope without a note or return address—the only contents, American bills of various denominations.

Moulin looked up at her. "Have patience," he said. "I am sure it will be here . . . Ha," he added, with a crafty expression. "I know what you wait for."

Two years had not changed the old priest. He still had the scruffy white hair and beard, the petulant blue eyes. Josette would not go back to the church, though Moulin had made it possible for her to do so if she performed a public recantation. Many of the Métis kept her company on Sundays, for they still regarded the South Branch priests with suspicion, and—in Father André's case—even anger for giving damning evidence at Riel's trial, effectively sending him to hang.

"How are your heretics?" Moulin asked, still occupied with sorting.

Josette had lost a good portion of her back fields to Mennonite farmers who now grew wheat almost to the small cabin that Norbert's relations had helped her rebuild on the site of their burned house. Moulin disapproved of her doing chores for food, washing their clothes, and caring for children not her own. Yet she liked these people who refused to worship saints or speak of sin.

Moulin had reached below the desk and brought out the latest edition of the *Saskatchewan Herald*. "*Regarde*," he said, pushing it toward her.

Gabriel's picture stared out from the front page. After getting over the shock of seeing his face, she quickly read the headline. *Gabriel Dumont, Louis Riel's Adjutant General, rides in Buffalo Bill's Wild West Show*. She looked up as if to say, "So, what of it?"

Moulin observed her with interest. "I know it is Gabriel who sends you money. The great rebel leader in exile. Why does he not return?"

"When he is granted amnesty, he will come back." It was something she had told herself many times over the last two years.

Moulin had found her envelope and held it for a moment before releasing it into her hand. "Perhaps Gabriel has a new wife." Josette turned to leave, the envelope finding its way into her skirt pocket. "The Wild West Show comes to Helena in a week's time," Moulin called as she went down the stairs.

Within two days, she had begged a ride with Maxime Poitras, on a trip south to trade his furs in Helena. Gabriel would be granted amnesty in time, but she was not one to tempt fate. Now that she had come with the children, she could not imagine facing him again. A month after the war, Gabriel had sent word to Madeleine and she had left for Montana, leaving their farm in the care of the Vennes. But a year later, there had been news of her death from consumption. What if he were still lost in grief, or Moulin was right and he'd taken a new wife?

In the arena below, the announcer had turned to the man on the roan mare. "Ladies and Gentleman! I present to you, the Adjutant General, leader of the half-breed rebels at Duck Lake and Batoche in the Territories. First Lieutenant to no other than the traitor Louis Riel. This is the half-breed Indian scout who gave an entire army of soldiers what for and yes, the gun he's about to show you is the famed *le Petit*—that's French for little one—not little if you ask me."

Gabriel made a show of lifting his gun to the crowd, his expression somewhere between distraction and annoyance. *He is not enjoying this*, she thought, her eyes not leaving him. He wore a fringed buckskin coat she'd not seen before, a slouch hat pulled low over his eyes. Did he still feel the wound he took at Duck Lake? It was impossible to tell. He had become fuller around the middle, his chest still broad and powerful, beard grey in places. His seat upon a horse and the grip on his gun were more familiar to her than her own self.

"Mr. Dumont has been in hiding from Dominion authorities," continued the announcer, "since the half-breed war and Riel's hanging for treason. He's here to show you how he drew a bead on those soldiers."

Gabriel kneed his horse into a gallop. A man dressed in cowboy attire had run into the middle of the ring and begun to throw glass balls into the air. Gabriel and Annie Oakley circled in opposite directions and—as the man tossed the balls up—shot them through the centre. When the balls shattered, members of the audience cried out, as if each one represented some rare and priceless thing.

"What of the horses?" Wahsis said to her. "They'll be hurt by the broken glass."

Josette whispered in his ear. "You see, they aren't galloping there, just on the outside."

Her eyes were still on the figure in the buckskin coat. When news had reached them of Madeleine's death, Josette would come out of her cabin in the evening and look down to Gabriel's Crossing, remember him coming out of the trees that fateful day of Riel's arrival. She would go out on the bluff and stare at the moon, as if she might invoke the memory of his face. Now here he was riding his horse in a Montana exhibition as if he had never known Riel or fought his war.

Gabriel and Annie Oakley rode out of the ring after the shooting display was over. Another act had started, but Josette got up quickly, leading Wahsis and Patrice through the fairgrounds. They passed a series of tipis outside the arena, families of the show Indians. A few finely dressed white women, the type Josette had seen in Prince Albert, were distributing small wrapped gifts they'd brought to a group of squaws and their children who ran barefoot across the camp. The Indian women ripped at the packages and stared at the strings of beads and trinkets with incomprehension, but nodded their thanks, thanks for handing back so little after taking so much.

Cleophile and Eulalie were lined up at a cotton candy emporium. Josette left Wahsis and Patrice with them and went quickly past a small slough, where the buffalo had been put to water by several cowboys, who kept them in a bunch with long prods. When she asked where she might find the performers, she was directed to a white walled tent at the edge of the pasture, where the land dipped down to a slough and a pretty stand of aspen. A wind had come up, the leaves fluttering. She thought of the aspen trees cut down in Batoche by settlers clearing more land to farm and of a line in a poem she had once found in one of Father Dubois' books.

But see! He casts one look upon the tree,
Struck to the heart, she trembles evermore.

Gabriel had come out of the tent, a saddle draped over his arm. He had his head down, and on his face was written the strain it had taken to ride and shoot that way, and perhaps the grief he still carried for what they had lost. He looked up and her hand went to the braid, loosely plaited and wound at the back of her neck, as the Mennonites wore it. Had she changed so much he didn't know her? The features of his face arranged in an expression of shock and then cautious relief.

They did not embrace, as she had imagined they would, but stood facing each other, as if there were still many miles between them. She told him of how the remaining Métis in Batoche were being driven out by the European immigrants. He spoke of his exile in the States, Buffalo Bill's offer to him only months after his arrival. He paused and she saw how Riel's hanging, followed so shortly by Madeleine's death, had devastated him. She saw that he was different, changed, and yet the same man, the best with a horse and a gun, one she had never stopped loving. It would be necessary to know each other again, start at the beginning.

Gabriel had moved closer as they spoke, asking of her grandfather. She told him that Big Bear was still in prison, serving time for the Frog Lake massacre, and Gabriel shook his head. "He did not go to Ottawa to meet the one who is higher."

She could not find the words to tell him that Ottawa had ordered the prison guards to cut her grandfather's long hair and keep him in chains, forced to hard labour.

They were silent for a moment. Gabriel lifted a hand to her arm, as if he were reaching to some apparition, a vision of her that might disappear like smoke. Through the thin cotton of her dress, his touch still managed to electrify her.

"There was news of you when someone came from the Saskatchewan," he said. "I had to know you would stay."

She began to tell him of her cabin, that she'd survived because of the money he had sent, but his face had softened as he looked at her, watching her mouth, eyes, memorizing her face.

"*Wâwâc*," he said in Cree. *Even now*.

She had forgotten how he looked at a person—cut away what wasn't true and let come what was. His eyes did it. They burned right through you.

The two of them walked out of the fairgrounds as the light changed and swung low over the aspen and the wide plains beyond, of Montana and the Territories and the world without end. It was not difficult to imagine how it might have seemed thousands of years ago, to a man or woman who stood on this hill, the snake bend of river, light reflecting from the sloughs, and buffalo that moved like clouds across the sun.

ACKNOWLEDGEMENTS

Song of Batoche is a work of historical fiction, but it is also about my ancestral history, and that of my people, the Métis. Most of the events are true to history, most of the characters, too. Some names were changed only because there were so many people with the name "Marie" and "Isidore" among the Métis. Josette, Norbert, and their children are products of my imagination.

Herb Wyile wrote in *Speaking in the Past Tense: Canadian Novelists on Writing Historical Fiction:* "A historical novel is kind of a work of impressionism." After years of researching Riel, I found him a fascinating character. My interpretation of him, although based on real events and dialogue from his writings, diary entries, and poetry, is very much a personal impression.

Riel's "relationship" with Josette is my own creation to give expression to his diary writings. The scenes that feature the two are fictional in nature, but were crafted to illustrate historical events, or to reveal what Riel was attempting to achieve with the Métis and the "Indians," in terms of his mission. Although these scenes are fictional, the content documents historical occurrences that include the perspectives of the Métis women, whose viewpoints I felt were often not considered in earlier accounts. Where names were not changed in the story, every effort was made by the author to contact descendants for permission to fictionalize these characters.

Gabriel Dumont's relationship with Josette is also conjecture, part of the story I wanted to tell—of vibrant three-dimensional characters who lived with problems and secrets that weren't all that different from our own.

As well as primary source material, I read many secondary sources while I was researching this story and thank all of the authors. They are too numerous to mention here, but any reader interested can find a comprehensive list on my website: maiacaron.com

Special thanks to the following:

Beverly Crier, Director SCN Culture, Language Archives & Museum, Samson Cree Nation, for help with the Cree words and phrases.

Johanne Brissette who assisted me with French usage in the novel. Any mistakes that remain in either the Cree or French are mine alone.

Diane Payment for her exhaustive research and her documentation of stories of Métis elders who lived during the Resistance. Her book, *The Free People*, was invaluable to me.

Don McLean, researcher for the Gabriel Dumont Institute and author of *1885: Métis Rebellion or Government Conspiracy?* His book helped me to flesh out Lawrence Clarke's incredible story, which had only been touched upon in earlier sources. For those interested, the book is available in pdf form on the Gabriel Dumont Institute website.

Lawrence Barkwell for *Veterans and Families of the 1885 Northwest Resistance*, also published by the Gabriel Dumont Institute.

Jean Teillet for her insight into Riel's Métis relations in Manitoba.

Ladonna Brave Bull Allard: an offering of tobacco for her information on Little Ghost and the Lakota Sioux.

The estate of Margaret Arnett MacLeod for permission to use excerpts from her book, *Songs of Old Manitoba*.

Thank you C.M. for everything and making it possible to write. My beautiful daughter, Shasta. My dad, Allan Caron, the best Métis. Auntie Jeanette, who gifted me with her haunting memories of growing up in Batoche. Dianne Shelton and Luanne Pucci who listened on the dog beach. Ronald B. Hatch and Meagan Dyer, you believed in this story and made it better. Murray Clark Johnson, who died before I could tell him: this one's for you.

ABOUT THE AUTHOR

Maia Caron is Red River Métis. Her extended Caron, Dumas, and Parenteau family were among the founders of Batoche, Saskatchewan. They fought with Louis Riel and Gabriel Dumont during the North-West Resistance of 1885. Maia is a member of the Métis Nation of Ontario and lives in Toronto. *Song of Batoche* is her first novel. For more information, please visit her website at www.maiacaron.com. Or follow her on Twitter @MaiaCaron.